LOYALTY

ALSO BY LISA SCOTTOLINE

LOYALTY

Lisa Scottoline

G. P. PUTNAM'S SONS
NEW YORK

PUTNAM
— EST. 1838 —

G. P. PUTNAM'S SONS

Publishers Since 1838
an imprint of Penguin Random House LLC
penguinrandomhouse.com

Copyright © 2023 by Smart Blonde, LLC
Map copyright © 2023 by Timlyn Vaughan Photography

Bunches of lemons image / Shutterstock.com

Library of Congress Cataloging-in-Publication Data

Names: Scottoline, Lisa, author.
Title: Loyalty / Lisa Scottoline.
Description: New York: G. P. Putnam's Sons, [2023]
Identifiers: LCCN 2022055464 (print) | LCCN 2022055465 (ebook) |
ISBN 9780525539803 (hardcover) | ISBN 9780525539810 (ebook)
Classification: LCC PS3569.C725 L69 2023 (print) |
LCC PS3569.C725 (ebook) | DDC 813/.54—dc23
LC record available at https://lccn.loc.gov/2022055464
LC ebook record available at https://lccn.loc.gov/2022055465

Printed in the United States of America

1st Printing

Book design by Lorie Pagnozzi

For my amazing daughter, Francesca, with all my love

To have seen Italy without seeing Sicily is not to have seen Italy at all, for Sicily is the clue to everything.

—GOETHE, *ITALIAN JOURNEY*

DRAMATIS PERSONAE

Dante, a boy kidnapped from Palermo

Renzo Gentili, a guard in the Ospizio di Santa Teresa, a madhouse

Teresa, Gentili's wife

Dottor Vergenti, administrator of the madhouse

Baron Pietro Pisani, administrator of the Real Casa dei Matti di Palermo and the real-life founder of "moral therapy" in Sicily

Franco Fiorvanti, the manager of a lemon grove outside Palermo

Roberto Fiorvanti, his twin brother

Sebastiano, a farmhand

Ezio, another farmhand

Baron Zito, the wealthy baron who owns the lemon grove

Gaetano Catalano, a lawyer from Palermo

Maria, his wife

Carmine Prizzi, his friend

Mafalda Pancari, a mother from the village of Porticello, outside Palermo

Salvatore "Turi," her husband

Lucia, their daughter

Alfredo D'Antonio, a cheesemaker from the mountain town of Mussomeli, in central Sicily

Bella, Flora, Valentina, and **Ginevra,** his daughters

N

Palermo

Porticello

Bagheria

Conca d' Oro

Marsala

Corleone

Mussomeli

Agrigento

Mediterranean Sea

Tyrrhenian Sea

Bronte

Mt. Etna

Ionian Sea

Sicily

PART ONE

They know how to read and write—that's the trouble.

—GIOVANNI VERGA, "THE GENTRY," *LITTLE NOVELS OF SICILY*
(D. H. LAWRENCE TRANSLATION)

CHAPTER ONE

It was the final night of the Festival of Saint Rosalia, and hundreds of people lined Via Toledo, cheering, praying, and singing hymns. Priests led the procession, holding tapers that glowed like halos in the darkness. Spectators looked up the street, craning their necks to see the ornate silver reliquary of the patron saint. The *carabinieri* faced that way, too, their plumed hats in a line, their horses shifting on polished hooves.

Only a bearded man looked away, down the street. Nobody noticed him in the shadows behind the crowd. He kept his eye on the wealthy families privileged to stand on the Quattro Canti, or Four Corners, which was the intersection of Palermo's two most important streets: Via Toledo, extending to the harbor, and Via Maqueda, bisecting the capital.

The procession moved down the street, and the crowd's fervor intensified, anticipating the reliquary. People kissed pictures of the young saint, held roses up to her, and cheered *Viva Palermo e viva Santa Rosalia!* Among the privileged on the Quattro Canti, the husbands surged forward to see better and the wives remained behind with the children.

The bearded man threaded his way to a little boy standing with his mother at the back of the Quattro Canti. He snuck up behind the boy and waited for the moment to pounce.

The saint's reliquary popped into view, and the crowd erupted in shouting, cheering, and weeping. The boy's mother burst into pious tears, and the bearded man made his move. He pulled a marionette from under his cloak and showed it to the boy. The boy reached for the marionette, and in one cruel motion, the man grabbed the boy and flung his cloak over him. The clamor of the crowd devoured the boy's startled cry. The marionette dropped to the cobblestones.

The man ran away with the boy. The mother looked around for her son. She called him but didn't see him anywhere. She whirled around, beginning to panic, then screamed. It was as if he had been swallowed by the crowd. She would remember this moment for all of her days.

The man jumped onto a bay mare and rode off with the boy. He galloped from the city proper and raced past prickly pear cacti, cypresses, and olive trees on a road illuminated by a crescent moon. In time, he approached a dilapidated building set off by itself, a boxy, broken shadow in the night. It was the Ospizio di Santa Teresa, a madhouse that held lunatics, lepers, and the poor.

The man entered the building's courtyard and halted the mare. He dismounted and threw the crying child over his shoulder, then banged on the door, which was opened by a guard. The kidnapper handed the boy over with a sack of ducats, then left.

The guard pocketed the ducats and took the boy inside the madhouse. The place was dark at this hour, though it was never quiet. The wails, rants, and cries of a hundred lunatics echoed throughout its stone walls. The guard crossed the entrance hall with the boy and entered the kitchen, where the only illumination came from the moon filtered through a dirty window.

"Sit, boy!" The guard dumped the boy onto the wooden table.

"Mamma?" the boy whispered, teary. "Where's Mamma?"

"She doesn't want you anymore." The guard picked up a knife, its sharp blade glinting in the moonlight.

"No!" The boy scrambled backward, terrified the guard would stab him. Instead, the guard used the knife to cut his own finger, drawing blood.

"Look what you did, boy! You cut me!"

"I didn't! Mamma! Papa!"

"Shut up!"

The guard picked up the boy, left the kitchen, and crossed the entrance hall. He reached the stairs and descended into a gloom that reeked of mice and chamber pots. He lumbered down a hallway lined with the cells of the male lunatics. The walls were of crumbling plaster, and the metal doors dented from within.

"Renzo? Renzo?" one of the lunatics shouted.

"Renzo, I'm hungry!" shouted another.

"Let me out! Please, I beg you!"

The guard reached the end of the hall and stopped at an open door, scattering the rats. He entered a cell that contained only a chamber pot and the frame of a bed with no mattress. A crucifix hung on the wall above an iron chain that ended in a leg manacle. A small window, set oddly high, admitted moonlight through its bars.

The guard tossed the boy onto the floor and picked up the manacle, realizing it was sized for an adult, not a child. He would have to come back with a rope.

"Mamma!" the boy called out, sobbing.

The guard whacked him across the face, knocking him unconscious.

"Mamma!" the lunatics shouted. "Mamma!"

CHAPTER TWO

F ranco Fiorvanti rose from the table, leaving his twin, Roberto, with his farmhands, Sebastiano and Ezio. It was almost midnight, and the three other men had just returned from the Festival of Saint Rosalia in Palermo. They'd brought home a jug of red wine, crusty peasant bread topped with sesame seeds, golden hunks of Canestrato cheese, roasted red peppers with garlic, and fresh green olives. Deliciously pungent aromas scented the small kitchen.

Roberto poured wine into a coarse glass. "You missed a great time tonight, brother."

"I couldn't leave the property." Franco crossed to the door, which stood open. "Our lemon house is almost full, and bandits would choose a night like this to strike."

"Roberto, your brother works all the time." Sebastiano dealt brightly colored Scopa cards.

Ezio drained his wineglass. "The Fiorvantis were no fun before you, Roberto."

Franco stepped outside, walked away from the farmhouse, and scanned the property with a manager's eye. The *latifondo*, an agricultural estate, was owned by Baron Zito, but he didn't live here and his villa stood empty and dark. Its lovely façade of gray-and-brown stone was flanked by two wings set sideways, and Palladian windows with potbellied railings faced the *giardino*, or lemon grove. A curved portico protected a grand entrance, the door painted a dark green like the shutters.

Franco's farmhouse was off to the side, allowing him to see all comings and goings, and behind was the *limonaia*, or lemon house, where they stored lemons until taken to market. A stone wall surrounded the villa, farmhouse, and outbuildings. Mules and donkeys grazed within, flicking their tails.

Franco's gaze shifted to the *giardino*. A cool breeze wafted through the lemon trees, rustling their richly green leaves and perfuming the air like a magical elixir. The Conca d'Oro, or golden bowl, was a luxuriant valley of lemon groves around Palermo, and Baron Zito's *giardino* spanned thirty hectares, or seventy-five acres.

Franco knew every tree. When he had first come here from Bronte, he had tended, pruned, and grafted them, as well as the olive trees surrounding them for protection against the wind. In ten years, he had risen from being a *bracciante*, a day laborer, to a *gabellotto*, a manager, and the *giardino* had become his passion.

"Brother." Roberto appeared at his side. "You seem restless. I know you're thinking about something."

"I'm always thinking about something."

"I'm never thinking about *anything*," Roberto shot back, and they both chuckled. They were identical twins and shared the same handsome face, with strong features. Most prominent were their eyes, which were the golden-brown of hazelnuts, and they each had a large nose, heavy cheekbones, and full lips. Their hair was thick, dark, and wavy, but Franco visited the barber more than Roberto. They were of average height, but Franco's work kept him fit, whereas Roberto's love for bread left him with a soft belly.

"I'm glad you came." Franco loved having his twin back, feeling incomplete without him.

"I am, too." Roberto grinned. "The city is so *big*, with so many people! Tonight, I felt like I was standing at the center of the world."

"You were, brother."

"Why did you want me to come here? I know you had a reason."

"Look." Franco gestured to the lemon trees. "Femminello lemons.

There's no more lucrative crop. They prevent scurvy, and the British Navy is crazy for them. Europe can't get enough, either. They ship easily and don't rot as fast as oranges. Palermo serves the busiest trade routes, and ships from here sail to England, Africa, Europe, even America, only forty-five days away by clipper, longer by merchant ship. We export tuna, spices, and silk, but lemons are—"

"Is this school?" Roberto wisecracked.

Franco remembered his twin's impatience with details and tempered his approach.

"All you have to know is that Sicily is the biggest exporter of lemons in the world, and Palermo grows the lion's share, here in the Conca d'Oro. We're sitting on a gold mine, and I have a plan for us."

"Okay, I'll pick lemons for you," Roberto said agreeably.

"You'll do more than that here. Look, Baron Zito's *giardino* sits in the middle of four others." Franco pointed east. "That way is Baron Piccolo's, there's Baron DiGiulio's, and to the north and south are Baron Moravio's and Marquis Silvestri's. They're all managed by *gabellotti* like me."

Roberto nodded.

"Remember when we were little? Everything grew on the other side of Mount Etna. Pistachios, lemons, oranges, grapes, everything. There was better soil there from the volcano. We lived on the wrong side, and we traveled with Papa to pick. We broke our backs."

"What of it?"

"Here, we're on the better side, to me. The western half of the island, with Palermo and the Conca d'Oro, teems with citrus, not just lemons. Oranges, blood oranges, limes, all kinds of fruit, vegetables, and flowers. You can grow anything here. The Arabs irrigated the valley, and for once, we benefitted from a colonizer." Franco could see Roberto listening. "But on the east side—the Greek side, where we grew up—it's harder, it's drier. The soil isn't as fertile, there's more hardship. Don't you get tired of being on the wrong side? Where there's such struggle?"

Roberto shrugged. "No, I'm content, like Papa was."

"Well, someday I want to *own* a *giardino*, not just manage one."

Roberto laughed, but Franco wasn't joking.

"Why not *us*, the Fiorvanti brothers? Why should we grow for others? Why not grow for ourselves? Noblemen aren't better than us, despite their titles. God loves all men equally." Franco felt himself falling under the spell of his own dream. "Like a woman in love, a *giardino* offers everything. Beauty. Sustenance. *Life*."

Roberto's eyes narrowed. "Are you in love?"

"No." Franco kept his secret, unripe for telling.

"Ezio thinks you are. He says you're seeing someone new."

"I'm always seeing someone new."

"He says this one matters. Last week, you smiled."

Roberto chuckled, but Franco wanted to change the subject.

"Roberto, lemons are the future. We can *master* the future."

"Now you're talking like Mamma. Crazy."

"She wasn't crazy. She just had dreams."

"Crazy dreams." Roberto shrugged. "Okay, I'm in. We'll be the famous Fiorvanti brothers. We'll be rich."

"It's not only for money. It's for dignity. Respect. *Equality*."

"Have you become a Communist now?"

Franco scoffed. "Politics is a corrupt conspiracy between colonizers and nobility against us. Sicily is still feudal. We're workers in their fields, fodder in their cannons. We're far behind the mainland and Europe in this way. I was reading—"

"I knew it!" Roberto wagged his finger. "This is because Mamma taught you to read. What a mistake!"

Franco let it go. "Roberto, other families have succeeded in business, not only nobility. The Florios aren't noble, but they're ascending the ladder. Baron Zito owns this *latifondo*, though he can't sell because it's feudal land. But there's talk of changing the law, and if that happens, I think I can convince him to sell me a small parcel."

Roberto cocked his head. "Where would you get the money?"

"Savings, since I left home."

"But why would he sell?"

"He doesn't like the country life at all, and he complains about the taxes."

Roberto smiled, narrowing his eyes. "Are you trying to *become* a baron?"

"Why not?"

"They were born noble. We were born handsome."

Franco didn't laugh. "I want to move up, Roberto."

"You want to be king of the mountain. Remember that game we used to play?"

"Yes, and back then, you wanted the same. So why not now?"

"This is life, not a game. Nobility is like the stars. They belong up there." Roberto waved at the night sky. "We belong down here with the women, the wine, and the cards. Which place is truly heaven?"

Suddenly they turned at the pounding of a horse's hooves, then a man materialized from the darkness, cantering toward them. Franco had been awaiting him. "Roberto, go inside."

"Why? Who's this?"

"Business. Go."

"Okay." Roberto turned away and walked back to the farmhouse, and the man halted the mare and dismounted, his cloak swirling around him. He breathed heavily, and his face was slaked with sweat, leaving spittle on his beard. The mare was exhausted, her nostrils as round as ducats.

Franco took the mare's reins and wiped foam from her neck. "Well?"

"Franco, it's done. I took him to the madhouse."

"Good." Franco's chest tightened. It was a dirty piece of work, but not as dirty as it could have been, since he hadn't followed orders. "Remember, Claudio, this is our secret. If you're ever asked, you must say you killed the boy."

"I will."

"And you weren't seen at the festival?"

"I don't think so."

Franco didn't like the answer. "Were you seen or not?"

"As I say, I don't . . . think so, but I can't guarantee anything. I waited until his mother was distracted, but there were so many people—"

"Look in my eyes. Were you seen? Yes or no?"

"No," Claudio answered, but his eyes betrayed him.

Franco felt stricken. He didn't know what to do. He couldn't risk being discovered or all would be lost. He willed himself to action. Quickly, he withdrew his knife from its sheath and plunged it into Claudio's chest.

Claudio's eyes flew open. He emitted a moan, dropped to his knees, and flopped over onto his side. Franco controlled the revulsion and horror he felt as he wrenched the knife from Claudio's chest. Blood spurted from the wound as the man's heart pumped its last.

"Franco!" Roberto rushed over.

Franco whirled around, shocked. "I thought you were inside—"

"No!" Roberto knelt beside Claudio, whose gaze fixed on the stars. "You *killed* him!"

"I had to." Franco felt sick to his stomach. He forced himself to think. He wiped his knife clean on the ground.

"How could you *do* such a thing?" Roberto looked up, distraught. "You stabbed him, unprovoked! Why?"

"It was the only way." Franco returned his knife to its sheath.

"What are you talking about?"

"You don't know how things are here."

"It's a sin!" Roberto's eyes filled with tears. "A mortal sin!"

Franco straightened, composing himself. "Roberto, what's done is done. I'll take the body, and you take the mare. She needs to be cooled down."

"Franco, this isn't like you!"

"No, it isn't like *you*." Franco picked up Claudio's heels and began dragging him away.

CHAPTER THREE

"So, tell me about this boy," Dottor Vergenti said to Renzo, as they stood in the entrance hall of the madhouse. It was Monday morning, and evidently a child had been relinquished over the weekend, which would necessitate extra paperwork. Vergenti was administrator of the madhouse, addressed as *dottore* though he wasn't a medical doctor. He had gotten this job through his relatives in city government. He used to teach Latin, and while he did like Latin, he disliked children.

"He's about five years old, maybe six. He's incorrigible. I told you what he did. He *stabbed* me!" Renzo held up a hand with bloodied gauze. "See for yourself!"

"*Madonna!*" Vergenti wrinkled his nose. "But how? You're built like an ox. He can't be very strong, at his age."

"He caught me unawares!"

"What's his name?"

"His parents didn't say. They barely stopped their carriage. They relinquished the boy after he tried to kill his little brother with a rock!"

Vergenti recoiled. "How horrible! Why didn't they summon the authorities?"

"I don't know, but the madhouse is the more humane solution, isn't it?"

Vergenti agreed. The madhouse was awful, but the prison was far worse. At least here, the government paid to feed them.

"Dottore, he's a bad case, I assure you. He needs to be admitted."

"We'll see about that." Vergenti thought of his budget, which was strict. "I must file a detailed report, you know. Tell me more about the incident. Where did he get the knife? He didn't have it on his person, did he?"

"No, I took him to the kitchen to offer him an orange. The next thing I knew, he grabbed the knife. The child is wicked!"

"Not wicked, insane," Vergenti corrected.

"You're right, Dottore." Renzo frowned. "Nevertheless, we can't be too careful. What if he had attacked *you*, at your age? Your reflexes aren't as fast as mine. Your wife would be left a widow and the madhouse without its leader!"

Vergenti knew Renzo was flattering him. He liked being flattered almost as much as he liked Latin. "I must examine the boy. Take me to him."

Renzo turned to the stairwell, and Vergenti trailed behind. They went downstairs and walked the dark hallway lined with cells. The stench of the chamber pots upset Vergenti's stomach, which was delicate.

The lunatics began shouting, "Renzo, let me out! Help me! Save me!"

Vergenti covered his ears. He never came down here, preferring his office, which was farthest from the patients, especially the lepers. He feared their contagion infected the very air. He waited while Renzo unlocked the cell and they stepped inside.

The boy was sleeping on his side, his hands under his face. He must have come from an upper-class family, because he had a fine brown jacket, a white shirt with a high collar, and dark green pants with polished shoes of black leather. He had well-formed features, smooth olive skin, and glossy dark hair, except for a red welt marring his left cheek.

Vergenti turned to Renzo. "What happened to his face? It looks like a blow."

"He came out of the carriage that way. Perhaps his father disciplined him."

The boy stirred, then woke up, his eyes rounding with fear. He scrambled away, dragging the rope tying his foot to the wall.

Vergenti forced a smile. "What's your name, boy?"

The boy's dark gaze shifted to Renzo and back again.

"Boy, don't be afraid. I repeat, what's your name?"

"I want Mamma," the boy whispered, tears filming his eyes.

Vergenti didn't have time for this. The child, the odor, the din. "Just tell me your name. That's all."

"Dante," the boy whispered.

"Good. What's your surname, Dante?"

Dante looked too frightened to speak, his terrified gaze fixed on Renzo.

Renzo advanced on the boy. "Spoiled brat! Show the doctor some respect!"

"Renzo, please." Vergenti was getting a headache. "Dante, your parents brought you here because you tried to harm your younger brother. Why did you do that?"

Dante's eyes widened. He shook his head, his lips still sealed.

"Speak, boy!" Renzo bellowed.

"Speak, boy!" one of the lunatics shouted. "Speak! Speak!"

"I have no brother!" Dante blurted out in bewilderment.

Vergenti turned to Renzo, puzzled. "They told you he had a brother, didn't they?"

"Yes, I *saw* his younger brother in the carriage. The boy lies!"

Vergenti patted his gray hair into place. "His young mind must be terribly disordered. How unfortunate."

Renzo stepped closer to the boy. "Stop lying! Tell the truth!"

"Boy!" the lunatics shouted. "Tell the truth!"

"Oh, that din!" Vergenti covered his ears.

One lunatic hollered, "He speaks the truth! I saw no carriage!"

Renzo bellowed, "Shut up, Big Nose!"

The lunatics fell quiet, except for one weeping.

Vergenti considered the situation. "It's hard to understand, Renzo. This boy seems well cared for, even loved. He shows no signs of beating, neglect, malnourishment, as we usually see."

One of the lunatics hollered, "I tell you, I saw no carriage! Carriages *never* come here!"

Renzo hollered back, "Big Nose, I'll beat you!"

Vergenti regarded the child. "He's frightened, so we'll show him he doesn't have to be. Renzo, untie him."

Renzo gasped. "Dottore, he bites, too! Did I tell you?"

"Renzo, please."

Renzo began to untie the boy. "Boy, don't you *dare* bite me!"

Suddenly the boy grabbed Renzo's hand and bit down.

"Brat!" Renzo yanked his hand away. "See what I mean, Dottore? I told you!"

Vergenti felt his face aflame. "My apologies," he said, edging to the door.

"The boy must be admitted!"

"I still need a diagnosis." Vergenti fled the cell.

"Make one up!"

AFTER THE MEN LEFT, DANTE sat curled into a ball, covering his ears. He didn't understand why he was here. Men in the other rooms shouted, yelled, and argued. One of them screamed day and night. Another cried, like Dante. He didn't want to be in this terrible place. He felt frightened all the time, especially of Renzo.

The night Dante came, he was afraid Renzo would run him through and through with the knife, like in *The Song of Roland*. It was about Christians and Saracens fighting at the battle of Roncevaux Pass. Count Roland had the best sword, named Durendal, given to him by Charlemagne himself.

Dante liked Count Roland, his best friend, Oliver, and all the others in *The Song of Roland*, which was his favorite book. Mamma would read it to him at bedtime, and he knew it by heart. He closed his eyes, pretending that Mamma was reading to him now and he was sitting on her lap.

"Mamma, read that part again, please. It's one of the best bits."

Mamma cleared her throat. "'High are the hills, the valleys dark and deep, grisly the rocks, and wondrous grim the steeps.'"

"Again," Dante said, as soon as she finished.

Mamma chuckled, and Dante's cheek rested against her dress, which felt scratchy because it was *brocade*, a word she taught him. She loved to teach him words, and he loved to learn them. Dante wanted to learn every word in *The Song of Roland*.

Mamma read the line again, then closed the book. "Bedtime."

"Mamma, isn't that one of the best bits?"

"Yes." Mamma set the book aside. "Why do you like it?"

"I can picture it in my mind."

"So can I." Mamma smiled, and Dante thought his mother was even more beautiful than Aude, Oliver's sister in the book.

"Mamma, Count Roland and Oliver are best friends. Will I have a best friend?"

"Yes, someday."

Dante recited, "'Roland is fierce and Oliver is wise, and both for valor may bear away the prize.'"

"*Bravo*, Dante." Mamma beamed, which made Dante feel as remarkable as the sun rising at night.

"Mamma, I think Count Roland is brave, but he's too proud. Oliver tells him to blow the horn for Charlemagne, but he doesn't listen."

"That's true. So, who do you like better, Count Roland or Oliver?"

"Oliver. I'm more like Oliver, I'm *wise*. Count Roland is *too* bold and fierce."

"I agree." Mamma smiled, brushing back his hair.

Dante kept his eyes closed, staying in his mind because it made him happy to be sitting in Mamma's lap again, telling her the best bits and hearing her say *I agree*. He didn't think there was any better sound in the world.

I agree

I agree

I agree

Dante covered his ears, keeping her words inside his head.

Until he fell asleep.

CHAPTER FOUR

Gaetano Catalano stepped into his well-appointed foyer, taking off his straw hat and hanging it on the rack. His sons were playing in the living room, and the delicious aroma of fried eggplant wafted from the kitchen. He looked forward to a wonderful lunch with his family before he had to return to the office. Gaetano was a lawyer at one of the finest firms in Palermo, which catered to an aristocratic clientele.

But his wife, Maria, was hurrying toward him, a frown creasing her forehead and clouding her warm brown eyes. A lovely woman, she had a fine nose and lips set on an elegantly long face. Her hair was dark and shining, and she wore a double braid around her head. Today she wore a dress in a blood-orange hue, coral earrings, and a gold crucifix he had given her.

"Darling, I have bad news." Maria lowered her voice. "There's been a kidnapping. A boy was taken at the festival."

"Oh no," Gaetano said, horrified. "Who was it, do you know?"

"No. He was on the Quattro Canti, so his family must be important."

"It happened on the Quattro Canti? That's an outrage!" Gaetano realized the kidnapping must've been why the meeting had been called tonight. He had gotten the notice about it earlier today, via secret courier.

"That's only a few blocks from where we were. It's so awful." Maria's dark eyes glistened. "They say he's young, five or six."

"Has there been a ransom demand?"

"No one knows."

"It's always the same." Gaetano clenched his jaw. Parents of kidnapped children feared retaliation if they reported the crime, and the police were unreliable, if not corrupt.

"Imagine that poor mother." Maria hesitated. "I admit, so often I feel, well, jealous. Do you remember what I said that night?"

"No," Gaetano answered, but he did. It hadn't been her finest moment.

"I said, 'I wish *we* were standing on the Quattro Canti.'" Maria puckered her lower lip. "But if we had been, it could've been one of our sons, kidnapped. I'm ashamed."

"Don't be." Gaetano kissed her, breathing in her jasmine perfume. He adored his wife and their life together in the Capo district. He could have afforded a better apartment but didn't want to move, though he couldn't share the reason with Maria.

"Darling, come in, let's eat."

"By the way, I won't be home until late tonight. I have a dinner meeting with a client." Gaetano didn't like lying to her, but he had to.

"Oh, that's too bad."

"I'm sorry." Gaetano followed Maria into their elegant dining room, which had a chandelier of Murano glass in ivory-and-melon tones hanging above a polished walnut table surrounded by carved chairs. A tall window with lace curtains admitted sunshine from the courtyard, shining on a large black lacquered breakfront, an Oriental touch Maria claimed was fashionable.

"Papa, Papa!" Gaetano's two sons, Paolo and Mario, came running toward him.

"How are my boys?" Gaetano clasped them to his sides, ruffling their dark curls. Holding them, he thought of the family who had just had a son kidnapped. "You know I love you, don't you?"

"Yes, yes!" The boys scrambled into chairs as the cook, Sofia, carried in the first course of *pasta alla Norma*, a traditional Sicilian dish of spaghetti with tomato sauce, strips of fried eggplant, and *ricotta salata*, or salted ricotta cheese.

"Sofia, thank you." Gaetano sat down, and the aroma made his mouth water. Sofia nodded, set the platter on the table, then went back to the kitchen.

"Gaetano, here." Maria served him a generous helping. "Will you say grace, please?"

Gaetano did, then twirled some spaghetti onto his fork and took a bite, tasting the rich sweetness of the tomato and the tang of the *ricotta salata*. But he didn't take his usual pleasure in the meal, preoccupied by the kidnapping. He knew how these cases went. Sooner or later, the kidnappers would demand a ransom and send the wealthy parents a lock of hair, a finger, or an ear. The ransom would be paid, and sometimes the boy would be returned alive. But some boys were never found.

Something had to be done.

Gaetano counted the minutes until his meeting.

THAT NIGHT, GAETANO WALKED THROUGH the winding streets and alleys of the Capo district, his fine boots clattering on the *balati*, the oversized cobblestones that paved Palermo. Ahead, he spotted the chubby form of his friend and fellow member Carmine, but neither man acknowledged the other on meeting nights, according to the rules.

The neighborhood was mostly empty, and the houses' closed shutters emitted light and sound through their slats. The air was cool and permeated with a fishy odor from the sea. A skinny cat trotted toward the market, which was closed now except to the city's vermin. Gaetano knew Palermo's dark side and loved her anyway. He couldn't do anything about her rat-and-mouse problem, but he could try to stop those who preyed on her children.

Gaetano turned onto the side street next to the Chiesa di Santa Maria di Gesù, dark at this hour. He reached a metal refuse bin and ducked behind it to a concealed side door. He opened the door, then closed it quickly behind him. He found himself in a tunnel that ran underneath the church.

It was chilly, dusty, and pitch-black inside, and he clambered down a set of ancient steps, running a finger along the rough wall for guidance. He reached the subterranean floor, hurried down a narrow hallway like a catacomb, and headed toward a pale light from flickering oil lamps. Voices echoed within the walls.

Gaetano entered a small room containing the members of the Beati Paoli, or the Blessed Society of Saint Paul, who sat around a table. They were aristocrats who worked for the common good in honor of Saint Paul, whom they revered. Some were moneyed enough not to be employed, and the others included a retired lawyer, a surgeon, a classics professor, and several businessmen. Gaetano and Carmine were the youngest members.

"Good evening, gentlemen." Gaetano greeted everyone. "Let's begin the meeting with our oath. Who are we, men?"

"We're the Beati Paoli!"

"And for whom do we fight?"

"For justice, for Sicilia, and for God!"

Gaetano sat down, leaning over. "We're meeting tonight about this awful kidnapping, and I would like to take the lead in this investigation. I know it's my first time, but with the help of Saint Paul, I think I can find the boy."

"By all means, you have my vote." Carmine smiled, his brown eyes warm. He was a lawyer, too, but his dimpled face looked like a schoolboy's. His hair was black and curly, and his dark skin evinced the African heritage of many Sicilians.

Don Ugo's hooded eyes met Gaetano's. "You're ready to lead. I trust in you."

"We agree!" Don Fulvio chimed in, and heads nodded around the table.

"Thank you." Gaetano eyed them. "I'll tell you why I feel so strongly.

This kidnapping occurred on the Quattro Canti, the very center of our city, on the night we celebrate our patron, Saint Rosalia. To me, it's a crime not only against the boy, but against all of us."

"Yes," Carmine chimed in. "The festival is the heart of Palermo. If you tear out our heart, how can we live? Who are we then?"

Don Leonardo clucked. "It's a lawless act against a child, an innocent."

"Yes!" Don Fabiano shook his knobby fist. "I want justice, for Palermo, the mother to us all."

Gaetano bore down. "Let me ask you, were any of you watching the procession from the Quattro Canti? We could have witnesses among us. I wasn't there, I was at the Cathedral with my family."

Carmine shook his head. "No, we were at the Cathedral, too. My mother-in-law likes to watch the reliquary leave."

"We were at the Cathedral," Don Leonardo answered for himself and for Don Manfreddi.

Don Fabiano shook his head. "Sorry, we didn't go to the festival this year. My wife was feeling poorly."

Don Vincenzo sighed. "We didn't, either. My back was acting up."

Gaetano thought it over. "Do any of you know of anyone who watched from the Quattro Canti? We know so many people who could have been there."

Carmine nodded. "I'll ask my wife. Discreetly."

"As will I," Don Fulvio added. "She gossips at the bakery every day."

"Good, thank you," Gaetano told them. "Now, I've been planning my investigation. If you'll allow me, I'll explain."

"Go ahead," Carmine said, and they all leaned in.

CHAPTER FIVE

Mafalda Pancari endured contractions all night, and her friends wiped her brow, offered her water, and prayed. They filled her warm little house to its walls, and those who couldn't fit inside prayed outside. They all knew how much Mafalda wanted this baby, having been childless for so long.

Mafalda didn't know if she could bear the pain any longer. Sweat plastered her nightgown to her swollen breasts and belly. She could barely breathe for the agony. Surely, childbirth would kill her. Surely, she would die. Women did all the time, two of them in the village last year.

"Please, God, help me!" Mafalda gritted her teeth. "I can't do this!"

"Mafalda, you're almost finished!" Her best friend, Concetta, held her hand. "It's time to push! Push, push!"

"Oh God!" Mafalda pushed with all her might. "It hurts so much—"

"Think about something else! Count! *Uno, due, tre . . .*"

"*Uno, due,*" Mafalda repeated, pushing. "I have nothing to count—"

"Count your blessings! What's your greatest blessing?"

"My husband, my Turi," Mafalda answered through clenched teeth.

"Yes, he's such a good man!" another woman joined in. "He'll bring home a good catch! Fish for everyone!"

Mafalda didn't want to think about fish now. "Concetta? Help me!"

"Turi is your first blessing! What else? Count your second!"
Mafalda pushed. "My parents in heaven, watching over me."

"Yes, good! What else, what's number three?"

"You and my friends."

"We love you!" Concetta said, and the other women chimed in, "Push, push!" "I see the baby's head!" "You're almost there!"

Mafalda yelled in pain. She pushed and pushed.

"One last time, Mafalda!"

Mafalda pushed once more, grunting, then heard the wail of a baby.

"It's a girl!" Concetta cried out, and Mafalda's heart filled with happiness, since she had prayed for one.

Silence fell in the bedroom, filled with the salty scent of blood and tears.

"But . . ." Concetta began to say.

"What?" Mafalda asked, alarmed. She couldn't see the baby because everyone was in the way. "Concetta, what's the matter?"

"Nothing, really. She's just a little . . . different." Concetta handed over the baby.

Mafalda accepted the baby, taken aback at her appearance. The infant was beautiful, but her skin was as white as flour. Her scalp was so transparent it revealed delicate blue veins underneath, and her fuzzy head was as pale as the moon. Mafalda had never seen such a baby in her entire life. Like most Sicilians, Mafalda was olive-skinned, and Turi was brown as a walnut from the sun.

Mafalda ran her fingertip along the infant's arm, smearing a red line of her own blood, as vivid on the baby's skin as red ink on white paper. Her gaze followed the red line to the purplish cord of blood that connected her to her baby, their God-given bond made flesh. In that moment, she fell in love with her daughter.

"I'll call you Lucia," Mafalda whispered to the baby. "You're pure light, from God."

Concetta beamed. "Yes, she's an angel."

The others joined in. "She's been touched by God." "She's a perfect little angel." "What a blessing!"

Mafalda hoped Turi would be happy, too. Her gaze went to the window, brightening. She realized that Turi should have been back already, since the men fished at night. "Where are they? What time is it?"

Concetta frowned. "Oh my, they're late."

"*Madonna*, they're an hour late!" The women burst into nervous chatter. "They should have been back!" "I lost track of time!"

Then they heard a shout, echoing from the harbor below.

MAFALDA STOOD ON THE DOCK with the other distraught wives, cradling her swaddled infant and trying not to panic. She was still in pain from the delivery and she'd wadded cloth in her underwear to catch the blood. Turi and the other men hadn't returned from the sea, and it was already nine o'clock in the morning. They'd never been this late before.

Villagers crowded the harbor, clustered on the docks, and overwhelmed the pebbled shore. Every able-bodied man in the village fished for a living, and now their wives, mothers, fathers, and children huddled together, clutching each other, weeping, praying, and calling for them.

"Giuseppe, Giuseppe!" Concetta shouted, alongside Liliana, Letizia, Mariana, Nicolina, and the other frantic wives.

Mafalda searched the horizon, but there was no sign of anything. The absence tore at her because the view was otherwise beautiful. Verdant mountains ringed a harbor shaped like a mother's outstretched arms, and the sky was the serene blue of Mary's cloak. The water glimmered like polished aquamarines in the sun, darkening to sapphire and lapis lazuli, like nature's own jewels. The waves rolled into shore, bubbling and frothy.

Every wife knew the dangers of the sea, and Mafalda's mind raced with the terrible things that could've happened. Storms could whip up quickly on account of the winds, as Sicily was at their mercy: from the north came the chilly *tramontana*; from the south, the *ostro*; from the east, *levante*; and from the west, *ponente*. A Rose of the Winds compass hung in every home, and even children knew the *grecale*, a dangerous wind from Greece that could take their fathers.

"Look, I see something!" Concetta shouted, pointing to the sea.

"What?" Mafalda gasped, horrified to spot a dark hump floating toward the dock, like a man's back. "No! No!"

The crowd erupted in chaos. Wives screamed their husbands' names. Villagers raced into the water and started swimming. A group of old men reached the floating hump and shouted what everybody feared. It was a dead body.

Mafalda prayed it wasn't Turi. Concetta prayed next to her, and so did the other wives. Everyone was in an uproar, screaming, wailing, and weeping on the dock, on the shoreline, in the water.

The old men swam the body closer, and villagers craned to see who had drowned. Then Mafalda spotted a bald head and she knew it wasn't Turi. She felt relieved even as she learned which of her friends had just become a widow.

"Gustavo!" Caterina wailed, falling to her knees on the dock.

The crowd surged to comfort her.

The wind picked up, and the waves grew taller and broke harder. Suddenly, everyone was shouting and pointing at the same time. Mafalda looked out to sea, appalled to find dark humps popping out of the water, filling the harbor like a tide of corpses. Amid the bodies bobbed broken blue-and-white wood, oars, and debris.

Mafalda, Concetta, and the other women ran screaming from the dock, reached the shoreline, and rushed into the water. Mafalda held Lucia high above the waves, crying Turi's name over and over. Everyone shouted, cried, and wailed, a cacophony of shock, horror, and grief echoing throughout the harbor.

Old men started swimming to the bodies, but Mafalda couldn't tell if Turi was one of them. The corpses kept turning this way and that, tossed about by the sea, revealing clothing, hands, a foot without a shoe. Body after body was brought to shore by whoever could swim. Rescuers staggered out of the water with corpses, weeping and exhausted. Wives raced into the waves, only to be knocked off their feet.

Husband after husband was taken to a widow. Father after father was lost to his family. The bodies of Concetta's Giuseppe and Nicolina's Stefano washed up hideously bloated.

Mafalda stood in water up to her belly, holding Lucia high and praying to Madonna del Lume to bring Turi to her. Suddenly she spotted a man's body carried forward by a wave, his arms floating. She recognized the diamond pattern of his shirt. It was Turi.

Mafalda wailed, agonized that she had become a mother and widow on the same day. But then she noticed Turi's arms, moving of their own accord.

"Turi, Turi!" Mafalda could see him swimming, then a large wave picked him up, carried him on its crest, and brought him closer.

"Help him, please! Help!" Mafalda cried again, and older men heard her, raced into the water, and swam to Turi. They helped him out of the water between them.

"Turi!" Mafalda rushed to embrace him, and he staggered toward her, falling into her arms, chilled and soaking wet.

"*Madonna, Madonna,*" was all Turi could say, over and over, and Mafalda helped him to shore, still holding the baby. They eased as a family onto the coarse sand, where Turi gave in to hoarse, heartbreaking sobs. He seemed not to notice his newborn daughter, but Mafalda understood. All around them was wailing, crying, and grieving.

Mafalda held him and Lucia, thanking Madonna del Lume and praying for the safe return of the other husbands.

An hour later, she knew the awful truth, and so did the entire village. Turi was the sole survivor of the disaster.

And Mafalda didn't know if they were blessed or cursed.

CHAPTER SIX

Alfredo D'Antonio was a blessed and happy man with daughters named Bella, Valentina, Flora, and Ginevra. Each was beautiful in her own way and had a wonderful personality. Alfredo loved each one, and the fact that they were goats made no difference to him.

"Come, Bella," Alfredo said, and she walked over, always first to be milked. The others waited patiently, chewing their hay in the shed. They knew Alfredo was trying to get to them quickly, aware they were uncomfortable with full udders.

"Good girl, Bella." Alfredo helped her to the milking stand, and Bella began to nibble hay from a hanging net. He didn't have to lock her in with any device, as his girls made the job easy for them both. The milk they produced had a lot of fat, which enabled him to earn a living by selling their cheese in Mussomeli.

Bella, Valentina, Flora, and Ginevra were Girgentana goats, a breed unique to Sicily, with creamy-white coats that curled around their bodies. Their eyes were a warm amber, and their longish ears flopped. Their pinkish noses were refined, and their mouths curved into permanent smiles. Most remarkable were their horns, which spiraled into the air like tall corkscrews, almost seventy centimeters high. Alfredo loved their soft white beards, and he had a beard, too, so the whole family was bearded.

He pressed his thumb and index fingers up into Bella's udder, which felt warm and heavy on his knuckles. He began to squeeze and release her teats, in alternating fashion. Her milk began to flow, and he reached for his tin bucket and resumed milking, finding his rhythm.

"Bella, which story would you like? How about 'The Cat and the Mouse'?" Alfredo liked telling stories while he milked, and if he told a medium-sized one, Bella's teats would be flat by the time he was finished.

He cleared his throat. "Once upon a time, there was a cat who married a mouse. One day, the cat went out to get some pasta, and the mouse fell into a pot of boiling water and died. The cat cried, tearing out his fur, and the door asked him what was the matter. The cat told the door, and the door got so upset it started slamming. Oh my, then the window asked what the fuss was, and the door told him, whereupon the window got so upset it began opening and shutting."

Bella shifted on her hind legs.

"Now, seeing this, the tree asked the window what was amiss, and after the window told him, the tree hurled itself onto the ground in grief. You can imagine what happened next, when a bird landed on the tree. The bird asked the tree why it wept on the ground, and the distraught tree told the bird, whereupon the bird plucked out its own feathers, one by one!"

Bella's milk flowed nicely, and Alfredo continued the story.

"The bird flew to a fountain to get a drink, and when the fountain asked where its feathers were, the bird told him. You can guess, the poor fountain dried up on the spot. Well, a cuckoo flew to the dry fountain, and after the cuckoo heard the tale, she was so sad she burned her own tail. A Monk of Saint Nicholas passed by and asked the cuckoo why her tail was on fire. The cuckoo told him, and the Monk became so distressed he went to Mass without his robes on—"

"Signor D'Antonio, are you home?" a woman called from outside the milking shed.

Startled, Alfredo released Bella's teats. No one ever came here, much less a woman. Ginevra raised her head to the sound.

"Coming!" Alfredo rose, dried his hands on his pants, and left the shed to find an attractive woman standing outside in a red dress. Her dark hair flew in the wind, and she held it back with her hand, smiling.

"Signore, I don't know if you remember me. I bought cheese from you last week. My name is Signora Tozzi. I hope you don't mind my coming to your home."

Alfredo did. "How did you know where I live?"

"I asked around."

Alfredo didn't like that. "How can I help you?"

"Do you have any more cheese?"

"No."

Signora Tozzi's shoulders let down. "You don't have *any*?"

"No, I make it fresh. I'll be at the piazza soon again."

"When?"

"I go twice a week. Sometimes one time."

"But the others are there every day."

"It takes time to make the cheese. You have to let the curds drain."

"Oh no." Signora Tozzi's lower lip puckered. "My husband isn't feeling well. I think I mentioned that last time."

Alfredo remembered. "A stomach problem?"

"Yes, he improved on your cheese, so I need to buy more."

"I don't think my cheese helped. Cheese doesn't improve stomach problems."

"I think it made a difference, I truly do." Signora Tozzi smiled. "I tasted some, and it was delicious, unusually so."

"*My* cheese?" Alfredo asked, incredulous, then caught himself. He wasn't a good salesman. "I mean, I know it's good."

Meanwhile Ginevra ambled out of the stall, and Signora Tozzi squealed in delight. "Look at those horns! They're *magical*! I've never seen a goat like that! Where did you get her?"

"From Agrigento." Alfredo could tell that Ginevra didn't like Signora Tozzi. "The Girgentana is a rare breed, and their milk has a lot of fat."

"How did she get here?"

Alfredo hesitated. "My family is from there."

"And you say her milk is special?"

"No, I said it has a lot of fat."

"I think that's what cured my husband's stomachache!"

"No, your husband got better on his own. Or perhaps you took good care of him."

"Are you flirting with me?" Signora Tozzi asked with a giggle.

Alfredo felt taken aback. He had forgotten how to flirt, if he had ever known. He still loved his late wife, Felicia. "I should get back to milking."

"What time do you come to the piazza, when you come?"

"Around ten."

"I'll be the first in line! Thank you!"

Alfredo nodded.

"Goodbye!" Signora Tozzi turned away, and Alfredo headed back into the shed, followed by Ginevra. He sat down next to Bella, resumed milking, and tried to remember the story.

"Oh yes, anyway, as I was saying, the Queen saw the Monk of Saint Nicholas without his robes and demanded to know why, or she would cut off his head. The Monk told the Queen the story about the cat and the mouse, and the Queen burst into tears, ran to the kitchen, and sifted flour all day."

Alfredo tried to find his milking rhythm, thrown off by Signora Tozzi's visit.

"The King had never seen his wife in the kitchen before, so he thought she'd gone mad. He asked her if she was crazy, and she told him all about the cat and the mouse, the door and the fountain, and the rest.

Now, what did the King do? The King drank a cup of coffee. That's it, that's all. Now, girls, you can take from the story what you will. I think the moral is, Be a King. Don't let things bother you."

But Alfredo couldn't heed the moral. His fingers trembled, and he stopped milking. He felt suddenly afraid. He lived his life bearing a secret. It was the most dangerous of secrets, he had been told from his earliest years.

His parents had made him and his older sister, Annalisa, swear never to breathe a word. Annalisa had taken the secret to her grave, and Alfredo would take it to his, sealed behind a plaque reading **Alfredo D'Antonio**, which wasn't his real name. His sister's real name wasn't Annalisa, nor were his mother's and father's Pieri and Gianluca. They had chosen their names as arbitrarily as Alfredo had chosen the names for his daughters who happened to be goats.

They'd changed their names to live in peace, and that was all his grandparents had wanted, and his great-grandparents before them, and so on. Alfredo's line went back for generations in Sicily, and so did his family secret.

Alfredo's secret was that he was a Jew.

His parents had told him the history so many times he knew it by heart. Jews had lived in Sicily before Christians, settling on the east coast, then spreading outward, flourishing under Muslim rule. Palermo became a Jewish center, but everything changed under Aragonese rule. In 1492, King Ferdinand and Queen Isabella of Spain issued the Alhambra Decree, or the Edict of Expulsion, which expelled Jews from any Spanish territories, including Sicily. Sicily's Jews, numbering thirty thousand, fled the island. Their temples were converted to churches, and Jews who didn't leave were converted to Christianity or executed at Palazzo Chiaramonte Steri in Palermo.

Alfredo's ancestors wanted to stay in Sicily, but they didn't want to convert. They wanted to live in the country they loved and worship the G-d they loved.

So they did, keeping to themselves for generations, guarding their secret.

Sicily had never before had *conversos* or *marranos*, the Spanish derogatory terms for those who practiced Judaism in secret, but it became a matter of life and death. Alfredo's family adhered to the Law as best they could without a rabbi, a synagogue, a Torah, or a kosher butcher. His parents warned him to keep to himself, lest anyone discover his secret. They always lived outside of town, and to avoid suspicion, they attended Mass at the Madonna dei Miracoli church in Mussomeli. They mouthed the Latin prayers and took the Eucharist. They knew G-d would understand.

Now they were all dead, leaving only Alfredo, who had no children except Ginevra, Bella, Valentina, and Flora. He kept his family's Hebrew Bible hidden in a box, with a frayed *tallis* in a satin sack. He used to have a skullcap, but Ginevra ate it. He had his family's silver menorah, but no candles narrow enough to fit. He didn't dare buy any, lest he give himself away. He hadn't heard of a single other Jew in the entire province, much less met one.

So he kept to himself and made his cheese, leaving only to sell it or to buy necessities in Mussomeli. He prayed on the Sabbath, by himself.

He kept his faith.

He felt happy and blessed in his life.

His real name was Abraham.

He was the last Jew in Sicily.

CHAPTER SEVEN

Dottor Vergenti smoothed down his white coat, scanning the examining room with annoyance. The madhouse was formerly a convent, so its physical layout was poorly suited to its current use. The examining room used to be a pantry, so it fit only a small table, a chair, and a scale. Shelves that used to hold groceries were empty except for a single textbook. The room was located next to the kitchen, so it smelled like bean soup and mouse droppings, making Vergenti's nose twitch. Today he had to diagnose the boy, Dante No-Surname.

He slid the textbook off the shelf and thumbed to the chapter entitled CAUSES OF MADNESS. He found the list, PHYSICAL CAUSES OF MADNESS, and read it: HEREDITY, MASTURBATION, SUNSTROKE, SYPHILIS, ALCOHOL ABUSE, ABUSE OF MERCURY. He frowned. None applied to the boy. He read the list, EMOTIONAL CAUSES OF MADNESS: FAMILY PROBLEMS, POVERTY, UNRECIPROCATED LOVE, JEALOUSY, RELIGIOUS FANATICISM, SUPERSTITION, AMBITION, HURT PRIDE, BEREAVEMENT, PERSECUTION. Maybe the boy's diagnosis was jealousy, of the younger brother. He put the textbook back on the shelf.

Vergenti turned when the nurse entered the room. Her name was Teresa and she was married to Renzo.

"Good morning, Dottore." Teresa had dark eyes, a wide nose, and a ready smile. A topknot tamed her black hair, and her ample body filled out a white blouse and a voluminous brown skirt under her muslin pinafore. "Renzo stayed this morning to help us, then he'll go home. He's bringing the boy down."

"How thoughtful."

"Dante's a difficult case, sir. I believe he's dangerous, though he's quite young. Not only did he stab Renzo, he threw food at me, and feces."

Vergenti loathed the shit-throwers. "I'll make quick work of the examination."

"Good." Teresa nodded, and Renzo entered the room holding Dante, who squirmed in his grasp. Tearstains streaked the boy's cheeks, and his hair was in disarray. His shirt and pants were dirty, and he was barefoot.

Vergenti frowned. "What happened to his shoes?"

"God knows." Renzo rolled his eyes. "Boy, stop it, stop it! Stay still!"

"He had a brown jacket, too. Where is it?"

Teresa interjected, "I gave it to the laundry after he soiled it."

"Oh." Vergenti knew Renzo and Teresa had three sons, but he didn't accuse them. The husband-and-wife team was invaluable to him, since he never went near the lunatics. "Renzo, set him down, please."

"What if he bites me again?"

"I need to evaluate him." Vergenti was required to diagnose the child, so the madhouse would receive its allotment for the boy's support.

"Write that he's violent and incorrigible."

Vergenti patted the examining table. "Dante, sit down here and be still. I would like to talk to you."

Dante struggled in Renzo's arms, his eyes wide with fear.

Renzo snorted. "He won't listen to anybody. He acts like a prince."

Teresa shot him a look. "Renzo, set him down."

"Are you crazy? He'll run away!" Renzo set the boy down, and Dante bolted from the room, tripping on his leg rope.

"Oh no!" Vergenti sighed in dismay.

Teresa shook her head, clucking.

"Get back here!" Renzo grabbed the child. "Stand still!"

Teresa looked back at Vergenti. "You see how hard he is to manage?"

Vergenti's patience evaporated. "Renzo, put him on the table."

"Yes, Dottore." Renzo brought the child to the table and sat him down. "Listen to the doctor, boy, or we'll send you to the lepers. Your fingers will fall off, then your toes. You'll be Prince of the Lepers."

"Let me talk to him, Renzo." Vergenti stood in front of the boy, who fidgeted in Renzo's grasp. "Now, I want to ask you a question, Dante. You must tell me the truth. Why did you try to harm your brother? Were you jealous of him?"

"I have no brother," Dante whispered.

"Lying is against the rules." Vergenti picked up his pen and pad, then made a note, *lies compulsively* and *disobeys rules*. Also *throws food and feces*, which revolted him even to write. "Dante, are you jealous of your little brother? Yes or no?"

Dante shook his head, frowning.

"Didn't you wish your brother away? Didn't you want your parents to yourself? That would be a natural wish of any firstborn child." Vergenti made a note, *delusional and wishful thinking*. "Your parents brought you here—"

"That's not how I came," Dante interrupted, still in a whisper.

"Then how did you come?"

Renzo interjected, "You're inviting him to lie, Dottore!"

Teresa chimed in, "Dottore, the boy is delusional. Asking that question will only encourage him."

"Please, silence." Vergenti turned to the child. "Dante, how did you get here?"

"A marionette—"

"A *marionette*? You mean, like Pinocchio?"

Renzo guffawed. "Pinocchio! He's a liar, he admits it! Prince Pinocchio!"

Vergenti wrote *marionette* on his pad. "So you're saying a marionette brought you? Was it Pinocchio himself?"

Dante shook his head. "It was dark, and he carried me on a horse."

"The marionette?" Vergenti made another note, *marionette on horse.* Then *driven to lunacy by jealousy.* "What happened to the marionette?"

Suddenly Dante spit in his face, and Vergenti staggered backward, dropping the pen and feeling his gorge rise. The child's sputum could carry tuberculosis, malaria, leprosy. *Plague.*

"Told you!" Renzo lifted Dante from the examining table.

Vergenti vowed never to see the boy again.

DANTE SAT IN HIS CELL, worried he'd made a mistake in spitting at the doctor. He was trying to be fierce like Count Roland, but maybe he was wrong. He'd been thinking he was too much like Oliver, because Mamma liked Oliver better. But the doctor kept saying he had a brother, and Dante knew he didn't. Then he remembered Papa liked Count Roland because he was fierce.

He thought about Papa now. It was Dante's birthday, and Papa was holding out a box wrapped in silvery paper. "Son, what do you think it is?"

Dante reached for the gift, but Papa moved it away with a smile. "Wait, can you guess?"

His mother chuckled. "Don't tease him, dear."

"I can't guess!" Dante wanted his gift. "Please, may I have it?"

"Fair enough." Papa handed him the present, and Dante sat on the floor and tore off the silvery paper. Inside was a box, and he lifted the lid to find a beautiful sword. It had a long blade of silver paper glued onto wood, with a silvery hilt and a real point at the end.

Dante cried, "It's Durendal!"

Papa grinned. "Now you have your own sword, like Count Roland."

"Thank you!" Dante scrambled to his feet and whipped the sword around boldly. "Papa, the pagans are coming for the rear guard!"

Mamma put up her hands. "Dante, be careful!"

Papa laughed. "Darling, he's fighting the pagans, can't you see?" He grabbed a poker from the fireplace and wielded it like a sword. "You Christians will not defeat us!"

"I will spill your bright blood, pagan!" Dante swung his sword.

"Count Roland, you're no match for me!" Papa struck the sword with his poker, and the battle was joined in the living room.

"I'll spare none of you!" Dante moved right, thrusting his sword. "'Lift up, my lords, your burnished blades and fight!'"

"'You shall learn the name of my good blade!'"

"Mountjoy!" Dante yelled, which was Roland's battle cry.

"Dante, enough!" Mamma caught him by the arm.

"Mamma, no, he's escaping! He's cunning and treacherous!"

Papa burst into laughter. "Darling, I'm cunning and treacherous!"

"Enough, you two!" Mamma took the sword from Dante. "Let's have some cake, and you can play later."

Papa winked at Dante. "We shall meet again!"

"You shall rue the day!"

And they both laughed.

CHAPTER EIGHT

It was early morning when Franco arrived at Villa Zito in Bagheria, having ridden through the night to avoid the heat. The town was east of Palermo on the coast of the Tyrrhenian Sea, and many nobles maintained summer residences here, among them Villa Butera, which was owned by the Prince of Butera, and the bizarre Villa Palagonia with its statuary of goblins and monsters. Villa Zito had been in Baron Zito's family for generations and was his favorite of his three residences.

Franco cantered up the long road to the villa, which cut through a luxuriant garden dotted with cypresses, red camellias, pink and white roses, giant aloe, agave with yellow flowers, and trees full of purple plums. Franco thought it was a shame not to grow lemons here, but Baron Zito refused, saying Villa Zito would never become a business, a true lady among prostitutes.

The villa itself was situated on a gentle bluff overlooking the water, privileging arrivals by sea. It had a limestone façade that absorbed the glorious sunshine, rising three stories high. Each window was topped by engravings and had its own balcony with a potbellied railing of wrought iron, trailing pink frangipani. Large porches anchored both sides, cooling the villa even in a Sicilian summer.

Franco headed for the stables, where Baron Zito would have just returned from his morning hunt. He reached the courtyard and stone barn to find the Baron watching his British trainer lunge his white stallion. Baron Zito was about the same age as Franco's father, but he looked younger, having enjoyed a privileged life. He stood tall and lean, and his refined features decorated a long face framed by light brown hair. His britches were grass-stained, which meant he had fallen.

"Good morning, Baron Zito." Franco dismounted, patted the mare's wet neck, and handed her to a groom.

"Good to see you." The Baron's light eyes went flinty in the sunshine. "How was the trip here?"

"Fine, thank you." Franco knew what the Baron wanted to hear about the kidnapped boy and would tell him obliquely, since they weren't alone. "Baron Zito, I dealt with that matter you asked me to. It's all taken care of."

"*Bravissimo*, Franco!" The Baron threw open his arms and hugged Franco, which was unusual for him. "What a load off my mind! So that ends the matter?"

"Absolutely."

"I knew I could count on you!"

"Thank you." Franco basked in the Baron's approval, feeling closer to him than before. The Baron would never know the boy was hidden in the madhouse, rather than buried in the dirt. Nor would he learn of Claudio's murder, which Franco had been trying to push from his mind.

"Franco, look, I took a tumble this morning." Baron Zito chuckled, gesturing at his britches. "Arabo saw a deer and took me for quite a ride. I know he's young, but I thought I was a better horseman. Perhaps you can give me a lesson someday?"

"Anytime, but if Arabo wants you off, then off you'll go."

"That's the truth!" Baron Zito beamed, clapping him on the shoulder. "Niall says if we tire the animal, he'll mind his manners."

"I disagree." Franco disliked the British prig to whom the Baron had entrusted his magnificent Arabian stallion. "I would never lunge Arabo. He doesn't need it. He's too smart to go around like a windup toy."

Niall interjected, "It tires him!"

"It *bores* him!" Franco shouted back. "Hell, it bores *me*."

Baron Zito laughed. "It bores me, too!"

Niall scowled. "Franco, what do you know? You're not trained."

"What Sicilian is?" Franco burst into laughter, and so did Baron Zito, since they shared something that the Englishman never could. Native blood.

Niall shook his head. "Franco, you grew up on donkeys!"

"*Horses!*" Franco simmered, knowing he would never forget this slur.

Niall turned away and raised his whip, about to bring it down on Arabo.

"No!" Franco rushed forward to stop him.

"Don't tell me how to discipline my horses!"

"They're Baron Zito's, not yours!"

Baron Zito stepped between them. "Franco's right, Niall. There will be no more whippings for Arabo." He took the lunge line from Niall and handed it to Franco. "Arabo belongs to you from now on."

"What?" Franco asked, astonished.

"*What?*" Niall recoiled, appalled.

"Franco, please accept him as my gift, for your loyalty." Baron Zito met Franco's eye in a meaningful way, and Franco realized that Arabo was his reward for murdering the boy, whom he hadn't killed. But he had killed Claudio, and the dirty business tainted the offer of even this splendid stallion.

"Baron Zito, no, I can't accept such a generous gift. What about your son, Davide? I thought he was taking lessons on Arabo."

Baron Zito scoffed. "That boy will never follow through. He's gallivanting around Paris. Arabo's better off with you. Take him."

"Thank you," Franco said after a moment, tugging the lunge line, and Arabo walked over, lowering his head.

Baron Zito smiled. "See? He obeys you already, son."

Son. Franco loved when Baron Zito called him that.

"Take the saddle, too. It was custom-made for him. Now, I'm off."

Baron Zito motioned to a groom, who brought Franco's mare forward. "Goodbye, Franco!"

"Goodbye!" Franco stroked Arabo's wet neck, which felt warm and strong under his palm, and he admired the stallion's darkly intelligent eyes and elegant, dished face, a hallmark of his noble breed. Arabo's white coat glistened like marble, showing a muscular topline, and the prospect of owning him overshadowed Franco's misgivings about why he was given him.

He mounted Arabo and gathered his reins, feeling instantly powerful. He surveyed Villa Zito from the higher vantage point, straightened in the saddle, and somehow knew he could attain the life he dreamed of.

The groom handed him the mare's reins so he could lead her, and Franco nudged Arabo into a trot around the front of the villa, so man and horse began a conversation that would last a lifetime.

Suddenly Franco spotted a kitchen maid running toward him in a black uniform and puffy white cap. It was Nenella, his Violetta's best friend, and his heart soared, knowing it had to be a message. He and Violetta sneaked trysts in the kitchen pantry, but Franco hadn't expected to see her today, since it wasn't one of his scheduled visits. He yearned for her with an intensity that surprised even him.

"Franco!" Nenella hurried toward him, out of breath. "We saw you arrive from the kitchen."

"Can you get me into the pantry?"

"No, Livia's watching. Go down the road, Violetta's waiting for you. Don't keep her long! I'm covering for her!"

"Thank you!" Franco cantered off. Midway down the road, he heard her calling his name and halted Arabo.

"Franco!" Violetta emerged from behind a bush, and the sight of her filled his heart. Her puffy white cap couldn't hide her beautiful face, nor her black uniform the lovely body.

"Violetta! Get on the mare! I've missed you!"

"I've missed you, too!" Violetta hiked up her skirt, clambered onto the mare, and took the reins. "Let's go!"

They took off together, riding side-by-side, and Franco found himself laughing, a lightness lifting his soul. He'd been with many women, but never experienced this feeling. Violetta's white cap flew off, and her remarkable red hair tumbled out, flying behind her like flames.

"To the right!" Franco called out, and they cantered to a grassy patch under umbrella pines. They reached the spot breathless, Violetta dismounted hurriedly, and Franco jumped off, scooping her into his free arm and covering her face with kisses, then her warm neck, which smelled adorably of flour.

"I love you," he told her, meaning it, for the first time in his life.

CHAPTER NINE

Gaetano set out for the police station, first thing in the morning. He couldn't wait to begin investigating the kidnapping. He hurried up Via Toledo and tilted the brim of his hat down against the sun. He shuddered to think that the kidnapping had occurred on this street, only a few blocks back.

He joined the men walking to work and the women to market, tugging children along the street, the busiest in Palermo. Everyone threaded his way around brightly painted donkey carts, bulky black carriages with matched horses, and carters pushing barrows of broccoli, artichokes, and fennel, from which Gaetano caught a whiff of anise.

He passed every kind of shop and business: hat shops, shoe stores, a book-and-map seller, an apothecary, a butcher shop with live roosters hanging upside down, a water seller with flavored waters in decanters, and a stationery store with a scribe in front, writing letters for those who couldn't, since the majority of Sicilians could neither read nor write.

A bakery released the aroma of baking bread, and a toy store attracted delighted children with dancing puppets of kings, knights, witches, and wizards. Gaetano heard snippets of passing conversations, mostly in the Sicilian dialect of his fellow *Palermitani*, with their characteristic accent, but also in the Italian, French, and English of the traders, merchants, and soldiers who swarmed the island like flies. Everyone came to Palermo to make his fortune, but foreigners came to take one home.

Gaetano reached the Questura, the police station, with its amber façade and arched windows facing the Piazza della Vittoria, full of lush palms, pepper trees, and large agave. A group of *carabinieri* stood chatting outside its entrance, and Gaetano knew a few of them, since he represented civil and criminal clients. He tried to have a friendly relationship with the *carabinieri*, but they loathed lawyers.

"Good morning, gentlemen." Gaetano smiled. "I need to see Marshal Rosselli. Is he in?"

"Yes, I'm sure he's awaiting you." The officer chuckled.

Gaetano kept going and entered the marble vestibule, which was dim. Dust motes swirled, agitated by motion in a room accustomed to none. He went to the reception desk, where an officer sat doodling on a piece of paper.

"Excuse me, I'm here to see Marshal Rosselli."

The officer didn't look up. "And the nature of your business?"

"I'll explain it to him," Gaetano answered, then heard Marshal Rosselli's laughter. He left the desk and hurried to the sound, past the arched courtyard filled with palms and ruins of the old convent of Saint Maria Maddalena. He spotted the Marshal heading down the marble hallway into his office, cigarette in hand.

"Marshal Rosselli, may I have a word?"

"Make it quick, Gaetano." Marshal Rosselli led him into a cluttered office and took a seat behind an ornately carved desk covered with papers. On the wall behind him hung a crucifix, a portrait of the Viceroy, and a painting of Jesus Christ. A chair was opposite the desk, but the Marshal didn't ask Gaetano to sit down, so he stood as if in court.

"Marshal, I'm sure you heard about the kidnapping at the Festival of Saint Rosalia. Have there been any developments?"

"None." Marshal Rosselli was diminutive in his fancy uniform, with an oiled gray-and-black mustache and silvering hair under a braided cap.

"Has the family contacted you?"

"No." Marshal Rosselli exhaled cigarette smoke, watching it swirl. On the side wall hung a map of old Palermo with its distinctive carve-out for La Cala, the harbor.

"You have no leads, truly?"

"Truly." Marshal Rosselli leaned back in his chair. "Nor do I expect to. I don't need to tell you how this goes, do I? These things take time. We won't hear anything for a season, or more. The parents will stay quiet. They don't want their child murdered. They'll call us if they need us, but until then, we have a conspiracy of silence."

Gaetano bit his tongue. Sometimes he suspected that the authorities conspired with the kidnappers, but he couldn't say so without proof. "Did any of your officers notice anything suspicious that night?"

"No."

"But there were so many on duty. I was at the festival with my family, and your men were on horseback and on foot. There had to be some on the Quattro Canti."

"As you know, my jurisdiction is limited. The officers you saw may not have been mine." Marshal Rosselli waved his hand, trailing a smoky snake. "They could have been from the Bourbons, the province, or the Church herself."

"Have you heard anything from other jurisdictions about the kidnapping?" Gaetano knew there was overlap of authority in Palermo, with the ironic result that nobody had authority over anything.

"No."

"How many of your officers were on the Quattro Canti?"

"I don't know."

"Can you estimate? Was it between five and ten, or ten and fifteen?"

"I don't require my officers to stand at fixed locations like statues."

"One would think that they have stations."

"Only one like you, unacquainted with policing in the capital city." Marshal Rosselli snorted, emitting twin jets of smoke. "We remain flexible to respond to whatever situations present themselves at the festival. It's not only the biggest celebration in Palermo, it's the biggest in Sicily."

Gaetano knew that, which was why he'd thought there'd be better security. "But there must be a shift schedule."

"No." Marshal Rosselli shook his head. "The schedule changes so much during the festival that we don't write it down. The demand for manpower is impossibly high, and we're always shorthanded. As you may know, there are only about five hundred *carabinieri* for the entire island, which has about two million people. Did you know that?"

"No," Gaetano answered, though it didn't seem on point.

"So, I deploy as I see fit."

Gaetano tried a different approach. "Were the mayor or other city officials on the Quattro Canti?"

"No. He and his family attended Mass at the Cathedral. My wife and my family were also at Mass."

Gaetano took yet another approach. "But those on the Quattro Canti had to be given permission to be there, didn't they?"

"I dispensed no such permission. That's not my duty or concern."

"Who would have given them permission?"

"I doubt it's so formal, Gaetano." Marshal Rosselli shrugged, his gold epaulets shifting up and down. "Anyway, many of the best families leave for the seaside in the summer."

"Some return for the festival."

"Then they leave again." Marshal Rosselli spread his palms. "It's simply impossible to tell where they would be at any given time."

"It's difficult, not impossible." Gaetano couldn't suppress his exasperation. "I don't understand why you're so unbothered by this crime."

Marshal Rosselli bristled. "What do you expect me to do? Investigate the kidnapping of an unknown child?"

"Yes, exactly," Gaetano shot back. "You can't sit here and do *nothing*."

"I wait for the parents to contact me. You lack the experience to see the wisdom in my approach."

Gaetano thought it was lassitude, not wisdom. "I'm trying to help an innocent boy."

"It's my job. Why are you trying to do it?"

Because you won't, Gaetano thought but didn't say. If the police did their job, there would be no need for the Beati Paoli.

"Indeed, why *are* you involved, Gaetano?"

"I represent an interested client."

"Who?"

"It's confidential."

"How hypocritical." Marshal Rosselli lifted an eyebrow. "You expect me to share information, yet you do not."

"We're not in the same position. You're a public official, and I'm a private lawyer. You're inquiring into a private business relationship, and I'm asking about a matter of public interest."

"Hmph! Your client must be wealthy to hire a fancy lawyer like you." Marshal Rosselli cocked his head. "If he is, perhaps he's friends with the victim's family. Perhaps *he* knows who the victim might be. I should invite your client here and interview *him*."

"That won't be possible."

"This meeting is over." Marshal Rosselli stubbed out his cigarette in a crowded ashtray. "Good day."

"Good day," Gaetano said, turning to go.

But he was just getting started.

CHAPTER TEN

Mafalda nursed Lucia at the table across from Turi, who slumped in his chair. His eyes remained downcast, and lines creased his forehead. His pasta with sardines and broccoli rabe with garlic and oil cooled on his plate.

"Turi, don't you want to eat?" Mafalda asked gently.

"I'm not hungry." Turi raised his glass of wine and drained it quickly. "Giuseppe's funeral is tomorrow."

"I know," Mafalda said, sympathetic. Giuseppe was Concetta's husband, and his would be the first of two funerals tomorrow, held in the morning and the afternoon. They had to be separated because the village undertaker had only one hearse.

"I tried to help them, I did. So did Giuseppe. He and I were the best swimmers. I tried, so hard."

"Of course you did," Mafalda rushed to say. Turi had barely slept since the disaster, nor had he taken interest in Lucia. He seemed not to care that the baby had even been born, much less that she was so pale.

"We managed to get to Fabiano, but the waves were relentless. They engulfed him. It was all we could do to keep our heads above water." Turi raked a hand through his hair. "The storm came so fast, the waves grabbed the oars from our hands. The sea broke our boat like a stick."

"I'm sure." Mafalda worried he was ruminating too much.

"Giuseppe was holding one of the boards, calling to me, and I tried to swim to him but I couldn't, the sea was churning. Then another wave lifted the boat into the air and crashed it down on him." Turi shook his head in anguish. "He went below the waves and never came back up."

"How terrible." Mafalda felt a deep pang, experiencing Concetta's loss as if it were her own. She'd brought Concetta some food, but she was starting to wonder where their own next meal would come from. So did the town, since the good boats had been destroyed and only the old men were left to fish.

"It was so dark, the lamps went out, and the moonlight wasn't bright enough to see anything. We were at the center of the storm."

"Madonna del Lume protect us," Mafalda said under her breath.

"But she *didn't*." Turi looked up, his dark eyes glistening. "She didn't protect us. She turned her face—"

"No, Madonna del Lume protects us always. She loves us."

"Then where *was* she?" Bitterness twisted Turi's lips. "I watched every man drown, one after the other. I prayed to her, I cried to her. She abandoned us."

"She saved *you*," Mafalda said reflexively, regretting the words as soon as they left her lips.

"How do you think I feel about that, my love?" Turi's eyes brimmed with tears. "How can I witness the grief of so many? Why didn't she save Giuseppe? Concetta's heart is broken, and she has four children. And Fabiano, and Leo? Why did she take my friends and save me?"

"We have a baby now, Turi. Maybe that's why."

"I don't want her then. You keep her!" Turi grabbed the wine bottle and left the table.

THE PARROCCHIA MARIA SANTISSIMA DEL Lume sat atop the tallest hill in town, bathed in sunshine on the piazza. It was a beautiful edifice, dominated by a triangular cornice with **MARIA S.S. DEL LUME** written in colorful mosaics, flanked by towers. Its stone façade glowed a beautiful alabaster hue, radiating the warmth of the sun, and its carved wooden doors stood open for the funeral Mass.

Families filled the piazza, a throng of women and children dressed in black, dazed with grief. They hugged, kissed, and comforted each other in subdued tones, bearing the loss as one village.

Mafalda and Turi reached the crowd with baby Lucia, swaddled in a white blanket. Mafalda spotted Concetta's hat at the front, but she was too far away. The friends had barely had a chance to speak, and Mafalda grieved for her. In ordinary times, they would be clucking over Lucia and sorting old baby clothes. The white blanket Lucia slept in was from Concetta.

Mafalda spotted heads turning in their direction, then women talking behind their hands. She heard a sob and looked over to see elderly Nicolina Castro scurrying toward her in widow's weeds. Mafalda met her to pay her respects. "Nicolina, I'm so sorry about—"

"Thank you," Nicolina interrupted, reaching for Turi. "Turi, I want to know if Stefano said anything before he passed. Did he have any last words? Did he call for me? Did you speak with him? Or hear?"

"Nicolina, I'm sorry." Turi winced, stricken. "He was in another boat. The storm was so loud, the wind was howling, I didn't hear anybody, I couldn't."

"What happened exactly? Who was in his boat?" Nicolina's hooded eyes spilled tears. "Turi, you're a good swimmer, and my Stefano, he's an older man, I understand why he didn't come back alive, I just want to know he didn't suffer. Do you think he suffered?"

"No, no, I don't, I believe he went quickly, I believe they all did." Turi nodded, his eyes brimming, and Mafalda touched his back. Other widows in the crowd were trying to get his attention.

Caterina waved at him, angry. "Turi, why did you go to sea that night? I knew the wind was from the northeast! I could tell by the trees!"

Mariana frowned, moving aside her black mantilla. "I thought the same thing! Why did you go, Turi? It was the Greek wind!"

Turi wiped his eyes, straightening. "Caterina, Mariana, everyone, I'm so sorry for the loss of your husbands, who were my dearest friends. Please accept my deepest sympathies." He raised his voice, hoarse with grief. "Believe me, I have asked myself, many times over, why we set out, and this is my answer. We underestimated the sea, we failed to respect her, and we let our guard down—"

Mariana interrupted, "Did you discuss it before? Tell us what was said!"

Caterina chimed in, "Turi, I don't feel sorry for you! You're alive to tell the story! My husband is dead!"

Liliana nodded, sobbing. "Did you try to save them? Why didn't you save my Marco?"

Turi began to shake, and Mafalda put an arm around him. "Caterina, Mariana, everyone, Turi feels terrible. It wasn't his fault."

Caterina shouted back, "He saved only himself!"

Mariana chimed in, "He could've done something!"

Liliana shook her head, sobbing. "He *should* have!"

"Ladies, no!" Father Benvolio scurried over, round as a meatball in his black cassock, waving his stubby arms. "Ladies, gentlemen, be calm. We'll have none of this discord, not in front of Madonna del Lume. She wouldn't want this, she loves us all."

Mafalda felt grateful. "Father, thank you, my Turi is heartbroken. People shouldn't blame him."

"I know." Father Benvolio placed an arm on Turi's shoulder. "Turi is our brother. This terrible disaster was not his fault. We mustn't harbor ill will against him."

Turi hung his head, sniffling, and Mafalda noticed Concetta making her way toward them in her black dress, a strange expression on her face.

"Concetta, I'm so sorry—"

"Shut up, Mafalda!" Concetta pointed at Lucia. "I blame that *thing* you hold! You got that baby in exchange for our husbands! You made a deal with Satan! You couldn't conceive before, we all know it! That's why the baby's unnatural!"

"*What?*" Mafalda asked, shocked. "Concetta? What are you saying? You know I didn't—"

"The calamity struck the night she was born! That's why Turi lived and not our husbands! That baby's a *monster*! Look at her!" Concetta yanked the blanket from under Lucia, causing the baby to fall from Mafalda's arms.

"No!" Mafalda caught Lucia a split second before she would have hit the cobblestones. The baby cried, and everyone got a good look at her. Gasps circulated, eyes flew open, and fingers pointed.

"Look at that *thing*!" Concetta shouted. "Has anyone *ever* seen a baby like this? She's a *specter*! She's an omen, she's bad luck! *She's* the reason our men died!"

"No, no!" Mafalda cradled the crying Lucia, horrified. "She's an innocent baby, an angel—"

"No, a *devil*! She's not *human*!"

Mafalda edged backward. Angry villagers encircled her, advancing. Father Benvolio tried to hold them back, but they pushed past him. Turi tried, too, but they weren't after him anymore. They wanted Lucia.

Mafalda felt a bolt of sheer terror. She turned away with the baby, ran from the piazza, and raced home. She was almost there when she realized something.

Turi hadn't come with her.

CHAPTER ELEVEN

Alfredo ambled down the sunny cobblestone street in Mussomeli with Beatrice, his donkey. She clip-clopped beside him, carrying packets of cheese in her side baskets. She was cute and chubby with large eyes and long ears with black tips. Her coat was a soft grayish brown with a black line down the back. Alfredo loved her, but he considered her a cousin rather than a daughter.

A few people walked on the street, and he kept his head down by habit. No one greeted him, nor did he greet them. He passed small stone houses with rough wooden doors, and he could hear people talking as they had their breakfast, a nice sound.

The street sloped steeply downhill, and at the bottom was the Madonna dei Miracoli church and the piazza with the open-air market. The other vendors were already selling from tables piled with oranges, lemons, plums, peaches, peppers, broccoli, squash, grapes, and nuts. Lupini beans and olives soaked in briny tubs.

Alfredo was last to arrive because he lived out of town. He didn't get a table because no space was ever left, so he sold his cheese from Beatrice's back. He was surprised to see a line forming in his customary spot, with Signora Tozzi at the front.

She waved excitedly when she spotted him, but Alfredo only blinked. The other vendors were friendly with their customers, but he wasn't.

He didn't speak unless someone asked him a question about his cheese, which rarely happened. There were only so many questions one could ask about cheese.

"*Ciao*, Signor D'Antonio!" Signora Tozzi called, still waving.

"*Ciao*," Alfredo finally called back. The vendors lifted eyebrows and exchanged looks. He reached the piazza and walked past them, but before he got to his spot, Signora Tozzi and her ladyfriends clustered around him.

"Signor D'Antonio! I'm so happy you're here! My husband feels much better. He thinks it's the cheese."

"It isn't."

"I've been telling my friends about your goats, too." Signora Tozzi's dark eyes danced. "Tell everyone how magical they are, with those horns!"

Alfredo shook his head. "They're not magical."

"Yes, they are!" Signora Tozzi clasped her hands together. "And the cheese is magical, too!"

"No, it's not." Alfredo concluded that Signora Tozzi had a hard head. "Anyway, would you like some?"

"Yes, I'll take two packets!" Signora Tozzi thrust coins at him.

One of her ladyfriends called out, "I'll take two packets, too!"

"So will I!" said her third ladyfriend, pushing money on Alfredo. He sold cheese as fast as he could hand it over, and Beatrice kept looking around, wondering what was going on. The other vendors started talking behind their hands, and passersby became attracted by the commotion and started digging in their pockets for money.

Alfredo sold out, for the first time ever. He'd always gone home with cheese and eaten it himself. He'd eaten so much cheese he thought it flowed in his veins.

He looked at Beatrice, picked up her rope, and they turned to go home.

Feeling happy and lucky, for which he thanked G-d.

CHAPTER TWELVE

"Good morning, beautiful woman." Renzo greeted his wife by squeezing her breast when she entered the staff room. She was starting the day shift as he ended the night shift, so this was the only time they saw each other during the week. They used to make love behind the cubbyholes, and he wanted to revive the practice.

"Stop it, silly." Teresa brushed her blouse down and put her purse in her cubbyhole.

"You *do* look beautiful today." Renzo kissed her on the cheek, breathing in the soapiness of her skin. "Kiss me."

"Don't get any ideas." Teresa reached for her muslin apron.

"Why not?" Renzo chuckled. "We're married. I have a right to pleasure. So do you. What a coincidence."

Teresa looped her apron over her neck. "How was work last night?"

"Wonderful." Renzo opened his big arms. "Welcome to the madhouse!"

Teresa smiled, surprised. "What's gotten into you, Renzo? You're usually so crabby after your shift."

"Not anymore." Renzo beamed. "Things are looking up, don't you think? We can buy meat this month. We'll eat like kings."

Teresa frowned, tying her apron in the back. "Only because of Dante."

"Yes, we got Prince Pinocchio admitted and made a fortune. You should kiss me for that." Renzo took another swipe at her breast, but Teresa sidestepped him.

"I wish you had discussed it with me first."

"I knew you'd say no. You can't go against me now. You'd get me fired."

Teresa fretted. "I don't sleep well."

"You're not tired enough." Renzo grabbed her, kissing her neck. "I'll tire you. I'll *exhaust* you."

Teresa pushed him away. "Dante doesn't belong here. I feel sorry for him."

"I don't. Now he'll get a taste of the world."

"This isn't the world. This is hell."

"It won't kill him."

"It might," Teresa shot back. They both knew that another child, a deaf-mute, had died here last year after a beating, when his wounds turned septic.

"I had nothing to do with that. It was Augusto who did it, and he got fired."

"What if someone comes looking for Dante? What if he talks?"

Renzo waved her off. "Vergenti will never believe him."

"What about Big Nose? He said he didn't see any carriage."

"Vergenti didn't hear him. And what value would anyone place on his word against mine? Among lunatics, my credibility soars." Renzo laughed, but Teresa didn't.

"Still, he could tell the other staff. Someone might ask questions."

"Don't worry." Renzo had more important things on his mind. "My dear, since our success with Prince Pinocchio, I've been thinking we could do it again and—"

"Haven't you been listening?" Teresa glared at him as only a wife could. "Never, *ever* say that again. We'll never do it again. I've been praying for forgiveness."

Renzo chuckled. "You think we'll burn in hell?"

"I know *you* will." Teresa stormed out of the staff room, and Renzo watched her go, mulling it over. He'd lost faith in God long ago. A sane conclusion, for anyone who worked in the madhouse.

DANTE HAD JUST BEEN SERVED breakfast, a piece of stale bread and strawberry jam on a metal plate pushed through the door. He pounced on the plate, knowing he had to get it before the rats. He picked up the bread, swiped it through the jam, and stuffed it into his mouth. The strawberry tasted sweet, and he wished it would last forever, but it didn't.

Suddenly a rat scurried from the corner, its pointed nose twitching. Dante scooted backward with the plate. The rat raced toward him, then stopped at the rope attached to his ankle. There was a glob of strawberry jam on top, which must have fallen.

The rat started eating the jam with sharp white teeth. Dante knew how their teeth felt because the rats bit him at night, leaving welts on his ankles. He licked his plate quickly, getting the last of the jam. Meanwhile, another rat raced from its nest, then another and another, swarming on the rope.

Dante edged away, frightened. The rats finished the jam on the rope and chewed the rope itself.

Roland is fierce and Oliver is wise.

Dante was starting to think he should be both.

CHAPTER THIRTEEN

Franco trotted Arabo with Roberto lagging behind on the mare. They had left the *giardino* and were making their way to the village on a dusty road. Prickly pear cactus, its paddles gray-green with pink flowers, flanked the road with agave, aloe, and yucca. Sometimes Sicily looked like a desert to Franco, but she never lost her wild and primitive beauty.

The brothers still hadn't spoken, and Franco was beginning to think his twin would never talk to him again. "Roberto, pick up the pace, would you? We need to get to the piazza."

"We have something to discuss, don't you think? It's why I came with you on this stupid errand."

"This stupid errand is my job."

"Is *everything* about work? Aren't some things more important, like me?"

"Okay, fine." Franco halted Arabo. Roberto caught up, and the twins walked side-by-side on the horses.

"Franco, explain to me why you killed that man."

"I told you, it was necessary."

Roberto scoffed. "For a new horse? Is that why?"

"No, I wouldn't kill a man for a horse."

"I'm surprised, you love horses. Then why?"

"It's better if you don't know. Trust me."

"I used to." Roberto shot him a look. "You said it was business. What could possibly justify an unprovoked murder? Who was he?"

"I can't tell you that, either."

"I hope he wasn't a friend. You don't have enough friends to start doing them in."

"It wasn't."

"You mean *he* wasn't. You killed a human being."

Franco had thought he'd put the deed behind him, but Roberto wasn't helping.

"Did Baron Zito have something to do with it?"

"No," Franco lied.

"So your trip to Bagheria was coincidental? And the horse?"

"Yes."

Roberto lifted an eyebrow. "But when I woke up that morning, no one knew where you were."

"I don't report to my men, they report to me."

"Why did you go to Bagheria?"

"I report to the Baron routinely. He expects to hear about his *giardino* face-to-face. You haven't been here long enough to know."

Roberto fell silent a minute. "The man you killed looked young."

"He was. He had no family."

"Does that make it better or worse?" Roberto shook his head. "Now he'll never know life's pleasures, like finding out your twin is a murderer."

"I'm not a murderer."

Roberto scoffed. "If you murder someone, you're a murderer."

"A murderer is someone who does it routinely."

"No, that's a monster."

Franco swallowed hard.

Roberto sighed. "I'm leaving Palermo."

"Why?" Franco asked, dismayed. "Because of this? Please, don't. I need you here, I want you here, and it's good for you, too."

"Is it good for me? With you keeping secrets?" Roberto looked directly at Franco. "There are only two possibilities. The first is that you killed a man for your own reasons. The second is that you killed a man for the Baron and he gave you a horse for your trouble."

"If I tell you, I'm afraid you'll go."

"I'll go if you don't. Telling me is the only chance I stay."

"What if it's worse than you know?" Franco was thinking of the boy in the madhouse.

"Then I'll make the decision."

So Franco began the story, and by the time he had finished, they had almost reached the village. "Well, what's your decision? Will you stay or go back to Bronte?"

Roberto looked flinty-eyed and impassive. "I don't know. I have to think it over."

"Okay." Franco eyed the village, a huddle of brown houses on a hillside. His task was to hire *braccianti* to work on the *giardino*. Villagers would gather in the piazza every morning, hoping to get hired by *gabellotti* like him. Jobs were scarce, and poverty lived among the *contadini*, the peasants in the countryside. A day's pay for a father or husband could mean the difference between a family eating or starving.

Franco used to loathe choosing one man over another, unaccustomed to wielding power and feeling guilty afterward. Men he rejected would turn away crestfallen, beg for the job, or cry openly. Some would bring their children to the piazza, tell them to lift up their shirts and show Franco their protruding bellies.

Look, Signore. My boy needs to eat.

But Franco had grown used to making hard decisions, and he reflected now that doing so had hardened his heart over time, to the point where he could murder a man.

They entered the village and walked along the cobblestone streets. The houses were too small to blot out the sun, and their stucco baked in the heat, cracking to expose crumbling stone. Their doors stood ajar in hope of a breeze that would never come. The windows were shuttered, but Franco could hear talking, laughing, and arguing inside. These would be the families of the men in the piazza.

Look, Signore.

Franco could see the men ahead, already gathered by the fountain, since he was late. They would be desperate for work, having been rejected by the earlier *gabellotti* as too skinny, too old, or too drunk. They would have club feet, missing fingers, or one blind eye. But they had families, too.

Franco saw them spot him, on his fancy white stallion with his lookalike brother, and he knew they were seeing a second chance at salvation. They brushed off their clothes, tossed away cigarettes, and smoothed their hair.

Roberto looked over. "How many men do you need?"

"Only four, but I see fourteen. Today, you choose."

"Me? How do I decide?" Roberto frowned, but Franco was hoping that if Roberto lived his life, he would understand his choices.

"You'll see," he answered, without elaborating.

CHAPTER FOURTEEN

Sunlight flooded the book-lined law office, and Gaetano sat at his desk, trying to read a lending agreement between a bank and their client, a local nobleman. Don Matteo Vigiliano's firm represented many noble families, some of whom were unable to pay the increasing *donativi*, or taxes, on their estates. They had to borrow money, so it fell to Gaetano to make sure their lending agreements were in order.

But he couldn't concentrate, preoccupied with the kidnapping. He skimmed the first page of the agreement several times, retaining nothing. He turned to the first exhibit, which listed appraisals of the value of a villa and its parcel, outbuildings, contents, and fixtures. The numbers swam before his eyes. He gave up.

Gaetano rose and took his hat from the rack, which drew the attention of Bartolomeo, the other associate in the firm. They'd gone through school together, where Gaetano had been at the top of the class and Bartolomeo in the middle. Gaetano still sensed Bartolomeo's jealousy, which he'd given up trying to assuage, and his faith taught him to turn the other cheek. *Palermitani* hated with the same unreasoning ferocity with which they loved.

Bartolomeo frowned behind his thick spectacles. "Leaving already?"

"Yes, I have an errand to run." Gaetano headed for the door. "I'll see you after lunch."

"Don Matteo needs that lending agreement, you know."

"I'll do it this afternoon." Gaetano left the office.

His cheek was getting tired.

FIFTEEN MINUTES LATER, HE WAS standing on the Quattro Canti, where life had returned to normal. Men and women strolled this way and that, talking and laughing under straw hats and parasols as they headed home for lunch. Shopkeepers locked their doors, and carters pushed barrows of peppers, tomatoes, and melons to open-air markets. A line of donkeys burdened with boxes of lemons lumbered to the harbor, their journey from the Conca d'Oro at an end. A street sweeper set aside his broom amid a pile of broken wine bottles, discarded papers—and, oddly, a soiled marionette.

Gaetano eyed the four corners of the intersection. The one on the south was occupied by a church, but the other three held palazzos converted to apartments. Each had a balcony overlooking the Quattro Canti, and during the festival, they would have been full of people watching the procession. The westernmost corner was closest to the area reserved for the privileged, so it was the logical place to begin. Surely someone had seen a boy being kidnapped. All Gaetano needed was one witness.

He crossed to the building, went inside, and knocked on the first door, which was opened by an older woman. Her hair was fashioned into a silvery topknot that matched her steely spectacles. A deliciously garlicky aroma emanated from the apartment.

Gaetano introduced himself, then asked, "Signora, may I ask, did you watch the Saint Rosalia procession from your balcony on the last night?"

"Yes, I did, with my family." The woman cocked her head. "Why?"

"I wonder if you heard about the kidnapping that took place?"

"Yes, yes, I heard. Such terrible news." The woman's lined face fell. "I pray for the family."

"As do I. Did you see anything suspicious that night? Or did you hear anything unusual, like a child shouting for help? You had the perfect view of the Quattro Canti."

The woman's smile vanished. "No, I didn't see anything. Or hear anything."

"Are you sure?"

"Yes, yes."

"By the way, how many floors of this building are your apartment?"

"This one and the one above, where my son lives with his family. He didn't see anything, either. He was with me." The woman closed the door. "Goodbye."

Gaetano found the stairway, climbed upstairs, and knocked on the next door. An older man opened it but gave the same answer. Gaetano went up one more flight and knocked on another door, to the same end.

He left the house and went to the houses on the other two corners, knocking on as many doors as he could and asking the same questions. Nobody had seen anything suspicious, or at least they wouldn't admit it.

Gaetano found himself back on the Quattro Canti. He took off his hat and wiped his brow with his handkerchief. The conspiracy of silence was spreading throughout his city, to the honest and the dishonest alike.

But Gaetano wasn't giving up.

Not yet.

Not ever.

CHAPTER FIFTEEN

There was a knock at the door, and Mafalda froze, afraid. Things had worsened since that morning at the piazza, when Concetta blamed baby Lucia for the disaster at sea. Neighbors threw rocks at their house, shouted profanities, or cast on them the *malocchio*, the evil eye. The village had turned against them, their grief decayed to hatred.

"Turi?" Mafalda went to him, slumped at the table. "Would you answer the door?"

"No, you." Turi's head dropped back onto his elbow. The wine bottle was empty.

"I can't. It's not safe." Mafalda understood why Turi was drinking, but it left her on her own. They had no more food, and she couldn't venture out to pick chicory. Her milk for Lucia was running low.

There was another knock, and Turi rose unsteadily and went to the door. Mafalda hurried to the corner, standing in front of Lucia's box on the floor, where she was sleeping.

Turi opened the door, and Mafalda's heart sank at the sight. Standing on the threshold was her mother-in-law, Petra. The older woman's eyes were dark and round, her thin lips pursed. Her dark-gray hair was pulled in a taut bun, and she was small and wiry in her black dress. She wore a large gold crucifix around her neck, but no other jewelry.

"Mamma!" Turi threw himself into her arms like a little boy.

"My son, oh, what have you been going through?" Petra hugged him, rocking him back and forth. "What happened? It's so awful. I heard all about it."

"Mamma, I tried to save them, I did try—"

"Don't blame yourself, it's not your fault." Petra kissed his cheeks, wiping his tears with her knobby hand, then turned to Mafalda. "You're the one I blame, you and the horrible baby you birthed. I live two villages over, and you didn't even get word to me. Let me see her right now."

Mafalda gasped. "She's not horrible—"

"Let me see." Petra flew to Lucia's box, shoving Mafalda out of the way.

"It's only that her skin is lighter—"

"Holy Virgin Mary!" Petra plucked Lucia from her crib. "She's a ghost! A specter! It's inhuman."

"No, no, that's not true," Mafalda rushed to say, and Lucia awoke crying. "She does everything normal babies do. She nurses happily, she looks around. I even think she's starting to know me." She turned to Turi, who stood aside. "Turi, please tell your mother our baby is normal."

"Mamma." Turi put a hand on his mother's shoulder. "I know she looks ugly—"

"She's beautiful!" Mafalda held out her arms. "Give me my baby."

"Take her!" Petra shoved the crying baby at Mafalda. "What did you do, Mafalda? Did you make a deal with the devil? That's what they say, you traded the men for your baby. Did you, because it took you so long to conceive?"

"No, no—"

"Why else would He send you such an unnatural child?" Petra made the sign of the cross. "Why else would He send you this demon? Why else would He deliver us this horror?"

"She's not! We love her and—"

"Turi!" Petra whirled around to face Turi. "Your wife has ruined you.

Everyone's saying it. This woman birthed a sacrilege, and you're paying the price. The village is paying the price. Men *died* because of her."

Turi edged away. "Mamma, I tried to save them, I tried—"

"Of course you did, but this evil is too dark a power. There was nothing you could do. It's her fault." Petra grabbed Turi's arm. "I *told* you not to marry her. She didn't even have a dowry. She was beneath you, beneath *us*, and now look. Disgrace! *Infamia!*" Petra raised her voice, red in the face. "The village hates you, Turi! It's only a matter of time until they *kill all three* of you! Don't you see you're in danger because of *her*?"

Turi answered, "Mamma, this will blow over—"

"No, it won't!" Petra pointed at Mafalda. "You *go*! Mafalda! *Go!*"

"What?" Mafalda reeled, stunned. "We're married. If we go, we go together."

Turi's eyes brimmed. "Mamma, she's my wife. I won't put her on the street."

"Put me *on the street*?" Mafalda felt dumbfounded he would consider such a thing. But it sounded as if he had, before now.

"Throw her out, son!" Petra wagged her knobby finger. "It's the only way to save yourself! They'll *kill* you, Turi!"

Turi sobbed, dropping his face in his hands.

"Turi?" Mafalda took his arm, but Petra pushed her away.

"Get out, you bitch! Right this minute!"

Turi staggered to the table, collapsing into his chair.

Petra pointed to the door. "Mafalda, go or I'll kill that baby *myself*!"

"*What?* She's your grandchild!"

"I'll twist her head off like a chicken's!" Petra flew at Mafalda, reaching for the baby.

Mafalda ran to the door with Lucia and escaped into the night.

CHAPTER SIXTEEN

Alfredo walked with Beatrice and her cart, traveling a ridge in the mountainside. The footing was rocky, but the donkey didn't take a wrong step, as this was her favorite errand. They were going to the hay dealer's, and Alfredo felt as happy as a father taking his daughter for a cherry *granita*.

His cap shaded his eyes, and he scanned the vista of hills rolling to the horizon. Shadow and light chased each other across the hillsides, as clouds passed under the sun and the wind whisked them away. Slabs of gray, brown, and tan rock veined with copper, orange, and gold studded a landscape gray-green with prickly pear cactus, olive trees, and hardy vegetation.

Beatrice lifted her head, catching the scent of hay. They reached the dealer, whom everyone called Pietro Hay to distinguish him from Pietro Cobbler and Pietro Baker. Nicknames were customary because so many men in town shared the same first names, there being only so many saints and apostles.

They entered Pietro Hay's farmyard, which contained an old donkey and a mule with a swayback. The animals didn't expect to be acknowledged, so they stayed inside themselves. Alfredo felt a pang, having learned long ago that not everybody saw animals for who they truly were, and all lives were poorer as a result.

He headed for the hay shed, which had an open front, three stone walls, and a slanted roof of gray metal with blankets covering rusty holes. Pietro Hay was pulling down the last bale of Alfredo's order, since he had seen him coming.

Pietro was Alfredo's age, and to Alfredo, the two men looked alike. Both were short, their faces wide and weathered, and their eyes crinkled at the corners. They both wore rough shirts and pants older than most people.

"*Ciao*, Alfredo." Pietro Hay straightened, the metal hook in his hand. "I have your order ready."

"*Ciao*." Alfredo stopped the cart, and Beatrice began nibbling hay on the ground. "But today I want the good hay, not the moldy."

"What?" Pietro Hay eased his cap back, blinking. "The good is too expensive for you."

"Not this time. I can pay." Alfredo's chest filled with pride. He could feed his girls the best because he had sold all his cheese. Ducats jingled like music in his pocket. "I want the good hay."

"The moldy hay is good enough."

"The moldy hay is moldy." Alfredo didn't want to argue. The two men had never exchanged more than twenty words, so there was no reason for any to be cross. "This time, the good hay. The usual amount. Ten bales."

Pietro Hay shrugged, then walked to the good hay and began to pull down bales. He carried them back one by one, and Alfredo loaded them onto his cart, making sure each was without mold. By the time the job was finished, both men were sweating.

"Here we go." Alfredo dug in his pocket, pulled out the ducats, and handed them over, savoring the moment.

"I might try some of your cheese." Pietro Hay dropped the coins into his pocket. "My wife heard about it, and her friends say it's very good."

"It is. *Very*." Alfredo was trying to be a better salesman. He had been practicing.

"Maybe you could bring some next time you come. My wife heard it grew hair on a bald man." Pietro Hay leaned over and waved Alfredo nearer. "She's losing her hair. To restore hair, should she eat the cheese or rub it on her head?"

"Neither. It doesn't grow hair."

"Next time, I'll give you a bale of hay for a packet of cheese. Is that a fair deal?"

"Not for you." Alfredo wasn't about to cheat him. "The hay costs more. It's not one-for-one."

"We'll call it even, since it's hair-growing cheese."

"But it's not." Alfredo wondered about people. Truly, animals were more sensible.

"You want the good hay, next time, too? If you do, I won't put out the moldy. Now I have to put it back."

"I'm sorry, I'll help you."

"No need." Pietro Hay eyed him, hands on hips. "What about next week? You want the good?"

"No. I sold out this time, but I might not next."

"That's wise." Pietro Hay nodded. "Always expect the worst."

CHAPTER SEVENTEEN

A few meals later, the rats had done their job, and Dante's rope lay on the floor in two pieces. One was attached to the wall, and the other to his ankle, so he wasn't tied up anymore.

He crouched in the corner closest to the door. He was supposed to put his dinner plate back through the slot, but he didn't.

He reminded himself to be as fierce as Count Roland *and* as wise as Oliver.

He was going to escape.

BOOM! RENZO POUNDED ON THE door. "Boy, where's your plate? If I don't get that plate, you don't get dinner!"

Dante didn't answer. He stayed in his corner by the door.

"Boy, wake up! Wake up!"

Dante didn't reply.

"Prince Pinocchio!" Renzo pounded on the door. "I can't see you, it's too dark!" Then his voice switched to a sinister whisper. "Are you dead, boy? Did you save me the trouble?"

Dante heard the jingling of keys. He got ready, crouching.

"Don't make me come in there!"

Dante heard the key going into the lock, then being twisted.

"Boy—" Renzo opened the door.

Dante scooted past him, out of the cell.

Startled, Renzo shouted, "Hey!"

Dante raced down the hallway. He saw a stairwell ahead and ran faster than he ever had in his life. He reached the staircase and tore up the stairs.

"Get back here!" Renzo lumbered after him.

Dante made it to the top of the stairs and found himself in an entrance hall with a big door. All of a sudden, he remembered it was the way he'd come in.

"I'll kill you!" Renzo's threat echoed in the stairwell.

Dante bolted to the door, turned the knob, and pushed hard. The door flew open, and he raced outside into the darkness, running for his life.

"Mountjoy!" Dante shouted, Roland's battle cry. "Mountjoy!"

CHAPTER EIGHTEEN

Twilight had fallen, and Franco checked the last donkey cart, which was loaded with lemons for the trip to La Cala, the harbor. It would take about three hours to get there, traveling at night to avoid the heat. Franco usually felt satisfaction in delivering his lemons, but tonight he was unhappy. He still didn't know if Roberto was leaving, and they were barely speaking. Their parents had gone long stretches without speaking, and Franco didn't know if it was a Fiorvanti or a Sicilian tradition. He suspected both. For a talkative people, silence was the ultimate weapon.

"Men, to your positions!" Franco mounted Arabo. "Sebastiano in front! Ezio and *braccianti* along the sides!"

Roberto turned to him atop the mare, his expression hard to see in the dark. "Where do you want me?"

"In the middle."

Roberto obeyed, saying nothing.

"*Andiamo*, men!" Franco trotted to the rear, and the caravan lurched into motion, the donkeys tossing their manes and snorting dust. There were fifteen carts, which he considered the perfect length, and his men were spaced along the line for security. The value of the lemons made them a target for brigands, so each carried a *lupara*, or a sawed-off shotgun.

The rising moon shed a gentle light on the caravan, and they set out through the Conca d'Oro with the fragrance of lemons perfuming the air. Lush *giardini* flanked the dirt road, and Franco noticed a repainted shed and a fixed fence here and there. Still, every trip reassured him that Baron Zito's *giardino* was the best run.

Clouds drifted in front of the moon, and the sky turned a velvety black. The horizon vanished into the mountains, and the caravan snaked along. The breeze cooled, and birds and bats flapped overhead. Deer, hare, and lizards hurried through underbrush.

Franco relaxed, his hips rolling with Arabo's regular gait. His thoughts turned to Violetta and he remembered their glorious afternoon at Villa Zito, making love in the garden. She was everything he wanted in a woman, and he could imagine living happily with her the rest of his life.

A gunshot shocked him out of his reverie.

Suddenly five brigands on horseback materialized out of the darkness, shadows thundering toward Roberto. The one in front brandished his *lupara*. He must have shot at Roberto but missed. He wouldn't get a second chance.

Franco kicked Arabo into a gallop, straight at the brigands. He raised his gun but didn't fire. He had only one shot before reloading.

The brigands kept coming. Franco heard Sebastiano and Ezio shouting behind him. Then the pounding of a horse's hooves. He knew who was following him.

Franco fired at the brigand in front. The man jerked back at the shoulder but stayed on his horse. Franco couldn't reload at speed but raced toward them anyway.

The brigands pulled up their horses, confused. Franco heard them shouting to one another. They didn't expect him to keep coming, on the attack. Three brigands turned around and took off in retreat.

Franco chased them past olive trees and cypresses, driven by fury. His breath came in ragged bursts. He could feel Arabo's heart pounding through the saddle.

The last of the brigands turned tail, racing away.

Franco galloped faster, chasing them.

"Franco, no!" Roberto shouted, as the brigands vanished into the darkness.

Franco came to his senses, slowed Arabo, and turned around, cantering back to his brother.

Roberto threw up his hands. "Franco, you went *after* them? Why? Are you crazy?"

Franco halted Arabo, breathing hard, and the twins faced each other on horseback, identical silhouettes under the moon.

"Franco, you idiot, what were you trying to do? Send a message that you're crazy, so they won't do it again?"

"No. That didn't occur to me." Franco's breathing returned to normal, and so did his heartbeat.

"Why then?"

"If you think about it, you'll know why. Just as I knew you were the one who followed me." Franco realized something. "I went after the brigands because they went after you. You did the same for me. Because we *are* one another."

Roberto fell silent.

"Let's go." Franco patted Arabo on his neck. "We have to get to La Cala."

"Okay, partner," Roberto said softly.

The Fiorvantis walked back to the caravan, side-by-side.

CHAPTER NINETEEN

Gaetano loved the Cathedral of Palermo, having grown up in its shadow. Its serene verdigris dome soared above the capital, and the morning sun brought into relief the myriad engravings, inscriptions, and carvings on its honey-hued limestone. Tall Gothic towers anchored its west side and ziggurats lined its long roof, next to small domes of yellow-and-blue majolica tiles. The cornice over the main portico sat atop three Moorish arches, and the center arch sheltered the entrance.

Families gathered in front of the Cathedral, Gaetano's among them. His wife, Maria, liked that the most important families worshiped here, and today that served his kidnapping investigation. It was reasonable to assume that the victim's parents would be among the congregation, so Gaetano was on the lookout for a family that seemed unusually upset. Or else, he would see if a family he knew was attending Mass without their little boy.

Gaetano scanned the faces for signs of distress. Appearances were important in Palermo, and the congregation was a moving sea of black mantillas and feathered hats. Perfumed women wore their loveliest dresses with fine coral, pearls, and gold jewelry, and men had on panama hats or straw boaters and tailcoats. No one seemed upset or shaken.

Gaetano knew it would be difficult, since *Palermitani* were expert at keeping secrets. He spotted Carmine and other members of the Beati Paoli, and none of them acknowledged the others, a case in point.

The crowd quieted as it entered the Cathedral, which was grand inside, lined with statuary and crypts adorned with gold, melon, and gray marble, as well as crimson porphyry. The congregation settled in the pews, and Gaetano and his family took their seats behind the new heliometer, a line of pure bronze inlaid into the marble floor and decorated with zodiac signs, which tracked the passage of the sun.

Mass began, but Gaetano didn't listen as he scrutinized the families around him. No one seemed upset, and nothing told him that a child who should be there was missing. It was difficult, like proving a negative. Lawyers attempted to do so every day, but his legal degree hadn't prepared him for a kidnapping investigation.

Mass ended in a collective release of goodwill and chatter, and Gaetano left the pew with his family. Maria took the boys to play on the heliometer, but he spotted his boss, Don Matteo Vigiliano, gesturing to him by the holy water font. Don Matteo had a lined face and a hawkish nose, and he was thin in a custom-tailored frock coat, with a cravat of pure silk.

Gaetano walked down the aisle to meet him. "Don Matteo, good morning."

"To you, too, Gaetano. I missed you in the office the other day. I was looking for that lending agreement."

"I'm sorry, I haven't finished it yet."

Don Matteo frowned. "I thought it was done."

"It's taking longer than I expected." Gaetano couldn't tell him the real reason he was busy. "I'll have it on your desk tomorrow morning."

"Unfortunately, I'm having lunch at the client's house today. I would have liked to review the agreement. Is there any change in its material provisions?"

"None, sir."

"Tomorrow morning will do then." Don Matteo nodded curtly. "Goodbye. Please give my regards to your family."

"Thank you, sir, and to yours." Gaetano managed a smile, then his gaze fell on his reflection in the pool of holy water.

His brow eased, and his face relaxed into a smile.

He was getting an idea.

CHAPTER TWENTY

T wilight washed the sky in periwinkle, and Mafalda cuddled Lucia under a tree atop a hill. It had been days since Turi and his mother had turned her out, and Mafalda had no tears left to cry. She had left Porticello and was traveling along the northern coast, following the steep, rocky cliffs of Sicily's shoreline, which dropped dramatically into the Tyrrhenian. She had never expected to be on her own, but Madonna del Lume watched over her, mother to mother.

Mafalda survived by foraging for wild chicory, berries, and mushrooms. Prickly pear cactus grew everywhere, and she picked its oblong fruit. She'd open the prickly pear with a sharp rock, eat its sweet magenta flesh, and suck out its delicious pear juice. She drank from random pools of rainwater or troughs for animals. She traveled at night to avoid being seen, scratching her ankles on nettles.

Tonight, she felt an unusual chill in the air, signaling a *tramontana* wind, which meant a storm was on the way. She would need shelter, and her gaze traveled to the lights of Saint Elia, a fishing village like Porticello. She had been there once with Turi. A sliver of moon illuminated a few meters in front of her, and that was all the light she needed.

Mafalda rose and tucked Lucia into her sling, made from the baby's blanket, then started walking. A cool breeze blew off the sea, which she had come to regard as a friendly guide. Living beside the Tyrrhenian afforded her a panoramic view of its majestic sweep, and the myriad variation in its colors came as a revelation, from showy turquoise to tonight's rich purple-black, like a ripened grape. She had breathed sea air all her life, but now she detected its bold salinity as well as its fishy smells.

Suddenly Mafalda heard a noise behind her and turned around, but she didn't see anything amiss. The moonlight ended in a raggedy fringe of darkness. She continued walking, but after a few paces, heard a noise again. She whirled around, alarmed. Nothing. She cradled Lucia and quickened her pace.

Mafalda kept her eyes on the ground, looking for a stick or a rock. She bent down and grabbed a rock without breaking stride. She kept going along the sea cliff, then heard the noise again. It was labored breathing, a primal animal sound that raised the hair on the nape of her neck.

Her mind raced. The other night she'd heard wolves howling, not far away. And a wolf could have been attracted by Lucia's milky smells or her own earthier odors. Blood still leaked from between her legs from time to time.

Mafalda didn't run, fearing the animal would chase her. She grabbed another rock on the fly, then dropped both into her pocket. She used to have good aim, playing *bocce* with her father when she was little.

Mafalda, don't think about it. Aim the ball and let it go.

Mafalda kept going, gathering rocks along the way. In no time, she had two pockets full. The huffing of the wolf's breathing grew louder. She bellowed at the animal like a man, but the wolf kept tracking her.

Mafalda reached into her pocket, grabbed two rocks, and threw them at the wolf. She heard the animal yelp, but it didn't run away. She reached into her pocket again, whirled around, and threw another spray of rocks. No whimper. She had missed.

Her heart began to hammer as she hurried along. The lights of the town twinkled ahead of her, at a lower elevation. Its harbor was lit, and she could see fishing boats rowing out to sea, their oil lamps bobbing up and down. She wanted to get to the water, but the cliff was too high.

She took more rocks from her pocket, turned around, and whipped them at the wolf. The animal didn't yelp, and Mafalda broke into a light run, holding the baby to her chest. Thorns scratched her ankles. She tripped, almost falling. She knew she mustn't end up on the ground or she and Lucia were done for.

She threw one rock, then another, hurrying forward. Some found their target, most didn't. She could hear the panting, closer and closer. She emptied one pocket of rocks and started digging into the second. Lucia began to cry, awakened by the motion.

Mafalda started to panic. She grabbed the leftover rocks and started throwing them at the wolf. She kept missing, and the wolf kept coming. She was getting nearer to the town and spotted what she had been hoping for. Around the harbor was a strip of beach.

She was down to one rock. She gripped it tightly, then broke into a run for the beach. She could hear the wolf panting louder, loping behind her.

Mafalda had one last chance. She threw her final rock. No whimper. She missed. She was out of rocks and out of luck.

She raced for the beach as fast as she could, her legs pumping and her skirt flying. She wrapped her arms around Lucia. She ducked under umbrella pines and tore through thornbushes.

The rocky shoreline turned sandy. The cliff sloped down, getting lower and lower until it wasn't far above the beach. The beach was getting closer and closer, a light strip in the darkness.

The wolf huffed at her heels. Mafalda couldn't let it take her down.

She raced to the lowest point of the ledge.

And jumped, wrapping her arms around the baby's sling.

MAFALDA LANDED ON HER KNEES near the water, with the baby on her lap. Her leg was stuck under her, but she hadn't broken any bones.

The wolf didn't follow.

A wave lapped at Mafalda, soaking her dress, and she wept with relief.

Lucia only gurgled.

CHAPTER TWENTY-ONE

Alfredo led Beatrice along the sunny street, amazed at the crowd awaiting him on the piazza. Signora Tozzi was at the front with her ladyfriends, but the other women were new. They overran the tables of the vendors, and Giuseppe Dry Beans was moving his stand back. Antonio Wet Beans and Bernardo Greens stood together, unhappily eyeing the commotion.

"*Madonna*," Alfredo said under his breath.

Signora Tozzi began waving, then so did her ladyfriends and the other women. Alfredo reached the piazza and started selling cheese before he was even in his spot. Women pushed money at him, and he pushed cheese at them. He sold out in no time, leaving the women who didn't get cheese with frowns.

"You need to make more cheese next time!" an old woman shouted.

"Yes, a lot more!" her ladyfriend chimed in, and another woman knocked over Marco Citrus's stand. Oranges started rolling all over the piazza, and Marco Citrus bolted to get them, cursing in front of the women.

A third woman added, "I need that cheese! My back hurts! Alfredo, when will you return? I'm in pain!"

Alfredo felt sorry for her. "It's only cheese, Signora. It won't help your back."

"Yes, it will, I heard! Won't you please make more? And come back sooner?"

"I can't. It takes time. You have to let the curds drain, and I have only so much milk."

"Get more goats!"

Alfredo wasn't about to explain they were his daughters, not acquired like possessions. He bred them when he wanted to grow his family and he didn't keep a buck because of its musky stink. All of that was nobody's business.

"Alfredo, I heard your cheese is magical! That it comes from magical goats!"

Alfredo stopped replying because they didn't listen anyway. He picked up Beatrice's rope and turned to go, but Donato Nuts stopped him.

"Alfredo, what are you doing to the cheese? They say it's charmed."

"They're mistaken. I tried to tell them, but I give up."

"If you want my advice, you should make more cheese."

"I can't." Alfredo didn't want his advice. He didn't even know Donato Nuts, who had never before spoken to him.

"Then increase your prices. If they think it's charmed, they'll pay extra."

"That would be cheating," Alfredo told him, and Beatrice looked over in disapproval.

"No, it wouldn't. Charmed cheese should cost more than regular."

"But it's not charmed, and it costs me the same to make, day-to-day."

Donato Nuts frowned. "Don't be so stubborn, Alfredo. I'm trying to help you. If you put nuts in your cheese, you could help me."

"But I don't want nuts in my cheese."

"Why not? Pine nuts would taste good in cheese. Almonds, too. I have Tuono and Avola." Donato Nuts leaned closer. "You should share your good fortune, you know. We can make a common venture, the two of us. What do you say?"

"I say, no, thank you." Alfredo turned away and headed up the street. He had sold out of his cheese again, but he was getting a bad feeling.

So was Beatrice.

CHAPTER TWENTY-TWO

Dante squatted in the corner, more terrified than ever. He had tried to run away that night, but he hadn't even gotten out of the courtyard. Renzo had caught him and put him in a different cell, with three men. One man was so skinny that he looked like a living skeleton, with dark sunken eyes and a long, bony nose, and he screamed himself hoarse, making it impossible to sleep. Renzo called him Opera Singer, and Dante had never been so tired.

The second man had a pimply face and shiny black eyes that glowered at him. Renzo called him Biter, and Biter had already bitten Dante's arm like a piece of meat. The third man had white hair and cracked spectacles, believing himself to be King Roger, so Renzo nicknamed him Raving King Roger. Raving King Roger would order Dante to serve him roast duck, draw him a hot bath, or fetch him a book from the library, as if they lived in a castle. Dante couldn't, and Raving King Roger would threaten to cut off his head.

Dante closed his eyes, trying to rest, but Opera Singer was screaming. Biter was sitting on his haunches, eyeing him like a guard dog. Raving King Roger was arranging an imaginary napkin, getting ready for breakfast, which was about to come through the door.

Dante dreaded mealtimes because of Renzo's game.

"Breakfast!" Renzo opened the slot in the door and pushed in three plates of bread and jam, even though there were four in the cell.

Biter scrambled to his plate.

"*Aaahhh!*" Opera Singer scurried forward, taking his plate.

Raving King Roger whirled around to Dante, his blue eyes flashing behind his cracked glasses. "Boy! Serve me this instant or I'll have you put in the Iron Maiden! Nails will pierce your chest, front to back!"

Dante reached for the last plate, but Raving King Roger snatched it from him.

"How dare you? I'll have you *shot!*"

Dante edged back to his corner.

The flap opened at the top of the door, and Renzo peeked through. "Prince Pinocchio, you hungry?"

"Yes."

"Then beg!"

Dante's stomach growled. "May I have breakfast, I'm begging—"

"Say please, you spoiled brat! You're no prince in here!"

"May I have breakfast, *please*? I'm begging!"

"No!" Renzo guffawed again. "You think you make the rules? You don't!"

Suddenly, someone else peeked through the flap. Renzo's wife, Teresa. "Dante, is that you?" she asked, her eyes rounding.

"Yes, may I have breakfast, please?" Dante started to the door, but Biter growled at him.

Raving King Roger pointed at the door. "Boy, leave! Servants aren't to linger! I'll have your head on the chopping block!"

The flap closed, and Dante edged back into his corner, his stomach rumbling.

"*Aaaahhh!*" Opera Singer was screaming, so Dante couldn't hear what Renzo and Teresa were saying in the hall.

"RENZO, WHAT'S DANTE DOING IN *there*?" Teresa threw up her hands. "I thought you put him back in his cell. He shouldn't be in with adults. They'll drive him crazy, and Biter is *dangerous*."

"He tried to run away. This is what he gets."

"It's only because he misses his family. He's a child. We should let him go—"

"We *can't*. We made a deal. We've been paid. You spent the money quickly enough." Renzo simmered. "I'm tired of the same argument. Don't bring it up again."

Teresa pursed her lips. "Okay, let's compromise, since you like deals so much. I agree to let Dante stay in the madhouse, but I will *not* let you keep him in that cell. Children are not to be housed with adults."

Renzo snorted. "Listen to you, quoting chapter and verse."

"Put him back in his old cell."

"No. The Prince needs to be taken down a peg. He'll stay until I say."

"End of the week, get him out."

"End of the *month*. Don't test me, wife."

"Don't threaten me, husband." Teresa locked eyes with him, and Renzo looked daggers at her, but he wouldn't let her stop him.

He had plans.

Big plans.

CHAPTER TWENTY-THREE

Franco set the basket of fresh lemons in the donkey cart, taking off his cap and wiping his brow. Roberto, Sebastiano, and Ezio were picking with the *braccianti* in the oppressive heat. Sebastiano and Ezio, who usually sang as they worked, remained silent, and Roberto had run out of jokes. There was no breeze, and the humidity soured the lemons' perfume.

Franco heard men calling his name. "Mariano? Onorato? I'm here!" he called back.

"Who are they?" Roberto asked, wiping sweat from his face.

"*Gabellotti* from Moravio's and Silvestri's."

Mariano and Onorato appeared on mules at the end of the row, then approached them, eyeing the *giardino*. Franco knew they were assessing his lemons, determining whether they were free from disease and if grafting had been successful. He sent Sebastiano, Ezio, and the *braccianti* back to the house for a break, and the *gabellotti* dismounted.

Franco gestured to Roberto. "Mariano, Onorato, meet my brother, Roberto."

"Franco, Roberto." Mariano smiled, and Onorato nodded.

Roberto shook their hands. "Nice to meet you."

"You, too." Mariano's smile showed missing teeth. His features were coarse, his eyes almost black, and a scar puckered his left cheek. Dark curls sprayed out from the sides of his cap. "You and Franco look so much alike."

"I'm handsomer," Roberto shot back, as Franco knew he would. It always got a laugh and did today, too.

"Good to see you, men." Franco didn't know what they wanted. Visits from other *gabellotti* weren't common, none of them had time. "How can we help you?"

"We heard about what happened with the brigands."

"Yes, but it went fine."

Mariano grinned. "Fine? We heard you ran them off, the two of you."

"It was fine," Franco repeated, not wanting to share his business.

Roberto interjected, "Franco ran them off. I followed at a cowardly distance."

They laughed, then Mariano's smile faded. "Tell us what happened. It's why we came."

"I'll tell it." Roberto launched into a comically exaggerated version, and Mariano and Onorato laughed. But by the time Roberto had finished, the humor had vanished.

Mariano met Franco's eye. "There are too many attacks in the Conca d'Oro. You know the same stories I do. Men have been *killed* taking lemons to market. No one is safe anymore." He pointed to his scar. "I got this from a brigand. He tried to cut my eye out."

"I'm sorry, and I know it's true. I see the crucifixes beside the road."

Mariano shook his head. "This has to stop. My farmers lose money. That means they can't pay rent."

Roberto interjected again, "We had this problem in Bronte, but I thought it would be different here. There's no police, even in Palermo?"

"None," Franco answered. "We're on our own."

Mariano straightened. "Franco, we have a solution. We should help each other, coordinate our trips to Palermo. We would all be safer, and our lemons would get to market. It only makes sense. We harvest at the same time and we make trips to market at the same time. We go *from* the same place *to* the same place. We would do better collectively."

Franco listened without interrupting. Roberto did, too.

"Franco, everyone knows what you did that night, chasing the brigands. If we were going to pick one leader, it would be you. We would like to join you and make trips to Palermo with you. There's safety in numbers, as you know. Donkeys herd for a reason."

Franco shook his head. "No."

Roberto looked over, lifting an eyebrow.

"Why not, Franco?"

"We're competitors. I have no interest in protecting your lemons to market against mine. I doubt Baron Zito would, either."

"The Baron needn't know."

"I make the decision on my own."

"You're saying no? Even if it means we're all safer? That nobody will get a scar like this one? Or lose his *life*?" Mariano's eyes widened in frustration. "Franco, it's for the collective good. Our lives are more important than lemons, aren't they?"

"We all have this problem and must solve it our own way." Franco gestured at his lemon trees. "Look, we have the same problems in the *giardini*. We all experience blight and have trouble getting grafts to take. Yet I have methods I don't share with you, and I saw you looking when you came in."

"Fair enough." Mariano shook his head. "But here's something you're not considering. There's little work except for what we offer. That's why the piazza is crowded when you hire *braccianti*. Men need to feed their families, and they're becoming brigands to do it. Franco, they'll attack you again. You're a target now. They need to save face."

Franco had noticed an increase in the frequency of attacks.

Roberto interjected, "Mariano, I agree with my brother that cooperating with competitors goes against business sense. Worse, I think if you combine your trips to market, it will make too long a caravan. A herd protects because it's a bunched formation. A long line is the opposite. I have a better idea."

Mariano blinked. "What?"

"Me." Roberto spread his palms. "I'm the idea. Just now, when I told the story about the attack, I exaggerated the number of brigands, because more brigands are more threatening. What we need is an army of guards to protect you on the way to market, even to protect your farms."

Mariano shook his head. "We already have *campieri*, two armed men to protect the *giardino* while we're on the trip."

Roberto raised an index finger. "Mariano, I mean thirty men or more, and *not* men who grow lemons. We need men who shoot, like me. I'm an excellent shot. I hunted all the time with my friends, also excellent hunters. I can send for them."

Franco could see only one drawback. "It's dangerous, Roberto."

"So? I don't mind risk, do I?"

"It's not a card game. I don't want anything to happen to you."

"I'll be fine, don't worry." Roberto patted Franco's shoulder. "This way, I can be my own man, but work with you. We'll be partners with different areas of responsibility. Don't you agree? We can both be king of the mountain."

Franco smiled. "I agree."

Mariano brightened. "How would we pay such an army, Roberto?"

"Easy." Roberto shrugged. "I'm betting you're a Communist."

"I am," Mariano answered proudly.

"Signor Collective Thinker, you're going to like my answer. You pool your money. Every farm contributes to a pot proportionally, according to its size. The pot is mine, and in return, every trip to market receives protection from me and my guards. This is a beautiful plan." Roberto bowed with a flourish. "Pleased to meet you, I'm Commendatore Roberto. I'm as rich as sin. Men envy me, virgins bed me. My future's as clear as the sky. Are you in?"

"I'm in." Franco chuckled.

"We're in, too," Mariano answered, then turned to Franco. "But I have a question. Franco, why is it okay for competitors to cooperate by hiring guards, but not by traveling to market together?"

"I want you bankrupt, not dead."

Mariano laughed, and so did Roberto and Onorato.

Franco laughed, too.

But he wasn't kidding.

CHAPTER TWENTY-FOUR

Gaetano hurried along the piazza to the Cathedral. He was going to investigate the kidnapping, following up on the idea he'd gotten after Mass. Tucked under his arm was his leather envelope, with fresh paper inside. He'd left the office in a hurry, having placed the finished lending agreement on Don Matteo's desk. He'd told Bartolomeo he was leaving for a doctor's appointment.

He reached the entrance of the Cathedral and let himself through its massive doors, taking off his hat. He paused at the font of holy water, making the sign of the cross. He walked up the center aisle to the altar, his footsteps echoing on the marble floor. It was between Masses, so it was quiet, and only a few parishioners knelt in the pews, their heads bent in prayer, rosaries dripping from their fingers.

Gaetano genuflected when he reached the grand altar, flanked by marble arches. Its majestic apse was illuminated by a candelabra that cast the crucifix in amber and gold. He spotted one of the junior priests, Father DiGregorio, short in his stiff vestments.

Gaetano motioned respectfully to the priest. "Father DiGregorio, excuse me, may I have a minute?"

"Of course, Gaetano." Father DiGregorio crossed to the marble rail.

"I wonder if you could help me. I'm here on behalf of a client." Gaetano had begun to think of the boy as his client, so he considered this the truth. "I know many children in Palermo are baptized at the Cathedral. In fact, my sons were baptized here."

"Yes, we have a beautiful font."

"I know you keep records, because I remember signing a book on the day my sons were baptized."

"Yes, of course. The records are in the rectory." Father DiGregorio gestured behind him, since the rectory was attached to the Cathedral.

"I'm interested in seeing the baptismal records from five and six years ago, for a client matter." Gaetano knew that in all likelihood, the name of the kidnapped boy would be in the baptismal records, since he was probably from one of the best families in town.

Father DiGregorio frowned. "That would be quite a number of books."

"I know, I expected that. I'd be happy to examine them here. I needn't take them from the premises. I'd like to see them now, if possible, since time is of the essence."

"I understand." Father DiGregorio nodded. "I'll speak with someone to obtain permission. It may take a moment or two. Excuse me."

"Thank you."

Father DiGregorio turned away, and Gaetano's gaze strayed to the transept that held the gleaming silver reliquary of Saint Rosalia, ornately carved and taller than a man, restored there since the festival.

Gaetano walked over, reached the nave, and knelt on the kneepad. He had grown up on Saint Rosalia's story, as did all *Palermitani*. She was born Rosalia Sinibaldi, the beautiful daughter of a duke, but instead of marrying, she chose to serve God and to live in a cave atop Mount Pellegrino. She died there in 1170 and performed a miracle during the 1600s, when she appeared to a soap maker and told him to carry her bones through the city to stop the plague. He did, which was why her relics were paraded at her festival every year.

The story resonated for Gaetano in a way it hadn't before. Saint Rosalia was a young girl alone in a cave, and the kidnapped boy would be alone in a strange and hostile place, too. Gaetano prayed to Saint

Rosalia to help him find the boy, then crossed himself and ended his prayer, looking over as Father DiGregorio reappeared.

With a smile.

GAETANO WAS SHOWN TO A small, windowless study in the administration section of the rectory, containing a medium-sized wooden table, four chairs, and austere white walls adorned with oil portraits of clergy in splendid vestments. Stacked on the table were twenty-four oversized books, one for each month of the year, five and six years ago.

Gaetano sat down, slid the paper from his leather envelope, and extracted a quill from the well. He picked up the first book, from January, five years ago. He opened the book, feeling a tingle of excitement. It was a long list of names, showing the gender of each baby, the date of each baptism, the parents' names and signatures, and home addresses. The entries were chronological by baptismal date and written in different inks and hands, made by different priests.

Gaetano's pulse quickened. It was exactly what he had hoped for. He intended to copy down the names of the male babies, along with the information about their families. Then he would visit the families, interview them, and see if each boy was home or if there was any sign he had been kidnapped. It would take work, but sooner or later Gaetano would end up finding the family of the kidnapped boy.

His gaze fell on the first baby boy baptized that year: GIOVANNI DITOLO. Gaetano started copying, and when he had finished, his papers were puckered with black ink and he had the names of one hundred and twenty boys, along with their parents and addresses.

He slid the pages into his leather envelope. His list was long but he was already thinking about how to organize his search. He wanted to find the boy as quickly as possible and he couldn't wait to start interviewing families.

Luckily, Gaetano had an army to help.

An army of good.

"GOOD AFTERNOON, BARTOLOMEO."

Gaetano hung his hat on the rack, and Bartolomeo looked up from behind glasses that magnified his eyes. He occupied the better desk by the window, and a shaft of light fell on his papers, the light reflecting upward onto his stern expression.

"You were gone a long time."

"Yes, I suppose." Gaetano went to his desk and spotted a note from Don Matteo that read, *See me about the lending agreement.* "Is he in?"

"No. He left for the day. The note isn't good."

Gaetano disliked that Bartolomeo had read his note. "Did he have the lending agreement in hand?"

"Yes, and he wasn't happy." Bartolomeo cleared his throat. "He told me I did an excellent job on the Whitaker tax matter."

Gaetano's chest tightened. "Congratulations."

"May I ask, are you well?"

"Yes, why?"

Bartolomeo lifted an eyebrow. "You were at the doctor's so long."

"Oh yes." Gaetano slid his note into his leather envelope. "I guess we ended up talking."

"Why did you go? Have you been sick?"

"No, I go every year." Gaetano wasn't a good liar. "That's probably why we talked so long. He's chatty."

"Who's your doctor?"

"Dottor Marconi, on Via Maqueda."

"Oh, I use him, too. He's not that chatty."

"Then I guess I'm the chatty one." Gaetano headed for the door.

"Where are you going now?"

Gaetano left, ignoring the question. He was out of lies.

And he had work to do.

CHAPTER TWENTY-FIVE

Mafalda settled herself and Lucia under an umbrella pine against a crumbling stone wall outside the village of Saint Elia. Her makeshift camp had a magnificent view of the jagged camelback of Cape Zafferano, jutting out into the sea, and the familiar natural terrain of rocks, prickly pear cactus, and palm trees around her.

Mafalda had realized she had to improve her aim to protect herself, so she practiced throwing every day while Lucia napped under the tree. She picked up a rock from the pile she had accumulated and sized up the distance to her target, which was another rock on a boulder.

She threw the rock, but missed. She picked up another rock and threw it. She missed again, but got closer.

She threw another rock, then another, missing both times. She wiped her brow. She had to do better. She picked up another rock, struck by a thought. Maybe she needed someone to throw the rock *at*.

Petra, her mother-in-law.

Mafalda threw the rock and hit the target with a *crack*.

And she smiled.

IT WAS THE MIDDLE OF the night, and Mafalda walked through the village, holding Lucia. The houses were dark, and no sound came from within. Nobody was out except for a stray tabby that ran by, its tail in the air. She found the piazza, washed herself and the baby in the fountain, and looked around for morsels of food. Her stomach growled, and she was losing weight. She had to eat to keep her milk up.

Suddenly she heard footsteps and glanced over her shoulder. At the end of the street was the dark figure of a man. His silhouette was brawny.

Mafalda started walking faster, holding Lucia tighter. She knew what horror could befall a woman alone. She looked around for a rock, but there wasn't one. She spotted an alley ahead and hurried that way, trying not to panic.

She turned into the alley, but it ended in a high gate with bars. She was trapped.

The footsteps kept coming her way, the man speeding up. She couldn't run or he would catch her. She was struck by a bolt of fear.

She edged down the alley toward the gate. The man appeared at the entrance to the alley, a shadowy figure backlit by the moon.

Mafalda raised a palm. "Stop! If you come near me, I'll scream!"

The man raised his arms. "I mean you no harm. My name is Francesco, and I need something from you."

"What? Tell me from there!"

FRANCESCO LED MAFALDA TO HIS house and admitted her to its warm room. It was dark inside, but she could discern a bed with the sleeping form of Francesco's wife. Otherwise there was a table, chairs, and a small copper brazier.

Francesco lit a candle, then woke his wife, who stirred, revealing a tiny baby sleeping beside her. "Anna, I'm home."

"Francesco!" Anna reached up to embrace him, and Mafalda felt a pang at seeing the love between the couple. She used to have such love, but those times were gone for good.

Francesco gestured to Mafalda. "Anna, I have someone for you to meet."

"Who, now?" Anna sat up, covering herself with the sheet. She was a small woman with a delicate face in the candlelight. Her long brown hair trailed over her shoulders in ringlets.

"Anna, this is Mafalda. I brought her home to help us."

Anna's gaze took in Mafalda and Lucia, then she smiled. "Oh my, you have a baby, too?"

"Yes, a girl." Mafalda kept Lucia's face turned to her chest. "She's asleep, I don't want to wake her. I was traveling through town when I met Francesco. He said you needed a wet nurse."

"I do, but where are you from? Where's your husband?"

"I left him."

"With a baby?" Anna's lower lip puckered with sympathy. "Why?"

"I'd rather not say." Mafalda would have to keep to herself if the situation was going to work. She and Lucia would be safer here in the nighttime, rather than outside with the wolves. "Anyway, I can be your wet nurse."

"You can? I make some milk, but not enough." Anna reached on the night table for an *ex voto*, a small, silvery plaque shaped like a female breast. "I bought this to bring to church for Saint Agatha. I pray to her to help me."

"Anna, we can't wait anymore," Francesco interjected, shaking his head. "My son needs more milk."

Mafalda added, "Anna, I'd be happy to nurse your baby. What's his name?"

"Salvatore."

Mafalda felt a pang, thinking of Turi.

"We call him Salvo."

Thank Madonna. "I'd like to come at night, nurse the baby throughout, and leave in the morning."

"Fine, I can nurse in the day, then sleep without interruption."

Francesco turned to Mafalda. "How much would you charge? We don't have a lot of money."

Mafalda felt for them. "I'll settle for dinner every night, fresh clothes, and diapers."

Francesco's eyes widened with relief. "Then we have a deal!"

Anna beamed. "That would be wonderful! I could give you Salvo's baby clothes, and we can become friends, and the children can grow up together—"

"No, I'm a private person. I'd rather keep my baby to myself."

Francesco shrugged. "Fine. This is too good a deal to pass up."

Anna's forehead buckled. "But may I ask why, Mafalda?"

"Some people think my baby is ugly, but I think she's beautiful. I want her to grow up seeing people smiling at her, not frowning. She's innocent and she deserves to feel loved. I hope you can respect my wishes."

"I understand." Anna smiled, her sympathy plain. "Every woman in the village has opinions about my Salvo. They say he looks like a skeleton. They criticize me for not having enough milk. They say I'm eating the wrong food or praying to the wrong saints. I'll respect your wishes, mother to mother."

"Thank you."

"Would you like to see Salvo?" Anna gathered up the sleeping baby and brought him into the candlelight, which glowed on his warm, olive skin. He was thin, but had fine little features and shiny black hair.

"He's beautiful." Mafalda felt a tingling in her breasts, her milk letting down. "I can nurse him now, if you wish."

"Oh my!" Anna saw wet spots forming on Mafalda's blouse. "How lucky you are!"

How lucky you are, Mafalda thought, then shooed it away.

CHAPTER TWENTY-SIX

Alfredo's happiest moments were making cheese at the end of the day, while the girls slept on the floor. He had begun the process the previous day, heating the milk in a big pot on the brazier, then mixing in the culture and rennet. The pot would sit for twelve hours, so the curds separated from the whey, then he would scoop the curds into a colander, putting a bowl underneath to catch the remaining whey. The curds would sit another day, then he would get ready for the final stage, tonight.

Alfredo scooped curds onto a cheesecloth and mounded them gently with a spoon. He pulled the four corners of the cheesecloth together, making a ball. He tied a knot in the cheesecloth, to be hung up over the sink to drain even further.

Suddenly he heard scuffling outside.

Bam! A loud bump came from the door.

Alfredo jumped, startled. Instinct told him he needed protection. He scurried to the sink and fetched his paring knife. He brandished it and crept to the door, but heard the commotion subsiding. Whoever had been here was leaving.

Alfredo waited until it was completely quiet. He cracked the door and peeked outside. It was dark. No one was there. All he could see were the shadowy trees along the dirt road that led to town.

He looked down to find a large rock. He picked it up and brought it inside, barring the door for the first time ever. The latch was old, but it worked.

He brought the rock to the table. He could see in the candlelight it had a note tied around it with a string. He took out the note, and though his reading wasn't the best, he could tell what it said:

STAY AWAY FROM THE PIAZZA

CHAPTER TWENTY-SEVEN

Renzo carried the breakfast plates down the hall, past lunatics shouting for help, which was music to his ears. His mood soared because he was going to start his new scheme after his shift today. Soon he'd be making cartloads of money.

"Breakfast is served!" Renzo reached the cell, opened the flap in the bottom, and shoved three plates through. Opera Singer stopped screaming, Raving King Roger barked orders, and Biter growled. Prince Pinocchio was silent.

"Prince Pinocchio, breakfast!" Renzo pushed through the last plate, then opened the top flap so he could see what was happening inside.

Biter reached breakfast first, growling. Opera Singer grabbed his plate and so did Prince Pinocchio. Raving King Roger snatched Prince Pinocchio's and a fight broke out between the lunatic and the boy, which delighted Renzo.

"Fight, Prince! He's an old man!"

Prince Pinocchio grappled with Raving King Roger. Bread flew off into the air, and the metal plate clattered to the floor, dripping strawberry jam. Raving King Roger dove for the bread, but Prince Pinocchio got there first.

"*Bravo*, Prince Pinocchio! You're learning! Finally!"

Renzo let the flap close, then left to start his day.

And his new future.

DANTE SAT IN HIS CORNER, trying not to hear the screaming. He squeezed his eyes shut and imagined *The Song of Roland*, but lately he kept remembering that Oliver and Count Roland died in the end. Dante had cried the first time his mother had read him the end of the story.

Mamma had smoothed his tears away. "It's very sad they died. I agree."

I agree, which helped a little. "I wish they lived. They were the heroes. The heroes always live. You're supposed to, when you're in the right. You're supposed to win."

"I know, but that doesn't always happen." Mamma looked sad, too. She was always sad when Dante was sad, so he didn't have to be sad alone, which was the worst feeling in the world.

"It's not fair."

"But, Dante, there's something about the ending that I like." Mamma turned to a page and ran her fingernail down the lines. "Right here, it says, 'He that has suffered learns many things in life.' I think that's true, and that's what happens in the story. Roland and Oliver suffer, and they learn from their suffering."

"What does 'suffering' mean?"

"Suffering is how you feel when things go badly for you."

"Like when I want cake and you say no?"

Mamma smiled. "No, worse. If you were to go hungry, or thirsty, or lose people you love. When Roland loses Oliver, and Charlemagne loses Roland, *that* is suffering."

Now, in his cell, Dante heard his stomach growl. He didn't have enough to eat or drink, and he had lost Mamma and Papa.

He supposed he was learning the most you could ever, ever learn.

CHAPTER TWENTY-EIGHT

Palm trees lined the elegant street, and Gaetano approached the fancy house. He had his list of one hundred and twenty boys, and he was going to visit the families, interview them, and try to find the one who'd had a son kidnapped. The name of the first boy on his list was Carlo Zarella, and his parents were Antonia Tinto and Lorenzo Zarella. They lived in the district opposite from Gaetano's own, and he was starting here to avoid word getting back to his wife, Maria.

It was midmorning, a time when he knew the family would be home. Men of the upper class didn't go out early unless they were hunting or riding in La Favorita park, and their wives would be getting the children ready for tutors. Gaetano wouldn't need to present a calling card. He was of the same class, so his calling card was his presentation, his dress, his manners, even his accent.

He knocked on the lacquered door, which was opened by the boy's mother, Antonia. She had a pretty face, with a smile that suggested she didn't have a care in the world, much less a kidnapped boy. Nevertheless, Gaetano was thorough and methodical by nature.

"Good morning, my name is Gaetano Catalano. I'm sorry to bother you. Would you be Signora Tinto?"

"Yes, I am. Pleased to meet you, Signore."

"Is your husband home?" Gaetano asked, to stay within the bounds of propriety.

"Yes, but he's indisposed."

"Perhaps I can speak with you briefly." Gaetano peeked past her, scanning the living room. There was a canopied bassinet, but he couldn't see much else. "I know you're busy, and my wife would have my head for interrupting you."

"I'm sure she wouldn't." Signora Tinto smiled indulgently.

"I'm an attorney, and baptismal records show you have a son named Carlo, is that correct?"

"Yes," Signora Tinto answered, surprised. "Why do you ask?"

"When a son is born, it's a good idea to have a Last Will and Testament in place, should the worst happen. I have one for my sons." Gaetano's heart pounded, because it was his first time telling his cover story. He knew it was credible because lawyers were seeking business so aggressively these days.

"Oh, I quite agree. We took care of that when Carlo was born. He's upstairs practicing his violin." Signora Tinto cocked her head, smiling. "If you listen, you can hear him play. I think he has true talent!"

Gaetano listened to the screeching.

Signora Tinto's eyes lit up. "Isn't he *wonderful*?"

"Yes, he is," Gaetano lied, for the common good.

GAETANO WENT NEXT TO THE home of little Cristiano D'Oliva, son of Attilo D'Oliva and Luisella Donato. It was two blocks up and its façade was similar to the last house. The door was of red lacquer, and the apartment was also on the first floor.

Gaetano straightened when the door was opened by a mustachioed man about his own age, who was just putting on a waistcoat to leave. Gaetano introduced himself, then said, "Good morning, I'm sorry to bother you. Are you Signor D'Oliva?"

"I am. Pleased to meet you."

"And I, you." Gaetano peered past him into the living room, where children's toy soldiers were scattered on the rug. "I got your name from baptismal records and I know you have a son, Cristiano."

"Yes."

"Well, my legal advice is that as soon as a son is born, a father must make sure a Last Will & Testament is drawn up. I'm a lawyer in general practice, experienced in drafting such instruments."

"Actually, we do have one, and I admire your initiative. I recognize a kindred spirit." Signor D'Oliva smiled, and a curly-haired boy came running up, chased by a fluffy yellow dog.

"Papa, Papa!" the boy squealed, gleeful. "I taught him to sit! I taught him!"

Signor D'Oliva chuckled, ruffling the child's hair. "Good boy! Now, Cristiano, let Papa speak to this nice man."

Gaetano mentally crossed off the name. "Signor D'Oliva, I won't take more of your time. Thank you very much. Goodbye."

Fifteen minutes later, Gaetano had visited two additional families on the list and had been delighted to eliminate two more boys, Saverio Gangi and Patrizio Santino. He had laid eyes on Saverio, who was leaving to go for a walk with his mother, and Patrizio, resting on the couch with a hot water bottle, fighting off a cold. Gaetano sent up a silent prayer for the boy's health and hurried to the office.

GAETANO KNEW THERE WAS TROUBLE the moment he got back to work and heard his name being said in Don Matteo's office. He went to the threshold to find Bartolomeo in a chair opposite Don Matteo at his antique desk. Leather-covered lawbooks on walnut shelves lined the exquisite room, their gilt-embossed titles winking in the sunlight. Red-striped curtains flanked the windows, and between them hung diplomas and an oil portrait of Don Matteo's late father, who had been a prominent judge in Palermo, like Gaetano's father.

Gaetano managed a smile. "Don Matteo, good morning. Do you need me?"

"I certainly do. Gaetano, sit down." Don Matteo gestured to the red-striped chair next to Bartolomeo. He frowned in his black waist-coat with leather trim on the collar. "Please tell me where you have been."

"I had to see a dentist."

Bartolomeo looked over, lifting an eyebrow. "I thought you said it was a doctor."

"That was the other day," Gaetano answered, then realized Bartolomeo had trapped him.

"What?" Don Matteo flared his hooded eyes. "Gaetano, why so many personal matters when we're busy here? Couldn't you have gone at a more opportune time? I've been trying to see you to discuss the lending agreement. You're never at your desk. Bartolomeo is taking up the slack. Doing a fine job of it, too, I might add."

Bartolomeo nodded. "That's very kind of you, Don Matteo."

"Thank you, Bartolomeo." Gaetano remembered the teaching of Saint Paul. *Your every act should be done with love.*

Don Matteo shook his head. "Gaetano, I was very dissatisfied with your job on the lending agreement. The provision provided the monies are due every six months, but you filled in the wrong dates, a careless error."

"I'm sorry—"

"Furthermore, do you know who caught the error? Not I! Perhaps I would have, if you had given me sufficient time to review the agreement, but you didn't. Baron Tedesco *himself* found the mistake! Can you imagine?"

Gaetano cringed. "I'm so sorry. You must have been embarrassed."

"*Mortified!* I have a reputation to uphold. Our papers must be perfect. You know how much business we get from Baron Tedesco. He has faith in us, and I don't want him to feel it's misplaced. There are many other lawyers in Palermo, and he can have his pick. And if he speaks ill about us to others, I don't have to tell you how deleterious to my reputation it would be."

"I promise you, it won't happen again."

"I would hope not." Don Matteo heaved a sigh. "Gaetano, this is highly uncharacteristic. Your work has always been impeccable. Am I asking too much? I'm far from a taskmaster, aren't I?"

Gaetano didn't know how to reply, as it was a compound question. "You're a pleasure to work for, sir."

"Good, then see to it!" Don Matteo slid a huge stack of files across the desk. "Now, get started on these agreements right away. They need to be updated by the end of next week, all of them."

"Thank you." Gaetano picked up the pile, heavy in his arms.

Bartolomeo interjected, "Don Matteo, I'm happy to help Gaetano."

"Bartolomeo, no, thank you. That's cooperative of you, and that's what I like to see. However, these agreements are largely similar, so the task is more efficiently performed by one lawyer." Don Matteo met Gaetano's eye, his gaze stern. "Make it your priority."

"I will."

CHAPTER TWENTY-NINE

The hustle-bustle of Palermo's harbor made Renzo realize how much action he missed at the madhouse. All manner of ships were sailing in and out of the harbor or anchored a distance away: trawlers, skiffs, clippers, merchant ships, and fleets of fishing boats with the night's catch. Plumes of smoke billowed from the steamers, fading in the salty gusts off the sea, which was a choppy indigo color with scalloped whitecaps. Fishmongers sold fresh squid, octopus, mussels, and tuna on tables on the docks. Housewives and servants clustered around them, carrying baskets.

Renzo kept going on his mule, heading to one of his favorite bars. He looked forward to seeing his old friends who worked at the harbor, one friend in particular. Palermo would have no shipping trade without men like them, but they earned a pittance for loading ships, greasing engine gears, washing docks, gutting fish, and carting away refuse.

Renzo dismounted his mule, tied her up, and went inside the bar. It was a dark single room with a counter on the left, and on the right were a few tables nobody used. Over the bar was a mirror so old that the silver paper had molded to black and gray patches, like a map of a nightmare world.

The bartender, Faustino, broke into a toothless grin. "Well, look at you! *Ciao*, Renzo!"

Renzo grinned back. "*Ciao*, Faustino. How have you been?"

"Good, and you?"

Renzo sat down. "Still at the madhouse."

"Have you gone crazy yet?"

"A long time ago," Renzo shot back, and they both laughed. "Listen, has The Pirate been in today?"

"No. Come to think of it, I haven't seen him in a while."

Renzo hadn't expected this. "Could he be at Sofia's?"

"No, they broke up."

"Good, he didn't deserve her." They both laughed.

"You might try Antonio's, a few blocks up. One of the other stevedores might know where he is."

ANTONIO'S SMELLED OF FRIED CALAMARI and body odor, its tables occupied by stevedores wolfing down their meals. Renzo scanned them, noticing that most were in uniform, which meant they were employees of shipping companies. The Pirate hadn't been legitimately employed, since he had a criminal record. It was a stevedore's apparel that tipped Renzo off to who might know The Pirate.

Renzo walked over to the stevedore in the back, sitting alone in a dirty white shirt. "Excuse me, sir, I'm looking for The Pirate. Do you know him?"

The stevedore didn't look up from his fish stew. "I know ten men who call themselves The Pirate."

Renzo had to think of the real name. "Claudio DiMoro."

"I know him."

"Do you know where he is?"

"No." The stevedore dunked bread into his soup.

"Do you know who would know?"

"No."

Renzo felt stumped. He needed The Pirate for his new scheme, since he was the one who had kidnapped Prince Pinocchio and paid Renzo to hide him in the madhouse.

"Why do you want to see him?"

"I want to talk to him. I'm a friend of his. My name's Renzo."

The stevedore glanced up with recognition. "Renzo-from-the-Madhouse?"

"Right."

"He mentioned you."

"And you are?"

"Call me Scales. I weigh cargo."

"Nice to meet you, Scales. It's too bad he's gone. There's something I need done."

"Like he did before?"

"Yes."

"I'll help." Scales kicked out the opposite chair, and it clattered away from the table. "Give me the details."

Renzo took a seat and told Scales his new scheme, that Scales would kidnap a rich man's son and bring the boy to the madhouse for the night, to be picked up the next morning. If the family paid the ransom, they'd get the boy back. If they didn't, the boy would stay away until they did.

Scales nodded. "If we split fifty-fifty, I'm in."

"Done."

"Does the boy stay in the madhouse, like the first one?"

"No, it causes problems."

"Do you have someplace better?"

Renzo snorted. "No, I have someplace worse."

PART TWO

The head of the Palermo police once remarked
to me, "Were a cross to be placed on every spot
where a victim lies buried in the plain of Palermo,
the Conca d'Oro would be one vast cemetery."

—DOUGLAS SLADEN, *SICILY, THE NEW WINTER RESORT*

There were a few locked cells, dark, sordid, and unhealthy;
designated either male or female. They were indiscriminately
crowded with maniacs, the demented, the furious and the
melancholic. Some of them were stretched out on filthy patches
of straw but most lay on bare earth. Many were completely
naked or wrapped in filthy rags; they were like beasts in chains,
inundated by annoying insects, enduring hunger and thirst
and heat and cold and mockery and anguish and beatings.

—BARON PIETRO PISANI, *GUIDE TO THE ROYAL MADHOUSE OF PALERMO*

CHAPTER THIRTY

Gaetano stood at the head of the table, addressing the Beati Paoli. Their faces went grave as he told them he'd been unable to find witnesses to the kidnapping, but they brightened when he finished with the baptismal records. By the time he had brought them up to date, they were skimming his list of boys' names.

"Gaetano, you've done a fine job!" Don Manfreddi smiled.

"Yes, *bravo*!" Carmine added, and everyone joined in.

"Thank you." Gaetano nodded. "But we have much to do, and it must be done quickly. Every day is another day the boy is kept prisoner."

"That's true," Carmine said, shaking his head. "How can we help, Gaetano?"

Gaetano gestured to the papers. "As I've said, there are one hundred and twenty families on this list. I've eliminated some of the names and I think we can narrow it down further, among ourselves tonight. I noticed when you were looking at the list, some of you were commenting that you know the family name."

Carmine said, "I do, one of them."

"So do I." Don Fabiano raised his hand.

"Me, too, my cousins are on the list," Don Enzo chimed in.

Gaetano felt encouraged. "That's what I hoped. The boy's family will come from ranks much like our own, professionals, well-to-do, maybe the nobility." He motioned to Don Vincenzo, sitting at the other head of the table. "Don Vincenzo, you must socialize with some of these families."

"I do, that's true." Don Vincenzo scanned the page in his hand. "I recognize the children of my friends among them. They have five- and six-year-olds."

Gaetano nodded again, pleased. "So, our first line of inquiry is to examine the list with care, identify the names each of us know, and task yourselves with interviewing the families."

Don Leonardo frowned. "How do we do that without revealing our purpose?"

Gaetano had expected the question. "Simply visit the family and inquire how they've been, how the children are, and what's going on in the household. Listen carefully to the answers to see if you're being told the truth."

"In other words, use our powers of observation," added Don Ugo.

"Then, I have a second way to narrow down the list." Gaetano turned to Don Fulvio and Don Fabiano. "Gentlemen, I know you're both bankers with positions of responsibility in your respective institutions. I'm asking you to look at this list and see if you recognize the families of your clients. I'm hoping you will identify those clients, and the next time you're at the bank, investigate their accounts and determine if they've made large withdrawals since the kidnapping, as if for a ransom. Obviously many people are making large withdrawals, especially with taxes"—Gaetano paused for the grumbling around the table—"but perhaps you can discern the reason for the withdrawal and determine whether it was valid. If so, it will enable us to identity families who are likely to have been victims."

Don Fulvio frowned. "I can do it, and I will. But you can imagine our clients are concerned with confidentiality. They may not give me a valid reason, if asked."

Don Fabiano shrugged. "True, but we know many of them well enough to know if they're lying."

"Good." Gaetano straightened. "The third way to narrow down the list is for the lawyers among us, like Carmine, Don Manfreddi, and me."

"Yes?" Carmine looked up, and so did Don Manfreddi.

"Most families of means contact a lawyer for a Last Will & Testament after a male child is born. You must have drafted such instruments. So, like the bankers, I'm asking you to go through these lists, identify any clients of yours, and see if they have made a will."

Carmine responded, "We can do it, Gaetano."

Gaetano came to his final point. "Lastly, even after we have reduced the list thusly, we'll still have many, many families to visit. It would take too long for one person alone, so I reorganized the families according to their neighborhoods. We can divide the neighborhoods among us and interview the families simultaneously. I've already started visiting families, to no avail yet. My cover story is that I'm a lawyer interested in getting new business."

Carmine smiled. "Good work, Gaetano!"

Don Manfreddi said, "You never know, you might get new clients."

Gaetano laughed. "If there are no further questions, let's get down to work and see how many we can eliminate tonight."

THE MEETING ENDED AT MIDNIGHT, and the Beati Paoli had eliminated twenty boys for a variety of reasons. Gaetano hoped the number would narrow in the days to come.

Gaetano let himself into his apartment quietly because everyone had gone to bed. He tiptoed through the dining room, where Maria had left a candle burning next to his favorite pastry, a Finger of the Apostle, a ricotta-filled confection with one end dipped in chocolate. He was about to take a bite when she appeared in her nightgown, her dark hair loose to her shoulders.

"Gaetano." Maria smiled indulgently, crossing her slender arms. "Any other woman would think her husband was having an affair."

"I'm sorry I'm late." Gaetano went to her, took her in his arms, and gave her a kiss on the forehead, then the lips. He breathed in her lemon blossom perfume, faint on her warm skin.

"Where have you been?"

"At work."

Maria lifted an eyebrow, her smile fading. "Funny, because Bartolomeo stopped in looking for you. He said Don Matteo was looking for you, too."

Gaetano cringed. "I'm sorry, uh, I had something else to do."

Maria put a hand on his arm. "Where were you? Where have you been lately? You seem preoccupied."

"Honestly, I do have something on my mind."

"What? Tell me." Maria searched his face, pained. "Are you ill?"

"No." Gaetano sat down and Maria joined him.

"What's going on then?"

"It's about the kidnapping."

"What kidnapping?" Maria asked, and Gaetano realized even she had forgotten about the boy. *Palermitani* moved on the way they always did after a crime, thanking God they weren't today's victims and hoping they wouldn't be tomorrow's.

"The one from the festival. It bothers me." Gaetano owed her an explanation, since the foundation of his love was his respect for her, and their marriage was one of best friends, as well as lovers. "I got baptismal records from the Cathedral and have been trying to figure out who the kidnapped boy is."

Maria frowned. "Gaetano, why?"

"I can't solve the crime if I don't know its victim."

"You're not the *carabinieri*. It's up to them to solve the crime."

"They do nothing, we both know that."

"But you have responsibilities at work. Bartolomeo says you were given agreements to edit. Is that the stack in the study?"

"Yes, I'll get them done." Gaetano was halfway through, working at home.

"He says Don Matteo is very unhappy with you lately."

"Don Matteo is fine with me. It's Bartolomeo who stirs up trouble."

"But I don't understand, Gaetano. This kidnapped boy, he's not your son."

"Morally, what difference does that make? We believe, Love thy neighbor as thyself. Saint Paul tells us, 'No one should seek his own advantage, but that of his neighbor.' That makes the boy a son to all of us."

Maria sighed. "I should have known when I stole you from the priesthood."

Gaetano had wanted to be a priest, but when he met her, he'd fallen completely in love. "I can't turn away from the boy."

"Nor can you forget about your own sons, and you're starting to." Maria shook her head slowly. "You haven't been home much lately, and you're distracted at mealtimes. You don't play with the boys or read to them anymore. They want your attention."

"They have you."

"A mother doesn't substitute for a father."

"You overstate it, Maria. I'm here and they know I love them. I'm not neglectful."

"Fine, but nevertheless, I . . . need you now." Maria touched his arm, and Gaetano saw a sly look cross behind her eyes.

"Why? What's the matter?"

Maria smiled. "I'm pregnant, dear."

CHAPTER THIRTY-ONE

Alfredo wasn't about to be bullied by the note on the rock, thrown at his door. He had a right to earn a living and a family to feed. He walked down the street to the piazza, leading Beatrice with the baskets of cheese.

He spotted the crowd on the piazza, led by Signora Tozzi, her lady-friends, and even more women. Two uniformed *carabinieri* were trying to get them in line, and so was Father Casagrandi, the priest at Madonna dei Miracoli church, which bordered the piazza. But as soon as the women spotted Alfredo, they started calling to him.

One of the *carabinieri* hurried toward him, waving. "Are you the man who sells the goat cheese? You've got customers waiting for you. They're not orderly."

"I can't help it."

"They say you put a charm on the cheese and it cures sickness."

Alfredo sighed. "I told them it's just cheese, but they don't listen."

"They call you Magic Alfredo. They think you're a wizard."

"Why?" Alfredo asked, blinking.

"Have you *looked* in a mirror?"

"No, I don't have one."

"Well, look here." The officer took Alfredo by his shoulders and turned him to face a glass window. Alfredo's reflection surprised even him. His hair was long, his beard overgrown, and his clothes shabby.

"Okay, I see your point, but there's no such thing as wizards."

"Tell *them* that." The officer gestured at the women. "They're making a fuss, and the other vendors don't want you at the piazza."

"Too bad for them." Alfredo straightened. "They threw a rock at my door, with a warning. You should do something about it."

"Like what?"

"Ask them who did it. Tell them not to do it again. You're the *carabinieri*."

"Don't be a baby. A man should expect a little rough-and-tumble in business. You see the disruption you cause."

"I don't like it any better than you do." Alfredo didn't think it was fair. "Anyway, I have to sell my cheese."

"What if you sold it here instead of the piazza?" The officer gestured to the side. "I can make the customers line up on the street."

"Fine, I'll compromise."

"Can I get a pack of your cheese?" The officer held out his hand. "Those women gave me a headache."

"Okay, but my cheese won't help." Alfredo gave him a packet, and the officer eyed the cheese, turning it this way and that.

"I've never had charmed cheese before."

Alfredo felt like nobody was listening to him. Meanwhile, the women were hurrying up the street and the other officer was running after them.

"Alfredo!" Signora Tozzi waved. "My husband is better! Your cheese cured him! You have to make more!"

"Magic Alfredo, Magic Alfredo!" cried her ladyfriends, and they surged toward him, thrusting coins at him and grabbing his cheese. He sold out even quicker than before, leaving the women without cheese sad and desperate. They began calling out ailments that sickened their children or husbands.

Alfredo tried to explain, yet again. "Ladies, I'm not a wizard or a doctor—"

"When will you come back?" the women called to him, heedless. "My daughter's fever is rising! What will I do?"

Alfredo turned away, upset, and picked up Beatrice's lead. The *carabinieri* had to hold the women back so he could leave, and some of them burst into fretful tears, which tore at his heart.

The last look he got of the piazza was of Donato Nuts, Mario Cow-Cheese, and Giuseppe Dry Beans scowling at him, their arms folded over their long aprons.

He wondered which of them had sent the note.

And what they would do now.

CHAPTER THIRTY-TWO

Franco dozed under a shade tree with Violetta, her cheek against his chest and his arm encircling her. Their nakedness felt natural and wonderful to him. They had sneaked a tryst on his routine trip to Villa Zito, making love where they had before, laughing until desire overwhelmed them, hungry for each other. Only afterward did they put down a blanket and return to each other's arms.

"I missed you." Franco stroked her hair, silky to his touch. He had shed his clothes, and she had tossed aside her black uniform and white cap. The breeze off the sea cooled their skin, and they had found a perfect spot overlooking the Tyrrhenian, which glimmered a beautiful turquoise hue. Waves splashed against the dark, rocky cliffside.

Violetta gazed out to sea. "Franco, do you ever want to leave?"

"Sicily? No. Why?" Franco propped himself up and looked at her. Dappled sunshine fell on her richly red hair, and a breeze blew a strand from her face, revealing large, round eyes that were an unusual reddish-brown. Her skin was smooth, her nose strong, and her lips full and pretty, but they were curving down in dissatisfaction.

"Look, out there." Violetta made a sweeping motion across the sea. "There's Greece, Africa, and Arabia, and there's Europe and the mainland. Don't you want to see any of them, ever?"

"No, I want to buy land and stay here. I want to move up the ranks, not across the sea."

"I've heard that speech." Violetta smiled. "Many times."

Franco smiled back. "Then why do you ask?"

"I'm hoping I can persuade you to change your mind."

"Why?"

"So I can see where I fit into your future." Violetta eyed him frankly. "We want a future together, don't we?"

"Yes." Franco knew she was talking about marriage, which she had been doing a lot lately. He wanted to marry her, but he wasn't ready to propose until he was more established.

"I feel restless. Day after day, nothing ever changes. I'm stuck inside because I'm a woman. We're not even supposed to walk in town without accompaniment. In Bagheria or in Palermo."

Franco had a vague memory that such inequality had bothered his mother as well, but at the end of her life, no one told her what to do. Not if he valued his head.

"Franco, I'm tired of staying in. And I'm tired of Sicily."

"But you love this country, don't you? I do."

"Yes, but I wish I could see the world. We're on the edge of it here, do you realize that? It's too tempting to live along the shore, but never cross the line. The world doesn't end at La Cala. That's where it *begins*."

"You want freedom." Franco understood, touching her face.

"Yes. Don't you?" Violetta frowned at him, and Franco felt strangely as if he were his brother, Roberto, content with less than he should be.

"As I've said, I want to own my own grove. I want the same opportunities as other men. I want equality, too."

Violetta brightened. "Freedom and equality go well together."

"Not always. Sometimes they're at odds."

"Not if we time it properly. Maybe after you get your equality, I get my freedom?"

"Is that really what you want?"

"Yes. I catch myself looking out the windows at the ships. Travel calls to me. My mother wants grandchildren and she drives me crazy. Wait till you meet her."

"I'll charm her." Franco knew Violetta's stories of fights with her mother. "Here's the key to mothers. When a woman has a child, she becomes not only a mother, but a boss. Accept your mother as your boss, and you'll get along better."

"But *I* want to be the boss."

"When you have a child, you will be. But not before. Not to her."

Violetta smirked, narrowing her eyes. "You think you know so much about women."

"I know everything about women. Mothers are just women at their bossiest."

Violetta laughed. "Then we agree? We'll travel together?"

Franco could see how much she meant what she said. "If I want you, I have to agree, so I agree."

Violetta chuckled. "This isn't a negotiation, it's a conversation."

"Okay, whatever you call it, I agree. We'll travel, that's our plan."

"A plan to be free?" Violetta burst into laughter. "You can't *plan* freedom."

"Yes, you can. You have to." Franco pointed to a clipper ship on the water. "See her? She's beautiful, isn't she? She can go anywhere she wants in the world, right?"

"Yes," Violetta answered, smiling. "Am I the clipper?"

"You are, but don't get ahead of me. She can go anywhere, but she doesn't travel aimlessly. She's anchored right now, waiting for her turn to enter La Cala. She follows a shipping schedule, a plan."

Violetta burst into laughter. "*Bravo*, Franco! I'll be your clipper, and you'll be my anchor."

"Exactly!" Franco reached for her, tenderly putting his hands on her smooth arms.

"Just don't anchor me too much," Violetta whispered, kissing him.

"Just don't sail too far," Franco whispered back, breathing her in.

CHAPTER THIRTY-THREE

Gaetano checked his pocket watch and decided he had time to interview a few more families before heading back to the office after a client meeting. He had already eliminated six more boys by meeting the child himself or seeing nothing amiss at the house.

Gaetano started with the home of the Michangeli family, which had a façade of soft ocher stucco and a front window with green shutters. He knocked, and the door was opened by a woman who struck him instantly as melancholy, which alerted his senses. Signora Vera Catena had a lovely face and a mouth shaped like a seraph's bow, but her smile seemed strained and her eyes had darkish circles. Her maroon dress hung on her, as if she had lost weight.

Gaetano introduced himself, then said, "You must be Signora Catena, Dante's mother."

"Yes, I am." Signora Catena emitted the slightest gasp, and Gaetano thought it came at the child's name.

"Is your husband at home?" Gaetano peeked into the living room and spied a toy sword in the corner. The room seemed still, quiet, and too neat for a home with children.

"No, unfortunately, my husband's away right now." Signora Catena's hand fluttered to her slim throat. "Perhaps I can help you. What's this about?"

"A private matter." Gaetano began to get excited, wondering if she was the kidnapped boy's mother.

"Does this private matter concern my family?" Signora Catena's weary eyes widened with hope.

"Yes." Gaetano felt like they were talking about the same thing, in oblique terms. "Perhaps we should discuss it inside?"

"I agree." Signora Catena opened the door, and Gaetano entered the house, surprised to find his boss, Don Matteo, and his wife, Donna Angelina, sitting in the living room.

Don Matteo rose. "Gaetano, what are you doing here? Do you have a message for me from the office?" He paused, puzzled. "Wait a minute. We decided to stop in only at the last moment. How did you know I was here?"

"I, uh . . . didn't," Gaetano stammered, caught. He was supposed to be at work.

"Gaetano, how nice to see you." Donna Angelina smiled, a kind, elegant woman with a sleek twist of dark hair.

Gaetano forced a smile back. "You as well, Donna Angelina."

Don Matteo frowned. "What are you doing here, Gaetano? I thought you were at a meeting."

Signora Catena interjected, "Do you know this man, Uncle Matteo?"

Gaetano's mind raced, and he got his bearings. So, Signora Catena was Don Matteo's niece. It was a coincidence, but not unlikely. Palermo's upper class traveled in the same circles. But Gaetano still had to explain why he was here.

Don Matteo was saying, "Gaetano works for me. I'm just not sure what brings him here, in the middle of a workday."

Gaetano defaulted to his cover story. "Well, sir, I've been visiting families with young sons, to see if they need new wills."

Don Matteo recoiled. "How did you know my niece had a son?"

"I obtained baptismal records and I—"

"Come with me. Excuse us, ladies." Don Matteo took Gaetano by the arm, walked him to the door, and brought him outside into the street.

"Don Matteo, I can explain—"

"Not here." Don Matteo eyed an alley up ahead. "Go that way, right now."

Gaetano did, his thoughts churning. He was in trouble, but he wasn't going to forget about the kidnapping investigation. Signora Catena's son Dante could still be the kidnapping victim, so either Don Matteo didn't know the boy had been kidnapped, or he did know and was keeping it secret.

Don Matteo led him into the alley. "Gaetano, what's gotten into you? Knocking on doors is *not* how we attract clients. What do you think you're selling? Pots and pans?"

"Many lawyers solicit—"

"Lesser lawyers, not *me*. Not *you*. You're Judge Catalano's son! That's not how we get clients! What's next, *advertising*?" Don Matteo threw up his hands. "Do you think you get a baron by knocking on a *door*? What the devil has gotten into you? You used to have excellent judgment."

"I thought I would help." Gaetano still needed information. "Signora Catena seemed sad, and I wondered why."

Don Matteo pursed his lips. "She's unwell. Not that it's any business of yours."

Gaetano bowed his head. "I'm very sorry to hear that. That must be difficult for her, not to mention her family. I didn't see the boy at home. Is he?"

"No, he's away with his father." Don Matteo shook his head. "To return to the point, I don't need your help to attract clients."

"You're right, I'm sorry, I should have thought of—"

"Wait." Don Matteo's eyes narrowed with suspicion. "I bet I know what you're up to. You're about to go into practice for yourself, aren't you? You must be soliciting clients for your own business."

Gaetano gasped. He hadn't anticipated this turn. "No, not at all—"

"How could I have been so blind? It's the only explanation that makes sense." Don Matteo started shaking his head. "Your frequent absences, your sloppiness of late. Are you sabotaging me? Is that what you've been up to? Sabotaging me so you can steal my clients? Do you think they'd come with you, young man?"

"No, I swear." Gaetano had no choice now but to tell the truth. "Don Matteo, I'll be honest with you. I'm here because I'm investigating the kidnapping of the boy from the Saint Rosalia festival—"

"What?" Don Matteo's eyes went wide.

"—and Signora Catena seemed melancholy, so I must ask you, was her son Dante kidnapped from the festival?"

"Of course not, I just told you, but you *lied* to me? Have you lost your mind? You used to be so trustworthy, so moral, like your father." Don Matteo eyed Gaetano with disappointment. "I can never trust you again, Gaetano. As a result, you can no longer work for me. Your employment is hereby terminated."

"Sir, please don't! I'm sorry and—"

"I've made up my mind. Bartolomeo was right about you. Do not return to the office. A courier will deliver your personal effects to your home. Please give the courier any client files in your possession."

Don Matteo stormed off.

Gaetano stood alone in the alley, feeling the walls closing in.

"GAETANO, NO." MARIA MOANED. THEY sat together at the dining room table, and the boys were playing downstairs at the neighbor's.

"Don't worry. I'll find another job."

"How could this happen?" Maria's lovely eyes filmed with tears. "We have two sons and a baby on the way. We need the money."

"We have savings." Gaetano had no inherited money, since his father had never taken a bribe like the other judges.

"How much?"

"Enough to support us until I find another job."

"Why don't we ask my father?"

"There's no reason to. I can support my own family."

"But if we ask my father, we won't have to worry. How long will it take you to get a new job?"

"Not long, I promise you. I'll begin looking today."

Maria bristled, wiping her eyes. "Will you have time, when you're not playing police? You put a stranger's child over your own."

Gaetano felt pained. They had been quarreling so much over this lately. "My investigation is part of who I am."

"It's not who you are, it's simply what you do. Why must it be your cause?" Maria's eyes flashed. "Are you making up for not entering the priesthood? Is that why?"

"No, but I'm doing it for the same reasons I felt called to the priesthood. I'm trying to serve the common good. I'm trying to do something for my fellow man. I'm *called* to save the boy."

Maria sniffled, frowning. "Anyway, now does it stop?"

"Stop? No, why would it? I can't, I told you."

"No?" Maria asked in disbelief. She rose, resting a delicate hand on the table. "You have to make a choice. That boy, or your family."

"Why?" Gaetano rose, opposite her. "I can do both."

"Can you? You got *fired*. You've worked there since law school. You had a future there—"

"I tell you, I'll find another job." Gaetano reached for her arm, but Maria pulled it away.

"Choose."

Gaetano's heart sank. "Maria, I can't, I won't—"

"Is it *that* hard a choice? You choose a stranger over your own blood?" Maria's eyes brimmed with tears, and she hurried to their bedroom, closing the door.

Gaetano hurried after her, because he loved her more than anything. Except God.

CHAPTER THIRTY-FOUR

Gaetano stood before the Beati Paoli, updating them on his investigation and giving them the latest tally. They supplied their tallies, but their progress was far slower, owing to work or familial obligations. They were attending to things he was ignoring, and he didn't blame them, but decided to ask for their help.

"Gentlemen. There's one last personal matter, if I may. I've had a setback in my professional life. I've been spending time away from the office, frankly doing these interviews, and Don Matteo terminated my employment. I'm hoping you might have leads on job opportunities."

"I know one," Carmine answered, as the men burst into chatter. "A friend of mine needs a new lawyer at his firm. It's general practice, like Don Matteo's."

"I have one, too," Don Fabiano chimed in. "One of my clients owns a ceramics business. He's decided to take on a business lawyer."

Don Ugo waved his hand. "I myself have an interest in a shipping company. You know Admiral Bentinck and the British garrison are overrunning Palermo these days. There are so many complex questions of international and maritime law that need answers. I feel certain you could do it, Gaetano. Would you like to learn a new specialty?"

"Yes!" Gaetano answered, encouraged. "I'm interested in all of these opportunities. Thank you!"

"It's the least we can do, since we got you fired," Carmine quipped, and everybody laughed, even Gaetano.

Love never fails, he thought.

"Gentlemen, let me add one last thing," Gaetano added, cheered. "I have a new baby on the way!"

"*Bravo*, Gaetano!" "Congratulations!" "What wonderful news!"

Carmine grinned. "It won't be long before he sits at our table! The Catalano family will run the Beati Paoli!"

Gaetano laughed, then led the oath. "Who are we, men?" he asked, and they responded as one:

"We're the Beati Paoli, the Blessed Society of Saint Paul!"

"And for whom do we fight?"

"For justice, for Sicilia, and for God!"

CHAPTER THIRTY-FIVE

It was a sunny morning, and Alfredo walked to Pietro Hay's, leading Beatrice as she pulled her empty cart. Buying hay was their favorite errand, but not today. He couldn't stop thinking about the trouble he'd had the last time he sold his cheese. When he'd sold out, the women were desperate, which made him feel guilty. He couldn't convince them he wasn't Magic Alfredo. He'd made enough money for the good hay, but he was unhappy. Beatrice was, too, not even lifting her head at the smell of hay.

They reached Pietro Hay's and entered his farmyard, passing his somber mule and donkey. Alfredo realized he didn't have any cheese for Pietro Hay, not that it would grow hair on his wife anyway. They stopped at the shed, and Beatrice rallied to nibble stray hay on the ground.

"*Ciao*, Alfredo." Pietro Hay walked over, hay hook in hand. There were no stacked bales waiting.

"*Ciao*." Alfredo wiped his brow and replaced his cap. "I'll take the good hay today. I'm sorry, but I don't have any cheese for your—"

"I have no hay for you." Pietro Hay straightened, hook in hand.

"But I have the money." Alfredo patted his pocket, and the coins jingled cooperatively.

"Nevertheless, it's promised to someone else." Pietro Hay's cap shaded his eyes, which were flinty. "He's coming to pick it up tomorrow."

"How much did he buy?"

"All of it."

"Really?" Alfredo eyed the good hay, estimating fifty bales stacked to the ceiling. "Who could need so much hay?"

"Someone with horses."

"How many horses?"

Pietro Hay shrugged. "I don't know, I didn't ask."

Alfredo felt disappointed. "Okay then, I'll take the moldy. Ten bales."

Pietro Hay shook his head. "The moldy is spoken for, too. The man bought everything."

Alfredo's mouth dropped open in astonishment. "Who *is* this man?"

Pietro Hay frowned. "Don't make this harder than it is, Alfredo. Just go. I can't sell to you anymore."

"Why not?" Alfredo asked, surprised. Then he realized what must have happened. "Someone told you not to? Who?"

"You know who."

"Donato Nuts? Mario Cow-Cheese? Giuseppe Dry Beans?"

Pietro Hay didn't reply, tilting his face down.

Alfredo felt a wrench in his chest. "We've done business for years. My girls need to eat. This is wrong."

"I know, I'm sorry."

"But you're the only hay dealer around." Alfredo felt desperate, like the women when he ran out of cheese. "Just sell me some moldy. I'll pay extra. Double."

"Please, go." Pietro Hay looked crestfallen. A tear rolled down his weathered cheek.

"Okay." Alfredo gave a gentle tug on Beatrice's rope, and they left the farmyard, bidding a silent goodbye to the sad mules.

ALFREDO HEADED FOR THE FARMSTAND by the road, having figured out what to do. He was going to buy vegetables and make a stew
for his daughters. Luckily, they were also goats, so they would eat anything, even his cooking.

The farmstand was run by Guido Onion, and Alfredo thought his
nickname was apt. Guido Onion sold onions, his bald head was shaped
like an onion, and he had an onion's personality. Guido dozed in a
wooden chair leaning against an umbrella pine, arms crossed and his
cap over his eyes.

Alfredo picked out four tomatoes, a long squash, some carrots, an
onion, and plenty of garlic, since Ginevra loved garlic. He cleared his
throat to wake up Guido Onion, who lifted his cap drowsily, blinking.

"Alfredo, put those back. You can't have them. Nothing here is
for you."

Alfredo's heart sank. The vendors on the piazza must have gotten to
him, too. "Please, I'll pay you triple. No one has to know."

"I said, no."

"But my girls need to—"

"Put my produce back or I'll *make* you put it back."

"You know this is wrong." Alfredo put the produce back in the correct bins.

"Go," Guido Onion said, pointing away.

CHAPTER THIRTY-SIX

Gaetano sat opposite the large desk of Don Attilio, the majority owner of the shipping company in which Don Ugo owned a minority interest. The well-appointed office had the best view of La Cala, and Don Attilio was a dapper businessman with oiled black hair and sharp blue eyes behind spectacles with gold rims. His lips flattened into a frown, and the interview wasn't going well.

"Gaetano, I have questions." Don Attilio looked up from the curriculum vitae. "You have no experience in maritime law or the law of international waters, is that correct?"

"Yes, but I've been studying at the law library. I memorized the major cases and I learn quickly."

"You do seem willing." Don Attilio hesitated. "And you're the son of Judge Catalano."

"Yes, I am." Gaetano hated to think what his father would say about the state of his legal career. He had been applying for jobs all over town, but he had received rejection after rejection.

"Judge Catalano's reputation was impeccable."

"Yes, it was." Gaetano warmed to the praise. "He was a wonderful judge and a wonderful father."

"And a man of absolute integrity." Don Attilio slid the curriculum vitae back across the desk. "Thank you for your time. I'm afraid I won't be hiring you."

Gaetano's mouth went dry. "May I ask why? My credentials—"

"Your reputation."

"My reputation is excellent. Don Ugo vouched for me, didn't he?"

"Yes, but you didn't work for him. His recommendation is entitled to less weight than your employer's. I checked your reference, and Don Matteo's law firm declined to vouch for your honesty."

Gaetano felt his face aflame. "Don Matteo and I had a disagreement, that's all—"

"To clarify, he wasn't there when I stopped in. I didn't speak to him. I spoke to Bartolomeo, who gave me an earful."

Bartolomeo. Gaetano shifted forward. "Don Attilio, if you were to speak to Don Matteo directly, I know he wouldn't speak that ill of me."

"Gaetano, my standard is high. I want a lawyer who represents my company with the utmost professional integrity." Don Attilio slid the curriculum vitae farther away from him, as if it were malodorous. "Best of luck in your future endeavors."

"Thank you, sir," Gaetano said, rising.

GAETANO WALKED AWAY FROM THE harbor, downcast. It was a beautiful day, with a salty breeze off the sea, and he had imagined working in this nautical setting. But he put that fantasy behind him. He found himself walking toward Don Matteo's to confront Bartolomeo, but Saint Paul prevailed.

Gaetano turned in the opposite direction, gathering his thoughts. He resolved to buy himself a coffee and start knocking on doors again to interview families. At least unemployment gave him more time to investigate.

Gaetano prayed he would find the boy *and* a job.

Be strong, Saint Paul had written.

Gaetano held his head high.

CHAPTER THIRTY-SEVEN

Summer turned to fall, and a new law presented Franco with the opportunity he'd been waiting for. Noblemen were now permitted to sell parcels of their *latifondi*, and anyone could buy land, even commoners. This morning, he had news he couldn't wait to tell Roberto, who would be home any minute from a harbor trip.

Sunlight filled Franco's kitchen, and he set out slices of cantaloupe, blood orange, grapefruit, and lemon-and-almond cakes decorated with tiny marzipan lemons. He heard Roberto returning outside and lifted the coffee pot from the brazier. He had timed breakfast as well as his mother would have, and she would have been proud he was making his dreams come true.

"Good morning." Roberto entered with a surprised grin, taking off his cap. "You greet me with breakfast? What do you want?"

Franco smiled. "I have news."

"What is it?" Roberto washed up in the basin, then dried off. "Am I to have a sister-in-law?"

"Sit, eat, then I'll tell you. How did it go?" Franco poured his brother a cup of coffee, then one for himself, sitting down.

"Perfectly! Not a single lemon lost. The brigands don't test us anymore. They know." Roberto crossed to the table, pulled out a chair, and sat down. "Sixty-two trips, so far. The pot is mine—rather, ours. These new men are solid, very solid."

"Good, good. So that brings you to how many men? Fifty?"

"No, forty-nine. One went away."

"Where?"

"Prison, you idiot." Roberto smiled, cutting a piece of cake. "Ours is the only business where you don't hire a good man, you hire a *bad* one."

Franco smiled, sipping his coffee, which tasted hot and delicious.

"And I have to be the worst. Here's my trick. We practice shooting every day, and I give them pointers. They see how well I shoot." Roberto wolfed down his cake. "Anyway, this woman of yours, will she say yes?"

"Of course."

"You *are* the second most handsome man in Sicily."

"You need a new joke."

"I need a new brother, then my jokes will be new. Hold on, look." Roberto pulled something from his pocket and tossed it onto the table with a metallic *clang*. It was a thick brass belt buckle embossed with an *F*. "I had it custom-made to wear with a bandolier belt."

"I hope you didn't pay much. It's ugly."

"It's beautiful." Roberto cut another piece of cake. "Now, here's the question. What *is* this object, really?"

"It's a belt buckle with an *F* for fool."

Roberto smirked. "Show some respect for my genius. The belt buckle isn't for me, it's for my men."

"Are their pants falling down?"

Roberto chewed his cake. "Trust me, every man will want this belt buckle."

"You're going to sell it to them?"

"No, I'm going to *give* it to them."

"Why, if it's expensive?"

"You know lemons, I know people." Roberto pointed to his temple. "That's why I'm excellent at cards. Lovemaking, too, but that's another subject. Men like to belong to something. I want my men to feel close to me, to our family. Hence the *F* for Fiorvanti."

"Like a brand on an animal?"

Roberto lifted an eyebrow. "That's *dark*, brother."

"Like a uniform, then?"

"No, this is a *reward*, it's *earned*. A man gets his belt buckle when I deem him worthy."

"Like a promotion?"

"Yes, but better. Something that shows everybody what a man's achieved."

"By looking at his crotch."

"If it isn't big enough already, it will be now." They both burst into laughter, identical echoes of one another.

"I like it." Franco smiled.

"So, you understand." Roberto smiled back, nodding. "Now everyone can see that a man is a respected member of our family. As our reputation spreads, every man will want one."

Franco felt a rush of happiness. "Mamma would love what we're doing."

"Papa loved us whether we did anything or not."

Franco let it go. "How many *giardini* do we protect?"

"Most of the big ones."

"I wish we had them all."

"It takes time. It's the reason I'm hiring now. It's cutting into my profits, but I'm going to grab all the best men—sorry, the worst men. Allow me to explain." Roberto drew a line in the air. "I need men in the right age group. Then I need those with a criminal record, or aspirations. After that, they have to be able to shoot. I want only men who meet all three qualifications. If I hire more now, I'll lose money, but I'll make it back later. And I'll have a head start against any competitors. I'll *own* the best worst men."

Franco smiled, impressed. "You're smarter than you look."

"So are you," Roberto shot back. "Now tell me your news. I tell you every woman I bed, how happy I made her, how lucky she was, her sighs and caresses, her filthy, sinful, delicious words—"

"First, business."

"—and I'm an excellent lover. I could give you pointers, but I won't. *I'm* king of *that* mountain."

Franco tried to focus Roberto's attention. "Listen, not all of the noblemen in the Conca d'Oro have money like Baron Zito. They keep up appearances, but they can't afford to maintain their estates. They owe taxes and creditors."

"I noticed. Palermo is populated by empty titles."

"Exactly." Franco's heartbeat quickened. "I heard Baron Moravio is selling a parcel of his *giardino*, six hectares. It goes up at auction next week. It's closer to the irrigation canals than Baron Zito's, so the soil is perfection. If we owned that parcel, I could make it produce better than it does now."

"Fantastico!"

"He's selling because he has gambling debts."

"I could give *him* pointers, too, but I can't educate the *world*." Roberto's eyes lit up. "Wait. It has a nice farmhouse, doesn't it? If you're getting married, I can live there."

"Yes, and you could run your business out of there."

"So how much will it go for? Can we afford it?"

"Yes, considering my savings, salary, and what you're earning." Franco rose to fetch the ledger from his bureau drawer. "I've gone over the numbers. I think we can make a reasonable bid."

"So we could *own* land, you and me?"

"Absolutely, I told you." Franco hurried back with the ledger.

Roberto groaned. "Not the ledger, the numbers, the lecture. Tell me about your woman instead. Ezio knows Nenella, and he saw them in the Capo market from behind. He said she has red hair and a nice ass."

Franco shot him a look. "Don't talk about her that way."

Roberto's mouth dropped open. "So it *is* serious!"

"We're talking business, Roberto."

"Will you introduce me to a redhead, too? So I can have one of my own?"

Franco ignored him, opening the ledger. "If we buy this parcel, I can support a family, and you can support a family, so—"

"Farmhouses *full* of redheads!" Roberto threw up his arms. "Redheads forever! Like poppies they'll grow!"

"First, you need to know the details—"

"I hate details."

"Rich men love details, and you're going to be rich."

"Can I be a baron? Baron of the Redheads?"

"Roberto, pay attention."

"Okay, but you're not getting a belt buckle."

CHAPTER THIRTY-EIGHT

Mafalda sat nursing baby Salvo by candlelight, and Lucia slept in Salvo's box at her feet. Anna was asleep, and the kitchen was quiet except for Salvo's suckling. Mafalda felt relieved and happy, now that she and Lucia were safe at night, and she grew accustomed to nursing another mother's baby. Her body produced enough milk to feed both, for which she thanked Madonna.

Mafalda had on a new dress in a floral pattern, and a pair of shoes only one size too small. Lucia had clothes, diapers, and a swaddling blanket from Salvo, and Mafalda used the blanket to cover the baby on the walk here. Anna made a big dinner every night, and Mafalda gained back the weight she had lost. Tonight, they had a mouthwatering red mullet with rosemary, fennel, and basil.

Mafalda began rocking Salvo as he nursed. The baby had gained weight, too, thriving in her care. She closed her eyes, letting the nursing relax her, but she didn't fall asleep. She thanked Madonna del Lume for Lucia, Salvo, Anna, and Francesco, who was away again. They had been her salvation.

Mafalda opened her eyes to a scream.

"What's the matter with her?" Anna stood holding Lucia, her mouth a horrified circle. "She's the color of milk! She's *milk*!"

"No!" Mafalda jumped up and set Salvo on the table. "You weren't supposed to look! Give her to me!"

"Take her!" Anna thrust Lucia at Mafalda, and the baby started crying, then Salvo did, too. The wailing reverberated in the tiny kitchen, and Anna picked up Salvo. "You lied to me! You brought a *demon* into our house!"

"She's a baby!"

"You lied!" Anna advanced on Mafalda, who edged backward. "What have you done to Salvo? Will he turn white, too? Is it your *milk*? Is that why you have so much? It's a spell, isn't it? You're trying to turn him into *milk*!"

"No, no! I fed him! I loved him! I took care of him!"

"Get out!" Anna pointed at the door, and Mafalda flew outside with Lucia crying. She ran through the village, reached the wall, and put Lucia in her sling. She stuffed their belongings, food, and water into her sack. Tears came to her eyes, but she wiped them away.

Mafalda would never think again about the baby boy and the home she was leaving, since neither was hers. From now on, she would avoid everyone. She would live in the shadows, behind the walls, or under the trees. She would survive like a she-wolf with her cub. It was the only chance Lucia had to grow up strong, proud, and safe.

Every mother's wish.

CHAPTER THIRTY-NINE

It was the Sabbath, and Alfredo needed G-d. He had no hay, and they were down to his last apple. He'd made his cheese, but fed it to the girls. He'd been looking forward to tonight, so he could conduct his service, as both rabbi and congregation. He prayed G-d would have answers for him.

The sun was sinking outside the window, and Alfredo lit a single candle on the kitchen table to substitute for a menorah. He used his threadbare white *tallis* to cover his head and shoulders. His Hebrew Bible lay open before him, and his girls and Beatrice were dozing.

Alfredo froze when he heard a commotion outside the door, which was closed. Ginevra and the others woke up, but not Beatrice.

"Alfredo, we want those goats! Hand them over and we won't hurt you!"

"No!" Alfredo hurried to bar the door, but Donato Nuts pushed it open, with Mario Cow-Cheese right behind him.

"Give us the goats!" Donato Nuts brandished a big knife, and Ginevra and the girls fled to the far corner of the room.

"Get away!" Alfredo stood in front of his girls.

"You heard me!" Donato Nuts shouted. "Your goats or your life! That's the deal!"

Alfredo felt a bolt of terror. "I'll die first! You'll have to kill me!"

Mario Cow-Cheese brandished a knife, too. "Give them to us! I can make cheese as well as you!"

"No, they won't produce for you!" Alfredo thought fast. "Why do you think everyone loves my cheese? Why do you think it cures stomachaches? You heard the women! I charmed the cheese! The goats produce only for me! I'm a *wizard*!"

Donato Nuts grimaced, nervously. "Are you really?"

"Yes!" Alfredo flared his eyes theatrically. "Why do you think I'm wearing this magic white robe? You interrupted me! I was working my spells and charms!"

Mario Cow-Cheese frowned. "Why didn't your charms work until now? Nobody bought your cheese before!"

"I didn't charm it before! I wanted to make more money, so I charmed my cheese! You see the results! You can't sell while I'm in the piazza! That's why you threw the rock at my door, isn't it? It was you both, wasn't it?"

Donato Nuts went red in the face, showing his guilt.

Mario Cow-Cheese glowered behind his knife. "Lies! If you're a wizard, prove it!"

"You want proof? Look *there*!" Alfredo pointed at his Hebrew Bible in the candlelight. "It's a book of spells and incantations!"

Donato Nuts squinted at the table. "It's a Bible, isn't it?"

"No, it only looks like a Bible! Go read the words! You won't be able to!" Alfredo knew they were unable to read Italian, much less Hebrew. "Those words can be read only by wizards!"

Mario Cow-Cheese recoiled. "What does it say?"

"It's for me to know, not you!" Alfredo stretched out his arms like the wizards in his folktales. "Beware of Magic Alfredo! I'll put a spell on you right now! I'll *curse* you!"

"No!" Donato Nuts headed for the door. "Don't curse me!"

"Me neither!" Mario Cow-Cheese hurried after him, but Alfredo chased them, holding his arms wide.

"I curse you! You'll never satisfy your wife again, if you did before!"

Donato Nuts ran outside, followed by Mario Cow-Cheese.

"I put a spell on you!" Alfredo flared his eyes like a wizard. "Neither of you will be able to make love again!"

Donato Nuts and Mario Cow-Cheese jumped onto their mules and rode away.

Alfredo watched them go, relieved but unhappy. It had been too close a call. Sooner or later, they would figure out he was a Jew, and he couldn't take that chance.

He went back inside the house and barred the door.

His girls herded around him, and he kissed each one on her knobby head. "Everything's okay now, my sweeties."

Beatrice woke up, blinking. Her expression asked, *What did I miss?*

Alfredo didn't have the heart to answer.

Or to tell her they had to leave.

Forever.

CHAPTER FORTY

Franco sat across from Baron Zito, who was behind his ornate desk with a black marble top, in his magnificent library. Bookshelves full of leather-bound volumes lined the walls, and couches and chairs were covered with a red-and-gold embossed fabric, coordinating with a rug in a red, orange, and blue pattern. The Baron's palazzo was in the most coveted location in Palermo, near bucolic La Favorita park.

"Franco, I'm hearing such good things about the *giardino*. All my friends with property in the Conca d'Oro are jealous." Baron Zito leaned forward, his light eyes glittering. "What's going on out there? Fill me in, disasters first."

"Baron DiMarco's *giardino* got blight, and it destroyed ten hectares."

"Too bad!" Baron Zito chuckled.

"Baron Moravio has to sell a parcel to pay off gambling debts." Franco didn't add that he was hoping to buy it himself.

"I *did* hear that! Moravio's a fool!" Baron Zito shook his head. "The lure of cards, I never understood it."

"My brother, Roberto, plays, but he wins."

"I'd like to meet him someday. Could you arrange that?"

"Of course," Franco answered, pleased.

"Okay, down to business. Tell me about our recent harvest."

Franco opened the ledger and took the Baron through a detailed accounting, which showed a steady increase in the *giardino*'s profitability. He had been surprised that Baron Zito had requested the ledgers, since he never had before. He'd called Franco so quickly that Franco hadn't been able to get a message to Violetta, since the household was back for the winter.

"Franco, this is wonderful news." Baron Zito leaned back in his chair. "You've done an excellent job, and my wife will be so pleased. The *giardino* was her dowry. This palazzo is from her side of the family, too." Baron Zito sniffed. "Villa Zito in Bagheria is more *my* style."

"All of your estates are beautiful."

"Thank you." Baron Zito loosened his dark silk cravat, which he had on with a custom-tailored waistcoat. "We're finished here. It's lunchtime, and you can go."

Franco stood up. "Thank you."

Baron Zito rose, pausing. "On second thought, would you like to join me for lunch? It'll be the two of us, and we can continue our chat. You can tell me how Arabo's doing."

"I'd like that." Franco perked up, since the Baron had never invited him to a meal. He brushed down his coat, wishing it were of a finer cut. "That's kind of you."

"Nonsense, you're excellent company. My son's in Naples again. You can take his seat."

Franco loved that Baron Zito offered him his son's seat, and they walked together through an enfilade of luxurious salons illuminated by beautiful chandeliers of Murano glass. Each room was furnished with inlaid cabinets displaying decorative dishes and the like, and one room could have come from China, with rich red silk covering its walls, black lacquered cabinets, and a round table that held a collection of carved ivory figurines and jade perfume bottles.

Baron Zito chuckled. "My wife thinks she's Chinese."

Franco smiled, and Baron Zito led him to the south side of the palazzo, then the dining room, which was elegant. It was dominated by a long table surrounded by twelve chairs with carved backs. There were walnut étagères and more inlaid cabinets displaying ormolu clocks, painted ceramic statuary, and marble eggs on stands. Friezes depicting knights jousting and carrying multicolored pennants adorned the walls and ceiling.

Baron Zito beamed. "Now *this* is my taste. I chose every item you see here. I'll bore you with each one's provenance over lunch."

"I won't be bored." Franco wanted to soak in every detail. He hoped for a beautiful villa of his own someday, but in the Conca d'Oro.

"I commissioned those medieval friezes. My wife thinks she's Chinese, but I think I'm a knight in shining armor."

"Aren't you? I am."

Baron Zito burst into laughter as a uniformed servant appeared and pulled out his chair for him. "Please, Franco, take Davide's seat."

"Thank you." Franco started to pull out the chair, but another servant rushed over and did it for him. Baron Zito gave him a good-natured wink, and Franco felt as if he was crossing an invisible line, ascending to the class he wanted to join.

Suddenly, there was the sound of fussing in the hallway, and Franco recognized one of the voices, stiffening as the women burst into the dining room, in mid-argument.

"Papa, Mamma is saying that—" Violetta stopped when she saw Franco. She looked even more beautiful without the puffy white cap and black uniform she wore to meet him, so her parents wouldn't know. Her red hair was now in a gleaming chignon, and she had on a shiny dress of violet silk with pearl-drop earrings.

Baron Zito gestured to her. "Violetta, daughter, say hello to our guest, Franco Fiorvanti. He manages our *giardino* in the Conca d'Oro."

"*Piacere*, Signor Fiorvanti," Violetta stammered, her thin skin flushing.

"*Piacere mio*, Baronessina Zito." Franco hadn't expected to see Violetta, since the Baron had said the lunch would be only the two of them, and Violetta hadn't expected to see him, since he hadn't been able to let her know he'd be here. He and Violetta had kept their relationship a secret from Baron and Baronessa Zito, knowing Franco wouldn't be their first choice for a suitor.

"Oh, I didn't realize we had company!" Baronessa Zito swept in with a flouncy *swoosh*, in a gold dress with black trim. She looked like an older version of Violetta, except her hair was dark brown. "Well! I'm sorry a guest has to witness a display by my ill-mannered brat."

"Mamma!" Violetta gasped. "Don't embarrass me!"

"You embarrass *yourself*, daughter!" The Baronessa's hooded eyes flashed with anger. "Honestly, you're impossible to be with anymore. You won't listen to reason or take the simplest direction."

"I don't need you to direct me, I'm a woman."

"You're a child!"

"I've grown up, and you don't see it!"

"When you act like it, I'll see it!"

"I do act like it! Ask *him*!" Violetta pointed a finger at Franco.

Franco's mouth went dry as dust. This wasn't the way he'd wanted to tell the Baron and Baronessa about the two of them, but it was too late.

"Him?" The Baronessa frowned in confusion. "Isn't he our *gabellotto*? I forget his name—"

"Mamma, it's Franco, and we're in love." Violetta raised her chin in defiance. "How about *that* for being a woman?"

Baronessa Zito recoiled, aghast. "Violetta, what are you talking about? That's not possible! How do you even *know* a *gabellotto*?"

Baron Zito rose, stunned. "Violetta? What's going on? You and *Franco*?"

"Yes, we're going to be married!" Violetta whirled around to face Franco. "Tell them about us, Franco! No more sneaking around! No more disguises!"

Franco stood up. "Baron, Baronessa, I love Violetta and I intend to

ask for her hand. I'm buying land from Baron Moravio and I can pro-
vide for her and make her happy—"

"Franco, are you *mad*?" Baron Zito's refined features contorted in
shock. "You and my daughter? *My* daughter and *you*?"

"Holy Virgin Mother!" Baronessa Zito's hand fluttered to her neck.
"We're ruined!" She turned to Violetta. "Violetta, have you let this
man *ruin* you? No, no, no, this can't be! You stupid, silly child! No man
of quality will want you now!"

"Shut up, Mamma!" Violetta shouted. "We love each other! We're
going to be married!"

"Not as long as I draw breath!" Baronessa Zito grabbed one of Violetta's arms, and Baron Zito grabbed the other.

"Daughter, you're not marrying *him*! I'll send you to the convent to
cool down!"

Franco rushed to help Violetta. "Baron Zito, I promise you, I'll
marry her and make her happy! She's not dishonored!"

Baron Zito blocked his path. "Franco, what possessed you to believe you could marry *her*? How did you think you could be my *son-
in-law*?"

I killed for you, Franco thought but couldn't say, astonished. "My
loyalty to you is absolute! I made your *giardino* a success! I serve your
interests every day in the Conca d'Oro! You say all the time I'm 'like
family'!"

"'*Like* family' isn't *family*! She's a *baronessina*, Franco! You're a
jumped-up *bracciante*!"

Franco reeled, feeling betrayed. "But you treat me like your son! You
sit me in Davide's chair! You said I earned a seat at your table!"

"You don't *earn* your way into a family! You're *born* into a family!"
Baron Zito stiffened. "It's not a promotion, it's a *birthright*! You're my
employee, not my *son*-in-law! Count D'Orazio asks me about her, so
does Marquis Caligiri! Violetta will *never* be yours!"

"She has to be!" Franco realized he'd been a fool. "We're marrying,
no matter what you say!"

"Shame on you, and Violetta! I order you never to see her again!"

"You can't!" Franco stood nose-to-nose with the Baron. "I tell you, I'm going to buy Moravio's parcel! I can support her!"

"You think *you're* buying land? I'll put a stop to that! I'll buy it myself! You're fired, Franco! Vacate the farmhouse immediately! Take your degenerate gambler of a brother, too!" Baron Zito motioned to the servants. "Get him out of here! And don't let him take Arabo! I'll sell that beast to the butcher!"

"Baron, no!" Franco shouted, but uniformed servants strong-armed him backward and the Baron and Baronessa pulled Violetta in the opposite direction.

"Violetta!" Franco shouted, while the servants hurried him through the enfiladed salons, down the marble staircase, through the courtyard, and out into the street, slamming the lacquered door in his face.

"Franco!" he heard Violetta scream, then even the echo was gone.

CHAPTER FORTY-ONE

Gaetano walked down the street, his leather envelope under his arm. He had applied to law firms all over town, but his reputation kept scuttling his chances. Meanwhile, he had eliminated more families on his list, but had many more to go.

He stopped to wait in line outside a coffee shop, but the line wasn't moving. He would've left if he had somewhere to be, but he didn't, unlike the men hurrying past in their frock coats. Their frowns were due to preoccupation, not disappointment. Palermo was a hard city in which to be unsuccessful.

"What's taking so long?" asked the young man in front of Gaetano.

"It's the news, haven't you heard?" a man called back from the coffee shop. "There was another kidnapping."

"What?" Gaetano interjected, shocked. "When?"

"Yesterday. A boy was kidnapped off the street."

"Where?"

"Via Argenteria Vecchia."

"No," Gaetano said, hushed. "That's around the corner."

"That's why they're gossiping inside, instead of making coffee."

"What are they saying?"

"They're talking how horrible it is and how nothing ever changes."

"Did anybody see anything?"

"I don't know."

"Thank you." Gaetano left the line, hurried off, and turned onto Via Argenteria Vecchia. It was in the jewelry district, and goldsmiths, silversmiths, and tinsmiths lined the narrow, curving street. A group of well-dressed women in fancy hats gathered in the middle, talking animatedly in front of a silversmith's. The sign in its window read CHIUSO, closed, which was strange at this time of day.

Gaetano had a hunch and made a beeline for the women. "Excuse me, is this jewelry shop where the kidnapping was?"

"Yes, isn't it terrible!" one of the women answered. She had on a hat of canary felt, and her face was a mask of concern. "I came here to check on a bracelet and heard the news."

"Do you know any details?"

"No. I heard only that his mother went inside for a minute, and the boy was snatched from where we're standing."

Another well-to-do woman shuddered. "The kidnapper must've been *following* them. That's evil, pure evil!"

A third woman clucked. "I let my son play outside while I'm shopping. I'll never do *that* again."

Gaetano's stomach tensed. "Do you know who the boy or his mother is?"

"No," the first woman answered.

"Were the *carabinieri* here?"

"I assume so."

"I don't!" The second woman shook her head. "I assume *nothing* with them. They do nothing!"

The third woman clucked again. "These criminals act with impunity. They're attacking our children, and no one cares."

"I do, I care!" Gaetano blurted out, and the women looked over as if he were vaguely crazy. "I mean, I feel bad about it, too."

The first woman's smile faded, and Gaetano edged away. Guilt engulfed him. If he had solved the first kidnapping, the second one would never have occurred.

Saint Paul, give me strength.

Gaetano prayed, and his soul calmed.

He knew exactly what to do next.

CHAPTER FORTY-TWO

The long, hot ride back to the Conca d'Oro intensified Franco's rage. Everything he believed had been wrong. He had thought Baron Zito's regard for him was genuine, but it wasn't. He had thought his loyalty would be rewarded, but he now knew it wouldn't be. He had believed that he could move up, but he saw now how crazy that was. There would be no going back to the man he used to be.

The moment Franco got home, he jumped off the borrowed mule, handed the animal to Sebastiano, and stormed inside the farmhouse, followed by an astonished Roberto.

"Franco, what's the matter? Where's Arabo?"

"I'll get the Baron for this!" Franco's head pounded. "He'll pay every day of his life!"

"What happened? You're acting crazy."

"I *am* crazy! I'm mad!" Franco started to pace in the tiny kitchen. "The arrogance! The betrayal! The *injustice!*"

"Calm down and tell me—"

"I got fired! We're not living here anymore, you and me!"

Roberto's mouth dropped open. "The Baron fired you? Why? You do a wonderful job and—"

"It's over! No more! I swear, he will pray for salvation from me! So will the rest of his kind! I have a new plan!"

"Stop." Roberto grabbed his arm. "Franco, whatever happened, I'm with you. You're not alone, you never were. I'm always by your side, I always have been. Whatever it is, we'll fix it together."

Franco felt his rage subside, touched. "Everything changes now, Robo."

"Robo?" Roberto smiled sadly. "You haven't called me that since we were little."

"Maybe because we're starting over, right now. You and me. This is a new beginning for us."

"Okay. Sit down. I'm getting you some wine."

"Get me water, instead." Franco eased into his chair and raked his hands through his hair, wet with perspiration. He was angrier at himself than at Baron Zito. "How could I have been so blind? I made a deal with the devil, and I was surprised when the devil reneged."

"Tell me what you're talking about." Roberto set a glass of water in front of him.

"I should've known better. I was such a fool. I was wrong about everything." Franco shuddered to think of what he had done. He had ordered the ruin of an innocent boy and killed a man to hide the crime. He had slain innocence to benefit corruption. He could no longer deny the depth of his depravity, but he could regret it, just as deeply. "I never should've done it. I never should've done any of it. The devil doesn't keep his bargains, does he?"

"No, he doesn't." Roberto sat down opposite him, and they both knew they were talking about the same thing, their darkest secret. Silence fell between them, and Franco picked up the glass, drank the water, and set the glass down with finality.

"Robo, it's time I told you, I was seeing Baron Zito's daughter, Violetta. She's the redhead. We hadn't told the Baron or Baronessa, and today, they found out."

Roberto's eyes flew open. "The redhead is Baron Zito's *daughter*? All this time, she's the girl you're crazy about?"

"Yes, I had it all planned, but it didn't happen the way I wanted. I was going to prepare him, but I didn't get the chance."

"*Prepare* Baron Zito? He'd *never* go for it, no matter how much you prepared him. Not you, not for *her*! No baron would!"

"I know that now." Franco met Roberto's eye, agonized. "You were right from the start. Way back when, remember? How could I think it would ever be otherwise? That men could be equal?"

Roberto met his eye, puckering his lower lip. "I love that about you."

"What do you mean?"

"I admire your belief in yourself. It's faith, pure faith. Nobody does great things without great faith. You thought you could change Palermo, by yourself. You were going to *will* yourself into marrying the Baron's daughter, all because you love her."

"I do, I love her."

"I'm sorry, for her and for you."

Franco sighed, composing himself. "Where are your men?"

"At Mario's. We're off tonight."

"Not anymore. Go get them." Franco rose. "We have to go to Palermo."

Roberto stood up with a puzzled frown. "But you just got back."

"Baron Zito's going to buy Moravio's parcel, so we can't. We have to stop him."

"How?"

"I'll explain on the way."

CHAPTER FORTY-THREE

aetano hurried uptown. His mind reeled after learning of the second kidnapping. He had to find out if Marshal Rosselli knew anything and if he was doing anything to investigate. Gaetano wasn't optimistic, but he was too thorough not to check.

He turned left toward the *Questura*, and a group of uniformed *carabinieri* collected in front of the entrance, as usual. Their heads turned when they spotted him. He saw them snicker, but that didn't stop him.

"Excuse me, gentlemen." Gaetano tried to get through them to the door. "I'm here to see the Marshal."

"No kidding," one of the officers muttered, and they all laughed.

Gaetano went inside and stopped at the desk, where the officer pointedly kept doodling. "Excuse me, I'm here to see Marshal Rosselli."

"No, you're not, Signor Catalano." The officer looked up, his eyes hard under the brim of his cap. "I've been given strict instructions. Marshal Rosselli will no longer entertain your inquiries."

"What do you mean? I need to speak to him about this second kidnapping. I assume you know the one."

"You've made a nuisance of yourself. Your visits disrupt his ability to do his job."

"Part of his job is to answer to the public."

"You take more time than any other member of the public." The officer rose and folded his arms in his thick uniform.

"Has he been to Via Argenteria Vecchia to investigate?"

"I'm not at liberty to share such information."

"Has he gone to the store? Spoken with the proprietor or any witnesses?"

"Are you deaf?"

Gaetano tried another tack. "Have you heard from the victim's family? Do we know who they are?"

"My patience has reached its end, sir." The officer walked around the desk and took Gaetano by the arm. "Allow me to escort you off the premises."

"I'm just trying to find out what's going on." Gaetano wrenched his arm free. "The second kidnapping might not have happened if the first one was solved. I'm trying to solve it, and you throw me out? This is Marshal Rosselli's job, and yours. Why don't you do it? Don't you care?"

The officer propelled Gaetano outside, and the other officers started laughing.

"Why do you men think this is funny?" Gaetano struggled for a civil tongue. "I just spoke to mothers on the street. They think you don't care. We must show them otherwise. These boys deserve justice."

The officer began to pull Gaetano away, but he pleaded his case to the *carabinieri* as if before a judicial tribunal.

"We have laws for a reason, but the law cannot enforce itself. If you don't enforce the law, there's no justice for the kidnapped boys—or anyone else. Don't you see? The purpose of law is to serve the common good. If laws are not enforced, society falls apart. *Palermo* falls apart."

"Leave or I'll arrest you!" The officer began to unhook handcuffs from his belt.

"Okay, I'll go." Gaetano noticed a crowd of families gathering around him. They talked behind their hands about him, gawking and pointing. Some laughed.

He turned away.

GAETANO HURRIED TO THE CAPO district, but he wasn't going home. The streets were congested with families emerging for the *passeggiata*, the evening stroll, happy and well-dressed like his family used to be. He kept his head down to avoid being recognized by his neighbors. He knew Maria would stay home, loath to stroll and socialize without him.

Gaetano entered the tobacconist's shop, aromatic with smoke. Boxes of cigars in glass cases lined one side, and the other side had tin containers of loose tobacco. He excused his way past the customers to get to the counter, where the young clerk's expression didn't change, even though he recognized Gaetano. The clerk was the secret courier for the Beati Paoli.

"Young man, good evening, I hope you can help me," Gaetano said.

"Good evening, sir," the clerk said, with a professional smile. "How may I assist?"

"The other day, I bought the wrong cigars and I'd like to return them tonight, at eight o'clock." Gaetano was saying that he needed another emergency meeting. "Will your manager be here then?"

"I don't know. That's very short notice. I may not be able to reach him in time."

"I understand, but it can't be helped."

"Are you certain?"

"Yes. You have my apologies. Thank you." Gaetano left the shop and started to head home, but stopped himself. If he did, he'd have a hard time getting out again for the meeting. He'd been telling Maria he was going to the library to study different areas of the law, but she wasn't that gullible.

Gaetano started walking in the opposite direction. The second kidnapping burdened his conscience, but then he had another thought. The second kidnapping could have been committed by the same person who committed the first. After all, if a kidnapper could operate with impunity, why wouldn't he?

If that was true, Gaetano realized that solving one kidnapping could help solve the other. The notion redoubled his determination, and he prayed he could find not only one boy, but both.

Fight the good fight.

Gaetano would fight on.

CHAPTER FORTY-FOUR

Darkness surrounded Baron Zito's palazzo, which was set by itself outside La Favorita park, quiet at this hour of the night. Franco and Roberto led Sebastiano, Ezio, and Roberto's men on horseback to the lacquered front door, then Franco gave the signal to attack.

Franco, Roberto, and their men started blasting away at the door. It exploded in broken wood and flying splinters. Ferrous smoke filled the air.

They charged through to the courtyard, shooting at the sky to strike fear. "Violetta!" Franco shouted, his cry echoing.

The palazzo awoke in alarm. Panicked cries came from inside. Lamps and candles were lit. Servants came running out in terror. The *carabinieri* wouldn't be here anytime soon, since the palazzo was far from the center of town.

"I'll get Arabo!" Roberto shouted, taking off.

"Nenella!" Franco spotted Violetta's best friend among the women fleeing in nightgowns. He raced to her side. "Where's Violetta?"

"The Baron put her in the convent!" Nenella cried, teary. "She was so upset!"

"Which one? Santa Caterina?"

"Yes!"

Franco's blood boiled. "Where's the Baron?"

"Bagheria!"

Franco expected as much. "Is Arabo in the stable?"

"Yes, but the butcher's coming in the morning!"

"Get everyone out! I don't want anybody hurt! Tell them to go home and say nothing! I'll make sure they get paid! Now, go!"

Nenella ran off as Roberto rode toward him, ponying Arabo.

"Franco, I got him! I'll take him out front, then meet you inside! The stable is empty."

"*Bravo*, Roberto! I'm going inside the palazzo!" Franco motioned to Sebastiano and Ezio, who were lighting torches wrapped with oil-soaked rags. "Men, my torch!"

"Here!" Sebastiano handed him a flaming torch, and Franco took off toward the main entrance. Roberto's men were already invading the house with torches, entering every doorway.

"Start at the top!" Franco shouted to them, clattered through the arched entrance, and spurred his horse to climb the staircase. Sebastiano and Ezio caught up with him and continued to the third floor, but Franco got off on the second, according to his plan of attack.

Franco rode through the beautiful enfiladed salons and set fire to each one, burning the drapes, the cushioned chairs, the tables, and the rugs. The fire burst into red, orange, and gold flames, heating the air and sending tendrils of smoke upward. He reached the pagoda room and set fire to the silk on the walls, shattered the glass display cabinets, and knocked over the table with the carved ivory and perfume bottles.

He tore ahead to the dining room and cantered around the magnificent table, running the flaming torch along the painted friezes, setting fire to the knights, princes, and make-believe battles. He torched the rug, and the dining room grew hotter. He cantered out and set fire to another set of enfiladed rooms, leaving a flaming wake.

He reached the stairwell. Heat seared the air. Smoke and particulate filled his nostrils. His horse tossed his head in fear, and Franco knew it was time to go. He clambered down the stairs, joined by Sebastiano and Ezio. They rode out of the palazzo and into the courtyard.

Franco, Roberto, and their men watched the palazzo burn. Fire raged from the windows. Glass exploded in the heat. The conflagration rumbled like thunder. Orange flames flew into the air and gray smoke billowed into the darkness.

Franco was filled with fury and joy. Priceless antiques were being destroyed, well-appointed rooms reduced to rubble. The costs would be astronomical, rebuilding financially onerous. The Baron would never be able to buy the Moravio parcel now.

Franco reveled in the conflagration, inflaming the dark side of his soul. It was the point of no return. Only hours earlier, he had wanted to copy this man and this house, but no longer. He would be his own man now, better than before.

Franco looked over to see orange flames flickering on Roberto's sweaty face.

Franco knew they looked identical, like an infernal mirror.

This was only the beginning, for them both.

CHAPTER FORTY-FIVE

Gaetano had time before the Beati Paoli meeting, so he squeezed in interviews with three more families and eliminated them. The *passeggiata* was winding down in the Capo district, but stragglers socialized in animated groups. He walked as quickly as possible, head down, since he was near his house.

Gaetano turned onto his street, spotted a group of people, and recognized his downstairs neighbor Alberto. It wouldn't do to run into him because they were friends and Alberto's wife, Egidia, probably knew about their marital problems.

Gaetano kept going, head still down, as the group began to dissipate. He got closer, but sensed something amiss. Their conversation sounded like nervous chatter, not happy socializing. There came a wail, and he realized Egidia was weeping.

Gaetano hustled to them. "Alberto? What's the matter?"

Alberto turned, with Egidia sobbing in his arms. "Gaetano! It's Maria! She fell. We got the doctor."

"*Madonna!*" Gaetano was already in motion. He ran to his house, burst through the front door, and raced upstairs to his apartment, opening his door to find Dottor Marconi in the dining room, closing his black bag.

"Gaetano—"

"Dottore, how is she?" Gaetano tossed his leather envelope on the table.

"She's fine now. She bruised her hip, but nothing is broken."

"Thank God." Gaetano sent up a silent prayer. "What happened, she fell?"

"Down the front stairs, coming home from the shops. She was with the boys." Dottor Marconi slid off his spectacles, folded them, and tucked them into his pocket. "She didn't hit her head."

"When did this happen?"

"About two hours ago."

Gaetano groaned. He had been knocking on doors when Maria needed him.

"The boys fetched Egidia."

"Where are they now? In bed?"

"Yes, Egidia tucked them in." Dottor Marconi put on his fine dark hat. "My nurse checked on them. She just left."

Gaetano felt sick to his stomach. "How's Maria? Can I see her?"

"She's sleeping. I gave her something for the pain."

"She's in pain?"

"Not much, and the tablet will help. She did lose some blood, but she won't require hospitalization. She can convalesce at home." Dottor Marconi's lined face fell, and his grayish eyes were solemn, and Gaetano sensed that something remained unsaid. It struck him that he was looking for the negative again, a natural assurance that should have been there, but wasn't.

"And the baby, Dottore? Is the baby okay?"

"I'm sorry." Dottor Marconi met his eye with sympathy. "Your baby was lost. She fell on her belly. There was nothing I could do."

Gaetano felt his heart stop. He didn't know what to say. He had to process what he was being told. The fall had killed their baby before it was even born. They had lost their child, a new boy or a girl. His heart broke for Maria, for the agony she must be feeling, for having gone through the ordeal alone.

Saint Paul, give her strength.

Dottor Marconi touched Gaetano's shoulder. "The undertaker just left. I hope you don't mind, I summoned him in your absence."

Gaetano reeled. He didn't want to picture the scene with the undertaker. The tiny baby, unformed. A black velvet sack, like they'd used for his parents. Did they have such things for babies? Small sacks of black velvet, containing heartbreak?

Saint Paul, give me strength.

"Gaetano?" Dottor Marconi pulled out a chair. "You should sit down."

"No, thank you." Gaetano didn't want to sit, like a spectator to his own life. His responsibilities had already been met by other people. His sons had fetched Egidia. Egidia had summoned the doctor. The nurse had contacted the undertaker. Others were filling the space he should have filled. Gaetano realized *he* was the piece that was missing. Somewhere along the line, *he* had become the negative.

"Gaetano, you must be strong. Maria will need you. I gave her instructions. She must rest in bed for at least two weeks. Summon me if there's bleeding or problems."

"I will, thank you." Gaetano rallied. "How much do the boys know?"

"That she fell and she's fine. That's all. I leave the rest for you." Dottor Marconi patted Gaetano's arm. "These losses are tragic, but not uncommon. They happen more often than you know. It's God's will. Some mothers take it harder than others. Maria will do fine."

"She's more sensitive than she appears. She makes it look easy, but it isn't."

"Nevertheless, there's no reason you can't have another child, in time." Dottor Marconi picked up his black bag. "I must go."

"I'll see you out." Gaetano walked him to the door. "Thank you, and good night."

Dottor Marconi left, and Gaetano looked around the living room, utterly at a loss. Maria's embroidery sat on the end table, a baby's face half-stitched on ivory linen. He didn't know when she'd started the design. He spotted a vase with drooping freesia, but he didn't know when she had bought flowers. He didn't even recognize the vase, so perhaps that was new, too.

Gaetano couldn't remember the last time he'd chatted with Maria in the living room or roughhoused with the boys on the rug. He had been reading a book about the Spanish Inquisition, but it was nowhere in sight. There was no evidence of him in the apartment. He'd become a ghost in his own home.

His heartbroken gaze fell on their ceramic statue of the Virgin Mary, a bronze crucifix on a stand, and their family Bible. He walked over and sank to his knees. Their four rosaries sat in little silver boxes, his had tiger's-eye beads.

He felt a wave of guilt so profound that he doubled over, covering his face with his hands. He had neglected his wife and his family. He had chosen to search for a missing child, and in the end, he had lost his own.

He would have to pray to God for forgiveness, for the rest of his life. He started now.

CHAPTER FORTY-SIX

Franco, Roberto, and their men left Baron Zito's palazzo in flames and galloped through the night. Franco's mind burned with fiery images. Something had been set free inside him, a dark energy empowering him. He was becoming the man he was truly meant to be. Now he was home in the Conca d'Oro, and it was time for the final step.

Franco held his flaming torch high, facing his farmhouse from atop Arabo. Beside him were Roberto, Sebastiano, and Ezio, and behind them were all of their men. Franco looked around, taking in the beautiful *giardino* in the darkness, one last time. No longer could he smell its lemony perfume. He breathed only oily smoke from his torch.

"Is everything ready?" Franco looked over at Roberto in the torchlight.

"Yes. The servants are paid and gone, the animals were taken to Mario's. We dug and watered the perimeter."

"What about our strong box?"

"Reburied at Mario's." Roberto met his eye. "Franco, are you sure you want to do this? The *giardino* is not the palazzo. You love this place. It's *yours*."

"No, it's not. It never was. The next one will be."

Roberto fell silent, awaiting Franco's order, and so did the men, their horses restless.

"Vai!" Franco shouted, spurring Arabo into a gallop. He galloped straight for the farmhouse, while Roberto and his men headed for Baron Zito's villa and its outbuildings. Sebastiano, Ezio, and the other men went with them, heading with torches for the *giardino*.

Franco rode inside the farmhouse and set fire to his table, chairs, and bed, maneuvering Arabo in the tight quarters. Arabo understood, his fine Arabian blood as hot as Franco's. They set fire to the farmhouse, charged outside, and headed for the *limonaia*.

Franco rode inside the *limonaia* and lit up the wooden walls, rafters, and boxes of lemons. He raced out and rode up and down the rows of lemon trees closest to his house and the *limonaia*, setting fire to limb and leaf. They went up, their leaves crackling and spitting. Birds and bats flapped and fled in panic.

The smell of smoke filled his nostrils. His eyes began to water. He charged on and on, setting fire to every tree, up and down, right and left, not stopping even when tears streamed down his face.

Orange and gold flames climbed the night sky. The lemon trees burned like hundreds of fireballs under the moon.

Franco knew he was crying, but he didn't stop.

His new life would arise from these ashes.

CHAPTER FORTY-SEVEN

It was nighttime, but Dante was awake and the cell was quiet. Opera Singer had fallen asleep, and the silence felt like a gift. Suddenly, he heard men in the other cells calling to Renzo, and he feared that Opera Singer would wake up. Luckily, Opera Singer stayed asleep, and Dante's ears picked up a sound he had never heard before in the hallway.

It was another boy, crying.

Dante thought his ears were playing tricks on him, at first. But in the next moment, he heard Renzo's heavy footsteps and the crying, louder and closer.

"Shut up, boy!" Renzo shouted, his voice echoing in the hallway.

Dante started to shake, and his eyes filled with tears. Renzo was carrying another boy down the hall.

Dante heard the door on his old cell open. Renzo was putting the boy in the cell and would tie him to the wall with the rope.

Dante covered his mouth so he wouldn't cry out. He felt like it was happening to *him*. He heard the cell door slam closed.

"Mamma, Papa!" the other boy wailed, the way Dante used to.

Dante bit his lip, still shaking. He felt terrible for the boy. He wanted to tell the boy that crying wouldn't do any good. That his parents wouldn't come. That putting jelly on the rope would only make everything worse.

Dante didn't want to hear the boy crying. He covered his ears, but he could still hear it through his fingers.

"Opera Singer, wake up!" Dante shouted. "Wake up!"

Opera Singer woke up and started screaming. *"Aaahhhhhh!"*

Dante covered his ears again, but he could still hear crying.

Then he realized that the crying was his own.

CHAPTER FORTY-EIGHT

It was dawn by the time Franco reached Piazza Bellini, one of the holiest places in Palermo. He slowed Arabo to a respectful trot and passed the Chiesa di San Cataldo with its red-domed roof, La Martorana with its tall bell tower, and the Chiesa di Santa Caterina d'Alessandria with its adjoining convent of amber limestone. Its cloistered walls imprisoned Violetta, and Franco was going to free her.

He dismounted, tied Arabo to a hitch, and hurried up the massive steps to the arched doorway, then bounded up a marble stairway to an entrance hall with white plaster walls. The convent was silent, and the air smelled of disinfectant.

Franco had never been here before, but the layout was plain. He pushed open a door into a hallway with white and gray floor tiles and a vaulted ceiling. Large glass windows overlooked a beautiful courtyard with a garden around a circular fountain. There was another door at the end of the hall.

Franco hurried that way, burst through the door, and found himself in a small visiting room with white plaster walls. It contained a row of stools in front of decorative iron grates made to look like grapevines, shuttered from the inside. There was a door on the right, and Franco hurried there.

"Please, open up, I'm here to see Baronessina Zito!" Franco knocked until the door was opened by a frowning old nun in the black veil and white habit of the Dominicans.

"Sir, what's this racket?"

"I need to see Baronessina Zito. She was brought here last night."

"Only immediate family may visit—"

"I'm her brother," Franco interrupted.

"Nevertheless, this is a cloistered convent. We have visiting hours."

"Please, I just got back in town. I traveled all night to see my sister."

The nun eyed him up and down, pursing thin lips. "Go wait at the first window. Keep your voice down."

"Thank you." Franco sat down and smoothed back his damp hair as the shutters opened.

"Franco?"

Franco could barely see through the decorative grate, but he could tell she was upset, her eyes puffy from crying. Her red hair was in its chignon, and she had on the lilac dress from yesterday.

"Darling, are you okay?" Franco put his hand on the iron grate, wishing he could touch her. "We have to get you out of here, and I have a plan. I'm—"

"Franco, did you set fire to the palazzo? And the *giardino*?"

"Yes."

Violetta gasped, her hand flying to her mouth. "How could you do such a thing?"

Franco blinked. "Because of what your father did to us, Violetta. And your mother, too."

"But they're so upset, it's so awful, and the palazzo is *ruined*! My father was shocked!"

"He shouldn't have been. He knew I wouldn't take it lying down."

"He didn't think you would burn the palazzo down!" Violetta's eyes rounded with disbelief. "He didn't know you were capable of such a thing!"

"Your father knows what I'm capable of." Franco bit his tongue, thinking of the Baron's order to murder the boy. This conversation wasn't going the way he had planned. "And I know what he's capable of."

"My father would never do such a thing, and I never would've thought *you* could do such a thing! You burned my house to the ground!"

"It was your parents' house—"

"I live there! My bedroom is there! All my things!"

"Your father was going to stop me from buying Moravio's parcel. Now he can't, and I'll get the parcel and a villa, too. We can start a new life and travel the world, the way you want to—"

"How can I start a new life with you now?"

"How can you *not*?" Franco's mouth went dry. "Your parents can't stop us anymore. We're going to be married."

"No, no, I can't, I can't now." Violetta sniffled, holding back tears, and Franco felt his heart break.

"Why not? I love you. We love each other."

"My parents are devastated! My mother fainted when she heard!"

"You hate your mother."

"No, I don't!"

"Yes, you do, you used to say so all the time. Same with your father. You say they treat you like a child. They do, I saw with my own eyes."

"Franco, all families fight. It doesn't mean we hate each other."

"But what about the way they treated us? Your mother called you a brat. Your father called me a jumped-up *bracciante*."

"They were angry, surprised, and they hadn't known about us! Anyway, I'm talking about the *giardino*. My mother had happy memories there. My grandparents loved it."

Franco's head was spinning. "Violetta, we can sort this later. Let's get you out of here, and we can talk reason—"

"I *am* talking reason. We can never have a future after what you've done. My parents will never accept you now."

"They'd never accept me anyway. You saw what happened." Franco felt himself losing control. "I was wrong to trust your father! I was crazy to believe he would see me as his son-in-law, ever!"

"Now I'm ashamed we were together. Not because of who you are, or even what you've done, but because of me. I was selfish, I saw only what I wanted. I brought such shame on my family. I brought such destruction into their lives."

Franco couldn't believe his ears. "Violetta, you don't mean this."

"Yes, I do." Violetta straightened. "I caused a calamity. I'm getting what I deserve."

"No, your parents caused it by not accepting us."

"You don't understand." Violetta eyed him through the grate. "Go away, and never come back."

"But, Violetta, I love you." Tears sprang to Franco's eyes.

"My parents say I never loved you, that it was childish rebellion."

"It *was* love," Franco shot back. "Violetta, don't you want to be free—"

"Yes, of you!" Violetta closed the shutters.

CHAPTER FORTY-NINE

Gaetano carried a breakfast tray containing hot coffee, slices of blood orange, and a fresh *sfogliatella*, a layered pastry shaped like a shell with candied orange and lemon peels, Maria's favorite. The boys were playing happily in their room.

"Good morning, Maria," Gaetano said quietly, opening the door to the bedroom. "I thought I would bring you something to eat."

"Good morning." Maria looked over without meeting his eye. Her face showed the strain of fresh grief, and her eyes were bloodshot. Her dark hair was in a long braid, and she had on her pink nightgown with lace at the collar.

"How are you feeling?" Gaetano set the tray down on the bed. "Any pain?"

"No more, I'm just tired." Maria wasn't given to complaint, but Gaetano knew she was in agony, emotional if not physical.

"Maria, I have so much to say to you."

"That's how I feel. I have so much to say to *you*."

"Would you like to eat first?" Gaetano asked, newly awkward around her.

"No, I'd like to talk first, but I don't want to argue." Maria met his eye with openness and honesty, and Gaetano felt the strength of his love for her, in that one look.

"Our arguing days are over, Maria. I was up all night, praying, and I have to say to you, first, I'm so very sorry." Gaetano felt tears in his eyes, unshed. "What happened yesterday was my fault. I should have been here. I love you with all my heart, and I love our boys. I will spend my life asking you for forgiveness. I will spend my life praying to God for His." Gaetano braced himself to say the next words. "I'm stopping my investigation about the kidnappings. I learned from this loss, Maria. My first duty is to you and to our family, I know that now. I lost my way, but I've found it again." Gaetano wiped his eyes, and at that moment spotted a suitcase packed in the corner of the room. "Maria, are you leaving me? I can make this right, I swear to you. Please don't go."

"I have to go, and I will." Maria held up her delicate hand. "I made up my mind, and you can't change it."

"Please don't, I'll beg you if I have to—"

"Gaetano, let me speak." Maria kept her hand up. "You always think you're in court when you're not."

"Okay." Gaetano cleared his throat. He felt as if his Adam's apple had lodged there. "I'm sorry."

"I was going to say, what happened to us wasn't your fault. It was God's will. He made that choice, and we may not understand it, but we have to respect it. I thought a lot last night, too, and I prayed, too. I learned a lesson from this terrible loss, this terrible, *terrible* loss of our baby." Tears filmed Maria's lovely eyes, but she didn't cry, either. "What I learned, what I'm *living* now, is how painful it is to lose a child. I didn't sleep much last night because I was understanding how that feels, and it made me think of the mother of the kidnapped child. I underestimated her pain, but now I don't. Now I understand what it's like to lose a child, because I have, too."

Gaetano felt the depth of her words, so he didn't interrupt her.

"I know you're motivated by a higher calling, to fighting the good fight, like you always say. I admit I was hoping you would change, and when you started your investigation, I disagreed with you. I thought you should have put us first and—"

"And now I am," Gaetano interrupted.

"—but you were right, and I was wrong."

Gaetano shook his head. "No, you were right, and *I* was wrong."

Maria smiled, sadly. "You were right to try and find that woman's child."

"What? Why?"

"I was at the bakery yesterday and I heard about the second kidnapping. I thought, 'This will drive Gaetano crazy.' But I didn't realize how that felt until I came home from the bakery and lost our child." Maria's eyes glazed with grief. "I had an epiphany, Gaetano. A conversion, like your Saint Paul. The scales fell from my eyes. You must do everything you can to find those boys."

Gaetano felt moved beyond words.

"You mustn't give up your investigation, ever. Whoever is kidnapping the boys isn't going to stop until someone stops them. It shouldn't fall to you, but it has. *This* is your calling, not the priesthood."

Gaetano felt the truth of her words resonating in his chest.

"One more thing." Maria gestured to her suitcase. "I'm leaving, but I'm not leaving *you*. I'm going to my parents in Messina with the boys. I need to rest and be taken care of. My mother can do it, and it will make her happy." Maria smiled briefly. "You have to find those boys and bring their kidnappers to justice. I know you can do it, because there's no man smarter than you, or stronger than you, or with more heart than you. You'll leave no stone unturned, and you'll finish the race."

Gaetano felt tears brimming, loving her with all of his heart and soul. She was giving him a gift of total understanding, acceptance, and love.

"And, Gaetano, you have to do it to honor the memory of the baby we lost. We have to find meaning in this terrible grief, and this is the way. Do it *for* the baby we lost." Tears spilled from Maria's eyes. "But *do it.*"

Gaetano swept her into his arms, and Maria collapsed, giving way to sobs that wracked her body.

The two of them cried together, mourning their baby.

Bound together by their love, and their grief.

CHAPTER FIFTY

Franco had just gotten back to the Conca d'Oro when he saw the *carabinieri* approaching in a straggly line, their stiff uniforms and plumed caps incongruous in the countryside, their horses' hoofbeats making puffs of dirt behind them.

Franco counted twenty-five officers, so his men outnumbered them. He and Roberto were sitting in front of Mario's house with the men, who were playing cards and cleaning their guns. They were better shots than the *carabinieri* and stronger, too, hardened by hours in the saddle.

"Here they come, men," Franco said to them.

Roberto looked over, flinty-eyed. "I hope you know what you're doing."

"I do." Franco rose, threw his cigarette to the ground, and crushed it under his boot. "Let's have some fun."

"You, fun?"

"I've changed, Robo." Franco winked, grimly. "Keep up."

"WHERE'S FRANCO FIORVANTI?" MARSHAL ROSSELLI demanded, his manner authoritative despite his faintly ridiculous appearance. His fancy uniform was soaked from perspiration, and his gold-braided cap slipped sideways. His silvering hair was damp, his face was sweaty, and his oiled mustache flecked with dirt from the road. He and his officers dismounted, forming a tired and plainly nervous group.

"Right here. I am he."

"I'm Marshal Rosselli, and Baron Zito has filed a complaint against you for the criminal arson of his palazzo in town, his villa out here, and his *giardino*. I've come to arrest you."

"I had nothing to do with such crimes. What makes you think I did?"

"We'll discuss the particulars back in Palermo." Marshal Rosselli gestured to an officer holding handcuffs.

Franco raised a palm. "Why make the trip when we can talk here? I didn't set those fires and I can prove it. I was here all night with my twin, Roberto, and our friends." He gestured to Roberto. "Isn't that right, Robo?"

"Yes. We played cards, then went to bed," Roberto answered, folding his arms.

The men chimed in, "We were here, all together." "Franco was with us."

Franco returned his attention to Marshal Rosselli. "See? What lies did the Baron tell you?"

"He says he fired you as his *gabellotto*, so you destroyed his palazzo, villa, and *giardino* to get even."

"Did he say anything about an illicit romance?"

"No. What romance?"

Franco chuckled. "Between me and his wife, of course."

"What?" Marshal Rosselli's eyebrows flew upward, and the *carabinieri* started looking at each other.

"I've been sleeping with his wife, Baronessa Zito. We've been sneaking around for almost a year. I've had her many times, in all of his residences. She dresses in disguises so we won't be detected, like the uniform of a kitchen maid. That's my favorite."

Roberto and his men snickered, and so did the officers.

Marshal Rosselli narrowed his eyes. "Let me get this straight. You worked for the Baron—"

"I did until he fired me, when he found out about his wife and me. We three were having lunch at the palazzo, and the Baronessa touched my thigh under the table. She can't keep her hands off of me."

"She can't?" Marshal Rosselli asked, shocked.

"Can you blame her? He can't get it up."

Roberto interjected, "Marshal Rosselli, look at my brother. Better yet, look at *me*. Wouldn't you rather screw us than Baron Zito?"

The men laughed again.

Only Marshal Rosselli frowned, at Franco. "Signore, if you're having an affair with his wife, it's worse for you. I'll believe you burned everything because you're jealous of him."

"No, *he* did it. He hired someone to burn it all down. He's the culprit."

"*Baron Zito* did it?" Marshal Rosselli recoiled, incredulous. "Why would he do such a thing?"

"To frame me, because I cuckolded him." Franco snorted. "Listen, if *my* wife were screwing the help, I'd *kill* the man. But Baron Zito lacks the balls. He uses you to arrest me. He warps the law to fit his own ends. He has no regard for justice. The nobility act high and mighty, but they don't know the travails of working men like you and me."

"You, what do you do?" Marshal Rosselli glanced at Roberto and the men.

"We protect lemons on the way to market. We make sure bandits stay away."

"Since when?"

"A while now. You need to get out more."

Marshal Rosselli bristled. "I work every minute in the capital city."

"I meant no disrespect. I know you're busy, so men like us step into the breach. You can't deny there's a difference between law and justice in Palermo. Law protects nobles like the Baron, and they use you to keep power. But justice protects men like me, and we rely on ourselves for its dispensation." Franco gestured to the *carabinieri*. "Men, we could use you, too. Anyone who wants to join us may apply. You see the best among us wear a special belt buckle."

"Signore, are you saying you want to *hire* my men?"

"Yes, if they want to do justice, for a change."

Marshal Rosselli shook it off. "This isn't on point. Why would Baron Zito burn down his own properties?"

"They're not his. They're the Baronessa's dowry, both of them. He did it to spite her."

"But it still costs him money."

"So? He has plenty. Can you imagine being cuckolded by me, a jumped-up *bracciante*?" Franco shook his head. "He even destroyed his beautiful *giardino* to spite me. It was my life's work."

Marshal Rosselli pursed his thin lips. "Baron Zito is furious about his financial losses, which he tells me are astronomical. A man in his position will not take that lying down. You're tangling with him."

"He's tangling with *me*." Franco decided to play his winning card, which was the boy in the madhouse, whom Baron Zito believed Franco had murdered. "You tell Baron Zito, from me, that if I go down, he goes down."

Marshal Rosselli blinked. "What do you mean?"

"It's not for you to know. Say those exact words." Franco met his eye. "After you do, he'll beg you to drop the complaint. In fact, he'll offer to wet your beak to do so."

"I accept no bribes," Marshal Rosselli shot back.

"I merely said he'd offer."

Marshal Rosselli paused. "One other thing. The Baron said you stole his stallion, a white Arabian named Arabo."

"That's another lie."

Marshal Rosselli pointed to Arabo, grazing with his mare in the pasture. "Isn't that him?"

"No."

"He looks like an Arabian."

"He's not."

"What's his name?"

"What's the difference? Go back to the Baron, Marshal. Tell him what I said, and tell him, too, that the days of feckless nobility running the country are over. Sicily will be led by men like me, who earn our bread. From now on, we'll make sure that every man has justice and equality. Thank you for your visit."

"Not so fast." Marshal Rosselli raised a hand. "You must come back with me and make a formal statement."

"What's the point? Don't you agree, men?" Franco looked back, and they all nodded.

"So you won't come voluntarily?"

"I won't." Franco straightened, and Roberto rose to stand beside him. Their men stood up and arranged themselves in a line, a show of armed force.

Marshal Rosselli eyed them, puckering his lips. "I'll be back."

"No, you won't."

LATER, ROBERTO TOOK FRANCO ASIDE, putting a hand on his shoulder. "You handled Rosselli well, but why did you make a job offer to the *carabineri*? I don't want them. Remember, I'm in charge of my men. We agreed."

Franco detected pique, which was justified. "You're right, Robo. I'm sorry, I got carried away."

Roberto's smile returned. "I get it. You need work. You've been unemployed since you burned down your *giardino*. We need to buy you a new one."

Franco chuckled. "The auction is tomorrow."

"By the way, what happened with Violetta? You've been quiet since you got back."

Franco's heart ached, but he kept that to himself. "It's over with her."

"Why?" Roberto frowned, sympathetic. "You couldn't get her out of the convent?"

"She doesn't want to see me anymore."

"Why?"

"She's mad I burned down her house."

"Women." Roberto rolled his eyes.

Franco chuckled, though it hurt.

Roberto touched his arm. "Franco, it was the right thing to do."

"It was also the wrong thing to do."

"Exactly!" Roberto smiled crookedly. "It was the right wrong thing to do."

Franco burst into laughter, despite his heartache.

"So anyway, what's the plan?"

"It begins tonight," Franco answered, then told him.

CHAPTER FIFTY-ONE

Gaetano rose to start the meeting of the Beati Paoli, then noticed that many of the members were missing. "Should I wait until the others get here?"

"I don't think so," Carmine answered. "Let's begin."

"But there's been a second kidnapping, and I'm not sure everyone knows about it. It could relate to the first, so we need to discuss it as a full membership."

"Nevertheless, they may not come." Carmine hesitated. "There may be the press of other business, and it was short notice."

Don Fabiano looked up. "Gaetano, not all these meetings you call have been true emergencies."

Carmine interjected, "Gaetano likes to keep us informed. I think that's a good thing."

Don Ugo added, "I think they're absent because of the fire at Baron Zito's palazzo near La Favorita. It's the talk of the town."

"What fire?" Gaetano hadn't heard, given what had been happening at home.

"It's a disgrace." Don Leonardo frowned. "A fire destroyed the Baron's palazzo, one of the nicest. Of historic import, too. Many of us who have palazzos near La Favorita want to find whoever is responsible. The rumor is that the cause was arson."

"Arson!" Don Fabiano exclaimed.

Don Ugo gasped. "A truly awful crime. That's Palermo's history, up in flames!"

Don Vincenzo chimed in, "What if the fire had spread to La Favorita, a *royal* park?"

Gaetano blinked. "To me, the destruction of a palazzo pales in comparison to a kidnapping. One is a crime against property, the other is against a person."

Carmine nodded. "I agree, and what's worse is that we live in a city where lawlessness is so rampant, we can't choose between crimes."

"I agree." Gaetano felt grateful for Carmine's support. "This is a terrible state of affairs, caused by the corruption of the *carabinieri* and the judicial system."

Don Vincenzo wagged a finger. "Nevertheless, a crime like arson is intolerable. I'm too old to have my children kidnapped, but I *am* at risk of having my palazzo set afire."

Gaetano blinked, surprised. "Crimes that affect us personally aren't more important than crimes that don't. It's irrelevant, as a matter of principled thinking. Otherwise our motives are selfish, not selfless."

Don Vincenzo recoiled. "I'm not selfish! I come to every one of these meetings!"

Don Fulvio shook his head. "Gaetano, I recognize that you're invested in this kidnapping case, but your interests aren't the only ones in the room."

Gaetano didn't understand. "It's not my interests, it's the interests of the boys."

Don Fabiano frowned. "But we cannot ignore our own interests, especially a fire. Palermo doesn't have the resources to fight fires if they increase. We cannot sacrifice the *capital*!"

Gaetano countered, "Nor can we abandon the kidnapped boys. If we had solved the first kidnapping, the second one might not have occurred."

Don Fabiano waved him off. "Gaetano, I fear you're becoming too emotionally involved in this matter. My cousin saw you outside the *Questura* making a scene, and I heard that Marshal Rosselli is refusing to see you. We must maintain good relations with the *carabinieri*, no matter what we think of them. Appearances matter."

Don Leonardo nodded. "Gaetano, I'm sorry, but I heard your wife left you and you've been unable to find another job. I think that's why you're so obsessed with this kidnapping case."

Gaetano stiffened. "I'm concerned, not obsessed, and she's only visiting her parents." He began seeing the Beati Paoli with new eyes. They were dedicated to the public good, but they were still aristocrats who were concerned about palazzos. He knew what he had to do, even as his chest wrenched. "I'm sorry for my words, which may have been imprudent. However, you're right, I do feel single-minded about the kidnappings. I care about them, above all. So I think it's time I went my own way."

"What?" Carmine asked, dismayed. "You mean you're quitting the Beati Paoli?"

"Yes," Gaetano answered, and frowns appeared around the table.

"Gaetano, please don't," Don Fabiano said, his regret plain.

Don Ugo chimed in, "Gaetano, perhaps we can prioritize the fire *and* the kidnapping."

Gaetano picked up his hat. "Gentlemen, thank you, but no. We cannot prioritize two matters equally, and we shouldn't try. The kidnappings are my priority, but that doesn't mean they're yours. I don't want to force that upon you, nor do I want to compromise my own beliefs. Thank you for your efforts to further the investigation. I admire and respect every one of you, but I have to go."

Gaetano felt tears in his eyes, knowing he was doing the right thing. "Gentlemen, I'll see you when we've finished the race."

CHAPTER FIFTY-TWO

Franco rose at the head of the table, having called a meeting of the *gabellotti* from the *giardini* guarded by the Fiorvantis. It was a temperate night, but the breeze was still hazy from the fire at Baron Zito's estate. A smoky odor tainted the air.

"Gentlemen, I called this meeting because of the horrific fire. As you know, it destroyed my farmhouse and the *giardino* I spent my life tending. It's devastating to me, as it is to Roberto. We're staying at Mario's, and we apologize for these circumstances. You know I like to offer you a nice meal, but that wasn't possible."

Roberto nodded, and Franco began to walk around the table as he spoke, so he could look each man in the eye.

"We know exactly who committed this crime. The culprits are the brigands and bandits from whom we protect you and your *giardini*. That's why they attacked Roberto and me. They seek to destroy us, but it won't work. We'll do whatever it takes to protect you, your *giardini*, and your lemons."

Franco cleared his throat. "I know your boss is like Baron Zito, a man no better than any other, given power by birth. I want you to go to your bosses and tell them that Baron Zito's estate was burned by bandits. Tell them bandits could burn their villas and *giardini* next. Tell them they need the Fiorvantis more than ever."

Most of the men nodded, quick to agree.

"I also want you to tell them our fee is increasing by twenty-five percent, and the justification is plain. Protecting their *giardini* and harvest has grown more dangerous, and the risk to us is greater. It's only fair your bosses pay more."

Franco paused for comment, but only Michele raised a hand.

"Franco, I can't afford to pay twenty-five percent more. As you know, we *gabellotti* are middlemen, answering to the nobles and managing the *contadini* who lease and farm the land. Our boss pays us a salary, but it's not much. The *contadini* pay us, too, but they're barely breaking even. We cannot pay more."

Men exchanged nervous looks, but Franco had a surprise for them.

"I understand, but let me be clear. The full twenty-five percent is not going to me or Roberto. We'll split it evenly with you, and your half will go directly back to you, into your *own* pocket."

Frowns turned to smiles, and eyebrows flew up in delight.

"Roberto and I are doing this because we share our bounty. That's how it is with family, isn't it? Loyalty is everything to the Fiorvantis, and I know it is to you, too."

"*Bravi*, Franco and Roberto!" one of the *gabellotti* called out, raising his wine bottle. Everyone chimed in, "*Grazie!*"

"Thank you." Franco waved to quiet them. "Look, I know this doesn't solve your problem. Remind the *contadini* that, if not for our protection, they couldn't make a living at all. Of course, the deeper pocket is your boss, and with him, use the destruction of Baron Zito's estates as an example. Twenty-five percent more is far less than the catastrophic loss of an entire *giardino*. However, if those asses turn you down, I will meet with them and convince them." Franco paused, smiling. "I can be very convincing."

The men burst into laughter, except for Michele, who was still uneasy.

Franco walked over to him. "Michele, if you have a problem, speak freely. I want to know what's on your mind."

"I can't get any more out of my *contadini*. If I try, they'll come after me with pitchforks."

"What about your boss, Baron DiGiulio?"

"He won't pay."

"Then pay it yourself. You're going to get half back, from us."

"I don't have it. My wife just had a third baby, and my mother is sick. Her doctor bills are terrible. I'm in debt." Michele hesitated. "Will you advance me my half, since you're giving it back to me anyway?"

"No, that's not how it works. All of the others are stepping up." Franco gestured to the table. "Raising the money isn't easy for any of them."

"But it's harder for me than the others. Their bosses are more responsible. Baron DiGiulio spends like crazy. He's vain and dreams of power. He wants to be mayor." Michele swallowed hard. "I can pay the old fee, but not twenty-five percent more. Can't I continue as before?"

"No." Franco placed a hand on his shoulder. "We act as one, like a family. If you don't wish to pay more, you're no longer a member of this family. You'll protect your own lemons from now on."

Michele looked over, and Franco could see fear in his eyes, flickering in the light from the bonfire.

"Michele, it's your choice. Stay or go."

"I can't stay under the new terms."

"Then go." Franco removed his hand from Michele's shoulder. "It was a pleasure doing business with you. I regret that we can no longer continue our relationship. Stay well."

"You, uh, want me to leave *now*?"

"Yes." Franco stepped back. "This meeting is for family only. Good night."

Michele stood up and walked away, his shoulders slumping. Everyone at the table watched him go.

Franco turned to the other *gabellotti*. "We wish our old friend Michele the best. If any of you feel the same way, you're welcome to leave now. In fact, you must."

The men looked at each other, and no one rose.

Franco picked up a bottle of wine and raised it high. "Let's drink a toast! To us, the Fiorvantis!"

"To the Fiorvantis!" the *gabellotti* cheered, raising their bottles.

Franco drank, then set his bottle down. "Now, about the auction . . ."

CHAPTER FIFTY-THREE

The next morning, Franco stood in front of Baron Moravio's property as if it were already his own. Its plaster façade had been freshly painted a melon hue, and its red tile roof had been repaired. The *giardino* was behind the house, and he could tell from the fragrance alone that its lemons were soft with juice. The auction was set to begin inside the villa, and Franco waited with Roberto and their men, armed with *lupare*, knives, and long wooden clubs.

None of the other bidders had arrived yet, but carriages began appearing on the road leading to the villa. Their black lacquer gleamed in the sunshine, and matched carriage horses pulled each one. They would be carrying lawyers or functionaries to bid, since aristocrats didn't bother to buy their own villas.

The first carriage reached the villa, and Franco stepped forward. The driver halted the horses, climbed down, took a footstool, and brought it to the carriage, opening the door. A young man in a well-tailored suit emerged from the carriage and stepped on the footstool.

Franco intercepted him. "Good afternoon. Are you here for the auction?"

"Yes, on behalf of a client." The lawyer pressed his steel spectacles up.

"Unfortunately, the auction's been called off."

"Oh no." The lawyer eyed Roberto and his armed men, catching on. "Will it be rescheduled?"

"No. Tell your client that Baron Zito's *giardino* was burned by bandits. Your client wouldn't want to suffer the same fate. Get back in your carriage and go home."

"Goodbye, sir." The lawyer ducked back inside the carriage, the driver grabbed the footstool, and they took off.

Franco walked back to Roberto, smiling. "That was fun. You take the next one."

"Lawyers scare too easy. It's barely sporting."

Franco chuckled, and they watched the next carriage pull up. The driver got down with the footstool, and the door to the carriage was opened for another young man with spectacles, plainly intimidated by Roberto's men.

Roberto walked over to him. "Don't tell me, let me guess. You're a lawyer."

"I am. And the auction?"

"Is canceled for the rest of your life."

"I completely understand. Sorry." The lawyer popped back into the carriage. The driver grabbed the footstool, hurried back to his seat, and they left.

Franco looked over to see another carriage heading for the villa, and his blood began to race. "That's Baron Zito's coach."

Roberto looked over, surprised. "He can still bid? Does he have *that* much money?"

"I didn't think so, but it's not going to matter." Franco clenched his teeth as Baron Zito's carriage pulled up. He didn't know the driver and took the footstool from him. "You won't need this, friend. Nobody's getting out."

A young man popped his head through the carriage window. "Excuse me, what's going on?"

"Leave. There's no auction today."

"Are you sure? I'm a lawyer and I've been sent to bid."

"Where are your spectacles?"

"I don't have any." The lawyer blinked, confused. "My vision is perfect."

"Then you can see it's foolhardy to leave your carriage."

Suddenly the door on the other side of the carriage opened, and a second passenger walked around to meet Franco. It was Niall, Baron Zito's horse trainer.

"Niall." Franco gritted his teeth. "Get out of here. There's no auction today."

"I'm here for Arabo."

"You're not taking him."

"Oh, I don't intend to." Niall pulled a pistol from his pocket and aimed it at Arabo, tied to a rail with the other horses.

Franco reacted lightning-fast, swinging the footstool at Niall's hand. The gun fired into the sky. Niall lost his balance, falling backward.

Franco hit him with the footstool, exploding in rage. He felt himself losing control but didn't stop. He hit Niall with the footstool again and again, until blood spurted from his skull in a gruesome fan.

"Franco, no!" Roberto grabbed his shoulder and Franco dropped the footstool, coming out of his fit of rage.

Niall lay motionless in the dirt, bleeding from the head. His eyes gazed sightlessly into the bright sun. Blood spattered his fine cravat and suitcoat.

The auctioneer came scurrying from the villa. "My God! You killed him!"

Franco picked up Niall's pistol, composing himself. "This is his gun. He tried to shoot me. It was self-defense. I had no choice."

Roberto nodded. "Absolutely right. I saw everything. He fired at you. You defended yourself. It's a miracle you're alive."

Sebastiano, Ezio, and Roberto's men chimed in that it was self-defense.

The auctioneer's hands flew to his cheeks. "What do I do now?"

"Sell me a house," Franco answered, pocketing the gun.

CHAPTER FIFTY-FOUR

Gaetano ran into Carmine in the Vucciria market, and the lawyers decided to have a bite together. The market was bustling, and the shade of its stalls provided a break from the sun. The market sold every kind of fruit, produce, fish, and meat, and the air was filled with irresistible aromas of frying fish, *sfincione*, or Sicilian pizza, and *panelle*, or fried chickpeas. He and Carmine sat down at a table with a plate of *panelle*, cut into sweet and savory squares.

"Carmine, it's good to see you." Gaetano had missed Carmine since he'd left the Beati Paoli.

"You as well. I'm sorry about what happened at the last meeting."

"Not at all. I hope you understand why I left." Gaetano took a bite of *panelle*, which tasted deliciously nutty and crunchy.

"I do. How's your investigation going?"

Gaetano gave him the tally. "I'm trying to figure out what to do with the second kidnapping. I don't know if it's related."

"We have too few facts."

"It's true. I don't know the age of the second boy, so I can't start over with another set of baptismal records."

"What a task!" Carmine frowned. "I'm worried about you, and the others were, too. After you left, they regretted what they'd said."

"I don't blame them." Gaetano wanted to unburden himself. "Carmine, Maria didn't leave me in anger. She left to give me time to do the investigation."

"Oh, how generous of her."

"Yes, and she needed to rest." Gaetano felt a stab of grief, which was always with him. "I don't know if you heard, but we lost the baby."

"I did, I'm sorry." Carmine lowered his voice. "It happened to us, too. Three years ago."

"I'm sorry." Gaetano hadn't known, since such matters weren't discussed publicly.

"It's God's will, I know, and we're lucky to have the new one." Carmine sighed. "Anyway, how's the job search?"

"Not good."

"Do you need money? I can lend you some."

"No, thank you," Gaetano answered, touched. He noticed Carmine was barely eating his *panelle* and sensed that something troubled him. "I've been selfish, talking about myself. What's new?"

"Something happened to me the other day, something truly horrific."

"Oh my, what?"

"I went to the Conca d'Oro to bid on a parcel for Baron Zito. You know, our firm has some of his business. He spreads it around the law firms in town."

"I know, they all do. We had some of his work, too."

"Anyway, there were thugs at the auction, intimidating people out of bidding, and one of them *beat* the Baron's riding instructor to death with a *footstool*." Carmine shuddered. "It was so sudden, so violent. I've never seen anyone *murdered*. It was self-defense, but still."

Gaetano gasped. "*Madonna!*"

"The riding instructor's name was Niall, and we shared the carriage from Palermo. He had a pistol on him, but I didn't know that. I was told he was going to pick up an Arabian horse and ride him back. He didn't say a word to me the entire trip. He shot at the man, but missed, and the man bashed his *head* in."

"What a scene!" Gaetano recoiled, appalled. "Why did this Niall try to kill the man?"

"I have no idea. Afterward I gave a statement to the *carabinieri*. They told me the thug's name is Franco Fiorvanti. Evidently, he's known to them, and the whole awful episode made me question what I know about Baron Zito. If you ask me, something's suspicious. Someone burns down his palazzo? Then his villa and *giardino* burn down, the same night?"

Gaetano hadn't heard about the *giardino*, too.

"Common sense tells me this Fiorvanti and Baron Zito have bad blood, but why would Baron Zito trifle with such a lowlife? It's hard to tell the nobility from the criminals anymore."

"My father believed that those with privileges should hold themselves to a higher standard."

"Mine, too." Carmine nodded. "And I told my boss I didn't want to do Baron Zito's legal work anymore. My boss said, 'Do it or leave the firm.' So, I'm leaving."

"Really?" Gaetano asked, surprised. "I admire your decision. Do you have other prospects?"

"I'm going out on my own, but I could use a partner." Carmine smiled in his boyish way, his dimples popping. "Would you work with me?"

Gaetano felt a rush of gratitude. "Carmine, I'm honored you asked, but I'd only weigh you down. I'd attract no clients."

"I don't need you to, I have clients. Good, solid businessmen and nobles who are right-thinking. Not the Baron Zitos of the world. Join me, would you?"

Gaetano hesitated. "What about my investigation?"

"Wedge it in around your work. You can earn enough to keep you going. We'll sort the expenses later."

"Carmine, thank you." Gaetano's spirit soared. "You've saved my life."

"Not at all." Carmine smiled, then dug into his *panelle*.

Gaetano thanked God for sending him this opportunity, so he could continue his work.

Rather, His work.

CHAPTER FIFTY-FIVE

Gaetano went to Via Argenteria Vecchia and knocked on every door, asking if anyone had seen anything the day of the second kidnapping. Every resident said no, as he expected they would. He was about to leave when he noticed the silversmith opening his shop, which had been closed for days.

Gaetano hurried over and went inside. The shop was tasteful, lined with display cases holding glittering silver earrings, necklaces, and other jewelry. The silversmith, an older man with a thin gray mustache, looked up from the counter. His features were as delicate as a watch mechanism, and he had on a gray frock coat.

"Can I help you, sir?" the silversmith asked politely. "We have fine silver jewelry, made by my son. Also lovely candlesticks, a nice gift."

"I'm just looking." Gaetano sensed that the man needed to make a sale, probably because he had lost money over the past few days.

"We have a wonderful selection of religious articles."

"I can see that." Gaetano gravitated toward the glass display of silver crucifixes, rosaries, and an array of silver *ex voti*, shaped like feet, eyes, ears, and a head, the last presumably for madness.

"Are you interested in an *ex voto*?" The silversmith crossed to the religious counter. "I have the best selection in Palermo. I can offer you a ten percent discount."

Gaetano needed information. "I noticed your shop's been closed. Were you ill?"

"No, I had a personal matter." The silversmith took an *ex voto* from the display and set it on the glass counter. It was shaped liked a human torso, showing internal organs and the digestive tract. "This *ex voto* is all in one, as you can see."

Gaetano recoiled, finding it oddly graphic.

"I just got this new one." The silversmith pulled out another *ex voto*, which was shaped like a swaddled infant. "This one is for a sick baby—"

"I know," Gaetano interrupted him, bereft. He had to rest his hand on the counter, momentarily unsteady.

"Sir, are you all right?"

"Yes, thank you," Gaetano answered, shaken.

"Take it," the silversmith said, after a moment.

"No, I can't. I don't have the money, and it's not why I'm here."

"Take it anyway, as my gift."

"I can't possibly accept it."

"I'll wrap it for you." The silversmith got white tissue paper from behind the counter, folded the *ex voto* inside, then presented it to him. "Here we go, sir. I'll pray for you and your child."

"Thank you." Gaetano's throat thickened. He couldn't begin to explain.

The silversmith smiled, sympathetic. "We must put our faith into practice every day, not only in church."

"That's exactly how I feel." Gaetano warmed to find a kindred spirit. "A loss to one is a loss to all, particularly when it comes to children."

"Yes, I believe that." The silversmith's eyes filmed, and Gaetano realized he had to have been thinking of the kidnapped boy, so he seized the opportunity.

"I heard that a boy was abducted near here the other day. I feel for the family and their lost child, now that I have lost my own." Gaetano was thinking of what Maria had said to him. "Please tell me what you know. That's all I ask. I'm trying to help them."

The silversmith frowned, pained. "I don't know anything."

"What did the kidnapper look like?"

"I didn't see him. I was in the shop with the boy's mother."

"What's her name?"

The silversmith hesitated. "Who *are* you?"

"Just someone who wants to help."

"Who sent you?"

"No one."

"You've taken this upon yourself?"

"Yes, I fear for the children of my city. They deserve justice."

The silversmith's face softened into knowing lines. "Now I understand who sent you, young man."

GAETANO HURRIED DOWN THE STREET to the fine house on the corner. The silversmith had told him that the kidnapped boy, named Vittorio Curcio, lived here with his older sisters and his parents, Vito Curcio and his wife, Eleanora Sebina. Trying to contain his excitement, Gaetano knocked on the door, which was opened by a young housekeeper in a neat white cap.

"May I help you, sir?"

Gaetano introduced himself. "I'd like to see Signor Curcio or Signora Sebina."

"They're not at home."

"When do you expect them back? I've spoken with the silversmith." Gaetano lowered his voice. "I know I can help them."

The housekeeper hesitated. "The family is away for several weeks. If you were sent by the silversmith, you'll understand why."

"Several weeks, really?" Gaetano asked, surprised. "Leaving for so long makes them harder to contact. Do you know if they've already been contacted?"

"My boss knows what he's doing, and that's all I'll say."

"Where did they go?"

"They have another home."

"Where?"

"I can't say. Goodbye." The housekeeper started to close the door, but Gaetano stopped her with his foot.

"But it doesn't make sense for him to go—"

"Move your foot, sir!"

Gaetano complied, and she slammed the door in his face.

CHAPTER FIFTY-SIX

It was almost midnight, and Franco, Roberto, and their men hid on horseback behind cypresses that flanked the dirt road. It was the route to Palermo, and this was the last night for Michele, the *gabellotto* who had left the family, to take his lemons to La Cala.

Roberto looked over, his silhouette indistinct in the darkness. "Are you sure about this, brother?"

"Yes. The others have to see the consequences." Franco wasn't surprised to hear Roberto balk. His twin had been remote since Niall had been dispatched at the auction.

"But Michele is harmless. Let him go."

"We can't. I told you, I'll take care of it."

They fell silent when they heard the approach of Michele's caravan. The donkeys snorted and brayed, and the *braccianti* sang a tuneless song. Franco peered between the trees and spotted the caravan. He counted six donkeys and seven men, including Michele in the lead. Franco, Roberto, and his men easily outnumbered them.

"Wait till I give the order." Franco watched Michele ride closer, unaware of the ambush awaiting him.

My wife just had a third baby, and my mother is sick.

Franco shooed the voice away. He straightened in the saddle and fixed on Michele. The man rode loosely, as if he had been drinking. The caravan grew closer, the singing louder.

The air carried the song of the *braccianti*, the sweet fragrance of the lemons, and the salty smell of the donkeys. The caravan was almost in range.

Franco raised his rifle, ready to give the order. Arabo shifted in anticipation, and the other horses tossed their heads.

"*Vai!*" Franco charged through the trees, followed by Roberto and his men. He shot Michele off his horse, and the *braccianti* scattered in fear. Roberto and his men ran them off, then gathered the donkey carts packed with lemons. The ambush was over in no time, and Roberto's men whooped, firing into the sky.

Franco rode over to make sure Michele was dead, but the man lay moaning in the dirt, his chest dark with spreading blood.

"Franco," Michele said, blood bubbling from his mouth. "Baron DiGiulio won't . . . take care of my family. Will . . . you?"

"Yes." Franco took out his pistol and shot him.

FRANCO LOOKED OVER AT HIS brother. They sat in front of Baron Moravia's villa, which they had gotten for next to nothing, as sole bidder. Roberto was brooding, which annoyed him. "Robo, what's bothering you?"

"You know."

"Michele, again? I told him we'd take care of his family, and we will."

"He was one of us."

"He quit."

"We gave him no choice. He couldn't pay the increase."

"He didn't even try to talk to Baron DiGiulio or the *contadini*. That's weak, and we can't have a weak man in our family." Franco touched his arm. "Did you see the way he rode that night? His answer to fear was the bottle. I'm glad he's gone."

"I don't agree."

"You don't have to," Franco shot back. "You said your men are your authority, and I conceded. Running the business is my authority. You must concede to me."

Roberto looked over. "But that makes you the boss. *My* boss."

"Yes, it does." Franco eyed him. "Robo, there can only be one man in charge. Otherwise it confuses the lines of authority. You're my deputy, but I'm the head of the family."

Roberto blinked. "Even over *me*? I'm your blood, your *twin*."

"Publicly, yes. Privately, I love you and consider you my equal."

"What's your plan now?"

"My original plan was to buy land, but my thinking is changing. I don't need to own the land to control it, and I control the *gabellotti* who manage the biggest *latifondi*. So I control the Conca d'Oro, as a practical matter. Who owns the land is a technicality."

Roberto fell silent. "You want to be king of the mountain."

"Yes."

"All this because you're five minutes older than me?"

"That's not why. It's because I want it more than you."

Roberto thought it over. "But we own the business and villa equally, right?"

"Yes."

"And we earn the same money?"

"Fifty-fifty."

Roberto broke into a crooked smile. "Franco, you want to work harder for *no* extra? Then I agree. Congratulations, you're a terrible negotiator."

Franco chuckled, then stood up. "Now, we have to get going."

"Where?"

"I'll tell you on the way. Get the men."

Roberto rose. "Okay, *boss*!"

CHAPTER FIFTY-SEVEN

It was morning by the time Franco, Roberto, and their men rode into Palermo, the sight causing a stir. Franco and Roberto led the way on Arabo and the mare, followed by ten armed men on horseback, blocking the narrow streets. Their sweaty faces, open shirts, dirty britches, and rough boots showed that they came from outside the city limits. Their guns showed that they came from outside any limits at all.

The clatter of so many hooves brought people to their windows to watch. Shopkeepers stopped sweeping and looked up. Women waiting at the bakery clustered together, talking behind their hands. Men ducked inside the shops or turned onto side streets, instinctively getting out of the way.

Franco acknowledged everyone with a nod, and Roberto was grinning like the mayor himself. Their men tipped their caps to ladies as they walked by. Franco could tell by the admiring glances of the women and the respectful expressions of the men that everyone regarded them as strong, bold, and daring. The Sicilian word for such qualities was *mafioso*, and it was a compliment.

Franco halted the men in front of Baron DiGiulio's villa, which was one of the best-maintained on the street, a limestone edifice three stories high. Its arched windows were tall, and it had balconies with ornamental ironwork and lovely red and white snapdragons.

Franco dismounted Arabo, handed Roberto the reins, and knocked on the red-lacquered front door. It was opened by an older house-keeper in a black and white uniform, and her mouth dropped open at the sight of Franco and the men.

Franco introduced himself, then said, "Good morning, I'm here to see Baron DiGiulio."

"You can't, sir." The housekeeper pushed a graying tendril back under her cap. "He never rises before noon."

"This is an important matter. Please wake him."

The housekeeper shook her head. "I can't. He'll fire me."

"If he fires you, I'll give you a job."

"You're joking, but I'm a widow. I need the money."

"I'm not joking."

Roberto interjected, "He *never* jokes."

The housekeeper whispered, "Baron DiGiulio isn't a nice man."

"Neither am I," Franco whispered back.

Suddenly, a beautiful woman appeared on the balcony in a red silk dressing gown, her long black hair curling to her shoulders. "What's going on?" she called down.

Roberto called up to her, "My brother, Franco, is here to see Baron DiGiulio, but I'm here to see you, Signora."

"Signorina!" the woman corrected him, giggling, then another beautiful woman appeared beside her on the balcony. The second woman wore a white dressing gown and had flowing red hair that reminded Franco of Violetta, engendering both desire and despair.

Roberto nudged Franco. "Brother, a replacement redhead!"

Franco ignored him. "I'm here for Baron DiGiulio," he called up, and soon he got inside.

BARON DIGIULIO WAS AN AGING aristocrat with a balding pate and slim features in a fleshy face with mottled skin. He met with Franco in his well-appointed study, wearing a dressing gown of gold-and-black brocade. He sat behind a rose marble desk with gilded legs, narrowing his gray eyes at Franco.

"Signore, you're rude to call uninvited, at this hour. My housekeeper should never have let you in. The woman cannot take direction."

"You should fire her."

"I will."

Franco got to the point. "My men and I guard lemons being brought to market. I don't know if you heard, but last night Michele was killed and the men taking your shipment to La Cala run off. Your lemons and donkeys were stolen by bandits."

"Who's Michele?"

Ironically, Franco felt angry at the Baron for not mourning a man he himself had murdered. "He's your *gabellotto*."

"How do you know what happened?"

"My men and I patrol the Conca d'Oro. I knew Michele. I found him and the others shot to death this morning."

"Can you help me get a new *gabellotto*? I never go out there."

"Of course, I know many experienced *gabellotti*." Franco would place his own man there, ensuring his loyalty. "I'll get back to you with a recommendation."

"How much are your services?"

"No fee for finding your *gabellotto*, but a fee for protecting your *giardino* and lemons to market. With some effort, I think I can recover the ones that were stolen."

"I bet you can." Baron DiGiulio lifted a knowing eyebrow.

"My fee is twenty-five percent more than before. These are dangerous times in the Conca d'Oro. My men and I run a lethal risk."

"It's a lot of money."

"Did you hear that brigands burned Baron Zito's villa and *giardino* to the ground? He lost everything."

Baron DiGiulio bristled. "Are you threatening me?"

"Of course not. I'm presenting a choice. Pay me for protection or don't."

Baron DiGiulio sniffed. "Why do I feel as if I'm paying you to protect me *from* you?"

"Ask yourself, I don't know."

"Hmm." Baron DiGiulio's hand went to his chin. "You know, I think my *contadini* should pay. They farm the land, and I doubt they pay enough for that privilege. What do you think?"

Franco thought that it was something only a *pezzo di merda*, a piece of shit, would say. "I don't care where you get it from."

"Did Michele pay your increase?"

"No."

Baron DiGiulio seemed to think it over again, and Franco took in the fancy quill-and-ink set and the paperweights of *millefiori* glass. Leather-bound books filled one shelf next to some silver awards that jarred a memory of something Michele had said.

"Baron DiGiulio, I understand you're considering running for mayor someday. I know everyone in the Conca d'Oro. I would encourage them to help elect you." Franco hesitated, for show. "If we were in business together."

Baron DiGiulio leaned back in his chair, folded his arms, and seemed to appraise Franco with new eyes. Suddenly, there came the lilting laughter of women in the next room, and only one man allowed himself to be distracted, looking away.

"Baron DiGiulio, have you made a decision?" Franco asked, on point.

FRANCO, ROBERTO, AND THEIR MEN rode on horseback through Palermo, turning heads. Roberto basked in the attention, and Franco felt satisfied, having made a deal with Baron DiGiulio and hired a housekeeper who couldn't take direction. Her name was Signora Esposito, and her bony little frame fit perfectly in his arms atop Arabo, even though she was cantankerous.

"Signore, go slower!"

Franco smiled. "We're walking."

"We're walking too fast! I'm worried my bag's going to fall."

"It won't," Franco told her for the third time.

Signora Esposito glanced over at the fabric satchel, strapped to Roberto's saddle. "If it does, you'll buy me new clothes. This uniform isn't my choice. I like to dress nice. Don't think I don't."

Roberto rolled his eyes. "Franco, does she remind you of Mamma?"

"Why do you think I hired her?"

Signora Esposito clucked. "*Madonna*, how do I tell you two apart?"

Roberto answered, "I'm fun, he's not. That's how you know."

Signora Esposito cackled like a little witch. "Ha! You boys found your match in me. I know how to handle naughty ones like you!"

Roberto smiled. "I'm nice, he's naughty."

Franco nodded. "That's true."

Signora Esposito cackled away. "Looks like I have twins to raise!"

Franco snorted. "I'm already raised."

"I'm not," Roberto shot back. "Signora Esposito, tell us about those beauties we saw on the balcony, starting with the redhead—"

"*Vai!*" Franco kicked Arabo into a gallop.

"Nooooo!" wailed Signora Esposito.

CHAPTER FIFTY-EIGHT

Gaetano spent the day interviewing families on the list from the first kidnapping, but the second kidnapping weighed on his mind. He kept thinking about little Vittorio, the second victim, and the family that had left the city. He couldn't wait until Carmine got out of work to talk it over with him.

Gaetano waited for him, sitting on a park bench opposite Carmine's office on the Piazza della Vittoria, only a block from the Cathedral and lined with government buildings, including the *Questura*. The office looked similar to Don Matteo's, which Gaetano pushed from his mind. He was excited about going into business with Carmine. Soon, he hoped to send for Maria and the boys, reuniting as a family.

"Carmine!" Gaetano called out, when his friend emerged from the building, beaming like a little boy.

"Gaetano, I did it! I'm free!"

"*Bravo!*" Gaetano rose and greeted him. "How did it go? Tell me everything!"

"Let's walk!" Carmine launched into the story of how he quit his job, and the two men fell into stride. Gaetano experienced the warm, good feeling that came from having a like-minded friend, and they walked down Via Toledo together.

When Carmine finished his story, he looked over. "So, what's new in the investigation?"

"There's a development in the second kidnapping, which I need help sorting."

Gaetano told him about his visit to the silversmith shop, then to the house of the second victim. It took until they had reached the Quattro Canti, and the intersection was flooded with pale golden light. Gaetano was standing where it had all begun.

Carmine stopped. "Gaetano, you're trying to find out the address of this second home, correct?"

"Yes, because it strikes me as strange that they left town, since the boy, Vittorio, was kidnapped in Palermo. It would make it harder to contact them with a ransom demand."

"I agree."

"They must have a second home somewhere, because many of that class do, and this second home may well be *closer* to the kidnapper."

"Yes, they must have some reason to believe it would be easier for the kidnapper to contact them at their second home, rather than in Palermo."

"That makes perfect sense. What's their name, by the way?"

"The boy is Vittorio, and his parents are Vito Curcio and Eleanora Sebina."

Carmine's eyes flashed with recognition. "I recognize that name, Curcio. I think the family might have been a client of my boss's. I think he drafted Curcio's Last Will & Testament."

"Oh my!" Gaetano cried, excited. "A Last Will & Testament would have a listing of the family residences, with their addresses."

"Yes, we have to get the will."

"Let's do it!" Gaetano looked at Carmine, and they realized the problem at the same moment.

"I just quit my job." Carmine moaned. "I don't have access to the files anymore."

"Don't you have anything to go back for? Any personal effects?"

"None. I brought them home at lunchtime. I knew I'd be meeting you after work. I went back only to say goodbyes."

"What if we go back right now and tell them you left something in the file room?"

"The office is closed for the day, and I turned in my key." Carmine's chubby face fell into resigned lines. "They wouldn't believe that anyway. Lawyers never go in the file room. The clerk does the filing."

"How about first thing tomorrow, we make up some reason why you need to see the client file?"

"What reason would I give?"

Gaetano wracked his brain. "Maybe say you'd like to use the will as a form? For when you draft wills in your own practice?"

"They're angry that I left. They're not going to help me." Carmine shook his head. "They're not going to show me forms. They're worried I'd poach clients."

Gaetano knew he was right. "Where's the file room?"

"On the second floor."

"Can we get in without them knowing?"

Carmine smiled. "The clerk always forgets to lock the back door."

Gaetano winked. "We can only pray."

AT MIDNIGHT, GAETANO TURNED THE corner around the back of Carmine's old law firm. There was a narrow cobblestone alley where garbage was stored, and he hurried ahead in the darkness, spotting Carmine coming from the other direction. The two men met in front of the rear entrance, a black door.

Gaetano clasped Carmine's arm. "Carmine, thank you for doing this."

"Of course. Pray God the door is unlocked."

Gaetano's heart began to pound as Carmine turned the knob. It made an unsatisfying *click*, and the door didn't budge.

"Oh no." Carmine grimaced. "He locked it."

"Are you sure?" Gaetano pushed on the door, but it stayed shut. "What bad luck."

"I say we try again tomorrow night, same time. One of these nights, he'll leave it unlocked. He always does."

"We can't wait. Every day we delay, the boys are in danger." Gaetano looked up at the building. There were three sets of windows, one on each floor. The sill of the lowest window was only slightly higher than he was tall. "If I stand on your shoulders, I can get in the first window."

Carmine recoiled. "You mean, break in?"

"I'm not *breaking in*. I'm going in through a window."

Carmine snorted. "It's unlawful."

"It's necessary. Think of what's at stake." Gaetano looked around. "No one's here. We won't get caught."

"It's still wrong."

"Is it possible you're more of a saint than I?" Gaetano chuckled. "I'm going in to get the Curcio file. Where's the file room, exactly?"

"On the second floor. When you go up the stairs, take a right and it's in the corner. You can't miss it."

"The files are alphabetical?"

"Yes, under the husband's last name."

"Give me a boost." Gaetano positioned himself under the window, and Carmine linked his hands. Gaetano took a leg up, then stretched as far as he could along the wall. The stone scraped his palms, but he got both hands on the edge of the windowsill.

"Okay?"

"Okay. Carmine, count to three, then push up as hard as you can."

Carmine counted off, then boosted Gaetano to the mullioned window. It opened partway, and Gaetano launched himself at the windowsill, clambered inside, and fell onto the parquet floor. He looked around, his heart pounding. He was inside a fancy law office, the desks and chairs shadows in the gloom.

He scrambled to his feet, hurried from the office, and found the entrance hall. There was a stairwell with a window at its landing, faintly illuminated by the lights in the piazza. He bounded up the stairs, turned, and hustled down a hallway to the closed door in the corner, which had to be the file room.

He entered the room, disoriented by its utter darkness. There was no window, and little light came from the hallway. His eyes became accustomed, and he saw file cabinets lining the room and a small wooden desk with a candelabra next to some matches.

He lit the candle and held it up to the file cabinets, reading the labels on the drawers. He passed the *A*'s, *B*'s, *C-Co*, until he reached *Co-Cu*. He yanked the drawer open, thumbed through the files, and spotted *Curcio*. He set down the candelabra and opened the file, thumbing through the correspondence on top.

He found a thick packet that read *Last Will & Testament of Vito Curcio*. He thumbed through the pages, scanning the provisos. He saw no reference to the family's addresses, then realized they could be attached as an exhibit.

"Hands up!" a man shouted, and Gaetano looked up, shocked to see Marshal Rosselli and the *carabinieri* aiming rifles at him.

"Marshal Rosselli, I was just trying to find—"

"I've had it with you! You're under arrest!" Marshal Rosselli and the *carabinieri* flooded the file room.

"No, wait, please, I just need to see the file—" Gaetano started to say, but Marshal Rosselli and the *carabinieri* dragged him into the hallway, where Carmine's boss was standing with a beautiful young woman. Gaetano realized the couple must have been together in one of the offices, heard him in the file room, and summoned the *carabinieri*.

"I know who you are!" Carmine's boss shouted at Gaetano. "I know what you're up to! Don Matteo fired you and now you're stealing our clients! You and Carmine! We got him, too!"

"No, we only wanted to see an address—"

"You're under arrest!" Marshal Rosselli and the *carabinieri* pulled him down the hallway, but Gaetano tried to hold his ground.

"I'm just trying to find the Curcio family! Their son was kidnapped—"

"Liar!" Carmine's boss hollered. "Don't let him see a thing! That's proprietary business information!"

"You're coming with us!" Marshal Rosselli and the *carabinieri* pulled harder, but Gaetano struggled in their grasp.

"Let me go, please, I need that address! I'm trying to find a kidnapped boy! I'm doing your job—"

"You're going to jail!" Marshal Rosselli and the *carabinieri* dragged Gaetano down the hall.

"No!" Gaetano exploded in desperation. He elbowed Marshal Rosselli in the face, hit the officer on his right, and fought his way back to the file room.

Carmine's boss hurried forward to stop him, but Gaetano punched him in the jaw. The boss fell backward, knocked off balance. The woman screamed.

Marshal Rosselli and the *carabinieri* seized Gaetano, then he felt an agonizing blow to the head.

He collapsed to the floor, in darkness.

CHAPTER FIFTY-NINE

The morning sun peeked through curtains of blue-and-green brocade, and Franco awoke in the big, soft bed, in sheets of ivory silk with intricate blue-and-green needlework. The canopy was of matching silk, and the headboard was embroidered with the Moravio family crest. Franco wasn't a baron, but he was living like one.

Franco tossed the covers aside and jumped out of bed. He picked up the dressing gown, put it on, and ripped off the pocket with the Moravio crest. "Signora Esposito!" he called out, since her room was down the hall.

Signora Esposito entered after a moment. "What happened to your dressing gown?"

"I improved it." Franco looked her up and down, her frame tiny in the black uniform of the Moravios' staff. "Do you like your new uniform?"

"Yes. Are we playing dress-up?"

Franco shot her a look. "How's your room?"

"I heard you snoring."

"Lucky you."

"I need staff."

"You *are* staff."

"No, I *manage* staff. I'm a household manager. I need a housekeeper, a cook, and a butler. Also, a valet to help you dress. Baron DiGiulio had two."

"I don't like men to see me naked. Maybe he did."

"There's no need for that." Signora Esposito wagged an arthritic finger. "I won't have you speak ill of my former boss, even though he's a bastard, a cheat, a liar, a snob, and an arrogant pig who passed gas without apology."

Franco laughed. "Anyway, no more staff. I don't want people around. Now, at the end of the week, I'm having an important meeting. I need you to put out a big dinner in the dining room with the best of everything."

"How do you propose I do that?" Signora Esposito folded her arms. "I don't know where to get fine provisions out here in the middle of nowhere."

Franco chuckled. "Can you do it or not?"

"I can, but it'll cost you."

"Fine. Also, I need something else, something special."

"Get your own prostitutes. I'm through with that. Your nose will fall off. You'll go blind. Mark my words."

Franco rolled his eyes. "I need you to get me pictures of Saint Rosalia."

Signora Esposito blinked. "You're a man of faith?"

"Not exactly. I believe in God, but He doesn't believe in me."

"He believes in all men, even naughty ones."

"Not this naughty."

"Anyway, where am I to get such pictures?"

"There's a church in the village nearby. Start there. Or send to Palermo. Every church has pictures of her. Figure it out."

Signora Esposito frowned. "This is an errand for a functionary, not a household manager."

"Can you do it?"

"It'll cost you."

Franco snorted. "Can I get coffee and breakfast? Or is that extra?"

"Meals are served in the dining room. It's ill-mannered to eat else-where."

"Okay, I'll dress and be right in."

"Bathe first."

"No. I bathe at night."

"*Braccianti* bathe in the evening. Noblemen bathe in the morning." Signora Esposito lifted a gray eyebrow. "Do you want to smell like a pig all day, Signor Head-of-the-Family?"

"Go make coffee."

"Hmph." Signora Esposito turned and left the room.

Franco smiled, watching her go.

He was home.

CHAPTER SIXTY

Gaetano was led past the detention cells, his hands cuffed in front of him. The *carabinieri* had questioned him all night and they hadn't been gentle. His head throbbed and his torso ached. The jail was filthy, and the air smelled like body odor and urine.

The prisoners shouted profanities at the *carabinieri*, and Gaetano realized he had crossed the line from lawyer to criminal. He was one of them now.

They reached the cell that held Carmine, who stood anguished at the bars. His chubby cheek was bruised, and there was a cut on his forehead. "Gaetano, are you okay?"

"Yes, you?"

"Better than you."

Gaetano was shoved into the cell by the *carabinieri*, and Carmine helped him onto the iron bench.

"I don't know how they caught us. The *carabinieri* came out of nowhere and found me in the alley."

"I know how." Gaetano told him everything, and Carmine's dark eyes widened with alarm.

"You hit *Marshal Rosselli*? You punched my *boss*? Gaetano, they know every judge in Palermo."

"I know, I lost control. I think you'll be okay, though. They can't charge you with anything. You didn't break and enter. You were in the alley on public property."

"I'm worried about you, not me."

They both turned when a group of *carabinieri* came down the hallway to renewed jeers and profanities. The officers motioned to Carmine. "Lawyer Prizzi, get up. You're going home!"

Carmine rose reluctantly. "Gaetano, I'll represent you."

Gaetano managed a smile. "Thanks."

The men in the other cells burst into excited chatter. "He's a lawyer!" "I knew it! I need a lawyer!" "Help me, would you?"

The *carabinieri* repeated, "Lawyer Prizzi, let's go!"

Carmine looked down at Gaetano, his anguish plain. "I'll see you as soon as they let me."

"Thanks. Open your law firm and be the best in Palermo. And do me a favor. Don't tell Maria I'm here."

Carmine frowned. "Gaetano, she'll want to know. The trial, she'll want to be there."

"Let me be the one to tell her. Go. Goodbye."

"Goodbye."

Gaetano watched Carmine being taken away, then leaned against the grimy wall, closing his eyes. He swallowed hard, sick at heart. His head pounded, and his body ached with each breath.

He knew what lay ahead for him, and it was grim. He would be going to prison for a decade or more. He wouldn't hold Maria in his arms or raise his sons. He wouldn't find the kidnapped boys and restore them to their families. He had failed, and the courts would jail *him* instead of the kidnapper. He wanted to pray, but his soul felt torn.

Tears came to his eyes, but he didn't cry. He let his thoughts run free, and soon he found a glimmer of faith, like light through a crack in a door.

He realized that faith was easy on the sunny days.

Faith was easy in the happy times.

Faith was easy at Mass, with Maria and his sons.

But faith was always there for him, whether in sun or in shadow.
Faith was at her best in darkness.
Then, faith shone.
Gaetano got down on his knees.
And prayed.

CHAPTER SIXTY-ONE

Franco surveyed the scene with a critical eye. The dining room was dominated by a long table of polished walnut with carved legs, surrounded by matching chairs. The place settings boasted china painted with a verdant forest, the silverware gleamed, and the crystal glassware twinkled in the candlelight. Majolica vases held bouquets of fragrant flowers. A bottle of red wine sat at each place setting.

The walls were covered with dark green silk, its sheen like the leaves on a lemon tree. Matching curtains flanked floor-to-ceiling doors, and paintings of the Conca d'Oro adorned the walls between brass sconces with glowing candles. A cool breeze wafted through the doors, each with a balcony.

Franco decided that everything was ready. Since the last meeting, all the *gabellotti* had paid the price increase. A few had persuaded their bosses on their own, and he had persuaded the rest, meeting with barons, counts, and a destitute duke. He had been very convincing, and tonight was the finale.

Roberto entered the dining room, grinning. "Well, are you happy?"

"Yes."

"Will you smile, so I know?"

Franco burst into laughter, looking him up and down. They were both shaved, showered, and dressed in stiff white shirts, fine black waistcoats, and new pants from tailors in Palermo. "We look good."

"I look better." Roberto glanced at Franco's boots. "You didn't get new boots. You disobeyed Mother Superior."

Franco chuckled at Roberto's nickname for Signora Esposito. "I hate to admit when she's right."

"She's always right, like Mamma."

"I know, I love her."

"I hate her."

Franco chuckled. "Why?"

"She favors you."

"You're right. So hire a Papa. Then we'll be even."

Roberto rolled his eyes. "She wants me to find a good girl, whatever that is. I *knew* she would be a nightmare."

"Or a dream." Franco smiled. "How are the men doing downstairs?"

"Having a great time."

"Good." Franco squeezed his shoulder. "Let's get them upstairs. Time to get started. This is the most important night of their lives."

FRANCO ROSE, EYEING THE *GABELLOTTI* around the table. Each looked up at him, dressed in his best clothes, dark eyes animated in the candlelight. The meal was over, except for *limoncello* made from his lemons and *cassata*, a delicious ricotta sponge cake topped with red and green sugary icing and candied fruits.

"Gentlemen, this will not be a meeting like the others, when we talk business after dinner. Tonight is a ceremony. You will be formally initiated into our Fiorvanti clan, our *cosca*."

The men straightened, their gazes riveted on him. Franco could see their respect for him had grown after the destruction of Baron Zito's estate and all that happened thereafter.

"I am the *capo di tutti capi*, the boss of this clan, and my twin brother is my underboss. I'm responsible for running the *cosca*, this clan gathered here and now, and you are each the *capo* of your family. I base this structure and nomenclature on my research into ancient Romans, who conquered our beautiful island." Franco had written his speech after studying in Baron Moravio's library. "It's fitting to harken back to the Roman Empire because it dominated through strength, honor, and loyalty."

Heads nodded around the table, solemn.

"You are men of honor. You will tell no one about what goes on here. This is *omertà*, our code of silence, but it's more than mere silence. *Omertà* is the quality of being *omu*, as we say, a man."

Roberto nodded, and his intense expression pleased Franco.

"These precepts aren't new to you. They're the way you've been conducting yourselves as *mafiosi* men, bold, daring, and strong. We're not lawless, but we don't follow the corrupt laws of the colonizers and nobility. We make our own laws and follow them. You will give me your obedience, your loyalty, and this family will always be there for you. If you should perish, this family will be there for your family. You can rest assured while you live, even thereafter. You'll never lose your place at this table, unless you breach the oath you are about to swear."

Two men made the sign of the cross.

"I will begin our ceremony with my twin, Roberto Fiorvanti. Roberto, please stand up."

Roberto rose uncertainly.

"We all revere our patron saint." Franco reached into an envelope on the table, withdrew a picture of Saint Rosalia, and held it up. "Roberto, let me have your hand."

Roberto extended his hand, palm down, but Franco turned it over, then picked up a knife and pricked Roberto's index finger, forming a droplet of blood.

Franco turned it so the blood dripped onto Saint Rosalia's picture, obliterating her face. "Roberto, repeat after me: I, Roberto Fiorvanti, swear an oath of loyalty to our clan tonight."

Roberto repeated the first sentence.

"I promise to serve our clan in any way I am told, and to respect the men of honor in our clan above all others."

Roberto repeated the second sentence.

"I swear that I will prove my honor and respect for our clan by *omertà*, my absolute silence about our family to those outside the clan."

Roberto repeated the third sentence.

"I promise to place our clan even above the saints in heaven, Jesus Christ, and God himself."

Roberto repeated the fourth sentence.

"The oath I swear tonight is sacred, and if I breach it or disobey, I deserve death."

Roberto repeated the final sentence.

"Roberto Fiorvanti, I accept the sacred oath you make tonight, on penalty of death." Franco held the bloodied picture to the candle and watched it burn. Charred paper fluttered to the table. "Roberto, you may sit down."

Roberto did, and Franco summoned the next man and administered the oath, then the next. Each swore his oath without hesitation, and his demeanor changed as he was elevated from *gabellotto* to man of honor. After the ceremony was finished, Franco dismissed the men, and Roberto escorted them downstairs with a new somberness.

Franco went to the balcony and looked at the magnificent *giardino*, inhaling the perfume of the lemons. The scent filled his lungs, and he savored the moment. The night sky was black and dense, and the moon didn't seem impossibly far away, shining its dark brilliance on lemon groves stretching beyond the horizon. He was exactly where he had always wanted to be, in the prime of his manhood. He stood above, at the apex of his career, the master of the Conca d'Oro.

Roberto materialized at his side, uncharacteristically silent.

Franco looked over. "Robo, I will swear your men in at a later time."

"I understand."

"We're going to control Palermo, then Sicily. The moon itself is within our grasp. And from now on, you're *Don* Roberto."

Roberto smiled. "And you are . . . ?"

"Who I've always been."

"God?" Roberto shot back.

CHAPTER SIXTY-TWO

Palermo's prison was a massive fortress of stone block with thick turrets and a high, crenellated wall. Gaetano was put in a cramped cell with nine other men, and the air was thick with argument, heat, and body odor. Gaetano had written to Maria using Carmine's address, without telling her he was here, and he still thought about his investigation. His failure to find the kidnapped boys plagued him. He questioned inmates accused of kidnapping, but had earned only punches for his efforts.

It was dinnertime, and his cellmates surged to the window, which had crisscrossed iron bars and was set high in the wall, so they had to stand on a wooden box to reach. Their families were bringing them food, since it wasn't provided by the prison. Carmine brought him lunch, and Gaetano subsisted on one meal a day, so by dinnertime his stomach growled with hunger. He lay down on his bed and began to doze off, but was awakened by someone shaking his shoulder.

"Gaetano, something came through the window for you." His cellmate thrust a small packet at him, wrapped in white tissue paper. He opened it to find his tiger's-eye rosary and a picture of Saint Paul, which could only have come from one person.

Gaetano jumped to his feet, hurried to the window, and climbed onto the box. Maria stood below, and his heart soared to see her again. Her dark hair glistened in its braid around her head, and she had on his favorite dress, the coral brocade. Her face was lovely, but her dark eyes agonized as she looked up at him.

"Gaetano!" Maria reached up for his hand. There was usually a box outside to stand on, but the guard must have taken it away. "I knew something was wrong. I could tell from your letters."

"Maria, I'm sorry." Gaetano reached down, but only their fingertips could touch. "How are you? And the boys?"

"I'm better, and they're fine, too. I brought you dinner, but they took it. I'll come every day and night to bring you meals."

"Maria, no. I'm going to be here for a long, long time. Fifteen years."

"It doesn't matter, I'll wait."

"No, you can't." Gaetano ached, wanting her to leave and wanting to look at her forever, both at once. "You should go back to your family—"

"You *are* my family. I'm where I belong, right now. Pray the rosary, Gaetano, and I will, too. We'll pray until the day we can be together again."

Gaetano felt tears filling his eyes. "The boys will be grown, I'll have missed everything. Please don't wait."

"Don't say that, darling. We vowed to remain husband and wife, before God. That vow can't be broken. It's sacred, and we'll keep it until the day we die."

"Yes, my love," Gaetano told her, a tear slipping down his cheek.

CHAPTER SIXTY-THREE

Franco hurried inside the convent of Saint Caterina and made his way to the visiting room, which was empty and quiet. He was hoping to change Violetta's mind, assuming she was still here. He was going to convince her to marry him, now that he had everything in place.

Franco knocked on the door next to the decorative iron grates. "Excuse me, I'm here to see Baronessina Zito. Is she here?"

The door opened, and the same old nun glowered at him under her stiff wimple. "You! You're not her brother. You lied to me."

"I'm sorry, Sister. Is she here? Please, let me see her."

"Yes, but you can't see her. You're not family."

"Please, we were almost married. Just tell her I'm here."

"No. Goodbye." The nun started to close the door, but Franco stopped it with his boot.

"Sister, I know your Order raises money for the poor. If you'll tell her I'm here, I'll make a generous contribution."

The nun arched an eyebrow. "How generous, exactly?"

FRANCO ALMOST FELL OFF THE chair when he looked through the grate. Violetta was dressed like a novice, in a white habit with a soft white wimple and long white veil. A simple wooden crucifix encircled her neck. She still looked beautiful, with her chestnut brown eyes and lovely mouth, but Franco feared she was lost to him now.

"You're taking the *veil?*" he asked. "You can't!"

"I can, and I will," Violetta said calmly.

"No, please, don't." Franco leaned close to the grate. "Violetta, will you marry me? I love you, and I bought Baron Moravio's villa and *giardino*. We—"

"No, I'm sorry."

"Please, marry me. I have a home for us now. For you."

"Franco, I'm taking the veil."

"It can't be. Don't do this. I'm begging you."

Violetta folded her arms, her manner cool. "This is our last meeting."

Franco's heart broke all over again. "Can you really mean this?"

"Yes, I realize the mistakes I made, with you."

"You didn't make any mistakes. You don't deserve to be in here."

"I'm trying to become a better person, so I *do* deserve to be in here." Violetta paused, softening. "What about you, Franco? Did you make mistakes?"

"Yes," Franco admitted, only to her. "I regret what I did and that I caused you pain. I'm sorry, I swear, but you have to leave. If not with me, then without me, but don't do this."

"Listen, I'm better now. I belong here."

Franco couldn't let it happen. "You wanted to be free, to travel, to see the world. Remember?"

"Yes, but I know myself better now."

"How?"

"Through contemplation." Violetta met his eye. "I'm happy, and you should be happy for me."

"This isn't *you*."

"But it is."

"Did you shave off your hair?"

"No, I just cut it short."

"No, no, no." Franco groaned. "I loved your hair."

"It's only hair, Franco." Violetta chuckled, like she used to.

"But it's *beautiful* hair."

"Don't make a fuss. It feels better."

Franco tried to collect his thoughts. "Violetta, you really want to stay? To live without love?"

"I have love." Violetta smiled. "I have love all around me, more than I had before."

"Not real love."

"Not *physical* love, you mean."

Franco whispered, "You *enjoy* physical love."

Violetta laughed, then covered her mouth. "I have so much else here. The world has opened up to me, one you can't even imagine. Now I understand the restlessness I always had, what was bothering me. I thought the answer was travel, but it wasn't." She leaned close to the grate, newly urgent. "Franco, if you knew what my life was like before, you'd understand that I'm freer here."

"But it's a prison."

"No, it's a *library*. It's a place of the mind. I have the privacy of my own thoughts. I never had that at home. My parents told me what to do, what to think, where to go, and whom to fall in love with. No one tells me that here, my mind is free."

"But your body isn't."

"It doesn't matter. If your mind is free, you can go anywhere, and I do good works now. I'm not idle anymore, I'm *useful*, and it brings me such joy, real joy." Violetta opened her palms. "I was the daughter of a baron, Franco. It was a privileged life, but it wasn't my own. Most of the nuns here are from families like mine. We feel the same way. I belonged to my father, and after that, I would have belonged to you."

"But I gave you freedom."

"Here, no one *gives* me freedom. I'm free, merely because I am. This is the first choice I've ever made, on my own, and believe me, my parents aren't happy, either. My father never expected me to take the veil. He wanted to marry me off to the Marquis Caligiri."

Franco felt anger flare at the Baron but didn't say so. He wanted to kill the *pezzo di merda*, but wouldn't harm him further, for Violetta's sake.

"Although he did remark that my conventual dowry was far less than it would have been."

"*Conventual* dowry? You have to *pay* for this?"

"Of course, I'm to become a bride of Christ, and the money supports our good works. I'm using my time to serve others. I work in the bakery."

"You're a confectioner-nun?" Franco asked, surprised. Confectioner-nuns baked fancy pastries, which were sold to raise money for the poor and for their own maintenance. The recipes were proprietary, and only convents were permitted to bake and sell such sweets, not bakeries, which sold everyone's daily bread.

"I'd love to be a confectioner-nun someday. I used to watch Nenella in the kitchen, but I wasn't allowed to cook, remember?"

"Yes," Franco answered miserably. "What do you bake?"

"Why do you ask?"

Franco shrugged, at a loss. "I guess I want to understand your life here. I want to imagine you baking. What do you wear? Does your habit get dirty, with flour or something?"

"I put on an apron, silly." Violetta chuckled. "I'm learning to bake *erbanetti*, those little cakes with pistachio paste on top."

Franco felt like crying. "I love everything pistachio."

Violetta smiled sadly. "I know, and when I make *erbanetti*, I think of you."

"Violetta, you're torturing me."

"I'm sorry, I don't mean to." Violetta straightened. "Franco, you have to move on with your life. Forget about me, about us."

Franco took the words like a blow. He'd won every battle except this one, and it was the one he cared about the most. "I want you, and only you."

"But I'm here, forever. You have to accept that."

"I can't."

"You will, in time."

"No, I won't." Franco's throat tightened. "I love you. Don't you love me?"

"Franco—" Violetta sighed, and Franco could feel her warm breath through the iron grate, like a kiss.

"Violetta, I'm asking you. Do you love me?"

"Yes," Violetta answered quietly.

"Then why not marry me?" Franco asked, anguished. "We could be so happy together. Why be apart?"

"I've made up my mind." Violetta's lips pursed. "Now, I'd better go."

"Why? Where? To make *erbanetti*?"

"Yes." Violetta rose.

Franco stood up. "Then I'll buy your *erbanetti* every month, for the rest of my life."

Violetta paused. "Franco, if you do, you won't see me. It's sold on the wheel in the entrance hall. We'll have no further contact."

"I know. I'll buy it anyway."

"Why?"

"I'll know it came from you, that it's your touch. A taste will be a kiss."

Violetta smiled sadly. "Goodbye, Franco."

Franco couldn't bring himself to say goodbye. He held back tears while she closed the shutters.

FRANCO BOUGHT HER *ERBANETTI* THAT very day.

And every month until he died.

PART THREE

Mafia is a way of thinking, a way of life
which is peculiarly Sicilian.

—GAIA SERVADIO, *MAFIOSO*

Mafia is the consciousness of one's individuality,
the exaggerated conceit in one's strength, which is
regarded as the sole arbiter of every dispute, of every
conflict of interest and opinions, which results in
an intolerance of anyone else's superiority,
or worse still, anybody else's power.

—GIUSEPPE PITRÈ, *USI E COSTUMI,
CREDENZE E PREGIUDIZI DEL POPOLO
SICILIANO*, VOL. II

CHAPTER SIXTY-FOUR

FIFTEEN YEARS LATER

Mafalda watched the sun send its final rays through the lemon trees, as she rested her head on her daughter's chest. Lucia had grown into a beautiful young woman, and mother and daughter had survived together, having only each other.

"Mamma, are you comfortable?"

"Yes, I'm comfortable." Mafalda wondered if her daughter knew it was their last day. They were each other's worlds, so Lucia probably knew it before Mafalda herself, in the way that daughters can sometimes be wiser than their mothers.

"How's the pain?"

"It will go soon," Mafalda answered, truthfully. The pain had started in her stomach a few years ago and spread throughout her body. She was wasting away, no matter what she ate. Her shirt and pants hung on her, as they dressed like men for safety, in clothes stolen from a laundry line.

"You can sleep now, Mamma."

Mafalda closed her eyes. Tears formed under her lids, but she didn't shed them. She wasn't sad to leave this life, knowing there was a better one in heaven. But she was heartbroken to leave her daughter, whose company she loved so much. Lucia's birth had changed Mafalda's life, and the change had been a blessing in every way.

"Mamma, I like it here, don't you? I smell the lemons."

"Yes, it's lovely." Mafalda breathed in the fragrance, so gentle and naturally sweet. They'd stayed in the Conca d'Oro because the *giardini* were so pretty and the irrigation canals were a reliable source of water. They could drink their fill, and Mafalda had to bathe, often sick in ways that embarrassed her.

"Are you hungry?"

"No, I'm fine." Mafalda's thoughts strayed to her only fear. "Lucia, I need to know you'll be okay without me. Then I can . . . sleep."

Lucia fell silent a moment. "I will be."

"You know what to eat, don't you? And what to avoid?"

"I know."

They ate plants that grew wild, like dandelion, chicory, wild parsley, celery, onions, and garlic. They ate prickly pears because the juicy pink flesh satisfied thirst as well as hunger. They found figs, on lucky days. They avoided most mushrooms out of caution. When they were near the sea, they ate samphire that grew on cliffs and sea urchins. They ate snails, rabbits, lizards, frogs, and, in leaner times, the bark of trees.

"Lucia, you know which trees have limbs that break in a storm. You know not to walk underneath?"

"I do."

Lucia had learned to identify trees of all kinds. Her favorites were Judas trees with their peach-colored blossoms and almond trees with their pretty white and pink petals, though they were so valuable they were grown behind walls with armed guards.

"Lucia, you know not to pick almonds, don't you? The guards will shoot you."

"Yes, Mamma."

"No oranges or lemons, either."

"I know."

Lucia took such joy in nature, and they reveled together in the wild-flowers of the countryside, the wild roses in red and bright pink, the fragrant freesia in pure white, and crocus, nasturtium, crane's-bill, Jove's-beard, grape hyacinth, geranium, and so many others.

"You know which bramble has the long thorns, don't you?"

"Yes, of course."

"And you must anticipate bad weather. Watch the sky and the clouds."

"I will."

Lucia had learned to predict the weather by the clouds and how to prepare for the winds that swept across the island: the dangerous *grecale* that had killed so many in Porticello, and the *scirocco*, a sandstorm from Africa that would send them running for cover. Afterward, they would shake red dust from their hair and wipe it from the folds of their ears.

"Lucia, watch out for wolves. You know what their tracks look like. You have to look in the daytime, so you know where they are."

"I do. I will."

"And listen for when they howl at night. You can tell where you are by the stars or the land. You know Cape Zafferano is on the one side and Mount Pellegrino on the other."

"Yes, I know."

"You have our knives, don't you?"

"Yes, in my bag."

"Always keep the bag with you. Practice your throwing every day." Mafalda had taught Lucia to throw a knife, the way she used to throw rocks. Lucia had excellent aim, even better than Mafalda's.

"People are your biggest danger. Stay away from them. Be careful in the villages. Even at night, if someone sees you, tell them you're a boy named Luca."

"I will."

"Don't kill anyone unless you have to defend yourself."

"I won't."

"Avoid shepherds altogether. They're strange and they drink."

"Okay, Mamma."

"Watch out for little children. You never know how they'll react to you."

"But remember that time? That little boy wasn't frightened."

"You were lucky. Stay away from dogs."

Lucia groaned. "Dogs are fine."

"Dogs are wolves."

Lucia sighed, and Mafalda smiled, knowing Lucia wasn't afraid to disagree, even with the only other person in her world. Mafalda didn't know what such a quality was called, but it would serve her daughter well.

"Lucia, always remember why God made you the way you are."

"I know, everyone has light inside their soul, and mine is on the outside, too."

"Yes." Mafalda wondered if she was the only mother who had lied to her child for her own good. She never understood why God had made Lucia such a color. She had hoped to know by the end of her life. Now that time was nigh, and she still had no idea.

"Mamma, you have a light, too."

Mafalda smiled, pained. "No, I'm just a mother. I have nothing and I've given you nothing, not even a home."

"Sicily is my home."

"But no family."

"You're my family. You're a wonderful mother, and I'm lucky I have you."

"You don't know any other mothers."

Lucia sniffled. "I don't have to. I know I have the best one. I have the perfect one for me."

Mafalda sniffled, too. A tear ran down her cheek. "I have the best daughter, too, the perfect one for me."

"Don't worry. You can go to sleep now." Lucia's chest heaved, and Mafalda knew her daughter understood. Neither of them wanted to be sad in their final moments together, so they watched the sun vanish, washing the sky with light to say goodbye.

"I love you, Lucia."

"I love you, too, Mamma."

Mafalda listened to her daughter's heartbeat, and their hearts beat as one, the way they had in the beginning, when they had started each other's worlds.

Then one heart stopped.

And the other kept beating.

Even though it was broken.

LUCIA DUG HER MOTHER'S GRAVE using a sharp rock, clawing at the dirt in the moonlight. The earth was fertile and rich, and she worked at a fever pitch, wanting to finish before dawn. She didn't have time to cry. She prayed to Madonna del Lume for the eternal rest of her mother, who was now in heaven. Praying and purpose kept her grief at bay.

After she had dug the hole, she lifted her mother's body inside. It was as light as a ghost, and she laid it on the earth, touched her mother's face tenderly, and kissed her on the forehead. She took her own rosary and put it in her mother's hands, already cooling.

Lucia climbed out of the hole, filled it with dirt, then tamped it down. She gathered rocks and placed them on top. She stood over the grave and prayed, holding her tears inside. She couldn't afford to break down. It was almost dawn. She could see the sky brightening.

Lucia put on her cap and tucked her braid inside. Suddenly, she heard a rustling in the cypress trees nearby. They formed a thick screen, and she couldn't see what was behind them. Instinct told her there was danger, and she never questioned her instincts. They kept her alive.

She grabbed her pack and hurried down the road. She forced herself not to look back or she would cry. The road snaked through walled *giardini*, and she picked up the pace. Men rose early to pick lemons, and she didn't want to take any chances.

She hurried toward a run-down building set off by itself behind a crumbling stone wall. Most of the windows were broken, and its red tile roof was in terrible disrepair. Bramble had overgrown the land, and an old green door in the back of the building hung open.

Lucia headed for the door, ran inside, and found herself in a dark hallway lined with empty rooms.

She ducked into one of them.

CHAPTER SIXTY-FIVE

Dante woke up, startled. It was dim in his cell, but he could see that a young man in a cap was standing inside, peeking out into the hall. His cell door was left open these days, since he was chained to the wall and couldn't escape. He guessed he was about twenty years old, judging from the changes in his body. He never cried anymore, like he used to when he was little, and sometimes he wondered if he was still human. He hurt anyone who came near him, so they called him a Monster.

Dante eyed the young man, doubting he was real. Sometimes he saw things that weren't there, which the nurse called delusions. There were fewer guards these days, and the madhouse had deteriorated over time. Opera Singer, Raving King Roger, and Biter must have been moved somewhere else, because it was always quiet on the hall.

Dante asked the young man, "Are you real?"

"Oh!" The young man turned around, startled. His cap covered his forehead, but his face looked uncannily light, the shade of moonlight itself. "I'm sorry, I didn't see you there. The outside door was open, and I thought this place was empty."

Dante knew that was true, so maybe the young man was real. The guard left the outside door open to let in fresh air, and delusions didn't need doors. "But are you real or not?"

"Yes, I'm real. Who are you?"

"They call me Monster."

The young man grimaced. "Don't you have a Christian name?"

"It's Dante," he answered, but it sounded strange. "You're so white, you can't be real. You must be a delusion."

"I'm a man, and my name's Luca."

"But you sound like a woman."

"I can't help it. Why do you look like that?"

"What do I look like?"

"You're dirty and hairy. I can barely see your face."

Dante didn't reply, but he wasn't surprised. They were too afraid of him to bathe or groom him, and he had lice everywhere, under his arms, in his beard, even in the seams of his brown muslin gown. He itched so much, he scratched his skin raw in places. He'd gotten used to his own stench.

"Dante, is this a prison?"

"No, it's a madhouse."

"So, you're mad?"

"I must be."

"Will anyone come to see you?"

"Not until dinnertime. The guard brings me dinner and bread for the next day. No one else comes."

"What about lunch?"

"He stopped bringing it after I bit him."

"I'm so tired, I need to sleep." Luca's shoulders sagged, and he blinked under his cap. "Can I stay here for a bit and rest?"

"Yes." Dante wanted him to stay. He liked talking with his delusion.

"Don't try anything." Luca eased onto the floor. "I can defend myself."

"I won't hurt you. I can't reach you."

"Don't call the guard, either."

"I won't. I'll wake you before he brings dinner, and you can go outside and wait until he goes away. I'll share my food with you."

"Thank you. That's kind of you." Luca's eyes glistened with tears that caught the moonlight. "My mother died, and I had to bury her. I've been up all night."

"I'm sorry. I don't remember my mother. She might be dead, too." Dante realized he hoped she wasn't.

"I'm sorry." Luca pulled his cap over his eyes. "I need to sleep."

Dante stayed in his corner, and Luca dozed off instantly. Dante watched him sleep. Luca breathed in and out like he was real, but his paleness was so unnatural. In time, Luca slid over and started sleeping on his side. His cap fell off.

Dante leaned closer to see him better. Luca looked like a woman, with a delicate brow, a heart-shaped face, a smallish nose, and pretty lips. His hair was long, also like a woman's, woven into a braid as white as the moon.

Dante squinted, trying to figure it out. Luca looked too much like a woman to be a man, but he was too pale to be a human. His skin was as white as the clouds, and his eyes were as blue as the sky.

Dante realized Luca could be only one thing.

"YOU'RE AN ANGEL, AREN'T YOU?" Dante asked Luca, when he came back in after the guard had brought dinner. They shared his meager portion of soggy *gnocchi* with rancid tomato sauce.

"No, I'm a man."

"You're not a man, I can tell." Dante chewed his awful pasta, which he barely tasted anymore. "So, the truth. Are you an angel? Or a delusion?"

"I told you, I'm a man." Luca licked tomato sauce from his fingers, but Dante stopped eating, giving voice to his fear.

"If you're a delusion, you're lasting longer than the others. It worries me. I don't want to be Raving King Roger. Please, tell me the truth."

Luca sighed. He took off his cap, showing his pale face, and his long braid fell out. "Okay, I'm a woman, and my name is Lucia."

Dante sighed, relieved. "But why are you all white? And why are you here?"

"It's the way I was born. I'm here to hide because people try to hurt me. This hall is empty except for you, and I need to stay out of sight."

Dante felt a twinge of sympathy, something he hadn't felt in a long time.

If Lucia wasn't an angel, she was as beautiful as one.

OVER THE NEXT FEW DAYS, Dante and Lucia fell into a routine, spending day and night together, sharing meals and getting to know one another. Lucia did most of the talking, telling Dante about her life and her travels, and Dante fell asleep every night, exhausted from learning about people, villages, flowers, trees, and birds. He mostly listened, lacking words or ways to explain things, but in time, he asked her questions, and she asked him about his past. She cried about her mother, which made Dante think about his own, and he started to remember more about his childhood. But what struck him most was that Lucia wasn't afraid of him.

She didn't treat him like a monster.

But like a man.

LUCIA HEARD DANTE'S WHISTLE, WHICH cued her that the guard had left dinner. She hurried back inside the madhouse, down the hallway, and into his cell. He was setting up their meal of spaghetti with olive oil and old garlic, but she couldn't bear to eat any more garbage.

"Dante, look." Lucia took from her pockets a fresh blood orange and a prickly pear. It was all she'd had time to pick.

"*Madonna!* I haven't had fresh fruit in so long. What's that green thing?"

"A prickly pear. It's from a cactus."

"I never had one before. Let me try it."

"Okay," Lucia said, amused. She'd stolen a precious blood orange, but he wanted the fruit that grew like weeds all over Sicily. She slid a paring knife from her bag and slit the thick green skin of the prickly pear.

"What does it taste like?"

"It's good, but I've eaten so many, I'm sick of them." Lucia peeled the fruit, revealed its bright magenta flesh, and handed it to him.

"It's such a pretty color!" Dante turned the prickly pear this way and that, and Lucia smiled to see him so delighted. She liked seeing things through his eyes, as if they were new again.

Dante bit into the fruit and the juice slipped down his chin, so he wiped it away with his hand, chuckling. "Oh my, this is delicious. I've never tasted anything so sweet and juicy. I can't believe all the things you know about."

Lucia chuckled. "Dante, everybody knows about prickly pear. You just haven't been outside."

"But you know everything, all the things you tell me, all about flowers and the trees, and how you lived all over." Dante smiled at her, his lips slick with juice, and through his messy hair she could see the warmth in his gaze, and something she saw every time he looked at her, as if his eyes shone, just for her.

"Dante, why do you look at me that way?"

"What way?"

"I don't know, I can't describe it." Lucia didn't know how to be anything but direct. "How do you feel, when you look at me?"

Dante smiled. "Amazed."

"You're saying that because I just taught you that word." Lucia smiled back. Whenever Dante learned a new word, he used it constantly.

"No, you're amazing. You know so much. You're beautiful."

Lucia's throat caught at the notion. The world's gaze made her feel terrible, but when Dante looked at her, she felt beautiful. Her mother used to say she was beautiful, but Dante made her *feel* that way. He even made her feel *desired*, a feeling she hadn't even known existed.

And it thrilled her.

THAT NIGHT, AFTER THEY HAD talked themselves drowsy, Dante leaned back against the wall, but Lucia started to move toward him in the darkness, without saying anything.

Dante pressed himself back against the wall and pulled in his legs. His chain clinked as it dragged across the floor.

"Lucia, what are you doing?"

"It's okay," Lucia said softly, but she stopped, kneeling in a square of moonlight coming through the window. The bars cast shadowy lines across her white hair and face.

"Don't come close to me."

"Tell yourself it's okay, Dante. It's just me. You know me. We know everything about one another."

"Still, don't." Dante clenched his teeth. "Why are you doing this?"

"I want to see your face."

"See it from there. Don't come closer."

"I can't, your hair covers too much." Lucia reached out to touch his hair, but Dante raised his hand reflexively.

"Please don't." Dante felt fury rumble inside him, like hunger growling to be fed. He feared he would bite her, harm her, kill her. "You don't know me."

"Yes, I do. We've talked about everything."

"We don't touch."

"Just relax." Lucia moved his hair from his face and smoothed it back.

Dante flinched, barely able to hold still. He'd never been touched so gently.

"I want to see your face. I want to know what you look like." Lucia stroked his hair and tucked it behind his ear. "Tell me what I look like."

"You're beautiful," Dante blurted out. "I mean, you look like an angel. You have a beautiful face, very delicate, and your eyes are so blue, like a warm blue sea. Your hair is long and white and shining. You're a beautiful, beautiful woman."

"Thank you." Lucia smiled with pleasure. She moved her hand to the other side of his face and pushed his hair back. "Now let me tell you what you look like. You have big round eyes, and they're a dark blue-gray. My mother calls them Sicilian eyes, and they change in the light. And your nose has a little bump, and your mouth smiles more lately." Lucia cupped his beard, and Dante cringed, his back against the cell wall.

"I'm a monster."

"No, you're just like me. I'm not the devil, or an omen, or bad luck, like everyone thinks. And you're not a monster. You're a handsome young man."

"I'm not." Dante grimaced, pained. "I'm not, I'm not."

"Yes, you are," Lucia said, her voice calm and steady. "They've locked you up in here, but they can't take away your soul. Everybody has a light inside them, Dante. I can see yours, through your eyes. You're human and you have a soul."

"Do you think?" Dante's eyes brimmed with tears though he hadn't cried in years.

"Yes, look." Lucia traced a teardrop down his cheek. "This is proof."

Dante emitted a hoarse sob that came from deep within, from a hope that had been buried so long he hadn't known it was still there.

"It's okay," Lucia whispered, then she placed her lips on his and kissed him so gently that Dante felt as if she were breathing life into his very soul. Teary and trembling, he kissed her back, *feeling* human and sensing that she was bringing him from darkness into light, from Monster into his very self.

"I love you," Lucia breathed, releasing him.

"I love you, too," Dante heard himself say, remembering the word.

And the emotion.

Because of her.

CHAPTER SIXTY-SIX

Franco raised his flute of *prosecco* to toast his happiest birthday yet. His success had surpassed even his dreams, and he had become the *capo di tutti capi*, or boss of all bosses, of the all-powerful Fiorvanti clan. They were the first Mafia family in Sicily, controlling the Conca d'Oro and Palermo. They had made a vast fortune, and tonight, Franco was going to tell Roberto his plan for an even bigger future.

Franco grinned. "Happy birthday to us!"

"Happy birthday to us!" Roberto grinned back, raising his flute.

"Happy birthday to both of you!" Franco's wife, Elvira, smiled sweetly. She was a quiet, dark-haired beauty with round, brown-black eyes and a body that was soft in all the right places. A perfect wife and mother, Elvira had given Franco three daughters and she knew when to look the other way.

"To the bosses!" added Roberto's wife, Bruna. Bruna was beautiful, but she was too skinny and cheeky for Franco's taste. She wore her black hair in a modern style and had expensive habits, like the glittery dress from Paris she wore tonight. Her only virtue in Franco's eyes was she had borne Roberto a fine son, Patrizio.

"Ah, the first course!" Franco turned as Signora Esposito entered the dining room. Her hair had turned white, but her wit was sharper than ever. She carried a plate of ravioli stuffed with ricotta, spinach, and pine nuts, covered with her *passata*, or tomato sauce.

Roberto clapped. "Here comes the best *passata* in the world."

"*Second* best," Franco corrected him. "Mamma's was the best."

"I disagree." Roberto motioned to Signora Esposito. "Mother Superior, serve me first."

"Sorry, but he's the boss." Signora Esposito went to Franco and served him steaming ravioli, the tart aroma of the tomatoes filling his nostrils.

"When do I get to go first?" Roberto asked, mock-offended.

"Never!" Franco and Signora Esposito answered in unison.

Signora Esposito moved around the table and served Roberto. "The key to my *passata* is my *strattù*, my tomato paste. My mother would make it with the other women, and the village would smell like tomatoes." Signora Esposito served Elvira. "She would make the *passata*, ladle it onto plates with salt, and leave it in the sun for days. She would stir it, she wasn't lazy. The extra water would evaporate, leaving only the best of the tomato, and the breeze off the sea would give it a special saltiness." Signora Esposito ended with Bruna. "Then, she would spread it out on fewer plates and start again. This is how you make the best *strattù* in Sicily, and when you make *passata* with it, only a fool could miss. And I'm no fool." Signora Esposito finished her speech, gave a little nod. "I tell you this secret on your birthday, boys. That's your gift from me. Expect nothing else."

Franco and Roberto burst into laughter, Signora Esposito left the dining room, and everyone dug into the ravioli. Franco savored the creaminess of the ricotta and the salt of the tomato, then cleared his throat. "So, I have an announcement about our expansion—"

"Franco, I have something first," Roberto interrupted, excited.

"Of course, go ahead. It's your birthday, too."

Roberto straightened. "I think we need to move into the sulfur business."

"No." Franco hated the idea, suspecting that its source was Bruna, not Roberto.

Roberto raised a hand. "Hear me out, brother. Sulfur is a precious mineral, in demand worldwide. England and Europe need it for sulfuric acid, gunpowder, and the like. It's a very lucrative market, and there's plenty of sulfur east of here, around Mussomeli in Caltanissetta province."

"Roberto, no. We're growers. We nurture beautiful trees in the fresh air. My plans for expansion take us west to Marsala. The Florios and others are growing grapes there to make Marsala wine, and we can protect grapes the way we protected lemons."

"The Florios, still?" Roberto shook his head. "We're not them."

"We're *better*. We protect lemons, so grapes are logical for us. We're not miners."

"We can become miners."

"Why? It's a dirty business, sulfur. You have to dig through hard rock. It's dark and smelly. It's poisonous, that gas."

Roberto touched his arm. "Think about it, for me. Mussomeli's only ninety kilometers or so away, and it's more like where we grew up."

"But there are no roads between here and there. The ride is long and hard. Going back and forth is crazy."

"I know, that's why I could move there, someday." Roberto glanced at Bruna, and Franco tried to keep his temper.

"Because she's from there? You want to move because of your wife?"

Bruna started to respond, but Roberto waved her into silence. "Franco, it's not for her, it's for me."

"What would I do when you're away? What happens to our business?"

"There are many who could take my place—"

"Not family. I have one twin."

"Nevertheless, they could do my job."

"I don't want them, I want you." Franco set down his fork. "It's out of the question."

"Why?" Roberto leaned forward in frustration.

"I told you, I need you here and I don't want to go into sulfur."

"What about what *I* want? I want to be boss."

Franco rolled his eyes. "Come on, Robo. We both know you're not a boss."

Roberto recoiled. "I know no such thing!"

"Be honest with yourself. Ever since you were little—"

"You act like I'm your little brother, but I'm your *twin*."

Bruna snorted, interjecting, "Roberto, Franco knows you can do it, he just doesn't want you to. He's holding you back."

"What?" Franco asked, offended. "How dare you? I love my brother!"

"You *use* your brother!" Bruna shot back.

"*What* did you say?" Franco felt a surge of anger and Roberto put both hands up.

"Franco, wait! She didn't mean it."

"Yes, I did!" Bruna sneered. "Franco, you love lording it over Roberto. We're not going to put up with it anymore."

Franco jumped up, pointing out the door. "Go see to the children! I need to talk business with Roberto!"

Franco's wife, Elvira, was already in motion, hurrying from the dining room.

"No!" Bruna remained seated, folding her arms. "I'm not going anywhere."

"Bruna, go, please." Roberto rose and hoisted her to her feet.

"No!" Bruna wrenched her arm away.

"Go *now!*" Roberto ordered, and Bruna left the dining room, cursing under her breath.

Franco turned to Roberto, angry. "Robo, I've *never* held you back, not for one minute. I've taken you with me every step of the way."

"Franco, I run the toughest, most violent men in Palermo. You didn't give me authority over them, I earned it. You must credit me for that."

"I do."

"No, you don't. You just said I can't be a boss, but I *am* a boss. *Their* boss."

"I meant the boss of the family. You can't succeed at the top."

"Stop it!" Roberto scowled. "I have the same blood and brain as you. If you can be a boss, *I* can be a boss."

Franco threw up his hands. "Robo, this is because of Bruna, isn't it? She sweeps in and changes everything?"

"We've been married almost fifteen years," Roberto said, incredulous. "When will you accept her?"

"She disrespects me. You heard how she addressed me."

"You used to appreciate a woman with a mind of her own."

Franco knew he meant Violetta. It still hurt, amazingly. "Is this why you go to Mussomeli so much?"

"We visit her family. What of it?"

"And that father of hers, he owns a sulfur mine, doesn't he?"

"You mean Don Bruno? Yes, there are a handful of families who own mines, but his is the biggest. He employs the most people, but he's not disciplined." Roberto touched his arm. "Remember how I used to tease you, that you cared about the details? Well, I see the benefit now. Don Bruno doesn't have that, even Pino knows it."

"Who's Pino?" Franco hated hearing about these strangers, whom Roberto liked so much.

"Pino works for Don Bruno. They give us entrée in Mussomeli. We can take over mining there and someday, throughout Caltanissetta."

"Since when are you so close to your father-in-law? You found a new Papa?"

Roberto sighed, wearily. "Franco, you can't always be king of the mountain. Nobody wants to be second-in-command forever."

"You make the same money, remember? Why can't you be content?"

"Wasn't that your point, so long ago? Who's the one with the crazy dreams now?"

Franco remembered, his temper brewing.

"Franco, I might as well tell you, I want to move to Mussomeli. Right away."

"No!" Franco shouted. "You'd be creating instability! You'd weaken our business! You'd jeopardize our family!"

"*I'm* our family!" Roberto shouted back.

"That's why I won't let you leave!"

"*Let* me?" Roberto threw up his hands. "That's why I have to go! You always put your interests above mine!"

"Of course I do, Robo! *I matter more!*"

Roberto gasped.

The twin brothers locked eyes, their expressions identically enraged.

Roberto stormed from the dining room.

Leaving Franco.

CHAPTER SIXTY-SEVEN

Gaetano thanked God that the day of his release was finally here. He had served his sentence and was leaving prison. He knelt in the chapel and prayed the rosary, thanking Saint Paul, too. His thoughts unspooled back in time to the beginning of his prison sentence. He'd been so depressed then, especially when he would hear about new kidnappings in Palermo. They seemed to happen every two years or so, leaving him wracked with guilt. But things began to turn around when his fellow inmates, who used to ask him legal questions, began asking spiritual ones. He preached the Gospel of Saint Paul and taught them that Saint Paul himself had been jailed, more than once. The inmates nicknamed him Saint, and he established a prison ministry, like the priest he had once wanted to be. It had been his salvation. And now, it was over.

Gaetano looked up at the crucifix of simple pinewood, with a figure of Christ carved by an inmate. The altar was a small wooden desk at the front of the room, and a chipped statue of the Virgin stood on a stool. The pews had no kneeling pad, and the window had no stained glass, but the chapel had become a spiritual home in a way the Cathedral of Palermo never could. Now, though, it was time to go.

Gaetano rose, crossed himself, and went to the door, opening it onto a delightful surprise.

"We wanted to say goodbye, Saint! We wish you the best!" exclaimed his cellmate the Baker, holding out a magnificent *cassata* with red and green icing. Behind him grinned his other cellmates, Long Hair, Talks Too Much, Little Mouse, Knob Nose, and Orange Eater, with many other inmates, along with Superintendent Coniglio and some guards.

"Oh my." Tears came to Gaetano's eyes. "How kind."

"We'll keep your lessons with us always. You have to come back and visit us."

"Yes, Saint, we'll miss you!" the inmates joined in. "Visit us!" "We'll pray for you!"

"Saint, wait!" Big Feet hustled to him, waving in alarm. "Before you go, will you see my cellmate? It's One-Eye. He's at death's door, and Father Terrino won't get here in time."

"Oh no." Gaetano felt a pang. "I'll come, but you know I can't administer Last Rites."

"Don't worry, he's had them twice already. It's a miracle he's lasted this long."

Gaetano turned to Superintendent Coniglio. "May I go?"

"Yes. We'll save your *cassata*."

"Sure we will!" the inmates called out. "We're thieves and robbers, trust us!" "Your cake is safe with us!"

Gaetano followed Big Feet and a guard down the hallway. Inmates called out farewells and regards, and he called back thanks as he stopped at One-Eye's door. The guard unlocked the cell, and they went inside.

One-Eye was old and bald, lying under a sheet in bed, his shoulders and neck wasted by disease. His gaunt cheeks had a grayish cast, and his eyes were closed, with one stitched shut.

"I'm here, One-Eye. It's Gaetano . . . uh, Saint." Gaetano went to the bedside and sat down. He didn't know One-Eye well, since the man kept to himself.

One-Eye opened his good eye. "Saint, I knew you would come . . . pray . . . with me."

"'Hail, Mary, full of grace, the Lord is with Thee.'"

One-Eye whispered along.

"'Blessed art Thou among women, and blessed is the fruit of Thy womb, Jesus. Holy Mary, Mother of God, pray for us sinners, now and at the hour of our death.'"

"Now and . . . at the hour of . . . our death," One-Eye repeated with a sigh.

"'Amen.'" Gaetano clasped One-Eye's hand.

"Saint, I have done things . . . many terrible things," One-Eye whispered, anguished. "I used to drink too much . . . I killed a man who insulted me . . . that's what brought me here . . . murder."

"God knows we make mistakes, One-Eye. All of us have, including me."

"I've done worse . . . even worse . . ."

Gaetano couldn't imagine anything worse than murder. "God will forgive you. I will pray for you."

"It all started . . . with that boy . . . kidnapped from the festival . . . of Saint Rosalia . . . what a sacrilege . . . I didn't take him . . . but I hid him . . ."

"*What* did you say?" Gaetano recoiled, shocked.

"I did wrong . . . to him . . . and to you. . . . I know why you're here . . . you were looking for him. . . ."

"You say you *hid* the boy?" Gaetano scrambled to collect his thoughts. "The kidnapped boy? Where?"

"The . . . madhouse . . . I was his guard. . . ."

"The *madhouse*? The one in *Palermo*?"

"Yes . . . I wasn't the one who took him . . . my partner did. . . . I confess, I locked him up. . . . I'm going to hell. . . . I'm frightened. . . . I'm sorry, so sorry. . . ." One-Eye breathed shallowly. "Saint, I repent . . . I want to redeem myself . . . I don't want to burn . . . Will I go to hell?"

"Who was your partner?"

One-Eye exhaled a rattling breath, then his mouth dropped open. His jaw hung unhinged, and his head fell sideways. He stilled, dead.

Gaetano crossed himself, shaken to the core. "Dear God," was all he could say.

Big Feet crossed himself, too. "May Christ have mercy on your soul, One-Eye."

Gaetano turned to him. "What's One-Eye's name?"

"Renzo Gentili."

"Who was his partner? Did he mention one to you?"

"No."

"Who was close to him, among your cellmates?"

"None of us. Nobody liked him. He was a mean bastard."

"How about anyone else? Anyone visit him?"

"He kept to himself. He didn't have any visitors, that I know of."

"But how did he eat?"

"He paid an old lady to come with food. She stopped coming two weeks ago."

"Do you know her name?"

"No."

Gaetano's mind raced.

The madhouse.

CHAPTER SIXTY-EIGHT

The afternoon sun heated the cell, the air stifling. The humidity intensified a stench that Lucia could never get used to, though Dante had. They'd finished a lunch of the prickly pears she brought and they sat side-by-side, holding hands with her head on his shoulder. She knew she'd get lice sooner or later, but she could no longer ignore the heavy manacle around Dante's ankle, his skin rubbed raw.

Lucia squeezed his hand. "You know, I've been trying to think of a way to get you out of here, and I've come up with one."

"What?" Dante shifted, looking over. "You mean, escape?"

"Of course. Don't you think about it?"

"Not anymore."

Lucia had sensed as much, but he didn't have to accept this awful fate. "Did you ever try?"

"I don't remember."

"Look." Lucia picked up his chain, its metal rough and scratchy. "This is iron, and there are blacksmiths in Palermo. They have plenty of tools."

"What's a blacksmith?"

"Someone who makes shoes for horses."

"Horses wear shoes?"

Lucia smiled, since most of their conversations went this way. "Yes, fancy horses have iron shoes hammered into the bottom of their hooves, and blacksmiths make the shoes. They have saws, rasps, files, pincers, all kind of tools. I could steal some tools and I bet one of them would cut your chain off."

Dante's face fell. "You mean I'd go? Leave the madhouse?"

"Yes." Lucia could see it made him nervous, that he'd grown too accustomed to this awful place. She squeezed his hand. "Dante, you can't really want to stay here. You're just used to it."

"But I'm mad, and it's a madhouse." Dante frowned, his confusion obvious. "I belong here."

"No, you don't. I don't think you're mad."

"I'm here, so I must be, and I have delusions."

"Have you had one recently?"

Dante thought a minute. "Not since you."

Lucia smiled. "So there. You were lonely, and your mind was trying to keep you company. I think you're sane, and you can't live in this awful place for the rest of your life. We have to get you out."

"I don't know where I would go. I don't have a house, I don't know who my parents are, I don't even know my own last name. I don't know who I am."

Lucia's heart went out to him. "You're Dante, and you can start a new life, with me. We would go together, anywhere we wanted to."

"But, where?"

"Wherever we wanted," Lucia repeated, with a grin. "We'd be free, together. Forever and ever. Tonight, I'll go into Palermo and get us some tools."

"You, in Palermo? Is it safe for you?"

"Yes, I'll be careful. Palermo is big, but I've been before."

"I don't want anything to happen to you, not for me. Not for anything."

Lucia smiled. "Don't worry. I'll leave before dawn."

_____

IT WAS ALMOST DINNERTIME WHEN Lucia heard a noise in the hallway, then the echo of men talking. Dante was dozing, so she got up and peeked out of the cell. A doctor in a white coat was walking down the hall toward them, with two uniformed guards.

"Dante, wake up. They're coming!"

Dante awoke, alarmed. "Go! Run!"

"I'll stop them!" Lucia stepped into the hallway, pulled a knife from her bag, and threw it hard. The knife whipped through the air, flying end-over-end until it reached its target, a textbook held by the doctor.

"Lucia?" Dante said, shocked.

"My God!" The doctor dropped the book in terror.

Lucia ran for the back door and raced outside to the broken part of the wall. Her chest heaved with effort, her legs pumped with power. She didn't stop running until she reached her hiding place, a shallow cave in a hill in the countryside.

She crouched against the wall, sweaty and panting. The cave felt cool, dark, and comforting. A mouse family lined up on a ledge, watching her with big eyes. She stopped panting, and her heartbeat returned to normal. She had left her cap in Dante's cell, but still had her knife bag, minus one knife.

She pulled her knees to her chest and wrapped her arms around them. She didn't know how long she could stay away from Dante. She couldn't bear it if they were going to harm him. She didn't know when it would be safe to go back or if she should go to Palermo tonight.

She bit her lip and tried not to cry, worrying about him.

"DANTE, I'M BARON PIETRO PISANI, the new administrator—"

"Get out!" Dante threw his dirty plate at Baron Pisani, enraged that he had scared Lucia away.

"No!" Baron Pisani's hands flew up, but the plate hit him in the chest, leaving tomato pulp clinging to his white coat.

"Go away!" Dante wished for something else to throw, but his chamber pot was empty.

"Dante, please." Baron Pisani looked worried under a pile of dark curls. "Are you okay? Did she try to harm you?"

"Go away!"

"Where did she get the knife?"

"Leave me alone!"

Baron Pisani motioned to the guards. "Go close the exit door. I knew leaving it open was a mistake—"

"Leave it open!" Dante lunged at the doctor, but the guards rushed into the cell, grabbed him, and slammed him against the wall. His head hit the hard stone, stunning him. He fell to the floor.

"Don't hurt him!" Baron Pisani pushed the guards away and rushed to Dante's side. "Dante, are you okay?"

Dante's head throbbed. He slumped against the wall while Baron Pisani examined the wound, his dark brown eyes animated with compassion.

"Dante, I'm sorry, I instructed the guards not to enter—"

"Leave the back door open!"

"I can't. I have a duty to protect you. That girl's a killer."

"No, she isn't!"

"She threw a knife at me."

A guard frowned, interjecting, "Baron Pisani, we must lock the back door."

Baron Pisani patted Dante's arm, something no doctor had done before. "I know you haven't been treated humanely. You'll be treated with respect from now on."

Dante glowered at him. "Then leave the back door open!"

Baron Pisani frowned. "What if she comes back?"

Dante couldn't live without seeing Lucia again. "I hope she does!"

"Who is she? Do you know her?"

Dante felt tears in his eyes. "I love her!"

Baron Pisani thought it over, then extended a hand. "Okay, the door stays open. Now, may I help you up? I want to get you to the infirmary. Guards, take off his loathsome manacle!"

DANTE SAT ON AN EXAMINING table, oddly stiff and rigid. He realized he was gripping the edge. He tried to accustom himself to the infirmary, which looked completely different. The examining table was new, a gleaming porcelain white, and the grimy walls had been wiped down. Shelves he remembered as cluttered and filthy had been cleaned. Fresh medical supplies in shiny jars stood in neat lines, with labels he couldn't read. The air smelled like antiseptic, not mouse droppings.

Dante's gaze fell on his own clothes, also new. He had on a white muslin shirt with buttons and dark green trousers. He wore proper shoes of brown leather, which felt stiff. A nurse had allowed him to take a bath with medicinal soap, then cleaned his wounds, applied unguents, salves, and bandages, and given him medicine. She had shaved his beard and was now cutting his hair.

Dante felt a tense and silent panic. He didn't know where Lucia was. She had told him she had a cave in the countryside, but he feared for her. He knew she wouldn't come back until it was safe, but he didn't know when it would be safe now. The madhouse was changing, the administrator was new, and he didn't know if they could escape together or even if he would ever see her again. He couldn't imagine life without her.

"Dante?" the nurse said softly.

"Yes?" Dante looked up, and the nurse smiled at him, her aspect kind. Her dark hair was tucked under a white cap and she had a soft body in her white uniform, like a freshly made bed.

"I'm finished. Would you like to see how you look?"

Dante nodded, nervous. The nurse picked up a large mirror and held it up to him, and he confronted his own face. His eyes were a dark bluish-gray, like Lucia had said, and his features were as she described, too. What he couldn't look away from was his eyes. He *knew* those eyes. He had seen them before. They were the eyes of his mother, and they sparked a memory.

I agree

I agree

I agree

"My mother used to read to me," Dante blurted out, his chest tight.

The nurse placed a hand on his shoulder. "Then you had a good mother."

"Yes. I did," Dante said, knowing it was true. His heart told him so.

For some reason he wanted to cry.

He needed Lucia.

CHAPTER SIXTY-NINE

It was a sunny afternoon in Palermo, and Franco felt free, walking around the city in a sort of disguise. He had on Roberto's cap, shirt, and pants with his *F* belt buckle. He could pass as his twin to even the most knowing eye, and today, he would have to. He entered a rougher part of town, with fewer people. The streets narrowed to alleys, shady and dark in sections.

Franco kept an eye on his prey, following at a safe distance. He knew her schedule, and she visited her fortune-teller every Thursday at four o'clock. She turned left down an alley that led to the fortune-teller's apartment, passing an old man looking in a shop window.

"Bruna!" Franco called out, sounding exactly like Roberto.

Bruna stopped, whirling around with a smile. The skirt of her yellow dress spun open like a flower. "Darling, what are you doing here?"

"I wanted to surprise you." Franco jogged to her, just like Roberto would have, and Bruna opened her arms to embrace him.

"I thought you were in Corleone."

"The weather turned bad, so I came back." Franco reached Bruna just as she began to frown, her dark eyes fluttering.

"Wait, you're not—"

Franco kissed her to silence her, pulled a knife from his pocket, and plunged it under her breast. Bruna emitted an agonized grunt, and

Franco hugged her tight, so any passersby would mistake them for lovers. He pressed her into the alley and pushed her against the wall.

"Franco," Bruna groaned, as her gaze stilled. Her head dropped over, and her arms fell to her sides. She sagged against the knife.

Franco eased her to the ground, turning away as he pulled out the knife to avoid getting blood on himself. He took her purse, hurried from the alley, and slipped the purse and the bloody knife to the old man, who had only been pretending to look in the shop window. The old man started running.

Franco gave him a head start before sounding the alarm. "Stop that man! He killed a woman for her purse! Murderer!"

Heads started turning on the street. Passersby ran to the old man and caught him. A crowd started to gather, calling for help.

Franco turned around and walked quickly away.

He picked up his *erbanetti* before he left the city.

FRANCO AWOKE TO HIS BEDCOVERS being yanked from his body. A distraught Roberto was standing over him, silhouetted in the dim light. "Robo?"

"Franco, what did you do?" Roberto shouted, his voice trembling with emotion.

"What are you talking about? What's the matter?"

"You know what I'm talking about! You *know*!"

"No, I don't!" Franco started to sit up, but Roberto pushed him back down, pressing on his shoulders.

"Yes, you do!" Teardrops fell from Roberto's face onto Franco's. "You did it!"

"Did what? What—" Franco started to say, but Roberto gripped his throat, choking him into silence.

"I know you did it! Don't lie to me!"

"No, no!" Franco croaked hoarsely. He hadn't seen *this* coming. He tried to pry Roberto's fingers from his throat.

"You did it!"

Franco struggled to breathe. He clawed at Roberto's hands, but his twin's grip tightened. He bucked, but his brother pressed down harder. "You did it!"

Franco kneed Roberto with all his might, and the blow shifted Roberto upward. Roberto released his grip, falling to the side. Hoarse sobs wracked Roberto's frame, and he doubled over.

Franco gasped for air, taking gulps to steady himself. Signora Esposito came scurrying in with a candelabra, and Sebastiano right behind her, raising his *lupara*.

"What's going on?" Sebastiano brandished his weapon, his aim uncertain. He looked around, wild-eyed. "Did somebody break in?"

"Lower your gun," Franco answered, trying to recover.

"I was on guard. I didn't see anybody but Roberto—"

"No one else is here. Go." Franco motioned him away, and Sebastiano turned to leave.

"Wait, Sebastiano," Roberto called out, wiping his eyes. "Sebastiano, where was my brother today?"

Sebastiano blinked. "Here."

"All day?"

"All day."

"Do you swear on your mother's grave?"

"Yes." Sebastiano nodded, and Franco thought it was convincing. Franco had sworn Sebastiano and Signora Esposito to secrecy, though he hadn't told them where he had been today or why. He'd sent Elvira and the children to her mother's yesterday.

Roberto turned to Signora Esposito. "Signora, where was my brother today?"

Signora Esposito looked taken aback. "Here, as Sebastiano said."

Roberto sniffled, wiping his eyes. "I don't believe either of you. I think you would lie for him."

Sebastiano shook his head. "I swear to you, Roberto. I wouldn't lie to you or your brother. I swore an oath of loyalty to the family."

Signora Esposito's eyes narrowed. "Roberto, I don't like you accusing me of lying, after all I do for you. You should apologize to me."

"I'm sorry." Roberto shook his head, then buried his face in his hands.

"What happened, Roberto?" Franco touched his brother's shoulder, but Roberto shifted away.

"Bruna's dead."

"*What?*" Franco asked, sounding shocked, even to his own ear.

Sebastiano gasped, his hand flying to his mouth.

"*Madonna mia!*" Signora Esposito sank into a chair, making the sign of the cross on her nightgown.

Roberto raked his hands through his hair. "She was stabbed to death. They caught the killer. He took her purse. He was seen by people on the street."

Franco moaned for show.

"I went to meet her, after I left Corleone. The *carabinieri* were still on the street. Her blood was on the ground in the alley. They told me what happened. The killer is in jail." Roberto broke into new tears. "He lives near the fortune-teller. They tell me he begs on the street. He must have approached her for money."

"That's horrible," Franco said, his tone sincere.

"It's a terrible neighborhood." Roberto covered his face. "I used to tell her that."

Franco stole a glance at Sebastiano, who looked horrified, and tears trailed down Signora Esposito's lined face. Franco knew this was a difficult moment for them and he couldn't take any chances. "You two should go and give us some privacy, please."

"Yes." Sebastiano helped a stricken Signora Esposito to her feet, and she came over and kissed Roberto on the head.

"Roberto, I'm sorry. I will pray for Bruna's soul."

"Thank you." Roberto gave her a hug.

"Good night." Signora Esposito allowed Sebastiano to escort her out of the bedroom, closing the door.

Franco rubbed Roberto's back. "Robo, I'm sorry."

Roberto looked up, glowering through his sorrow. "You didn't like her. Don't pretend."

"I didn't, but I certainly didn't want this to happen." Franco formed his face into a mask of regret. "I'm sorry for her, you, and Patrizio. Have you told him yet?"

"No, he's home with the governess." Roberto shook his head. "My poor boy."

"I love that boy." Franco did. Roberto's son, Patrizio, took after the Fiorvanti side, not the scummy Marescas. "How awful to lose your mother so young."

"I know, I know." Roberto wiped his eyes and trained his heartbroken gaze on Franco. "You didn't have anything to do with this, did you?"

Franco tried to look wounded. "No, of course not. Why would I do such a thing?"

"Because you don't want me to leave, and you blame her."

"I wouldn't, I swear to you. She's family."

"That's not how you think. You would say she's not family because she's not blood."

"She's family because she's your wife. Maybe she wasn't my type, but she was yours." Franco rubbed Roberto's back again. "You don't really like Elvira, do you? She's not your type, is she?"

"No." Roberto sniffled. "I don't even think she's *your* type."

"But you accept her as my wife, and therefore, she's our family. We built our family together, you and I. We may disagree, like we did on our birthday. But I learned something from our fight." Franco looked into his brother's eyes, so like looking into his own. "I have to give you room to make your own decisions. You can do whatever you like. Our family is what matters."

Roberto nodded, wiping his tears.

"I'm sorry for everything I said, Robo. I didn't mean it. I was angry. I'll always be your brother and I'll always love you. If you want to go, you should go."

"I don't know what to do, now. Maybe it *was* a crazy idea." Roberto teared up again, grief-stricken. "Patrizio will be so upset. His mother, gone. How do I tell him? You have to be there when I do."

"We'll get through this together." Franco pulled Roberto to him, feeling a rush of deep love. Roberto rested his head on Franco's shoulder, the way he used to when they were little.

"I loved Bruna, really loved her. I loved her for who she was. The woman she was. Do you know what I mean?" Roberto looked up, his bloodshot eyes brimming with tears.

"Yes, I loved Violetta that way, and always will," Franco answered, and it was his first true statement in the conversation. "But, Robo, you have to go on, for Patrizio and for yourself. You have to get through this awful time, and I'll help. I'll make the funeral arrangements. You take care of him."

"Thank you." Roberto nodded, weepy. "Where's Elvira?"

"At her mother's. Now, who's this scum who killed Bruna?"

"His name is Gabriele Provenzano. He's in custody." Roberto straightened. "I want him out, first thing tomorrow. I'll kill him myself. It's my right."

"Of course." Franco gave him a final squeeze. "I love you, Robo."

"I love you, too."

Franco heard the words, and they eased his heart. He resolved to find Roberto a better wife, one who fit into the family. No woman would ever come between them. They were twins, together forever.

His plan had worked.

Again.

CHAPTER SEVENTY

Dante blinked, not sure what to do. Baron Pisani stood in the hallway in front of his cell, his hand extended. The cell door was wide open, and Dante was no longer manacled to the wall. He was free to go, yet he stood still in his stiff brown shoes.

"Dante?" Baron Pisani's eyes were kind, his manner patient. "Would you like to come outside with the others?"

Dante was afraid and didn't know why. "What others?"

"The men you know as Opera Singer, Biter, and Raving King Roger. They're in the backyard."

"Really?" Dante hadn't been sure they were alive.

"Yes, but from now on, we'll call each other by our Christian names. No one will ever call you Monster again. Opera Singer is Beppe, Biter is Favio, and Raving King Roger is Ruggiero."

Dante forgot the names instantly, feeling jittery. He glanced into the hallway, surprised at how bright it was from this angle. He had never stood this close to the door, since his chain hadn't reached this far.

"Come with me." Baron Pisani motioned.

"I wish Lucia were here." Dante thought about her during the day. He barely slept at night, listening for her footsteps, which he knew like the beat of his own heart.

"Come outside, then you can tell her you did."

"Do you think she'll come back?" Dante found himself asking, though Baron Pisani didn't even know Lucia.

"Yes. Let's go outside. See what I have planned for you. You can trust me. Remember you asked me to leave the door open, and I did? We must start trusting each other."

Baron Pisani motioned again, and Dante walked into the hallway, then turned toward the outside door. They went down a short length of hallway, took a turn through an open door, and stepped outside.

Baron Pisani went ahead and Dante stood in the sun, feeling its warm golden rays on his face, for the first time since he was a boy. His eyes adjusted to the light, and he looked around the yard. There was a freshly mown lawn with patches of pink and white wildflowers, and oddly, in its center sat a polished black piano, a sight so strange Dante wondered if it was a delusion. Around the piano were three old men: one lying flat in the grass, the second twirling slowly, and the third standing with his arms folded, looking up at the cloudless sky. They were clean-shaven, bald, and dressed in street clothes.

"Baron Pisani, are they . . . ?"

"Yes. Beppe, Favio, and Ruggiero."

Dante couldn't believe it. They looked so different without beards and gowns. "They're so . . . old."

"Yes, you're the youngest by far."

"Opera Singer isn't shouting anymore."

"No, he stopped." Baron Pisani smiled.

"Which one is he?"

"The one on the ground."

Dante looked over. "Is he dead?"

Baron Pisani chuckled. "No, I assure you. He's more alive than he's been for nineteen years. That's how long he's been here. We have the records."

"How long have I been here?"

Baron Pisani hesitated. "Fifteen years."

Dante couldn't begin to conceive of that amount of time, though he had lived it. It was his entire life to date, as far back as he could remember. "I don't know my last name. Do you?"

"No, but we'll talk about it soon. I'm waiting until you're ready. Okay?"

"Okay." Dante nodded reluctantly. "Why is the piano here?"

"You'll see." Baron Pisani motioned. "Step a little farther out."

Dante did. "Now what?"

"Now do whatever you want to. Walk around, dance, spin in circles. You decide. That's what being free means." Baron Pisani folded his arms, taking on a professorial air. "This is the beginning of my moral therapy. You'll be treated as a man and respected as such. You'll make choices for yourself. You'll be exposed to the arts and taught to read."

Dante took a few more steps. He swung his arms and kicked his legs, surprisingly light without the manacle and chain. The sun still warmed his face, a soft breeze cooled his brow, and the chirping of birds filled his ears. The air smelled rich and earthy.

His heart felt light until he spotted a broken section in the crumbling stone wall around the yard, which must have been where Lucia came and went. He walked toward the break in the wall, reached it, and ran his fingers over its cool, rough stones and damp olive-green moss.

Baron Pisani caught up with him. "Well, what do you think?"

"I wish she'd come back."

"She will. Don't worry." Baron Pisani patted his shoulder. "It's better outside than inside, isn't it?"

"Yes." Dante chuckled. "This is crazy."

Baron Pisani grinned. "No, this is sanity."

Dante smiled back, focusing on the Baron for the first time. "Are you really a baron?"

"Yes."

"How is it you came here?"

"Well, I was lucky to be born into privilege, and I studied music, law, and archaeology. My late son, Antonio, was an excellent musician, but when he passed away about ten years ago, I became deeply melancholy." Baron Pisani met Dante's eye. "I discovered that the way to move through my melancholy was to help others, and I became interested in treating melancholy and other mental illness. I'm not a physician, but I developed a theory and instructions on moral therapy that can help patients find joy . . . Oh, wait, here he is. Look."

Baron Pisani stopped talking when a man in a frock coat entered the yard with some papers and sat down at the piano. He began to play, and the music delighted Dante.

"That's beautiful!"

"It is, isn't it? This is part of my therapy. Music speaks to us all, to our soul."

Dante listened to the notes going up and down, sparking a vague memory. "I think I've heard music like this before."

"Maybe you did, when you were little." Baron Pisani put a hand on his shoulder. "Try and remember."

Dante found himself closing his eyes, and in the next minute, he could almost see himself sitting next to his father, watching another man play piano. "My father took me to see a man play."

"A concert. Our pianist is playing Schubert. He's one of my favorites."

"I don't know that name. I don't even know my father's name."

"Stay with the music. Listen to the notes. See if it brings back any thoughts at all."

Dante listened to the music, and in time he felt as if he were resting his hand on his father's arm again, feeling the scratchy wool of his sleeve while a piano was playing on a stage.

"Listen," his father whispered, an index finger to his lips.

Dante listened. His father tapped his foot.

"Sir, stop tapping," hissed a man in front of them, turning around.

"Sorry," his father whispered, winking at Dante. Then, that quickly, the memory vanished, and Dante felt as if he had been in some lovely trance, only to find himself in the backyard of a run-down madhouse.

"Baron Pisani, why am I here? Is it the delusions?"

Baron Pisani's face fell into grave lines. "Dante, I want to discuss this when you're able to, in my office."

"But Lucia's real, right? You saw her."

"Yes, she's real." Baron Pisani patted his shoulder. "We'll discuss this soon, I promise you."

DANTE SAT BY THE BREAK in the wall all day long, listening to the music. He kept his distance from the others, and they kept their distance from him. Baron Pisani and the guards watched them, and in time they began bringing the others in. The sun dipped behind the wall, and the piano player stopped playing, gathered his papers, and left.

Baron Pisani appeared at his side. "Dante, it's time for dinner. You can come outside again tomorrow. Every day, if you like."

"I have one last thing to do before I go in."

"What's that?"

"Stand aside, please."

Baron Pisani complied, and Dante summoned all the breath in his body, cupped his mouth, and let his heart speak for him:

"Lucia!" he called out, yearning.

BUT SHE DIDN'T RETURN THAT NIGHT.

CHAPTER SEVENTY-ONE

It was a busy morning in Palermo, and people stopped to watch as Franco trotted into the Piazza della Vittoria next to Roberto, followed by Sebastiano, Ezio, and four of Roberto's men. Heads turned, conversations stopped, and mouths dropped open. Men looked at them with a combination of admiration and fear, and women gathered children against their skirts. The Fiorvanti family was notorious, and Franco and Roberto easily identifiable.

Franco acknowledged them briefly, but Roberto was driven by grim purpose, heading to the *Questura* to kill the man he believed had killed Bruna. The *carabinieri* began to look their way, bursting into chatter. Officers ran inside, undoubtedly to tell Marshal Rosselli.

They reached the entrance of the *Questura*, dismounted, and tied their horses to the rail.

"You all know who I am," Roberto told the *carabinieri*. "My wife was murdered yesterday, and you have her killer, Gabriele Provenzano, in custody. I want him now."

"I'm sorry," said the tallest of the *carabinieri*. "We can't do that. You have to—"

Franco interjected, "If you don't bring him out, we'll get him ourselves. Your choice."

"Let me explain, please." The officer swallowed visibly. "Provenzano is dead."

"*What?*" Roberto and Franco said in unison.

"We found him in his cell. He killed himself."

"No!" Roberto shoved the officer aside and charged up the steps. "That's not possible!"

Franco went after him, elbowing the *carabinieri* out of the way, followed by his and Roberto's men. They entered the *Questura*, charged down the hallway, passed the courtyard, and burst into Marshal Rosselli's office.

Marshal Rosselli looked up, his wrinkled face going white. He stubbed out his cigarette hastily in a crowded ashtray. "Gentlemen—"

"Where's Provenzano?" Roberto demanded. "I want to see him! I won't believe he's dead until I see him!"

"It's true, I assure you he—"

"Where is he? Show me!"

"Downstairs." Marshal Rosselli rose slowly, leaning on his desk. "Oh, my hip!"

"You incompetent old man! How could you let this happen? I want to see him right now!"

"*PEZZO DI MERDA!*" **ROBERTO KICKED** the corpse of Gabriele Provenzano, which lay on the floor of a storeroom filled with bottles of antiseptic, floor wax, old straw brooms, and dirty mops. Provenzano was naked to the waist, and bruises encircled his neck, which bent at an unnatural angle. Veins in his eyes had burst, and his eyeballs protruded. His purplish tongue hung out sideways. He had soiled his pants, and the odor reeked.

Franco stood next to Roberto, and on the other side of the corpse was Marshal Rosselli, next to his second- and third-in-command.

Roberto seethed, raking back his hair. "How could you let this happen, Rosselli? He killed my wife!"

Marshal Rosselli spread his palms. "In truth, I'm mortified—"

"Where *were* you?"

"I don't work the night shift."

"Who does?" Roberto confronted the second- and third-in-command. "Do either of you? Or both?"

"I do." The second-in-command raised his hand timidly. He was young, his eyes terrified under his plumed cap.

"I do, too," added the third-in-command. He was older, with a solid demeanor and a brushy mustache. He had a large family to support on slim wages, which made him corruptible. He had strangled Gabriele Provenzano at Franco's bidding.

Marshal Rosselli interjected, "Don Roberto, I'm sorry to say, we don't patrol the cells. We don't have the manpower. We rarely have suicides, and Provenzano was known to us. He's been in and out of prison for assault and robbery."

"Not murder?"

"No. We believe he acted on impulse this time. He had been drinking when he was arrested."

"But why would he kill himself? Why?"

"Murder is a more serious crime than he'd committed before, and we believe he found out whose wife he had killed. The murderer of the wife of Don Roberto Fiorvanti would be a dead man, even in prison." Marshal Rosselli's gray eyebrows sloped down. "We didn't know the identity of the victim until you came here."

Roberto exploded. "You stole my rights! She was my *wife!*"

"We're very sorry." Marshal Rosselli bowed his head, and so did the second- and third-in-command, who each apologized, in turn.

"Who found him?" Roberto shouted, unappeased.

"I did." The second-in-command raised his hand.

"How did he do it? What did you see?"

"He was hanging from the top horizontal bar, which goes across the others in the back of the holding cell. He had twisted his shirt into a rope, tied it to the top bar and to his neck, then jumped off the bench."

"Didn't the other prisoners see anything?"

"We had none. It was a slow night."

"You just said you don't have the manpower to monitor them, now you tell me it was a slow night. You should have been watching him!"

Marshal Rosselli interjected again, "I assure you, we will from now on. I'm making changes here—"

"What about his family? Have they been here?"

Marshal Rosselli shook his head. "No, and we haven't informed next of kin. You got here only half an hour after we—"

"Where does he live? His family will pay for this! They're dead! *Dead!*"

Marshal Rosselli's eyes flared. "You don't mean that."

"Yes, I do!"

"Then I didn't hear it."

"You owe me that address!" Roberto grabbed Marshal Rosselli by his collar. "And don't try to stop me or I'll come back for you!"

THE PROVENZANO HOUSE WAS IN a terrible neighborhood, among houses in dire need of repair. Stucco crumbled on their façades and shutters hung crookedly. Refuse rotted in the gutter, and laundry on clotheslines would take forever to dry on the dark, narrow street. Most of the residents worked in the nearby tannery, and the air reeked of boiling animal skins, a peculiarly carnal odor.

They found the Provenzano house, and Roberto charged through the front door, followed by Franco. Women, children, and old people packed the hallways, talking, playing, and arguing. They scrambled to their apartments at the sign of trouble, slamming doors throughout the house.

Roberto bounded to the top floor and banged on the apartment door, which flew open to reveal an older woman, skeletally thin in a bed by the window. She turned her head but didn't try to get up. Her hair had fallen out in clumps, and she had no teeth, which hollowed

out her wrinkled face. Franco knew her husband, Gabriele, had taken
the blame for Bruna's murder to pay for her imminent funeral, an act
meant to atone for a lifetime of neglecting her.

Roberto stood stricken, his eyes brimming with tears. His chest
heaved, but he didn't move. He didn't have the heart to harm a widow
on her deathbed.

Franco took control of the situation. "Signora, we bring you bad
news."

"What?" the woman asked, hoarsely.

"Unfortunately, your husband is dead. He killed himself in a cell at
the *Questura*. He was arrested because he killed my sister-in-law,
Donna Bruna Maresca."

"*Dio.*" The woman shook her head. "I'm sorry he did this thing. I will
pray for Donna Bruna."

"Thank you."

"May God forgive him." The woman began to weep, a pathetic
whimper, and Franco went to Roberto and squeezed his shoulder.

"Robo, I think we should leave, don't you?"

Roberto nodded, wiping his eyes.

BRUNA'S FUNERAL TOOK PLACE ON a sunny morning, and it was
the talk of the Conca d'Oro, owing to its size and importance. Franco
sat across from the grave next to Elvira and his children, Roberto and
Patrizio, and the Marescas. Behind them was Signora Esposito and all
of the Fiorvanti family, then assorted noblemen, businessmen, merchants, politicians, judges, and Marshal Rosselli. Mounds of flowers
massed around the gleaming graveside, sent by everyone who wanted
to curry favor with the Fiorvantis, as well as those who were afraid
not to.

The priest concluded the ceremony and a teary Roberto rose from
his chair, placed a red rose on the casket, and kissed its grain. His
strapping son, Patrizio, did the same, bereft, and Franco felt a stab of

sympathy for him, seeing himself in a boy devoted to his mother. Elvira and his daughters sobbed quietly. Franco comforted them with pats, and they looked up at him with loving smiles.

The Maresca women came forward, weeping too theatrically for Franco's taste. Bruna's mother collapsed over the coffin, demonstrating where her daughter had gotten her insatiable need for attention. Her fingers had to be pried off the casket, and her sisters walked her away sobbing, leaving behind a stoic Don Bruno, who struck Franco as looking like a man who made his living underground. His eyes were slit like a mole's, his nose was pointed, and his hair thinned to mouse-gray. His form was small and round in a brand-new waistcoat, and Franco hoped never to see him or his horrible family again.

The mourners dispersed, and Franco returned to Elvira and the children, helping them to the carriage. Roberto and Patrizio went with them. The carriage waited for Franco while he paid the priest, the undertaker, the florists, and the extra mourners, then made sure his guests found their carriages and headed to his villa for lunch.

In time, only Franco and Don Bruno were left, standing uncomfortably side-by-side, each seeing to the last of his family. Franco was about to go, then turned to Don Bruno with a polite smile. "Don Bruno, I'll see you at the house."

Don Bruno clutched his arm. "Don Franco, you fooled your brother. But you don't fool me."

CHAPTER SEVENTY-TWO

"Dante, please come in." Baron Pisani stood behind his desk, across from a man sitting in a chair. The man had round brown eyes and a warm smile. His dark, wavy hair silvered at the temples, and he wore a fine cravat with a brown frock coat. Baron Pisani gestured to him. "Please meet Signore Gaetano Catalano, a lawyer."

Dante was about to greet him but Signore Catalano leapt up with enthusiasm, grabbed Dante, and hugged him.

"Thank God! I'm so happy to see you, Dante!"

Dante stiffened. "Uh, I'm happy to meet you, Signore."

"Call me Gaetano, please!" Gaetano released him, beaming. Tears glistened in his eyes. "What a handsome young man you are! God, it's good to see you!"

Dante didn't understand. "Do I . . . know you?"

"No! We've never met, but I've wanted to meet you for a very long time. I'm just so happy." Gaetano took a handkerchief from his pocket and wiped his eyes. "So very, very happy."

Dante hadn't known you could cry from happiness, but didn't say so.

They settled down, taking their seats, and Baron Pisani cleared his throat. "Dante, I'm going to come directly to the point. The other day, you asked me why you're here. The truth is, you're not mad and you never have been."

"I'm not?" Dante felt stunned. So Lucia had been right. "But my delusions? The biting?"

"I'm sorry to say, they're the *result* of your being here, not the cause." Baron Pisani's brow furrowed under his curls. "Living here for so long, being treated so inhumanely, *caused* them and your other behavior."

Dante couldn't collect his thoughts.

"Gaetano knows how you got here, so I'm going to let him explain."

Gaetano turned to Dante, his eyes wet but his smile gone. "You were kidnapped when you were five or six years old, taken from the Festival of Saint Rosalia. I've been searching for you, and one of your kidnappers confessed to me that you were here."

Dante recoiled, shocked. "Someone kidnapped me?"

"Yes, two people, I believe. One took you from the festival, and the other imprisoned you here."

Dante reeled. "Why?"

"Someone must've paid them to."

"Who?"

"That, we don't know."

"And they put me here, in the madhouse?"

"Yes, the man who kept you here, who perpetrated a fraud on the administration, was a guard named Renzo Gentili."

Renzo. Dante shuddered. "I know that name."

"What do you remember?"

Dante felt shaken. His memory shattered like broken glass. Only a sensation remained, one of dread. "He was mean, that's all."

"Do you remember anything about the man who kidnapped you from the festival?"

"No. I didn't even remember that happened."

"Okay. As I say, Renzo's dead, and his soul will be judged by God. I'm searching for the man who kidnapped you and anyone who paid him. I believe I can find them and bring them to justice."

Dante's head was spinning. "But my mother? And father? Where are they?"

"I don't know, because we don't know who *you* are. We don't have your last name because your medical records are missing. We suspect that was Renzo's doing, too."

"Oh no," Dante said, bewildered.

"But I have a way to find out your identity, so we can find your parents and get you home. Now—"

"Home?" Dante turned to Baron Pisani. "What about Lucia? She's still not back, and I can't leave without her."

Baron Pisani nodded. "Dante, we'll take things one step at a time. I'm overseeing the construction of a new madhouse, not far from here. I designed it myself, and those are the plans." He pointed to a drawing of a building, tacked to the wall. "This will be the Real Casa dei Matti di Palermo, the Royal Madhouse of Palermo. I'll put into practice my principles of moral therapy to treat mental illnesses. Most of the patients have already been transferred there, and this madhouse will be shut down."

"But if I leave before Lucia comes back, she won't know how to find me."

"I don't expect she'll come back so soon." Baron Pisani looked earnest. "I hope you'll come with me to the new madhouse, where I'll make sure you get the best treatment. I can help you heal from what living here has done to you. Or, you can also choose to go home to your parents."

Dante tried to absorb the information. "I don't know what to do yet."

"That's fine." Dr. Pisani nodded. "Now, would you like to try and find out your last name, and who your parents are?"

"Yes," Dante said, nervous.

Baron Pisani gestured to Gaetano. "Gaetano, take it from here?"

"Yes, thank you." Gaetano pulled a stack of papers from a leather envelope. "I have a list of the parents of the boys named Dante during the relevant time period, which I took from baptismal records. I'm hoping you'll recognize one of these names."

"I can't read."

"I know, I'm going to read them to you. Shall we? Here's the first one. 'Dante DiGiuseppe. Father, Fabiano DiGiuseppe, and mother, Laura Pantera.'"

Dante shook his head, no.

"'Dante Messina. Father, Michele Messina, and mother, Mellina Palumbo.'"

Dante shook his head again, no, and Gaetano read the next set of parents, then the next.

They came to the third page, and Gaetano read, "'Dante Michangeli. Father, Adamo Michangeli, and mother, Vera Catena.'"

Michangeli. Dante raised his hand, without knowing why.

Gaetano stopped. "What?"

Dante's mouth went dry. "Would you read it again?"

"'Dante Michangeli. Father, Adamo Michangeli, and mother, Vera Catena.'"

Dante knew the names. He *recognized* them. They were the names of his parents. His lips parted, but he didn't know what to say. His throat was so tight he couldn't speak.

"Dante?" Gaetano touched his arm, excited. "Is that them? Is that *you*?"

"Yes!" Dante answered, with conviction. His own name resonated in his chest. Tears filled his eyes. "I'm . . . Dante Michangeli!"

"*Bravissimo*, Dante Michangeli!" Gaetano leapt to his feet and threw the papers into the air. "Thank God! Thank Saint Paul!"

"*Bravo*, Dante Michangeli!" Baron Pisani shot up from his chair, pumping his arms.

"I'm Dante Michangeli! I'm Dante Michangeli!" Dante began jumping up and down.

And he realized that now *he* was crying from happiness.

AFTER THEY HAD CALMED DOWN, Gaetano looked over at Dante, flushed and happy. "Dante, your baptismal record has your parents' address, too."

"Where do they live?"

"In Palermo. Would you like to go meet them?"

Dante felt excited, but tense. "When?"

"How about tomorrow? I would accompany you." Gaetano turned to Baron Pisani. "Would that be permissible? I could take Dante and return him here."

"For me, yes," Baron Pisani answered, beaming. He turned to Dante. "I leave it to you, Dante. I believe you can handle this matter. You deserve to make your own choices from now on."

Baron Pisani and Gaetano smiled expectantly at Dante.

CHAPTER SEVENTY-THREE

Franco set the candle on the kitchen table, unwrapped the cloth over a wedge of *pecorino siciliano*, and went looking for a cheese knife. It was the middle of the night, but he couldn't sleep. The villa was quiet, and the funeral guests had left. Roberto and Patrizio had gone back to Mussomeli with the Marescas for a visit.

"What are you doing in my kitchen?" Signora Esposito asked, entering in her bathrobe.

"Looking for a knife."

"Who are you going to kill now?"

Franco hid his surprise. The woman was uncanny. He didn't know what to say, so he said nothing.

"You went too far." Signora Esposito took a cheese knife from the drawer, then went for a plate. Her long white braid hung down her back like a fraying rope.

"I don't need the lecture."

"I'm telling you what you need to know." Signora Esposito set the cheese on the plate. "Your men tell you what you want to hear. I tell you the truth."

"Like you told Roberto?"

Signora Esposito eyed him, her dark irises cloudy. "You should know better than to bring that up. I lied for you before I knew why. You tricked me because I believed better of you."

Franco felt stung. "I did what was necessary."

"It was wrong."

"It's always wrong."

"This is different." Signora Esposito frowned, gesturing with the knife. "Bruna was family. A woman, a mother."

"What difference does that make?"

"She wasn't in your business."

"She threatened my business."

"She was off-limits. You never make a wrong move, Franco. Now you have." Signora Esposito sliced the cheese into neat pieces. "You know it, too, deep inside. I hear you, walking around at night. You haven't told yourself the truth yet." She looked up sharply. "What would your mother say? It would have killed her to see you break your brother's heart."

Franco scoffed, uncomfortable. "You didn't know her."

"All mothers have the same heart. You made a terrible mistake. I don't know how you come back from this."

"I already did. It's over."

"Because Roberto decided not to move to Mussomeli? Because you think it worked? *Bah!* Roberto's love for you blinds him." Signora Esposito pushed the cheese plate at him. "You want bread?"

"No."

"Olives? I got the ones you like."

"No." Franco took a bite of cheese, which tasted strong, salty, and deliciously herbal.

"Do you know what blinds you? Your selfishness. You don't see what your men see. They're not stupid. They know you didn't like Bruna. You killed your brother's wife."

Franco hated hearing it aloud. "They don't know."

"They suspect it and always will. What do they think of you now?" Signora Esposito arched a sparse gray eyebrow, wrapping the cheese. "What does Sebastiano think of you now?"

"I did what a boss does."

"You won't be the boss for long. The men respect you, but they *love* Roberto. They feel for him. They cried for him. I saw at the funeral."

Franco had noticed it, too. Roberto's men had mourned with him.

"Now they're not sure what you're capable of. They'll side with him over you. The wives are nervous, too. They thought they were off-limits, but now they can't trust you. They sleep with their husbands. They talk on the pillows."

Franco had seen the wives clucking around Roberto and Patrizio.

"Franco, after you lose the women, sooner or later, you lose the men. Do something to fix it, right away."

Franco waved her off. "They'll get over it. They know I put food on their table."

"So put more food on their table, especially Sebastiano's."

"Why? Has he said something?"

"No, but he wouldn't, to me. Use this time, while Roberto's with Don Bruno, who looks daggers at you."

Franco set down his cheese, his appetite gone.

"Franco, win the men back. Show them your appreciation. If they think Bruna was an exception, they'll let it go. They'll tell their wives to shut up." Signora Esposito wiped her hands on a dish towel. "You're the boss of Palermo, and power blinded you. You made the same mistake as Baron DiGiulio. Remember him, my old boss? Power blinded him, too. But *his* men didn't have guns."

"Thanks."

"So, are you going to do what I say?"

"I don't take orders from you."

"I'm trying to help you. But if you don't listen to me, I quit."

Franco felt hurt, which made him angry. "Then quit!"

"Are you sure about that?" Signora Esposito met his eye. "If I quit, then everyone will know you killed Bruna for sure. There would be no other explanation for my leaving, and I wouldn't explain."

Franco realized she had him.

"Do what I say. Or I quit." Signora Esposito turned on her little heel and headed for the door. "Your choice."

CHAPTER SEVENTY-FOUR

Dante walked down the street with Gaetano, going to see his parents after so many years. The prospect filled him with nervous anticipation, and Palermo bombarded him with noise and motion. People hurried this way and that, talking in different languages, sharing the street with carriages, donkey carts, bicycles, and horses. Fruit and vegetable vendors pushed barrows and called for customers, while shopkeepers hawked toys, frocks, and fresh fish. Houses and stores of all types lined the streets, with signs he couldn't read, flowers blooming on balconies, laundry flapping on clotheslines.

Gaetano looked over. "Your Lucia sounds wonderful."

"She is." Dante came out of his reverie.

"I'm sure she'll come back."

"I'm worried it might not be before I go to the new madhouse."

"You can leave word for her. You never know, you might want to move home with your parents. Do you remember anything about them?"

"Some things, about my father." Dante filled him in about the piano playing.

"And your mother?"

"Just that she used to read to me. My eyes remind me of hers, but I can't remember what she looked like."

"Dante, seeing your parents will be joyful, but difficult. Have you thought about that?"

"Yes, I'm just so surprised by everything. I'm trying to keep up."

"I understand. So much of your life was taken from you. The law let you down."

"But you didn't." Dante looked over, his curiosity stirring. Gaetano had told him about the search for him, begun so long ago. "You looked for me. You tried to get witnesses. You made those baptismal lists. You knocked on doors. You went to *prison* for me. You did so much, and I thank you. But I have to ask, *why?*"

Gaetano smiled. "Because it was the right thing to do. It wasn't me anyway. It was Saint Paul. He worked through me."

Dante didn't reply, since he didn't know Saint Paul as well as Gaetano.

"Your family's house is on the next block." Gaetano slowed his step, then stopped, astonished. "Wait, I know this house! I stopped here. I didn't recognize the name when you said it, before. I remember now, I *met* your mother!"

"You did?" Dante gasped. "What does she look like?"

"She's beautiful, but she had sorrowful eyes. I knew something was wrong. I asked but they hid that you had been kidnapped. She must have been afraid."

"Poor woman." Dante's pulse quickened. He realized he was only steps away from his mother and his father. The house looked vaguely familiar from the outside. "What was my father like? Was he nice?"

"I didn't meet him. My old boss, Don Matteo, and his wife, Donna Angelina, were there. Your mother is their niece."

"How funny."

"The more you know about Palermo, you'll see it's not. The privileged travel in the same circles. Let's go!"

Dante and Gaetano approached the house, which had a carriage and a mule cart in front. Laborers were loading the cart with boxes of books, and a well-dressed older man emerged from the house next to an attractive older woman in a black dress.

Gaetano waved to get their attention. "Don Matteo, Donna Angelina! Remember me, Gaetano Catalano?"

"You're out of prison, Gaetano?" Don Matteo looked over, frowning as they reached them. "Leave me alone. I have nothing to say to you."

Donna Angelina's lovely face fell. "Gaetano, I was so disappointed in you."

Gaetano stiffened. "We're here to see Signore Michangeli and Signora Catena."

Don Matteo's frowned. "Just go away. Our niece passed away six months ago. We're closing the house to put it up for sale."

Donna Angelina's eyes filmed, her mouth turning down. "Our Vera, what a loss."

No. Dante felt it as a stomach blow. His mother was dead. He had lost the chance to see her again, to know her at all. Tears sprang to his eyes.

Gaetano crossed himself. "I'm so sorry. You have my deepest sympathies. Nevertheless, we should talk to Signore Michangeli."

Don Matteo shook his head. "Why? Gaetano, what do you want with my family?"

Gaetano hesitated, then gestured to Dante. "This young man is Dante Michangeli."

Don Matteo's hooded eyes flew open with joy. "This is *Dante*? Gaetano, you found Dante? How?"

"*Our Dante?*" Donna Angelina threw open her arms, wrapped them around Dante, and pulled him into her perfumed embrace. "Thank you, Holy Virgin Mother! Our prayers have been answered! After all this time!"

"Dante!" Don Matteo hugged him, too.

Dante felt engulfed, trying to regain his bearings. "Don Matteo and Donna Angelina, how wonderful to meet you both. Is my father home?"

Don Matteo's eyes brimmed. "Dante, come inside."

BOXES WERE STACKED HERE AND there in the empty apartment, but Dante recognized the layout. There was a wall covered in blue silk and bronze sconces he remembered, and his father's piano was wrapped in white cloth. Rugs had been rolled up, and glass-front cabinets stacked with dishes that had pink flowers on the rim, which he remembered. The chandelier twinkled above the table, which had mesmerized him when he was little, its crystals like tiny stars in the darkness.

More teary hugs and kisses were exchanged, then Dante and Gaetano sat down with Don Matteo and Donna Angelina at the dining room table. Donna Angelina took Dante's hand, her hooded eyes glistening. "Dante, I'm so sorry, I have more terrible news. We heard your father passed away about ten years ago. He fell ill, in Naples."

"No, no." Dante felt rocked, after hearing about his mother. It didn't seem possible. He had no family but this old couple. His heart ached for all he had lost.

Gaetano put an arm around him. "I'm sorry, Dante. This is a shock, and it will take time to absorb. We can talk to Baron Pisani about it when we get back. Lucia, too, after she returns."

Dante nodded, numbly. He tried to think. "Still, I want to know about my parents. I remember some things, but not all. What were they like?"

Donna Angelina smiled shakily. "Your mother was like a daughter to me, sweet and loving. We were confidantes, since my sister was dead and I had only sons. Your eyes are so much like Vera's, and seeing you, I feel as if I'm seeing her again."

"I remembered my eyes are like hers." Dante could feel his mother's presence in the room, full of love. He even thought he detected a trace of her perfume, but that could have been his imagination. "And my father?"

"Adamo was a good man with a carefree heart. He was an excellent musician. He could play a variety of instruments, but he loved the piano."

"I thought so." Dante's gaze turned to the piano and a memory came to him. "I remember sitting next to him on the bench, but my feet didn't reach the pedals. He put empty boxes on them, and it worked."

"That sounds like him. He was so creative, so inventive."

Gaetano patted Dante's back, pained. "Dante, this is a lot of sadness to absorb, all at once. I'm sorry about your parents. I just wish I'd found you sooner."

"That's okay," Dante rushed to say, not wanting him to feel bad.

Don Matteo interjected, "Gaetano, I remember the day you came here, so long ago. Am I to understand you were knocking on doors to find Dante? And if so, why?"

Gaetano hesitated. "Yes, I remember that day. We talked in the alley."

"You can say it, I terminated you. You asked me if Dante was kidnapped from the Saint Rosalia festival, and I had to lie. We were told to, by the kidnapper. He sent us a ransom note, warning us that he'd kill Dante if we told anyone. We followed the instructions and paid the ransom, but the kidnapper didn't give Dante back. We heard nothing further after we paid." Don Matteo sighed. "Honestly, Gaetano, I couldn't risk Dante's life." Don Matteo turned to Dante. "I'm sorry, Dante. If I had told Gaetano the truth, we would have gotten you back. You would have enjoyed a happy childhood."

Donna Angelina dabbed her eyes with a lacy handkerchief. "We were wrong to keep the secret. We should have told the truth."

Dante's heart went out to them. "I don't blame either of you. I understand why you didn't say anything."

Don Matteo heaved a heavy sigh. "Nevertheless, it was a grievous error. Gaetano, how did you find Dante?"

Gaetano told the story while Dante, Don Matteo, and Donna Angelina listened. By the time he was finished, Don Matteo looked grave and Donna Angelina was teary again.

Don Matteo shook his head. "Gaetano, we can't thank you enough. If you want your old job back, you're welcome. Bartolomeo is still there, but I've learned he can be . . . annoying."

Gaetano smiled. "Thank you. I'll consider it."

Donna Angelina wiped her eyes. "Thank you, Gaetano. It means everything to have Dante back. But . . ."

"But what?" Gaetano cocked his head.

Dante blinked, wondering.

Donna Angelina fell abruptly silent, wiping her eyes.

Don Matteo looked over at her. "Dear?"

Donna Angelina looked back at Don Matteo. "Matteo, I believe we should be honest with Dante. We've just seen how keeping a secret can lead to tragedy."

"Yes, I agree." Don Matteo nodded, his lower lip buckling. "Perhaps it's time for the truth. But I think it's your place to tell him, not mine."

"Tell me what?" Dante interjected, newly urgent. "I've been kept in the dark for too long."

Donna Angelina shifted in her chair. "You see, Dante, your parents had problems in their marriage. Your father wasn't Sicilian. His people were from Naples, and he always went back and forth to the mainland. The marriage faltered, and well, your mother had an affair." Donna Angelina patted Dante's hand. "I'll come to my point. The man you know as your father isn't your natural father."

"What?" Dante recoiled, stunned. "Who's my natural father?"

Donna Angelina shook her head. "He's nobility, I'm fairly certain, but we don't know for sure. I was close to your mother, and she told me he gave her gifts and money. She fell in love with him, and he loved her, too, or at least she thought he did, until it went wrong." Donna Angelina began sniffling again. "Horribly, I believe your natural father was behind your kidnapping."

"No!" Dante reeled. "My natural father had me *kidnapped*? Why?"

Gaetano looked aghast but didn't interrupt.

"I know, it's awful." Donna Angelina held her handkerchief to her teary eye. "Your mother told me she wanted him to leave his wife, but he refused. The matter got ugly, and one day, she threatened to tell his wife. He cut her off, and the next thing we knew, you were kidnapped from the festival. We suspected he paid someone to abduct you, since you were proof of his infidelity." Donna Angelina wiped her eyes, leaving pinkish streaks. "After you were kidnapped, your mother told Adamo that you weren't his son, and the marriage broke up. He went back to Naples, and your mother spent the rest of her life praying you were alive. She died of a weak heart, which could no longer bear her burden of guilt and grief."

Dante shook his head, agonized. He could feel his lips part. He had no idea what to say, so he didn't say anything.

"Dante, your parents may be gone, but you're not alone. Don Matteo and I are your family. You must come and live with us. We have a beautiful palazzo, and you'll meet our children, your cousins. They're your family, too." Donna Angelina touched Dante's cheek tenderly. "The past belongs in the past. We have you back, that's all that matters. We'll take care of you. We love you."

Don Matteo nodded. "Yes, Dante, please, come home with us. You have a full life ahead of you. We'll get you tutors, and someday you can become a lawyer. You can even work alongside Gaetano, if he rejoins my firm. It's time for you to be happy."

"But what about my natural father?" Dante asked, beginning to seethe inside, feeling like Monster again. "I want to know who he is. He stole me from my mother, he ruined her life. And the man I called Papa, too. I loved him, whether he was my natural father or not."

"You don't want to lose more of your life, do you?" Donna Angelina's eyes brimmed anew. "You're young. You can live with us, find a girl, and start your own family. That's what your parents would have wanted. They adored you."

"Dante, she's right," Don Matteo added. "Come home with us."

Dante's heart darkened, and his disturbed gaze fell on the boxes, packed to go. He spotted something glinting inside one of them, recognizing it instantly. He crossed the room and slid the thing from its box. "Durendal, my old sword," he said, waving it back and forth. "My mother saved it all this time."

"Durendal?" Gaetano stood up. "You mean, from *The Song of Roland*?"

"You know that book?" Dante turned around, surprised.

"Every boy grows up reading it. I read it to my boys." Gaetano eyed

Dante, his compassion plain. "You've heard so much terrible news, more than I imagined. What are you thinking?"

Donna Angelina nodded, weepy. "Please, Dante, come with us. You're all I have left of my niece."

Don Matteo met Dante's eye with affection. "She's right, Dante. Please come with us."

Dante could see their offer was kind, but he couldn't choose kindness. Anger and resentment hardened his heart, empowering him in a dark way. He had been a monster once, and he would be one again.

Dante straightened. "Don Matteo and Donna Angelina, thank you, but I'm not ready to go home with you." He turned to Gaetano. "I want to find my natural father. I want him to account for what he did to me and my family."

Gaetano nodded. "Then I'm with you."

Dante remembered Count Roland's battle cry: "*Mountjoy!*" he said gravely, raising his sword.

CHAPTER SEVENTY-FIVE

A pergola filtered sunshine over the table in the courtyard, and Franco had called a breakfast meeting of the *capi* of the Fiorvanti family, in the wake of Bruna's murder. He had taken to heart Signora Esposito's advice, if not her threat to quit, and he was going to restore the shaken loyalty of his men. His *capi* had eaten their fill, and now it was time to put more bread on their table.

Franco stood up. "Gentlemen, good morning. Thank you again for your condolences at Donna Bruna's funeral. This is a difficult time, and I appreciate your sympathy."

"You're welcome," one of the *capi* replied, and the others joined in. "We're sorry for your loss."

"We have a family business, but it's not always about business. Today, it's about family. I called you here to tell you something personal. What I saw at the funeral opened my eyes. I saw each and every one of you, and your wives, grieving with Don Roberto and me. It made me appreciate you, anew."

Heads nodded around the table.

"The success of the Fiorvanti family is due to you. So I've decided to increase the percentage of your shares, from now on. You will keep an additional ten percent on the fees you collect, going forward. This extra payment will come out of my share, not Don Roberto's. I want you to know how much I appreciate your loyalty."

"Thank you, Don Franco!" The *capi* erupted into applause, and Franco could see that the gesture, and the money, had done the trick. But today would be his easiest hurdle, and Roberto's army would come later.

Franco smiled. "Men, we prosper together in the Fiorvanti family. That's what I want you to know, after this tragic event. We're heartbroken to see my beloved brother in such grief. When he comes home, we'll help him put this behind him. We'll go forward into the future, to even greater success."

"*Bravo!*" the *capi* chorused. "Thank you!"

Franco opened his arms. "You're welcome! And now, let's get to work!"

"SEBASTIANO!" FRANCO CAUGHT UP WITH him by the purple bougainvillea beside the villa.

"Yes?" Sebastiano turned, and if he harbored any ill will over the lie he'd told about Franco's whereabouts, he hid it better than Signora Esposito. His expression showed his characteristic reserve, which Franco valued. Sebastiano had dark eyes and a strong nose and mouth, but his features never betrayed his emotions.

"How do you think our meeting went?"

"Very well, Don Franco." Sebastiano nodded, and his black curls blew in the breeze. "Thank you for the increase. It was very generous of you, and everyone was delighted, as they should be."

"I have more in store for you." Franco clapped him on the arm. "We go back a long time. I remember hiring you on the piazza that day. You were a skinny orphan, but stronger and smarter than all of them."

"I had to be."

"I know." Franco's regard for Sebastiano had increased over the years.

The *capo* didn't hesitate to carry out even the most ruthless order, and Franco would never want him as an enemy. "Sebastiano, I need to confide in one man, above all others. I always have Don Roberto, but I need someone directly involved with my side of the business. I need a *consigliere*, a counselor. I want that man to be you."

Sebastiano's dark eyes flared briefly. "Don Franco, I'm at your disposal."

"Excellent, then." Franco extended a hand, and Sebastiano shook it, smiling in his tight way.

"I'm honored."

Franco knew he was making the right decision, even if wasn't for the right reason. "Now, let me tell you what I have planned for tonight. It's highly unusual. . . ."

EVENING CAME QUICKLY, AND THE courtyard behind the villa was transformed to host a dinner of a very different kind. It was only for women. Elvira sat at the head of the table, and the guests were the wives of Roberto's top soldiers. The latest delicacies had been served, the swordfish glazed with blood orange, tuna with lemons and parsley, and breast of chicken with sweet Marsala wine, bottled in the nearby town of the same name.

Franco was out of sight, watching from the window. Wives were rarely invited anywhere alone, but he had gotten permission from their husbands, who worked at night anyway. Their children made a racket in the living room, eating with Franco's children. The wives had almost finished their meal, and they talked animatedly, each in her best black dress, still mourning Donna Bruna.

Signora Esposito nodded to Franco, cueing him. He left the house and entered the courtyard, smoothing down his dark suit. The wives quieted as he approached, glancing at each other and pursing their lips. He could feel their tension, and he braced himself for his performance, which had to be convincing.

Franco reached Elvira and kissed her cheek, catching a trace of her floral perfume. "Good evening, dear."

"Franco." Elvira looked up at him with a smile he knew well, recognizing him for who he was, her powerful husband.

Franco eyed the women around the table. "Ladies, thank you for coming to our home. I hope you enjoyed your dinner, and I will speak only briefly. We remain in mourning for Donna Bruna, but Donna Elvira wanted you to come to dinner tonight, as a personal thank-you, from us."

The wives listened, and some nodded, but none dared to speak.

"Donna Elvira and I are heartbroken by Donna Bruna's death, but no one is more heartbroken than Don Roberto and my nephew Patrizio. I think you all know how close I am to my twin, my best friend, and how much I adore Patri." Franco put his hand on Elvira's shoulder. "Donna Elvira and I will do everything possible to help them when they return. We'll give them all the love in our hearts. I have always understood the importance of family, but never more so than now."

Franco paused, and a few of the wives tilted their heads.

"I want you to know how much I appreciate the special role you take in your families, as part of the Fiorvanti family." Franco kept his hand on Elvira's shoulder. "Donna Elvira is the perfect wife and mother, and I wouldn't be successful without her love and devotion."

The wives smiled, surprised, since it was unusual for a man to make such an admission, much less the *capo di tutti capi*.

"My wife would be the first one to tell you how much I loved my mother, and how close I was to her. And whenever I step out of line, I always have my mother here, in the spirit of Signora Esposito." Franco glanced at Signora Esposito, who rolled her eyes, and the wives laughed. Franco continued, "You are the wives, you are the mothers, and you are the hearts of our families. I want you to know how much I personally appreciate you."

Signora Esposito motioned to her staff, who appeared with gifts wrapped in silvery paper and began distributing them. The wives smiled, cooed, and clucked, and it was time for Franco to go.

"I'll leave while you open these gifts, because my wife deserves the credit. She picked them out at a fine shop in town, as an everlasting token of our gratitude." Franco nodded graciously. "Thank you, again."

Franco turned and walked away to the delighted squeals of the women opening their gifts. Each box contained a necklace of the finest coral beads with an ornate gold clasp, which had cost him a small fortune. Signora Esposito assured him that women loved coral, and Elvira had agreed.

Franco was sending the wives home happy. Tonight, the talk on the pillows would go his way.

But it was only a prelude to his meeting with Roberto's men.

CHAPTER SEVENTY-SIX

"Isn't it beautiful?" Gaetano gestured with pride to La Cala, the harbor. Clipper ships with soaring masts floated on a vibrantly blue ocean. Sunshine glittered like stars on the rippling waves, and fishermen hauled in their catch or mended nets with big needles. Women haggled over fish mounded slick on large metal scales.

"Yes," Dante answered, but he was angry inside. He couldn't enjoy the sight without brooding over what could have been. He should have seen the beautiful ocean every day. He should have eaten fresh tuna instead of rotted fish heads. He should have breathed a salty breeze, not fetid air. He had no pride of place, like Gaetano. He was a stranger in his own hometown. All because of what his father had done.

Dante hadn't slept last night, shaken after meeting Don Matteo and Donna Angelina. He grieved his mother and his father, too—or, at least, the man he called Papa. Lucia still hadn't come back, though he'd called to her from the backyard. He feared she would never return and now he understood why. Everyone on the street was dark, but Lucia would always be light. He felt lost without her, which intensified his bitterness. He could have offered *her* so much more, but for his father.

Gaetano pointed. "That's the prison where I spent fifteen years."

Dante looked ahead to see a massive building like a castle, with turrets on its corners. Latticed bars covered its windows, where inmates crowded to see their families, who stood outside on boxes to reach them. "Did you hate it, like I hated the madhouse?"

"No, I had friends here and still do. They're good men, even though they've done bad things. Today I'm hoping they'll help us."

"How?"

"You'll see." Gaetano ushered Dante across the street, and the families and inmates called to him.

"Look, it's Gaetano!" "Did you bring that macaroni Maria makes?" "We miss you!"

"I miss you all!" Gaetano called back. "But today I need help! May I interrupt your visits, friends?"

"Yes, of course! We're at your disposal!"

"Thank you." Gaetano addressed them all. "Friends, if you remember the day I left, a man named One-Eye passed away. Big Feet was one of his cellmates, and his cell was on this side of the building."

"Yes, it's me, Big Feet! I remember!"

"Big Feet, when One-Eye passed, he confessed to putting a kidnapped boy in the madhouse! Remember, you heard him confess?"

"Certainly!"

"Well, I'm here to introduce my friend Dante Michangeli. Dante is the young man whom One-Eye hid in the madhouse. Poor Dante lived there his entire life, though he's as sane as you and me!"

The inmates erupted in anger. "That's terrible!" "Poor Dante!"

Dante flushed. Everyone was staring at him. The inmates kept calling to him, and their families joined the chorus.

Gaetano faced the inmates. "Here's how you can help us, friends. One-Eye told me he had a partner, and the partner kidnapped Dante from his mother at the Saint Rosalia festival. We need to figure out who One-Eye's partner was. Big Feet, back then, you didn't know him." Gaetano paused. "Friends, think about the times you spoke with One-Eye or heard him speak to other people. Maybe you saw him with family or visitors, who brought him food or merely spoke with him. Try to remember. One of you must have seen One-Eye with *some-body*."

The inmates burst into puzzled chatter. "I can't think of anyone!" "I never saw him get a visitor!" "He was a loner, a *stronzo*!"

Gaetano turned to Dante. "Dante, would you make an appeal yourself? Men who have been imprisoned hate the law and the authorities. Sometimes they have information, but they keep their mouths shut."

Dante recoiled. "But why would they tell me and not you? They love you."

"Because you're the victim." Gaetano faced him forward. "Ask them. Speak from the heart. Tell them you want to know the partner's name."

Dante faced the inmates. He'd never spoken publicly. They were all looking at him, so were their families. Sweat popped on his forehead.

Gaetano patted his back. "You can do it, son."

Dante cleared his throat. "I'm Dante and I lived in a madhouse, even though I'm not mad. I *felt* mad, and angry all the time, driven by how horrible it was inside, locked in a cell day after day. Maybe you feel that way, too. We all have lived behind bars. We know how it feels, like our lives are passing us by and there's nothing we can do."

The inmates erupted. "Yes, that's true!" "I miss my family so much!" "My mother died when I was in prison!"

"My mother did, too!" Dante blurted out. "*And* my father! I missed growing up with them because One-Eye and his partner put me in the madhouse." He noticed the mothers at the wall shedding a tear. "Gaetano tells me one of you might know the name of One-Eye's partner, but you don't want to tell the law. But I'm not the law, and you can tell me. I'm the one who was wronged. I could be you or your son. I'm no friend to the law, because it didn't save me, either. Gaetano did. He stood up for me, and now I want to stand up for myself."

Gaetano smiled, easing Dante's heart, so he continued his appeal.

"Please, if you know the name of One-Eye's partner, I'm asking you to tell me. If you're as good as Gaetano says, then you'll want to do a good thing. If you think you can help me, please speak now. I'll be grateful to you forever."

Dante fell silent, and so did everyone else. The families were hushed, and some of the women began to tear up. One of the inmates cried, too. Still, no one said anything.

An inmate broke the silence. "If you know the name, tell him!"

Suddenly everyone started shouting, inmates and families alike. "Tell him! Tell him! Tell him!" They clapped to each word like a drumbeat. "Tell him, tell him!"

"I think I know who it is!" an inmate hollered over the din.

DANTE AND GAETANO STOOD ON the box to reach the window, and an old inmate pressed his grizzled face to the rough iron lattice, his knobby fingers gripping the bars. His hair was sparse and gray, his nose long and bony. They called him Pox because his skin was pockmarked, but his eyes were a sharp-edged blue.

Gaetano asked, "What do you know, Pox?"

"I was in the cell next to One-Eye's. I saw a man visit him, named Scales. His real name is Enrico Tonelli. I know him from around the harbor."

"How long ago was this?"

"I'm not sure."

"How often did Tonelli visit One-Eye?"

"I'm not sure. I saw him twice."

"Were the visits you saw close together or spread apart?"

Pox scratched his head. "Spread apart, maybe."

"Tell me more about Tonelli. How old was he?"

"I don't know."

"What did he look like?"

"Big and ugly, with a hole on the tip of his nose. That, I remember."

"Anything else you saw or heard between One-Eye and Tonelli?"

Pox mulled it over. "Tonelli worked at the harbor, but I remember I heard him say he was going to the mines."

"What mines?"

"Sulfur. I'm from out there, on my mother's side. There's a lot of sulfur mines out there, and the biggest is owned by the Marescas. My cousin used to work there. The boss is Don Bruno."

"Where's this mine?"

"Mussomeli."

CHAPTER SEVENTY-SEVEN

The night was cool and breezy, and cigarette smoke wafted from the table under the pergola. Franco had served the finest dinner, pasta with ricotta and pistachio pesto, sea bass with lemon and parsley sauce, roast chicken with couscous and mint, and an array of cheese, nuts, and sweets for dessert. But the men had eaten in virtual silence. They were Roberto's top soldiers, whose wives had come to the previous dinner. They'd thanked Franco for the coral necklaces, but the jewelry hadn't won the men over. Their stiff demeanor told him they still suspected him of Bruna's murder.

Franco stood up, and their flinty eyes and stony expressions flickered in the candlelight. "Gentlemen, thank you for coming. As I said, we all mourn the loss of Donna Bruna, the wife of our beloved Don Roberto and the mother of my nephew Patrizio. I know you love Don Roberto, but if I may say so, none of you love him as much as I do. Roberto and I are twins. The connection between us began as soon as life began." Franco gestured to his heart. "He and I feel deep love, and I hope you're reminded of it, every time you see me. I am Don Roberto, and he is me. Because this is true, you know that seeing him mourn at the funeral broke my heart. He's not only my blood, but *myself*."

The men remained impassive behind the screen of smoke.

"A long time ago, I asked Don Roberto to come to Palermo and help me build this family. He has been at my right hand every step of the way, and you have been at his. You're invaluable to our family, and Don Roberto never loses sight of that fact, nor do I." Franco allowed himself a slight frown. "Perhaps I've been remiss in not spending more time with you, but my twin is an excellent boss. I would never overstep my bounds with him. I don't tonight, either. I call you here only to speak very personally."

A few of the heads cocked, and the men looked intrigued.

"I know some of you may suspect I had something to do with Donna Bruna's murder. I swear to you now, I did not. I would never harm the wife of my brother. I would never do anything to hurt Don Roberto in any way." Franco lied with a level gaze. "I tell you the truth, and that is the truth. Don Roberto knows I had nothing to do with her murder, because he knows my soul."

The men blinked, stunned that he would discuss the matter so openly.

"But I will also tell you, I have new concerns about the Maresca family. Don Bruno has no love for me. You saw him at the funeral." Franco knew that if Signora Esposito had noticed, they had, too. "I didn't realize it was happening, but Don Bruno has been undermining me with my own twin. He's been trying to convince Roberto to leave us, move to Mussomeli, and join the Marescas in the sulfur business. Don Bruno has been doing so secretly, under the surface like a rat."

The men listened, and Franco could see they were thinking it over.

"Frankly, I underestimated the man. His family is growing in power and wealth in Mussomeli, but how long do you think he'll remain content out there, in that filthy business, when he sees how much we have in Palermo? How great our bounty in these beautiful *giardini*? How much we earn here in paradise?"

The men glanced at each other.

"Everybody knows that Palermo is the jewel in Sicily's crown. The Fiorvanti family controls Palermo. I believe Don Bruno has been trying to win over Don Roberto in order to take our business from us." Franco leaned forward, urgent. "We must unite as a family, reaffirm our loyalty to one another, and prepare for an attack by Don Bruno and the Marescas. Because that's what's going to happen next."

Franco was offering them someone to hate other than himself. Even he was starting to believe his own words. He was so convincing, he'd convinced himself.

"Don Bruno intends to take our business, and if he succeeds, I don't have to tell you what he would do. Once he takes power, he'll destroy me and Don Roberto. Don Bruno wants *war*."

Franco paused to let the word sink in, and the men started nodding. He sensed a tense undercurrent, now directed at their common enemy.

"I tell you, I wouldn't be surprised if Don Bruno *himself* had something to do with Donna Bruna's murder."

One of the men recoiled, and another shook his head.

"I see, you're asking yourself, 'Why would Don Bruno kill his own daughter?' Here's the reason. Don Bruno knew that if something happened to Donna Bruna, you would suspect me. He was trying to sow discord to weaken our family for attack. He sacrificed his own child for money and power. But his manipulations don't fool me, nor do they fool you."

Franco used the words Don Bruno had used with him, and the men mulled it over.

"Last night, my wife, Donna Elvira, gave each of your wives a coral necklace. Jewelry is a gift for women. What I give you is something more important. My loyalty. I will be loyal to you because of all you do for our family. We must be loyal to each other if we are going to defeat the Marescas." Franco took his knife, pricked his finger, then slid from his pocket a picture of Saint Rosalia. "Many years ago, you swore an oath to me and our family. I administered the oaths, but never swore one myself. Tonight, I do, to you."

Franco dripped his blood onto the holy picture, then put it to the candle flame. "I, Don Franco Fiorvanti, swear an oath of loyalty to you tonight. I promise to serve our family above all others. I will prove my honor and respect for our clan by *omertà*, my absolute silence about our family."

Franco raised his gaze to each man, in turn. Mouths dropped open and eyes glazed in the candlelight. They were astounded that their *capo di tutti capi* would humble himself before them.

"The oath I swear tonight is sacred, and if I breach it or disobey, I deserve death." Franco straightened as flame consumed the bloodied picture. Its ashes fluttered to the table. "That is my oath, to you."

"*Bravo*, Don Franco!" the men exulted. "We will fight for you and Don Roberto!" "We will defeat Don Bruno!" "We are the Fiorvantis!"

Franco savored his victory.

CHAPTER SEVENTY-EIGHT

Dante and Gaetano sat across from Baron Pisani's desk. Dante took the lead this time, filling the Baron in about Don Matteo, Donna Angelina, prison, then Renzo "One-Eye" Gentili and his partner-in-crime Enrico "Scales" Tonelli. Baron Pisani nodded and listened, and Dante finished by telling him their plans.

"Baron Pisani, we want to go to Mussomeli, find Tonelli, and make him tell us who paid him to kidnap me. We believe it was my father."

Gaetano added, "I'll protect Dante as if he were my own. We'll find Tonelli and Dante's father, then bring both men to justice."

Baron Pisani leaned back in his chair, his lips pursed. "I have grave concerns."

Dante felt his heart beat harder. "Baron Pisani, I'm driven to do it. I have to find these men. They stole my life from me. One was my *father*. I have to make them pay."

Baron Pisani eyed him. "Dante, you're talking about revenge. Gaetano is talking about justice. These are two different matters."

"No, they're not," Dante shot back.

Gaetano looked over, frowning. "Yes, they are, Dante. I'm not going to Mussomeli to kill anyone. We'll have them brought to justice."

"How, Gaetano? Who will arrest them?" Dante felt the anger building inside him. "How will we prove it? Where are the *carabinieri* out there? Why do you have any faith in them, after what happened here?"

"Those are excellent questions, and I'll find answers for them. But I used to be a lawyer and I believe in the rule of law. I'll figure it out."

"You still believe in *law*? After what it did to you? After what it did to me?"

"Nevertheless," Gaetano said, with characteristic calm, "I'm not going out there to murder anyone, nor will I help you do so."

"Why decide this now?" Dante strengthened his resolve. "I'm going to Mussomeli and I'm going to find Tonelli and my father. Then we'll discuss what to do with them. Agreed?"

Gaetano nodded gravely. "Agreed."

Baron Pisani clucked, shaking his head. "Gentlemen, I approach this from a therapeutic perspective, and my sole concern is Dante and his psyche." He turned to Dante. "I don't think this quest, as it were, is beneficial for you right now. I think it would be best if you transfer to the new hospital, allow me to treat you with moral therapy, and help you regain your mental health."

Dante felt stung. "But I'm not mad, you said so."

"But you are vulnerable."

"I *feel* up to it. I feel like I can't wait."

"You may not feel that way when you get there. What happens there can harm you further, and you're already upset. Agitated, angry. I can see it. It endangers your mental state to go."

Dante shook his head. "Baron Pisani, it endangers my mental state to stay. I can't ignore it. I can't wait another day."

"What's the difference, after all this time? I can get you more stable. Give me six months."

Dante felt it like a stab to the heart. "My mother died six months ago. If I had known about her then, I would have gotten to see her again."

Baron Pisani puckered his lower lip, his gaze softening.

"Baron Pisani, I can't allow more time to slip away. I feel as if this is unfinished business, the unfinished business of my life. Once I find my father, I can confront him." Dante glanced over at Gaetano. "I can ask him why he did what he did. I can tell him how much he hurt me. I can get answers I don't have now."

"But that confrontation may cause more trauma."

"I don't know what that word means, and I don't care. I don't want to let him get away with it—"

"Dante, give me three months, and I can help you heal—"

"I can't heal *unless* I know who I am. I can't heal *until* I know who my father is. I don't even bear his name. It's my right to know who he is, and knowing him is also knowing me. You said I should make my own choices, and I am."

Baron Pisani's bushy eyebrows sloped unhappily down.

"You can't keep me here, can you?"

"No. You're free."

Dante jumped to his feet. "Then we go, now."

Gaetano looked over in surprise, then rose. "Dante, now? I thought maybe tomorrow or the next day. We need time."

"Why? What are we waiting for?" Dante knew he was agitated, but it fueled his determination. "Gaetano, you don't have to go with me. I'll go myself. I want to go now."

Baron Pisani stood up. "What about Lucia, Dante? She's not back yet. Before, you didn't want to go in case you missed her. Now you want to leave right away?"

Dante's mouth went dry. "I didn't forget her. I'll never forget her."

"I thought you loved her. Don't you?"

"Yes," Dante answered, but he realized how dark his soul had become. "Everything's different now. What I've learned has changed me, inside. I don't feel the same. I feel like . . . I did when I was Monster."

Baron Pisani frowned. "That's *exactly* my fear. I can treat you so you don't feel that way—"

"But I *want* to feel this way. I can't feel love or light right now, and I'm no good to Lucia like this. I hope she comes back, but I can't wait another minute. Please tell her I love her."

"No, I won't. That should come from you." Baron Pisani met his eye, and Dante was struck with another realization.

"Lucia knows I love her. She knows who I am and she'll understand why I had to go. That's what love is. Love is faith."

Gaetano looked over. His gaze was troubled, but his eyes shone with new regard. "Dante, that's a beautiful definition. But I still don't think we should go tonight."

"I'm going alone then."

"Alone? You've barely been outside the madhouse."

"Then it's about time. You said you had horses. May I take one?"

Gaetano frowned. "You've never ridden a horse."

"I'll learn."

"How will you find Mussomeli? Sicily is a vast island, *truly* vast, and you can't read a map. There are few roads between here and there, only rugged terrain until you get to the mines." Gaetano shook his head. "How will you eat or drink? How will you survive?"

Dante realized the answer, with a rush of love. "Lucia told me how to live on the land, which plants to eat and which not to. About the winds, about the storms. About the *scirocco* and the *grecale*." He felt her stories coming back to him. "I know where to find water and how to avoid wolves. She taught me everything she knows."

"Hearing it is one thing, *doing* it quite another. Natural dangers are only part of the peril. There are bandits, brigands—"

"Is it worse than a madhouse?" Dante shot back. "Because if this hell didn't kill me, nothing can."

Gaetano blinked. "Okay, then I'll go with you," he said, after a moment.

Dante addressed Gaetano and Baron Pisani. "I'm grateful to you both, and I thank you. You saved me, but *this* is what I was saved *for*."

Baron Pisani's eyes glistened, too. "I respect your decision."

Gaetano nodded. "Then we go when you say."

"To Mussomeli!" Dante cried, with angry joy.

CHAPTER SEVENTY-NINE

Franco awakened to being shaken. "What?" he asked, coming out of a deep sleep in the bedroom.

"Don Franco," Sebastiano said, urgent. "You have to come downstairs."

"What's the matter?" Franco threw off the covers. Elvira was already awake, shifting upward in bed, and Sebastiano stood over them, silhouetted by light from the hallway.

"It's best if you see for yourself."

Elvira started to rise. "Should I come?"

"No. Stay here." Franco slipped into his robe. He headed for the door with Sebastiano. "Is Signora Esposito awake?"

"No, and I didn't wake her. This isn't for her eyes."

They flew down the staircase, across the entrance hall, and out the front door, which stood open. Standing outside was a young man leading a donkey, and lying across its back was a corpse. It was facedown, its arms flopped over one side of the animal and its legs over the other. The dead man had been beaten about the head, and blood matted his hair, stiff and black in the moonlight.

The stench told Franco the body wasn't fresh, and if the bloodied corpse disturbed the boy, it didn't show. He looked about thirteen, and his build was skinny, undoubtedly due to hunger, which made his dark eyes look sunken. His manner was matter of fact, and he wore the rags of a peasant.

Franco asked him, "Boy, what's the meaning of this?"

"I was paid to bring this body to you, Don Franco."

"Who paid you?"

"A man. I don't know his name. I come from Mussomeli. He works for Don Bruno."

"Don Bruno?" Franco's anger flared, and the boy recoiled in fear.

"Please, don't hurt me. I did it for the money."

"Relax. Who is he?" Franco gestured to the dead man.

"I don't know. I don't know anything, I swear."

Franco crossed to the corpse, grabbed a handful of its matted hair, and lifted up the head, recognizing its battered face. The realization sickened him. The dead man was Arturo Provenzano, the grandson of Gabriele Provenzano, the old man Franco had hired to falsely confess to Bruna's murder. Franco had met Arturo when he made the deal with Gabriele.

Franco's mind raced. Arturo's murder could only mean that Don Bruno knew Franco had killed Bruna. Roberto would know, too, that his beloved twin had killed his beloved wife. Franco felt his heart being ripped in half.

The boy held out a folded piece of paper in a trembling hand. "Don Franco, I have a note for you from Don Bruno. I don't know what it says. I can't read."

Franco opened the note, and his mouth went dry. The note was in Don Bruno's messy scrawl. It read:

I HAVE VIOLETTA

Franco masked his horror. Don Bruno and Roberto knew he had killed Bruna, so they were taking revenge on Violetta. Roberto was joining forces with Don Bruno against him.

Franco flashed back to his dinner speech to Roberto's men. The war he had fabricated had just become a reality. Violetta's life was in danger. His family and his business were in danger. Everything he had built in the Conca d'Oro was in danger.

His thoughts flew in every direction, like birds in panicked flight. He told himself to remain calm, and suddenly a plan came to him, all of a piece.

"Sebastiano, bury the body and water the donkey." Franco turned to the boy. "Help him and keep your mouth shut."

"I will, Don Franco. Please don't hurt me—"

"Calm down. You'll be well paid."

"Don Franco, thank you!"

But Franco was already hurrying inside the villa.

AN HOUR LATER, FRANCO HAD everybody in place, summoned to the villa for an emergency. All of his *capi* were present with every available man, as were all of Roberto's men. The Fiorvantis packed the courtyard behind the villa, spilling over the floral border into the rows between the lemon trees. Flaming torches flickered on their grim expressions and their guns.

Franco estimated that two hundred armed men stood before him, which had to outnumber the Marescas. Roberto would have only the Maresca clan to rely on, having been unable to summon his own men from the Conca d'Oro without tipping Franco off. Franco would also have the element of surprise, since Roberto would never expect his own men to ride against him.

"Gentlemen." Franco stood atop the table to be seen and heard. "I summoned you from your beds to tell you terrible news. Before I do, I admit that even though I predicted Don Bruno would move against us, I didn't know he would stoop so low."

The men exchanged quizzical looks, and murmuring rippled through the crowd.

"I have in my hand a note delivered to me tonight, from Don Bruno." Franco held up the piece of notepaper. "I'll read it to you, but brace yourselves for a terrible shock."

The men leaned closer. A hush came over them, and Franco unfolded the piece of paper.

"You can't see it from where you are, but I'll read it to you. The note says, 'I have Roberto.' See for yourself these awful words!" Franco held up the note, which he had forged, copying Don Bruno's handwriting exactly:

I HAVE ROBERTO

"*Madonna!*" the men erupted, electrified. "Don Roberto's been abducted!" "Don Bruno will kill him!" "We have to save him!" Franco's men raised fists and guns. Roberto's soldiers raged for the blood of Don Bruno.

"Yes!" Franco added fuel to the fire of their anger. "Don Bruno will kill Don Roberto! Don Bruno will kill my brother, my twin! We cannot let him! They'll have to kill all of us first! We'll have the blood of Don Bruno and his men! We'll kill each and every one of the filthy Marescas! We'll save Don Roberto!"

"Yes! Yes! Yes!" the men chanted, hoisting fists, guns, and clubs. Fury reddened their faces. Roberto's right-hand man, a muscleman named Mauro, was angriest of all.

"This is *war*!" Franco hollered. "We'll save Don Roberto! We'll protect ourselves and our families! We'll save our wives and children! We'll defend our business and everything we have here! This land! Our homes! Our *giardini*! Our family!"

"Yes, yes, yes!" the men shouted, whipped into a frenzy.

"We need your bravery! We need your loyalty! You are men of honor! Prove it tonight!"

"Yes!" the men shouted louder, firing into the sky, sending birds flapping in terror.

"I'll lead you in battle! We'll rescue my twin, and we'll destroy Don Bruno and the filthy Marescas!"

The men fired again, and gunshots filled the night. Ferrous smoke from the guns and oily torches billowed in the darkness.

"This will be our battle flag!" Franco waved the forged note. "We are the Fiorvantis! Now, to Mussomeli!"

"To Mussomeli!" the men cried, shooting into the smoke.

CHAPTER EIGHTY

Lucia crouched at the entrance to her cave, as night fell. The air was still, and the mouse family watched her from their ledge. Every night, she wrestled with herself, trying to decide whether to go back to Dante at the madhouse. She missed him, but she didn't want to get killed and she didn't want to kill anybody else.

She watched the sky darken, and the stars began to shine, each one coming to life, which was usually the time Dante called for her. Her ears pricked up, anticipating the sound. He hadn't called yet tonight, and it worried her. As long as he was calling her, he was safe, and the thought eased her aching heart.

Suddenly Lucia heard someone calling her, but it wasn't Dante. She thought her ears were playing tricks on her. She waited for the call, which came again.

"Lucia!" a man called, but she didn't recognize the voice.

Lucia jumped to her feet. If Dante wasn't calling her, it had to mean he had been harmed, or was gone.

She slipped her bag over her shoulder and hurried from the cave.

The mouse family watched her go.

LUCIA STOOD BEHIND A TREE and peered through the break in the wall behind the madhouse. The doctor was standing beside a small wooden table with a candelabra on top, his white coat bright in the gloom. She realized he must have been the one calling her.

Lucia shouted, "Where's Dante?"

"You, thank God! I'm Baron Pisani! Please come in!"

"Where is he? Did you hurt him?"

"No, I would never. Come in, I'll explain."

"I won't come *unless* you explain!"

"Look, a gift for you!" Baron Pisani showed her a box wrapped in shiny yellow paper.

"All I want is to see Dante. I have to know he's safe."

Baron Pisani set down the gift. "Lucia, don't be afraid. I know what you look like."

Lucia's face went hot. "Tell me where Dante is."

"He left to find his father."

Lucia blinked, not completely surprised. She knew it was true that Dante wanted to find his parents.

"Lucia, I answered you, so please come inside. He loves you, he told me to tell you."

Lucia softened. She knew Dante loved her, but it was reassuring to hear, and Dante must have trusted Baron Pisani to tell him so. She couldn't decide whether to come out from behind the tree, but Baron Pisani had kept his side of the bargain and she was a woman of her word.

And she could always kill him if she had to.

LUCIA HAD NEVER BEEN INSIDE such a house, which was strange indeed. There was a table and two chairs opposite. Books were everywhere, and pictures, official certificates, and a drawing of a building hung on the wall. She had no idea why anybody would live here, without a bed or a brazier for cooking, but that was her least important question.

"Baron Pisani, where's Dante?"

"Allow me to explain," Baron Pisani began, and he told her how Dante had come to the madhouse so long ago, then how a lawyer named Gaetano had helped him learn about his mother and father, now both dead, and also the horrible news that his father wasn't his natural father, and his natural father probably had him kidnapped and put in the madhouse.

Baron Pisani spoke with a calm demeanor that made Lucia trust him. His words rang true, and his compassion for Dante was plain. Remarkably, he didn't seem bothered by her color, so she began to relax. By the time he finished the story, she realized that he had gained Dante's confidence and might deserve hers, too.

"Poor Dante." Lucia felt heartsick for him.

Baron Pisani pushed the shiny gold box across the desk. "Now, please accept my gift."

"Thank you." Lucia picked it up, preoccupied by thoughts of Dante. "This is very pretty."

Baron Pisani blinked. "Open it."

"Why?"

Baron Pisani smiled. "The gift is inside. Tear the paper off."

Lucia took the paper off carefully, thinking of its many uses, since she never wasted anything. She unwrapped the paper and underneath was a box filled with tissue paper, for which she had many other uses. At the bottom of the box was something she had never seen before. "What's this?"

"They're dark spectacles. I had them made for you in Palermo. Allow me." Baron Pisani came around the desk, plucked the dark spectacles from the box, and leaned toward her.

Lucia recoiled reflexively.

"I'm not going to hurt you. I'm going to put them on you."

Lucia stayed still, and Baron Pisani hooked each side of the spectacles over her ears, then situated them on her face.

"They fit you perfectly! How do they feel?"

"Good." Lucia peered at him through the spectacles. "They make everything dark."

"Exactly. Wear them outside in the daytime. Here, let me put them away. You don't need them inside." Baron Pisani unhooked the spectacles and returned them to the box. "I think you'll like wearing them, and your eyes won't hurt in the sun."

"How did you know my eyes hurt in the sun?"

"It's common in people with your condition."

Lucia's mouth went dry. "What do you mean by 'my condition'?"

Baron Pisani's expression softened, and he leaned against the desk. "I have done some research, and I believe you have a medical condition that's congenital, which means you were born with it. That's why your skin is devoid of pigment, or color."

Lucia felt stunned. "You mean why I'm so white?"

"Yes, it's a medical condition. You were born that way, as some people are. Very few, but it's not unheard of. I found a case or two in the medical papers."

"Are they in Palermo?"

"No, in England. I couldn't find a documented case in Sicily."

Lucia didn't know whether to be sad or happy. "But my mother said it's because I'm blessed by God."

"You've been blessed by God in many ways, but your skin color isn't one of them. Your mother couldn't have known that. You'd have to be in the medical field to know." Baron Pisani hesitated. "Unfortunately, your condition can't be cured."

Lucia had no problem with her color, but other people did, and they made their problem hers.

"Lucia, I know how difficult it's been for you. I know your life has been threatened and that's why you defend yourself so readily. I know people might think you're a ghost, devil, angel, or a magical being. In fact, you're a woman of many talents. Among them, throwing a knife with deadly accuracy." Baron Pisani smiled. "Assuming you meant to kill my textbook, not me."

"Yes." Lucia smiled back, liking him.

"You're as delightful as Dante told me. You helped him very much.

He began to trust people, starting with you." Baron Pisani beamed, and Lucia warmed, realizing that she and Baron Pisani shared an affection for Dante.

"Baron Pisani, you said he left with a man named Gaetano to find his father, but where to? Palermo?"

"No, Mussomeli."

"What? That's so far away!" Lucia leapt to her feet and put her spectacles in her bag. "Why didn't you stop him?"

"I tried to—"

"Can you get me a horse? A fast one?"

PART FOUR

I am not prepared just now to say to what extent I believe in a physical hell in the next world, but a sulfur mine in Sicily is about the nearest thing to hell that I expect to see in this life.

— BOOKER T. WASHINGTON, *THE MAN FARTHEST DOWN: A RECORD OF OBSERVATION AND STUDY IN EUROPE*

What I tell you in the dark, say in the light, and what you hear whispered, proclaim on the housetops.

—MATTHEW 10:26–27

CHAPTER EIGHTY-ONE

Franco and the Fiorvantis raced across Sicily on horseback, two hundred armed men driven by bloodlust. They rode day and night, reaching the foothills of Mussomeli before dawn. They stopped in the vicinity of Don Bruno's villa, which was set off by itself among dry land that grew only hardy vegetation. They concealed themselves behind a screen of prickly pear cactus, the horses tossing their manes and jigging on nervous legs.

Franco caught his breath, his chest heaving. He was playing a risky game, given his lie. The Fiorvantis thought they were rescuing Roberto, not Violetta. Franco would have to improvise. He wheeled Arabo around to face the men, each sweaty face alive with anger.

"Fiorvantis, attention! When I give the order, we charge the house. The Marescas will be ready for us, but we outnumber them. Kill any man who moves! Show no mercy! Remember they'll kill Don Roberto! If Don Bruno's in the villa, leave him to me! The filthy Marescas end, here and now! This is our moment! Ready?"

"Yes, Don Franco!" The men hoisted their guns. "At your command!"

"Fiorvantis!" Franco raised his gun high.

"Fiorvantis!" the men chorused.

"Now, men! *Vai, vai!*" Franco wheeled around, kicking Arabo forward. They accelerated to a full gallop and charged across the countryside toward Don Bruno's. The villa zoomed closer and closer, surrounded by a low stone wall.

Marescas popped up from behind, firing. Franco and the Fiorvantis fired back, jumping the wall. More Marescas ran from the villa, firing back, but the Fiorvantis mowed them down with *lupare* and pistols. The fusillade rang out, unceasing. Bullets found their targets. Agonized shouts and screams filled the air.

The Marescas aimed at Franco, but Franco fired back, hitting one on his way to the villa. Sebastiano and Mauro galloped at his sides, shooting anyone who raised a rifle to him. The Marescas were dropping everywhere. They hadn't expected Franco to come with Roberto's men, too.

Franco, Sebastiano, and Mauro shot their way inside the villa and killed the men surrounding Don Bruno and Pino. Their pistols clattered to the floor. Pino returned fire, providing cover for Don Bruno, who tried to run out the back door.

"Take them alive!" Franco shot Don Bruno in the leg, bringing him down in the dining room. Don Bruno cried out in pain, trying to crawl away.

Meanwhile Pino fired, hitting Sebastiano in the shoulder. Roberto's man Mauro fired and hit Pino in the side.

"Bruno!" Franco leapt from Arabo, caught Don Bruno by the collar, and flipped him over, drilling his pistol in his cheek. "Where's Roberto? Is Violetta with him?"

"You'll never find them!" Don Bruno writhed in pain. "You killed Bruna! You killed my daughter!"

"Tell me where they are!" Franco shouted, spitting with fury.

"I hope Roberto kills her! I hope he kills *you*!"

Boom! Franco shot Don Bruno, then whirled around, knowing Roberto's man Mauro would be shocked, having just learned the truth.

"Don Franco?" Mauro asked, horrified. "Did Don Bruno say *you* killed Donna Bruna?"

Boom! Franco grabbed a pistol from the floor and shot him in the chest. Mauro fell off his horse, dead when he hit the floor.

Sebastiano had a pistol on Pino, who lay bleeding from his side.

"Pino!" Franco grabbed Pino by his bloodied shirt. "Where are Roberto and Violetta? Tell me or I'll kill you!"

"You'll never find them!"

"Tell me!" Franco pistol-whipped Pino, breaking his nose, which exploded in blood. "Tell me!"

"I never will! Kill me!"

"Have it your way!" Franco struck him again and again with the pistol, sending blood flying until Pino emitted his last breath.

"Sebastiano." Franco stood up, covered with blood. His chest heaved. His mind raced like a runaway horse. "Say nothing of what you just heard. The men don't know it's Violetta we're rescuing. They think it's Roberto."

"Understood, Don Franco." Sebastiano nodded. His shoulder wound was superficial, grazing his flesh.

"Roberto has Violetta and he's using her to lure me to him. The question is, where would they hide? It's mining country, so it's logical to hide in a mine."

"Yes, and Don Roberto knows the area better than we do."

"Right. Don Bruno owns the biggest mine, but they wouldn't go there, it's too obvious." Franco thought aloud. "They couldn't use a working mine, either. I think they'd go to an abandoned mine, one that's isolated. I saw some on the way."

"I did, too."

"I bet Don Bruno would have a map of the local mines, somewhere in here. Start looking. Turn this place upside down. I'm going out to talk to the men." Franco touched his arm, leaving a bloody fingerprint. Sebastiano left to look for the map, and Franco led the horses outside and scanned the scene.

The shooting was over, the Fiorvanti victory clear. The Marescas had been slaughtered, lying dead on the dry ground in front of Don Bruno's villa. Only a few Fiorvantis had been killed. The Fiorvantis turned to Franco as he emerged from the villa. Their stricken expressions showed that they feared the worst, since Roberto wasn't with him. The gunsmoke began to clear, revealing Mussomeli atop a nearby mountain, with its cluster of red-tiled houses, a church dome, and an abandoned castle.

Franco raised his bloodied hands. "Men, victory belongs to the Fiorvantis, but Roberto wasn't inside. Don Bruno was, and he's dead now. Pino is dead, too. I killed them because they refused to tell me where Roberto was."

"*Bravo*, Don Franco!" the Fiorvantis shouted, raising their guns. "Don Roberto needs us now!"

Franco waved them into silence. "But I have terrible news. We lost one of our best. Don Bruno killed Mauro!"

"No!" The Fiorvantis erupted in outrage, especially Roberto's men. "Not Mauro!"

Franco waited for the shouting to subside. "Mauro gave his life to rescue Don Roberto! We can't have let Mauro die in vain! We have to find Don Roberto!"

"Yes!" The Fiorvantis hoisted their guns. One man called out, "How will we find Don Roberto?"

"I have a plan!" Franco answered, though he'd changed his mind. "They're hiding Don Roberto, and the most logical place is in an abandoned mine. Sebastiano is looking for a map."

"Excellent thinking, Don Franco!" "That's what I would do!" "We saw some of them on the ride here!"

Sebastiano appeared with a rolled-up map. "Don Franco, I found it."

"*Bravo*, Sebastiano." Franco took the map, walked to a clearing, and unrolled it on the ground, weighing it down with two rocks. The map looked homemade and was roughly topographical, showing the location of Don Bruno's mine, working mines owned by other families, and abandoned mines in the area. Landmarks like Don Bruno's villa, the mountain, various large hills, and major rock formations were plain.

"Men, come look!" Franco motioned to the Fiorvantis. "This map will tell us what we need to know, and there are landmarks if you can't read."

The Fiorvantis gathered around, murmuring among themselves while Franco picked up a sharp rock and scratched three lines across the map, then three lines down, dividing the search area into nine squares.

"Men, I'll arrange you into nine groups. Each group will be assigned a square to search for Don Roberto. You'll take a look at your square and note its relationship to landmarks such as the villa, the mountain, the rock formations, and the like. Understand?"

"Yes, it's orderly!" the Fiorvantis chimed in. "We'll find Don Roberto in no time!"

One man called out, "Don Franco, which group will you join?"

"I'll ride from one group to the next, going back and forth to see if you've found Don Roberto. I may even head up the mountain to take in the entire vista." Franco straightened. "Fiorvantis, I place the life of my beloved Robo in your hands. I have absolute faith in you."

"Thank you, Don Franco!" "We'll rescue Don Roberto!" "We are the Fiorvantis!"

"Now, men, let's go! We haven't a moment to lose!"

CHAPTER EIGHTY-TWO

Dante and Gaetano left Palermo on horseback, galloping through the Conca d'Oro in the darkness. The dirt road past the lemon groves was rocky, pitted, and rutted, and Dante bounced along on a bay horse named Toto.

"Dante, put your heels down." Gaetano looked over from atop Argent, a gray Thoroughbred.

Dante complied, and soon got the hang of riding, moving with the rhythm of the horse. They passed *giardino* after *giardino*, and he marveled at the vastness of the open space. He was completely free, a revelation that would have made his heart soar, but his soul had darkened. "How much longer to Mussomeli?"

"It's in the next province south, Caltanissetta. We'll have to stop and water the horses."

"Can't we go any faster?"

"How?" Gaetano looked over, his smile faint in the moonlight. His hair blew back, and his cravat had come undone. "This terrain is hard and only gets harder. We can't risk injuring the horses."

"Are you absolutely sure this is the shortest route?"

Gaetano nodded. The route went through the rugged countryside and the foothills of the Sicani Mountains, and Dante had been astonished to see that Sicily was so large on the map. He didn't know anything about his own country, as a result of his father's wrongdoing. The revelation embittered him further.

Dante returned to his dark thoughts. Every stride brought him closer to Mussomeli and Enrico Tonelli, who would lead him to his father. Dante didn't know whether he wanted revenge or justice. He would decide when he got there. Lucia popped into his mind, but he couldn't think about her now. She was light, and he had become darkness itself.

The two men rode on and on, passing through Villafrati, Vicari, and finally Lecara Friddi, on the border of the province of Palermo. The elevation changed as they entered Caltanissetta province. The horses breathed with effort, and the air cooled.

Gaetano pointed out Mount Cammarata, but Dante barely looked over, singularly focused on their destination. They rode day and night through the countryside, and all around them were hills covered in brown dirt and wild grasses. Here and there were the entrances to caves, hidden in the stony faces of the hills. Most of the land was dry and uncultivated, rocky and overgrown with underbrush.

"That's Mussomeli!" Gaetano pointed at a town situated at the top of a mountain. The sky glowed faintly, silhouetting the houses, a church dome, and an old castle.

"Let's go!" Dante headed for the dirt road that zigzagged up the mountain.

"Right behind you!" Gaetano called back, rallying.

DANTE AND GAETANO ENTERED MUSSOMELI on horses exhausted from the trip. The sun was rising, shooting pinkish rays into the sky. Dark anticipation filled Dante, quickening his heartbeat. To be in the same town as Enrico Tonelli strengthened his resolve. Dante concluded that there was no difference between justice and revenge—or even if there was, he felt entitled to both.

They walked through the town on horseback, turning sharp curves and angular corners, traveling up and down grades. The cobblestone streets were lined with small stone homes, their shutters closed. Dante could hear talking inside one or two of the houses, and a yellow dog ran past, scattering a flock of pigeons.

Dante looked over at Gaetano. "Where should we start looking for Tonelli?"

"I gave it some thought." Gaetano smoothed damp hair from his forehead. "Mussomeli is small, and everyone goes to morning Mass, so we might try there first. We can begin asking around and see if anybody knows him. The church is just ahead." Gaetano motioned down the curving street. "I came here for a friend's wedding, and it's a lovely church, called Madonna dei Miracoli."

They continued downhill, and Dante could see a piazza where families were gathering in front of a church. They socialized in groups, dressed in humble clothes, the men in old caps and the women in worn black mantillas.

Dante and Gaetano came around the front of Madonna dei Miracoli, which had a gray stone façade dominated by a tall carved door, flanked by columns covered with verdigris. Above the entrance was a single window, and the church's fluted cornice was topped with a cross gilded in sunshine.

Gaetano dismounted. "Dante, I'll do the talking, okay?"

"Okay." Dante dismounted and held the horses, and Gaetano approached a group of townspeople with a friendly smile. The townspeople eyed them with curiosity, giving the impression that few strangers came here.

"Excuse me," Gaetano said, introducing himself. "I'm sorry to bother you, my friend and I are looking for Enrico Tonelli, nicknamed Scales. Do you know where he lives?"

The townspeople fell silent and their expressions changed instantly. Eyes narrowed. Lips flattened. Frowns creased foreheads.

"Never heard of him," answered one man.

Gaetano blinked, his smile still in place. "I need to speak to him about an important matter. Are you sure you don't know where he lives?"

"We don't know him," the same man answered, placing his arm around his wife and guiding her up the stairs to the church. The rest of the men began to turn away, and the women drew their mantillas around them, taking their children by the hand.

Gaetano stopped one of the men. "Please, tell me where Tonelli lives. I won't say how I know."

The man shook his head, turning away, and the townspeople hurried into the church. Families just arriving for Mass gave Gaetano wide berth.

Dante met Gaetano's eye, and Dante saw the lawyer redouble his determination. Gaetano strode up the steps to the church, where a priest was emerging to greet parishioners. He was an older man with curly white hair, steel spectacles, and worn vestments.

Gaetano introduced himself to the priest. "Father Casagrandi, I doubt you remember me, but we've met. I was at a wedding you performed many years ago. It was of my friend Ferdinando Cella and his wife, Donatella Borrelli, whose family is from here."

Father Casagrandi smiled. "I know the Borrelli family very well. My apologies, I don't remember you, and I admit, I'm astonished that you remember me."

"I never forget a priest." Gaetano smiled back. "You may know, the couple now lives in Palermo, where I'm from."

"Ah yes, I could tell by your accent. So how can I help you, Signore?"

"Please, call me Gaetano, and I'm here with my young friend Dante." Gaetano gestured to Dante. "We need to speak with Enrico Tonelli, nicknamed Scales. Do you know where he lives? I won't reveal to anyone that you told me."

"You may tell anyone you please. I'm not afraid of Enrico Tonelli. I answer to a power higher than the likes of him." Father Casagrandi pushed up his spectacles. "But Tonelli doesn't live in town anymore. Neither do any of his people. His wife left and took the children."

"Do you know where I can find him?"

"Yes, he works in Don Bruno's mine."

"Who's Don Bruno? I've heard that name."

"Don Bruno Maresca? He's the local boss, if you know what I mean. Tonelli lives at the mine, but he comes to the piazza to hire *braccianti*. I know he'll be there this morning because I saw him in town last night." Father Casagrandi winked. "A good shepherd keeps track of his flock, even the black sheep."

"Especially the black sheep," Gaetano said, and they both chuckled.

"He'll be at the piazza in an hour or so."

"Thank you, Father."

"I'll say a prayer for your endeavor. Bless you. Now, I must go." Father Casagrandi went inside the church, and Gaetano descended the steps toward Dante, who could barely contain his excitement.

"*Bravo*, Gaetano! Now we confront Tonelli!"

"No, we don't." Gaetano met his eye with new concern. "If Tonelli works for Don Bruno, we have to try a safer approach."

"How, then?"

"I'll explain over breakfast."

DANTE STOOD WITH GAETANO IN the sunny piazza, which was lined with small stone houses, their shutters open now. The town had come to life with families returning from Mass, and women headed to and from the bakery. Men took up chairs in front of the houses, rolling the first cigarettes of the day and starting card games. Children ran back and forth, kicking a ball. Two other *braccianti* waited by the tree, their raggedy clothes betraying their need for a job.

A man who could only be Enrico Tonelli swaggered into the piazza, leading a large mule. He had close-set eyes that narrowed to slits in the sunshine. His nose had a hole at the tip, and the skin on his face was dark and lined. His build was wiry, and he wore a dirty white shirt and brown pants. Faint yellow dust covered his beat-up boots.

Dante struggled to maintain his composure. He was about to meet the man who kidnapped him fifteen years ago, derailing his life. It took all of his self-control not to unleash Monster.

Tonelli pointed at Dante, even before he'd reached the piazza. "You."

"Me, what?" Dante asked, surprised.

"You want to work in the mine, right? What's your name?"

"Dante."

"You're hired, Dante. You can help our kiln men."

"My brother Gaetano needs work, too." Dante gestured to Gaetano, since they were pretending to be brothers, a story Gaetano had fabricated at the bakery.

"No to your brother." Tonelli dismissed Gaetano with a wave. "I don't need another man."

"Signore, please," Gaetano interjected quickly. "I need the job and I can do anything. Pick, carry, do office work. I can read and write—"

"Listen to that accent!" Tonelli snorted. "You literate, Palermo?"

"Yes, I was a lawyer before I went to prison."

Tonelli burst into derisive laughter. "A lawyer behind bars? You weren't a very good one then!"

"I don't disagree." Gaetano forced a chuckle.

"What'd you go in for?"

"I served fifteen years for breaking into a law office and hitting a few *carabinieri.*"

"Impressive!" Tonelli snorted. "You know, I spent time in prison myself."

"You did? Maybe we had some friends in common. Did you know Big Feet, Talks Too Much, Pox—"

"I knew Pox. Anyway, what are you two doing here?"

"We're on our way east and need to make some money. I can also keep ledgers and do bookkeeping. Or if you need legal advice, I can do that, too. I'd like to stay with my little brother."

"Okay, Palermo. You're both hired. What's your family name?"

"Catalano," Gaetano supplied.

Tonelli gestured to Argent and Toto, hitched nearby. "Are those yours?"

"Yes."

"Nice. Get on and let's go." Tonelli mounted his mule, and the other two *braccianti* rushed Tonelli, both talking at once.

"Signore, put me to use? I'm strong and I work hard!" "My family needs to eat! I'll do whatever you need done!" "Signore, Signore!"

"Get lost!" Tonelli shouted, kicking them away.

Dante and Gaetano crossed to the horses, exchanging looks.

CHAPTER EIGHTY-THREE

Lucia streaked across the countryside in the darkness, her path lit by moonshine. She had to catch up with Dante in his quest to find his father and Enrico Tonelli. She couldn't imagine why Baron Pisani had let him go so far. She honestly didn't know what men were up to. Women had so much more sense.

Her long white hair flew behind her, and her bag bounced across her body. She rode bareback, having learned to ride on the wild mules and donkeys roaming Sicily. Nor did she accept any bridle, grabbing the coarse black mane. Her horse was as black as midnight, named Mezzanotte.

Lucia galloped nimbly, making her way on terrain she knew better than her own body. She'd been to the mining region in Caltanissetta province, so she wasn't surprised when the elevation changed, the air smelled drier, and the vegetation turned scrubbier. The ground hardened, and each hoofstrike traveled up Mezzanotte's legs, roughening her ride.

Finally, she spotted Mussomeli in the distance. The sun was beginning to rise, lightening the sky to pinkish gray. If Dante was already there, she wouldn't be that far behind. She couldn't wait to see him again.

Suddenly, two wolves leapt from the underbrush, their fangs a white blur. Lucia screamed. She fumbled for her knife bag, but Mezzanotte reared, neighing and pawing the air.

Lucia flew off his back. The wolves kept coming. Mezzanotte galloped away, his hoofs thundering.

Lucia landed on the hard ground, striking her head on a rock. Pain arced through her skull. She felt stunned. She raised her hands against the wolves. She heard growling and felt the heat of their breath.

She lost consciousness.

WHEN SHE WOKE UP, SHE was looking at a wizard.

CHAPTER EIGHTY-FOUR

Lucia lay on her back, looking up at the wizard. He peered down at her, holding an oil lamp. His long white hair hung down, and his hooded eyes were animated with concern. He had wispy white eyebrows, a lined face, and a long white beard. He looked thin, little, and ancient in an old shirt and pants.

Lucia blinked, bewildered. "Are you a *wizard*?"

"No, I'm an old man. Are you a golem?"

"No, I'm a young woman. I don't know what a golem is." Lucia shifted to a sitting position and touched her head, which ached. Blood warmed her fingers, glistening darkly. She was on the cold floor of a cave. She remembered she had fallen off Mezzanotte when wolves attacked them. "My name is Lucia."

"Mine's Alfredo."

"What happened to the wolves?"

"I distracted them with some rabbits I had. I was out hunting when I saw your horse spook and the wolves attack. I had caught a few rabbits, so I threw them to the wolves and got you out of there."

"How?" Lucia asked, astounded.

"I put you on my cloak and dragged you here."

"How ingenious! You saved my life," Lucia told him, overwhelmed with gratitude. "They would have killed me."

"They would have, yes. They were hungry." Alfredo set down the lamp. "Why are you so white? I thought it was clay."

"I have a medical condition."

"Does it hurt?"

"Only my eyes, when it's bright, but I have dark spectacles now."

"How nice." Alfredo offered her a pouch of water. "Would you like a drink?"

"Yes, thank you." Lucia sipped some, passing it back.

"I have your horse. He's outside. He came to me, a very fine fellow. Unfortunately, he's lame behind."

"Is it serious?"

"No, but he needs to rest a day, at least. Where were you going?"

Lucia couldn't wait a day. "To Mussomeli, to catch up to my friend. He's looking for a man named Enrico Tonelli, who works in a mine."

"Oh, these days, there's one mine where mostly everybody works. It's in the foothills, so you don't have to go up the mountain to the town."

"Good." Lucia looked around the cave, which reminded her of her own, and he obviously lived here. There was a blanket, an old pillow, and a wooden box. "Do you have any family?"

"Not anymore. I used to have a wife, daughters, and a cousin. They passed away, and I never thought I would live on, after them." Alfredo managed a shaky smile. "I'm still surprised that I do, every day. I'm not sure why."

"I'm sorry." Lucia felt a sympathetic pang. "My mother passed away, too."

"I'm sorry for you, being so young."

"She got very sick." Lucia wondered if Dante was the reason she was still living.

"Here's what I tell myself. None of us is meant to live forever. We're meant to live only in the time we have, in love and kindness. That's all anyone can hope for."

"You're right," Lucia said, charmed by him. She didn't understand why he was in a cave, since he was the same color as everyone else. "Why do you live here?"

Alfredo hesitated. "I'm hiding."

"From whom? The *carabinieri*?"

"No, I've done nothing wrong."

"Then why?"

"I have a secret. I'm not safe in society."

"You can tell me." Lucia's heart went out to him. "I'd never hurt you."

Alfredo sighed, mulling it over. "Secrets wear on you. Once you keep them, you have to keep keeping them, and it gets harder to do over time, a fact I can't explain."

"I won't tell anyone. I don't know many people anyway."

"Okay." Alfredo hesitated. "My secret is, I'm a Jew."

Lucia blinked. "I don't know what that means. I never met one of you."

"I think I'm the only one in Sicily."

Lucia smiled, astonished. "I think *I'm* the only one of me in Sicily, too."

Alfredo smiled back. "I assumed so. I never saw anyone like you before."

"What's a Jew?"

"Judaism is a religion, like Catholicism, but it's not permitted. Jews were tortured, killed, and driven off the island during the Inquisition. Now none of us is left, except me. Or if there are, they're hiding, too. I have no way of knowing."

"How terrible!" Lucia felt their kinship, both outcasts. "This world can be unjust, and hard."

"Yes, but you're kind."

"As are you. Thank you again, for saving my life." Lucia looked around, realizing her knife bag was gone. "Oh no, my bag. I must have dropped it."

"I have it." Alfredo reached behind his back and handed her the bag. "You have quite a collection."

"It was my mother's. Anyway, I'm sorry to say goodbye, but I have to go. I don't want to fall farther behind my friend." Lucia stood up, but felt dizzy. "Oh, my head hurts."

"Are you okay?"

"Yes." Lucia looped her bag across her body. "Do you know where the mine is?"

"Yes, but you'll never find it on your own. There are some working, some not, many abandoned." Alfredo rose. "Allow me to take you there."

"Thank you. Is it far?"

"On foot, it will take all day."

Lucia reached into her bag for her dark glasses. "Let's go."

CHAPTER EIGHTY-FIVE

The sun ascended the sky, and Franco galloped to the mountain, leaving the men to search the mines for Roberto, where they would never find him. He had sent them on a chase that would keep them busy and free him to go after Roberto, alone. Only Franco knew where Roberto was hiding with Violetta.

He reached the foot of the mountain and rode up the skinny road that zigzagged up the mountain to Mussomeli, at the top. Townspeople rode donkeys or walked up and down, moving slowly in the heat. Their mouths dropped open as he sped past, a frantic stranger galloping on a magnificent white stallion.

Franco raced up the road, wheeled around the curve, and headed up in the opposite direction, higher and higher. Arabo matched his urgency, climbing with powerful front legs, his hooves clattering on the stones.

Franco reached the top of the mountain, then raced through the outskirts of Mussomeli, since his destination wasn't in town. He spotted a sign and learned its name: **Castello Manfredonico.** It was the abandoned castle he had seen from Don Bruno's villa.

Franco had realized that Roberto would hide there the moment he'd spotted the castle. He knew Roberto was sending a message only Franco would understand, from their childhood game.

I'm king of the mountain!

Castello Manfredonico rose dramatically at the mountain's very peak, its massive amber-and-tan limestone built into the mountainside itself. Its walls soared into the clouds, massively tall and shaped roughly like half of a pentagon, with a crenellated top. Its thick stone façade was unbroken except for pairs of arched windows set high in a sheer wall that disappeared into the mountainside. A walkway with a crenellated wall encircled part of the castle, and the narrow road to its entrance zigzagged upward in long, stepped stretches, a steep grade with a low wall on either side.

Franco galloped Arabo up the road to the castle, and the horse devoured the punishing grade. They reached the landing, pinwheeled around the turn, and tore up in the opposite direction, climbing higher and higher. Franco rode up flight after flight, his heart pounding harder and harder. Arabo slipped near the top, but Franco urged him upward.

The wind gusted hard, buffeting Franco's ears and lashing his hair around. He galloped higher, harder, and faster, man and horse racing up, up, up, until they reached the castle and there was nothing around but blue sky.

Franco sped through the immense arched entrance to the castle, its thick wooden doors standing open. "Robo!" he shouted, his voice echoing within the medieval walls.

"You remembered!" Roberto called back, his shout coming from within.

Franco slid his *lupara* from his shoulder and galloped through enfiladed stone rooms, each empty, dark, and crumbling. The ceiling was lofty and sharply peaked, the wooden rafters rotted and worm-eaten. Birds and bats fled, flapping in his wake.

Franco rode toward an archway that led to a courtyard flooded with sunshine. It was at the far side of the castle, and he sensed that Roberto would be there with Violetta. "Robo, let her go!"

"Come, get her!" Roberto shouted back, and Franco raced toward his brother, raising his rifle. He reached the sunny courtyard and halted Arabo, whirling around in horror at the sight:

Roberto had his gun trained on Violetta, who stood trembling atop of a crumbling wall, at the edge of the rocky cliff. Her lovely eyes were red with crying. A bruise marred her cheekbone. Her short red hair ruffled in the wind. Her white nightgown billowed against her body. Franco hadn't seen her in fifteen years, but she was as beautiful as ever.

"Robo, no, let her go, leave her out of this. She's done nothing wrong—"

Roberto snorted. "My Bruna did nothing wrong, but you killed her. Don Bruno figured it out. The funeral for Provenzano's widow was too expensive, and he started asking questions."

"Robo, let her go, I'll give you whatever you want. You want to be *capo di tutti capi*? You win, you're king of the—"

"No, it's too late. Now I want to kill the only woman you ever loved."

Franco's heart stopped. "Please, kill me! Take me instead!"

Roberto burst into derisive laughter. "You think I'm stupid? It's a trick!"

"No, Robo, it's no trick! Shoot me instead!" Franco meant every word. "I'm who you want, not her!"

"You're wrong, brother! I want you to know my pain before I kill you!"

"No, wait! I'm putting my *lupara* down!" Franco set down his rifle and raised his hands. "Look!"

"You always carry a pistol in your waistband!"

"Not this time! Look, none!" Franco turned around. "Shoot me, Robo!"

"Franco, you would really die for her?" Roberto asked, incredulous.

Franco's gaze found Violetta's, sharing her terror. "Yes!"

Violetta lowered her head, beginning to pray.

Franco fell to his knees, pleading. "Take me instead."

Roberto eyed him. Neither brother took a breath. Silence fell, except for Violetta's whispered Latin, and Franco knew his twin was making his choice.

"Roberto, I'm on my knees, begging you. You win."

"I have no choice." Roberto raised his gun and shot Violetta. The bullet hit her squarely in the chest. Her nightgown exploded in blood and tattered muslin. Her hands flew up reflexively.

"Violetta!" Franco ran to her, but she fell backward off the cliff, her arms outstretched and her nightgown flapping like the wings of an angel.

Roberto ran toward Franco, tossing his gun aside. Franco whirled around and charged Roberto. The twins collided in the courtyard, their identical faces red with primal fury. Each brother knew the other's moves, the roughhousing of their boyhood turned lethal. They were evenly matched, each as strong as the other.

"I'll kill you!" Franco grabbed Roberto by the leg, trying to pull him down.

"I'll kill *you*!" Roberto thwarted him, wrenching Franco's arm backward. He pulled Franco to the ground, and they fell wrestling to the stones.

Roberto punched Franco in the chin. Franco's head rocked backward but he jabbed Roberto's temple. Roberto flew off balance, stunned. Franco looked for his gun, but it was too far away. The twins grappled back and forth, rolling on the gritty floor.

"Franco, you lied to me! You killed my wife! You betrayed me!"

Franco didn't reply, conserving his energy. The twins punched, kicked, and wrestled, grunting with effort and rage. Franco realized they were nearing the edge where Violetta had fallen. He grabbed Roberto by the shoulders, trying to roll him there. Roberto headbutted him, leaving him reeling.

"I hate you!" Roberto's eyes filled with enraged tears. Emotion distracted him. His grip loosened just the slightest.

Franco recovered, seizing his chance. He gripped Roberto's throat and scrambled on top of him. He squeezed his brother's neck as hard as he could, trying to strangle him.

Roberto's face reddened with pain and anguish. The veins on his forehead bulged with blood. He clawed Franco's hands and pried off one of his fingers. It wasn't enough.

Franco squeezed harder. He would never forgive Roberto for killing Violetta. Roberto had to die, and Franco had to kill him.

"Franco?" Roberto eked out, guttural. He flailed at Franco's arms. His blows lacked force. He tried to scratch Franco's face. He was too weak.

Franco kept squeezing, emitting an agonized sound he didn't recognize as his own.

Roberto's eyes jittered side to side, frantic. He tried to move his head to say no.

Franco could feel his brother's warm flesh under his palms. He watched his twin's eyes until they stilled gazing into his own.

Roberto's hands dropped to the side. His big chest ceased moving.

Franco released him with a grunt. He fell back on his haunches in horror. His chest heaved. His breaths were ragged. He couldn't believe what he had done.

He looked at Roberto's face and saw his own, in death. He had killed the brother with whom he had started life, in the same womb. He had strangled his twin, destroying his other self.

"Robo?" Franco whispered, like he used to at night, in their childhood bed.

Roberto didn't answer.

Franco was king of the mountain.

He screamed at the top of his lungs, in horror and victory.

CHAPTER EIGHTY-SIX

Dante and Gaetano made it to Don Bruno's mine, and Tonelli had gone inside the office, telling them to wait for him in the clearing. Oddly, nobody else was around the mine site, which was buried in the foothills of the mountains. There was a vast clearing between a steep hill and a ramshackle wooden office, an equipment shed, and a barracks with corrugated tin walls and a rusted, sloping roof. Set off by itself beyond that was a large kiln.

Dante looked over at Gaetano. "When do we confront Tonelli?"

"Maybe tonight, when we're sure he's alone."

"Why not now? I think we're the only ones here."

"A miner's in the office with him."

"We can take them, two on two."

Gaetano frowned. "First, we need to understand what's going on. I don't know why no one else is around, unless they're underground. Pox said this was the biggest mine, so I expected a lot of miners."

"So did I." Dante's eyes watered, and his nose stung. The acrid stench of sulfur hung in the air, worse than a hundred chamber pots. The clearing offered no relief from the beating sun, containing only a weigh station, with a large scale next to a rickety table and chair. The table faced the desiccated brown hill, strewn with rocky dirt and devoid of any vegetation. The mine had been dug into the hillside, and it had three entrances reinforced by heavy wooden planks. Each entrance was small, dark, and shaped like a horrified mouth.

Gaetano gestured. "Here he comes."

Gaetano and Dante looked over as Tonelli emerged from the office with a sweaty miner in white shorts and a white scarf around his head. The miner's skin had an odd grayish pallor, and his bloodshot eyes were sunken in a gaunt face. He had lean, ropey muscles, but was skinny and bandy-legged. His ribs showed.

"Gaetano, Dante, listen." Tonelli held a crude pick. "We're short-handed today because Don Bruno took our men while I was in Mussomeli. It happens, we're at his disposal. So, Dante, instead of helping our kiln men, you're going to pick. Understand?"

"Yes." Dante accepted the pick, which was hefty in his hands, even lethal. It had a rough wooden handle and sharp iron point, a weapon for revenge *and* justice.

Tonelli gestured to the miner. "Dante, this is Constantino. He's a picker and he'll take you down Shaft One and show you what to do." Tonelli turned to Gaetano. "Palermo, you're the scale man, at the weigh station."

"Fine." Gaetano nodded.

"Let's get started. Dante, go with Constantino. Palermo, come with me."

DANTE FOLLOWED CONSTANTINO TO THE mine entrance, then doubled over after him to fit inside the mineshaft. There were steps going down, but they were short, uneven, and slippery, so he ran his fingertips along the rough stone wall. It was pitch-black inside except for Constantino's oil lamp, which cast flickering light. Wooden tree trunks shored up the mineshaft on the sides and the top.

They descended the stairs, and soon Dante didn't have to double over, though he had to stoop. The fumes stung his eyes, and his nose ran. His throat burned, he coughed. The air felt as hot as the noonday sun, and sweat soaked his clothes. He understood why Constantino wore only shorts. He took off his shirt and pants, bunching them under his arm.

The sulfurous odor and heat intensified as they went lower, making it hard to inhale a full breath. Dante felt like his lungs were burning and coughed until his throat was sore. They kept going lower down the mineshaft, and the air grew even hotter.

"Stop here." Constantino raised the oil lamp and illuminated a wall of grayish-white rock, craggy and pitted. He pointed to a skinny vein of faint yellow crystal, glinting in the lamplight. "See this, Dante?"

"Yes."

"The yellow is sulfur ore. This section is picked over, but down below it's not. Pick out the ore in as big a piece as you can. Don't pick surrounding rock. Don't hammer the ore or you'll break the crystals. The more you break the crystals, the more dust it makes and the harder it is to breathe."

"Okay." Dante just wanted to get through the day so he could take a pick to Tonelli.

"Let's go." Constantino resumed their descent, speaking over his shoulder. "It's good for you, starting when everyone's away. The boss won't expect much. I can't stand the guy, he's a *stronzo*. You'll see. All the pickers hate him." Constantino snorted. "Anyway, picking is hard work, but you're strong. There's water down there. Drink as much as you want. Take breaks, but not too many."

"Can I go to the surface on the break?" Dante could barely fill his lungs. His hair dripped with sweat.

"No. Believe me, the trip up and down takes more effort than it's worth. You're better off down."

"But the smell—"

"You'll get used to it. You missed the lunch break, so you'll be called to dinner. No naps and no smoking."

"I don't smoke." Dante heard whispering below.

Constantino bellowed, "Quiet!"

The whispering silenced.

"Okay, take this." Constantino handed him the oil lamp. "Keep going down. Stop when you get to the laborers. They're gathering the ore I picked this morning. I'm going to Shaft Two, so Shaft One is your responsibility."

"Okay."

"Don't drop the lamp. It can start a fire. Work hard, but not too hard. Don't make me look bad. Don't let the laborers get away with anything. Now get to work. Move over."

Dante flattened against the wall, and Constantino squeezed past him with difficulty, stepping on his feet. Constantino ascended toward the surface, and Dante raised the lamp and made his way down the steps, descending into the mineshaft. The air got hotter still, and he had to stop to catch his breath.

His nose kept running, and his eyes watered. He wiped his face on his shirt and stuck it back under his arm. There was no air anywhere, only a yellow dust.

He felt sick to his stomach, but kept going. He knew he was getting closer to the laborers when he heard scuffling and spotted moving shadows.

He raised the lamp, illuminating them.

And gasped with shock.

CHAPTER EIGHTY-SEVEN

Gaetano familiarized himself with the weigh station. On the desk was a thick black ledger to record the weight of the sulfur ore, the picker who picked it, the mineshaft it came from, and the time of day. Next to the desk on a wooden platform was an old industrial scale of questionable accuracy. Affixed to the platform was a makeshift grotto with a homemade sign that read, **Santa Barbara, Protettrice dei Minatori**, Saint Barbara, Protectress of Miners. Yellow dust blanketed the statue of the saint in her white gown and faded red cloak.

Sun blasted the clearing. Constantino had just emerged from Shaft One, then descended into another shaft. Gaetano shuddered to think how awful picking would be for Dante, yet another travail in his young life.

Gaetano heard someone coming out of the mineshaft and straightened. A figure emerged and Gaetano looked over expectantly, then recoiled. It was a little boy in white shorts, carrying a massive basket of ore on his bent back. He looked about six years old, but his skin was whitish gray, his eyes sunken, and his cheeks hollowed. The right side of his little body had an overdeveloped shoulder and biceps, while his left side was positively spindly. He had a small rib cage, a distended belly, and his legs were bowed.

"Let me help you!" Gaetano jumped up, hustled to the boy, freed the loop from his right arm, and lifted the basket from his back, horrified to find his spine horribly hunched.

"Signore, what are you doing?" The boy looked up with confusion. His face was dirty and covered with fine yellow dust. "Who are you?"

"I'm trying to help you."

"I'm supposed to bring it to the scale!"

"That's okay, allow me." Gaetano carried the heavy basket with effort and set it down on the scale's metal plate, which creaked. The sulfur ore was in powdery chips, nuggets, and pieces ranging from pale yellow to vivid gold, emitting a noxious odor. Some chips were crystalline, and their facets glinted like golden diamonds in the sun.

"I'm supposed to do it! I'm supposed to!"

"It's okay, don't be upset." Gaetano eyed the scale, shocked to find that the ore weighed fifty kilograms. "This is *way* too heavy for you."

"I can do it! I do it all the time!"

"But it's too much." Gaetano looked over to see Tonelli was swaggering his way, with a scowl.

"Palermo, what are you doing? The *carusu* brings the ore to the scale. You weigh the load and record it in the ledger. Then he picks it up and takes it to the holding bin near the kiln."

Carusu. Gaetano translated the Sicilian term, which meant "dear one." "He's a *carusu*? He's a laborer!"

"Yes, a *carusu* is a mine boy. The *carusi* gather the ore and bring it to the surface." Tonelli put his hands on his hips. "You stay at the desk. You're not supposed to help. You'd be doing it a hundred times a day."

"But he's a *child*!"

"They all are. We have thirty of them, ten per shaft. That's who does this job, in every mine in the province."

"This can't be!" Gaetano said, aghast. "This is a job for men, not little boys. It can't be legal."

"There's no law against it. Anyway, their parents signed them over to us. If you don't believe me, I have a file in my office with a *succursu di murti* for each boy."

Gaetano translated the Sicilian term, "death benefit," which suggested the contract was a form of life insurance. Even if the contract was legal, it was nevertheless immoral. "Where do the children come from?"

"Mussomeli. We pay the parents up front, and the boy works off the debt."

"How long does it take?"

"Ten years, then they go home."

"*Ten years?*" Gaetano asked, appalled. "That's a childhood!"

Tonelli scoffed. "It's a good deal for them."

"How?" Gaetano could only imagine the desperation of parents who indentured their own children. He knew dire poverty existed in Sicily, but had never imagined this particular misery.

"The parents get money to feed the rest of the family. The *carusi* learn a trade and sleep in the barracks. We don't charge much for food and board."

"They pay *you?*" Gaetano tried to understand. "Why use children? Why not men?"

"The *carusi* go up and down all day long. They have to be small. Adults are too tall."

"But you see what it does to them." Gaetano didn't elaborate, since the boy was listening. "He looks malnourished. Isn't that why his belly is so big?"

"No, that's worms."

"*Worms?*"

"Enough!" Tonelli waved him off. "Shut up and weigh the ore."

Just then, another little boy staggered out of the mineshaft, his small body doubled over with the burden of the basket. Gaetano moved to help him, but Tonelli grabbed his arm.

"Don't you dare, Palermo. If I see you out of that chair, I'll fire you *and* your brother." Tonelli shoved a finger into Gaetano's chest. "Understand?"

"Okay." Gaetano had to concede, for Dante's sake.

"Now get to work. I'm keeping an eye on you." Tonelli tried to grab the *carusu*, but missed. "I'll beat you, you little—"

"No!" Gaetano intervened, stepping between them.

"*What?*" Tonelli met Gaetano's eye, and the two men stood face-to-face, close enough for Gaetano to smell the wine on Tonelli's fetid breath.

"I said, no. I will not allow you. Beat me if you want to, but not that boy."

Tonelli punched Gaetano so hard that he reeled backward, falling to the ground.

Tonelli turned on his heel and stalked back to his office.

Leaving Gaetano in pain, but satisfied.

THE NEXT *CARUSU* TRUDGED TOWARD the weigh station, looking only seven years old. His nose was running, his eyes were reddish, and he had the same gray pallor, curved spine, and lopsided little body as the others. His skin glistened with sweat mixed with sulfur dust.

"What's your name, son?" Gaetano asked, while the *carusu* put the load on the scale.

"Daniele," the boy answered, managing a smile. "Are you the new scale man, Signore? The old one never talked."

"Yes, and I like talking to you. Are you from Mussomeli?"

"Yes."

"How long have you worked here?"

Daniele frowned, confused. "Uh, I don't know."

"You work very hard, don't you?"

"Yes, I'm strong."

"I see that." Gaetano weighed the load, a whopping forty-one kilograms, then made the necessary notations in the ledger. Daniele seemed to take it as his cue to go, picking up the load by looping the strap over his right shoulder and lifting it from the knees, showing why the right sides of the boys' bodies were overdeveloped. He staggered from the weigh station with his basket, heading for the loading area at the kiln.

Gaetano spotted another *carusu* heading toward the weigh station, maybe eight years old. The boy hunched from the weight of the load, with the same awful pallor and disfigured form. The *carusu* set the load on the metal plate.

"What's your name, son?" Gaetano asked, delaying the notation that would cue the boy's departure.

"Agostino," the *carusu* answered, and Gaetano's ears pricked up at the familiar accent.

"Are you from Palermo?"

Agostino hesitated. "Uh, yes. I think so, I don't know for sure."

"Your accent is from Palermo, like mine. Don't I sound like you? I can hear the difference, can you?"

Agostino nodded shyly. "Yes, I say words wrong. There are a few *carusi* like me, who say our words wrong. They tease us."

Gaetano's mind raced. It seemed strange that poor parents from Palermo would send a boy to a mine out here. "How did you get here?"

Agostino shrugged his lopsided shoulders. "Signor Tonelli brought me, I think?"

Gaetano blinked, putting it together. If Tonelli had kidnapped Dante, then maybe he had kidnapped these boys, too.

"Signore, aren't you going to weigh my load?"

"Oh yes." Gaetano glanced at the scale, which read forty-eight kilograms, then made his notations. He didn't delay because Tonelli could be watching from the office. Agostino shouldered his load, then trudged on his way.

Another *carusu* was already approaching. Gaetano quickly tore a page from the back of the ledger, then wrote the names of the boys he had seen so far, underlining Agostino.

The afternoon wore on, and *carusi* brought up basket after basket, going back down the same shaft as soon as they had unloaded the ore. Gaetano elicited conversations from each boy, seeing some more than once. He wanted to learn as much as possible about them, as well as hear their accents.

The sun finally began to dip, and Gaetano pulled out his list of names, skimmed them, and analyzed the results. He had met all thirty *carusi*, but only twenty-three of them were from Mussomeli. Seven of the *carusi* had Palermo accents, including Agostino. They confirmed they were from Palermo and that Tonelli had brought them to the mine.

Gaetano's heart lifted. He had heard about so many kidnappings while he had been in prison, and he may have just solved them. Tonelli must have kidnapped the boys from wealthy *Palermitani*, hid them in the madhouse with Renzo, and brought them here to work with the local boys.

Gaetano couldn't wait to tell Dante.

They had to rescue the *carusi*.

CONSTANTINO EMERGED FROM THE MINESHAFT, covered with sulfur dust and carrying an oil lamp. He walked tiredly to the weigh station, setting down the lamp. "Have the others come back from Don Bruno's yet?"

"No, it's been quiet."

"They're usually back by now. We need to run the night shift."

"There's a night shift?"

"Yes. It's cooler. The pickers prefer it." Constantino wiped his watery, red eyes on his arm. "Something's wrong. I'd better go to Don Bruno's and see what's going on. Tell Tonelli when he wakes up. He always sleeps all day after he goes to town, since he spends the night in a brothel."

"Okay." Gaetano masked a surge of excitement. "What about Dante?"

"He'll be up any minute. The *carusi* will tell him when. They come up in about an hour and get themselves to the wash station. They know where their food is. They put themselves to bed. Most of them fall asleep before dinner."

"I bet." Gaetano couldn't hold his tongue. "Don't you feel bad for them?"

"No. It's a shit job, no matter how old you are."

"But they're just children. They don't have a choice."

"And I do?" Constantino snorted, then walked away.

CHAPTER EIGHTY-EIGHT

Dante was on fire, filled with fury. His eyes and throat burned, but there was no time to lose. He and Gaetano armed themselves with picks, hurried to Tonelli's office, and peeked in the window. It held a cluttered table and chair, a filthy file cabinet, and a cot against the wall, where Tonelli slept with his mouth open.

Dante's heart pounded. It was time for justice *and* revenge. He glanced at Gaetano, filled now with righteous anger of his own. Gaetano had told him about the kidnappings of the other boys, and the lawyer had the spirit of an avenging angel.

Dante and Gaetano hurried to the office door and burst inside, slamming the door against the wall.

Tonelli woke with alarm, scrambling to a sitting position. "What—"

"You kidnapped me!" Dante raised the pick, his muscles engorged after the day's labor. "I should kill you for what you did! I should kill you right now!"

"No, don't, please!" Tonelli cowered, putting up his hands. "I don't know what you are talking about!"

"Yes, you do! You kidnapped me from the Saint Rosalia festival and gave me to Renzo in the madhouse!"

"Wait, listen! I know Renzo, but I didn't kidnap you. A stevedore named Claudio kidnapped you."

"I don't believe you!" Dante raised the pick higher.

"Stop! No! It's true, I swear." Tonelli backed up in terror. "Claudio did it, not me! I think he's dead, he disappeared after you were kidnapped! Renzo couldn't find him, he told me!"

"Why would Claudio kidnap me? Why?"

"He was paid to! He told me so himself! He did it for the money!"

Dante sensed Tonelli was telling the truth. "Who paid him to? Who?"

"A *gabellotto* named Franco Fiorvanti! Now he's Don Franco, the boss of Palermo!"

"Why would he do it? What did Don Franco have against me?"

"I don't know! Back then, Don Franco oversaw Baron Zito's *giardino* in the Conca d'Oro!"

"*Baron* Zito?" Dante wondered if Baron Zito was the nobleman who had an affair with his mother. "Did Don Franco kidnap me *for* Baron Zito?"

"What do you think? If you work for a baron, you do what he says!"

Dante's mind raced. Baron Zito could be his natural father. "Where's Baron Zito?"

"I think he has a villa in Bagheria, by the sea. I heard Don Franco burned down his palazzo in Palermo. That's all I know! I swear, I'm innocent!"

"*Innocent?*" Gaetano interjected, stepping forward. "There are thirty *carusi* here, and seven are from Palermo. You kidnapped them. They told me you brought them here. I think you worked with Renzo after Claudio did. I bet Renzo stowed them in the madhouse until you brought them here as *slaves*."

"I didn't do it, I swear to you!"

"Prove it! You told me you have contracts for each boy! Where?"

"Top drawer!" Tonelli pointed with a shaking hand while Dante brandished the pick.

Gaetano tore open the drawer, rummaged through the folders, took the one labeled *Succursu di Murti*. "I don't even have to open the folder!

I'll find twenty-three contracts, not thirty! You have contracts only for the local boys, not the kidnapped ones!"

"Okay, yes! So what?" Tonelli sneered. "What are you going to do? Call the authorities? Good luck!"

"*I'll* kill you!" Dante raised the pick.

Gaetano stopped him. "Dante, don't. We'll find a way to bring him to justice. The law will deal with him."

Tonelli burst into derisive laughter. "Ha! What law? Don Bruno's the law, Palermo!"

"I'm taking every boy!" Gaetano shot back. "All thirty of them! I'm tearing up your ridiculous contracts."

"The hell you are!" Tonelli reached under the cot, pulled out a pistol, and aimed it at them. "Drop the pick!"

Suddenly a strange *whoosh* came from the doorway.

Dante turned toward the sound. A gleaming knife whistled past him and sped end over end toward Tonelli. Tonelli fired his gun, but missed Dante. The bullet blasted the wall, sending wood flying.

The knife found its target with lethal accuracy, burying itself in Tonelli's chest. His gaze fixed instantly. He was dead before he could utter a sound.

"Lucia!" Dante cried, astonished. His heart leapt to see her in the doorway.

With a wizard.

CHAPTER EIGHTY-NINE

Franco held Arabo's reins, walking back to Don Bruno's villa with Roberto's body lying across his lap. He still couldn't fathom that Roberto was dead, much less that he had killed him. He felt something come loose inside him, whatever it was that tethered him to reality, a thread that kept him moored to his fellow man. He felt himself spiraling away from humanity, entering a dark world of his own making, in which evil ruled over good, might made right, and the only law was his word.

Franco had thought that he wanted such a world, but he felt crazy, unbound by anything now that he was no longer tied to his twin, his brother, his other self, with whom he had shared a bloody and twisted cord that bound them to their mother.

Franco approached Don Bruno's villa and he could see the Fiorvantis thronging in front, holding flaming torches and oil lamps in the twilight. Their heads began to turn to him, one by one, then they surged toward him. Franco realized he was weeping as the Fiorvantis reached him and discovered Roberto was dead, releasing an outpouring of shock and grief, a veritable tide of tears.

"No, no, no!" they wailed.

"Don Roberto is dead!"

"They killed him!"

"I'm so sorry," Franco heard himself say, and it was true. He was sorry Roberto was dead, and he was sorry that he had killed him, and he was sorry that he *had* to kill him. Somehow all of these things were true even though they were contradictory, in this dark kingdom in which he would reign.

Franco allowed Sebastiano to take Arabo's reins, then dismounted, falling into the arms of his men, who gathered him up, held him close, and shared his agony. Roberto's men tenderly took Roberto's corpse into their arms. They all moved together toward the villa in a mournful throng, each feeling the agony of the other, like a real family.

Franco came to his senses, realizing he had to preempt any suspicion. "I can't go another step," he heard himself say, stopping to tell the story that would preserve the grim world he wasn't sure he wanted to rule. "Men, I am sorry, so sorry. I tried to save Don Roberto, but I was too late. Don Bruno's men killed him."

"Oh no!" "Oh God!" "*Madonna!*" they shouted, grief-stricken.

"Let me tell you what happened. I was watching you from the mountain, then I noticed the old castle at its peak. I said to myself, 'Castles are the safest place anywhere, always built on the highest ground, and Don Bruno's men would know this castle.' I asked myself, 'What if they took a lesson from history? What if they brought Roberto up there to hide him, and not a mine?' So I rode there, and I was right."

"I never would've thought of that!" "You're right, Don Franco!" "What happened next?"

"I rode into the castle calling for Don Roberto. I heard a scream that cut my heart. I knew it was him, I know his voice as my own. I raced through the rooms, then there was a strangled cry. I saw Don Roberto, my brother, my *twin*, being murdered."

"Oh no!" "They killed him!"

"I found them bending over Roberto, *strangling* him." Franco felt tears brim in his eyes. "It took two of them. He was so strong, he was fighting them. I shot one and strangled the other with my bare hands."

"Justice was done!" "They got what they deserved!"

"After I killed them, I threw their bodies off the cliff. Their bones broke on the stones. Now they're food for wolves. There are no more Marescas!"

"We killed them all!" "Don Roberto and Mauro sacrificed themselves!"

Franco raised his hands. "We'll unite in mourning, and we'll go back to Palermo and bury our beloved Don Roberto, Mauro, and our other dead." Franco wiped his eyes. "We'll honor them and their memory. We'll pray for them. We'll take care of their families."

"Yes, that's our oath!" "We take care of each other! In life and death!"

"We'll be stronger than ever. We'll go on to greater success, in Don Roberto's memory. We'll be better than before, for him and for Mauro. For all the brave Fiorvantis we lost today. We'll go back to Palermo, a family united!"

"Don Roberto would want that! So would Mauro!"

Franco quieted them. "But we have one last thing to do."

"What do you want?" "We're at your disposal!"

Franco pointed at Don Bruno's villa. "Blow that place to the sky! Find me black powder, men! Don Bruno was a miner, he must have some! Sebastiano, you're excellent with explosives! Go set it up! Now! Go!"

"Yes, Don Franco!" Sebastiano and the Fiorvantis ran to the villa in a frantic horde. They raced all over the property, bolting into the villa and outbuildings.

Franco reached the villa just as Sebastiano shouted he'd found black powder. The news whipped the Fiorvantis into a frenzy. They ran back to the wall and distanced themselves from the villa, crazed with anticipation. They thronged behind Franco, their emotions at fever pitch.

"Don Franco!" Sebastiano hustled out of the villa with an oil lamp and a spool of fuse line. Quickly he unrolled the fuse line all the way to Franco, then handed him the oil lamp. "For you!"

"*Bravo*, Sebastiano!" Franco raised the lamp and hurled it down. The glass shattered. The burning oil sparked the fuse line with a *hiss*.

The spark traveled up the line, setting it aglow centimeter by centimeter. The Fiorvantis cheered and hollered, reveling in the suspense. The flame on the fuse disappeared into Don Bruno's villa. The Fiorvantis screamed like madmen.

Boom!

The villa exploded into a massive fireball rocketing into the sky. Red and orange flames shot into the darkness. The ground shuddered like an earthquake, and the noise deafened the Fiorvantis. They covered their ears, shouting and laughing. The percussive wave rocked them as they stood cheering.

The sheer power of destruction thrilled Franco. Fiery pieces of rafters, tables, clothes, and carpets flew upward. Bits of stones, dishware, glasses, statues, and papers blew everywhere. Don Bruno's villa rained from the sky, falling in flames.

The Fiorvantis exulted in triumph. They fired guns, pumped fists, and danced before the conflagration. The air reeked of fire and ferrous smoke. Birds fled in terror. Thick black clouds billowed into the sky, obscuring the moon and stars.

Franco had absolute power.

Alone.

CHAPTER NINETY

Dante squeezed Lucia's hand, and Lucia looked over with a beautiful smile, her skin luminous in the night. Gaetano and Alfredo chatted, and the four of them climbed the mountain to Mussomeli, leading thirty deliriously happy boys, dancing, singing, and shoving each other in fun, tireless even though they had worked all day in one of the most hellish places on earth.

The moon shed light like a blessing, and Dante lit the way with his lamp, so they kept their footing on the grade. The breeze was fresh, cool, and mercifully free of sulfur fumes. They left Don Bruno's mine far below, and Dante and Gaetano were returning the twenty-three boys to their families in Mussomeli and taking the other seven back to Palermo.

Suddenly a thunderous *boom* echoed in the valley.

Dante looked over to see a huge fireball below. Smoke billowed into the sky. "What happened? Something blew up?"

Gaetano shook his head. "I hope not the mine. It would produce sulfur gas."

"Not the mine." Alfredo pointed his knobby finger. "That's Don Bruno's villa!"

"*Fantastico!*" Lucia laughed, and they all joined in.

THE CHURCH BELLS RANG AS they reached Mussomeli and walked down the street to Madonna dei Miracoli. The doors were open, and Father Casagrandi stood on the steps. Townspeople thronged in the piazza, celebrating the downfall of Don Bruno, drinking, singing, dancing, and playing tambourines, mandolins, and accordions.

"Down with Don Bruno!" they shouted, pumping their fists. "He got what he deserved!" "Thank you, Madonna dei Miracoli!"

Dante felt happiness surge through him, putting his arm around Lucia, who had put on her cap and tucked her hair underneath. Gaetano clapped Alfredo on the back, and Alfredo did a little jig. They watched the boys race to the piazza, and the townspeople cheered at their approach.

Gaetano viewed the scene, his heart wrenching. Astonished parents threaded their way to their sons, and mothers burst into anguished tears at their boys' condition. Still they scooped them up, hugged them, and covered them with kisses, reuniting as families.

Dante and Lucia gathered the boys from Palermo, telling them their reunion would come soon enough. Gaetano picked up Agostino, giving him a kiss on the cheek. The other boys clustered around Alfredo, grabbed his hands, and tugged his clothes, since he'd stopped trying to convince them he wasn't a wizard, as they deserved a bit of magic.

The foursome made their way to Father Casagrandi, who greeted them with glee, spotting Gaetano. "How did you get the boys back? Did *you* blow up Don Bruno's villa?"

"No, Father." Gaetano launched into the story, and when he was finished, Father Casagrandi hugged him, then tried to get the crowd's attention.

"Everyone, listen to me, please!" Heads turned to Father Casagrandi, chatter subsided, and music stopped. "Allow me to introduce Gaetano, Dante, Lucia, and Alfredo! They freed our boys from Don Bruno's mine! They risked their lives to bring your sons home! Show them your gratitude, please!"

"*Bravi!*" "Thank you!" The townspeople burst into cheers and applause.

Gaetano beamed, Alfredo bowed, and Lucia kept her head down, hiding her face, which came off as modesty. Dante was thrilled to be with her again, but there was still no room for love in his vengeful heart.

He couldn't wait to confront and kill Baron Zito.

His father.

His enemy.

ALFREDO STOOD AT THE EDGE of the celebratory crowd. He had been away from town for so long that he felt nervous around people, self-conscious in his long beard, scraggly hair, and old clothes.

"Alfredo." Father Casagrandi came over with a smile. "Thank you for bringing home our boys."

"You're welcome."

"You used to come to Mass with your wife, didn't you? When I was a young priest?"

"Yes," Alfredo answered, surprised. "How do you remember?"

"I just do. I also remember your goat cheese. The women said it was charmed. I couldn't talk them out of it."

"Neither could I."

"It was delicious. They used to bring it to me." Father Casagrandi patted his round tummy in his black cassock. "Do you still make it?"

"No."

"Oh, that's too bad. People said you moved away. Where to?"

"The foothills."

"You know, if you came back to town, you could sell a lot of cheese. I miss it very much. In our old age, smaller pleasures assume greater importance, don't you think?"

"Yes." Alfredo had the same thought, every time he saw the sun rise.

"If you move back, I know a nice room you can rent. One of my parishioners needs a tenant."

"I don't have the money for rent."

"If you sold cheese, you would. I could help you reestablish your business."

Alfredo thought it was a kind offer and felt a twinge, thinking about making cheese again. He missed his daughters deeply, a loss made acute tonight, by the little boys doting on him. "Well, I'd have to go to Agrigento first, for some girls, and again, that costs money."

"Okay, we can take up a collection, and put it together with a contribution from the church."

"I would pay you back, with the proceeds from the cheese."

"Okay." Father Casagrandi cocked his head. "Will you consider it?"

"I don't know." Alfredo felt doubtful, but not only about his cheese. It was about his secret.

"Why not?"

Alfredo hesitated. Telling Lucia had lightened his burden, but telling the priest was another matter. "Father, you don't know everything about me. If you did, you might not want me back, or my cheese."

"What, Alfredo?" Father Casagrandi touched his arm with concern. "Do you wish to make a confession?"

"Yes," Alfredo shot back. "I'm a Jew."

"What?" Father Casagrandi's eyes widened. "You are? But you came to church."

"I was afraid not to. I've kept my religion secret, in fear." Alfredo folded his arms. "Now, do you still want me in town?"

Father Casagrandi's expression softened. "Alfredo, you're welcome here, and if you move to town, you'll be under my protection. I can't promise everyone will welcome you, but I can promise I won't allow even an unkind word against you. I preach love toward all men. I hope my congregation does the same, too."

Alfredo didn't know if he was sad, happy, or both. He knew only that he was proud to be a Jew and proud to say so, at long last.

Gaetano walked over. "Alfredo, did I hear you say you're Jewish?"

"Yes." Alfredo braced himself, knowing Gaetano was a man of deep Catholic faith.

"I had no idea." Gaetano smiled. "I'd like to talk to you about that."

"Really?" Alfredo asked, uncertain. "Why?"

"I'm a follower of Saint Paul, and he was a very devout Jew, of course. He was a scholar of the Torah, born Saul of Tarsus. He could read the Hebrew Bible and spoke Aramaic, Greek, and Latin. I've studied his life extensively and I've read a lot about Judaism. I'd like to talk to you about it." Gaetano looked around the noisy piazza. "Where can we go get a coffee, I wonder?"

"Maybe Father Casagrandi will lend us his office," Alfredo said, though he was getting an idea. Maybe life could be better for him, in the time he had left.

"For coffee?"

"Not exactly," Alfredo answered, with a sly smile.

AN HOUR LATER, ALFREDO STEPPED out of the Madonna dei Miracoli with Gaetano, feeling and looking like a new man. Gaetano had cut his hair to a normal length, and he had trimmed his beard to look distinguished. Alfredo had on a fresh shirt and pants borrowed from Father Casagrandi, with a jaunty bandanna around his neck.

Father Casagrandi applauded. "Alfredo, you look twenty years younger!"

Dante looked over, astounded. "Alfredo? What a change!"

Lucia hugged him. "You're so handsome!"

Gaetano beamed. "Doesn't he look wonderful?"

Alfredo chuckled. "It's a miracle!"

Father Casagrandi clapped him on the back. "Alfredo, I see my parishioner now, with the room to rent. I'd like you two to meet." He motioned to get someone's attention, and Alfredo looked over, surprised to see Signora Tozzi, attractive in a red dress, her dark hair threaded with gray.

"Alfredo, is it you? It's good to see you, looking so well!" Signora Tozzi burst into a dazzling smile and reached him with a kiss for both his cheeks, and Alfredo caught a whiff of jasmine perfume, which made him momentarily woozy.

"Signora, it's good to see you again."

"Please, call me Simona. I'm sorry you left town, so long ago. I know it was because of me and my friends, behaving badly over your cheese."

"Not really," Alfredo said, touched, but he turned to Father Casagrandi. "You see, Signora knows. If I make my cheese again, everybody will think it's charmed. Last time, that went badly for me."

"I promise, it won't happen again. I'll make sure."

"So will I." Simona's dark eyes twinkled. "Please come back to town, Alfredo. I'm a widow now. We could . . . keep company."

Are you flirting with me? Alfredo remembered she had asked him once.

"Okay!" he blurted out, his heart speaking for him.

Full of love and kindness.

And hope.

CHAPTER NINETY-ONE

Franco got home in the middle of the night, feeling as if he was in a sort of dream, sleepwalking through his own life. A bereft Elvira greeted him with his crying children and Roberto's son, Patrizio. The family undertaker was summoned, and Roberto was dressed and laid out in Franco's magnificent library. The next morning, a delicious repast was set in the dining room and florists delivered massive flower arrangements, one after the other, filling every corner of the villa.

At midday, the onslaught of guests began, and the Fiorvantis arrived to pay their respects to Don Roberto, and so did families from Partinico, Monreale, Corleone, and other towns around Palermo. Franco was the grieving host, busy with guests, family, and business, though he detected the envy of the other families as they took in his villa, *giardino*, and men. He sensed they'd move against the Fiorvantis soon, exploiting the instability after Roberto's death. Franco would be ready for them.

The night before the funeral, he found himself exhausted, and the villa had finally emptied of everyone except immediate family. He and Elvira went up to bed, and Franco crawled into the sheets. He was exhausted but couldn't sleep. He kept thinking of Violetta. Her tear-filled eyes. Her bloody nightgown. Her arms flung out like an angel as she fell. Then he saw Roberto's face. The veins bulging in his forehead. His eyes boring into Franco as they stilled, in death.

Franco tossed and turned, then gave up. He rose, retrieved his robe, and slipped it on, going downstairs. He passed the library, which held the body of his brother. He didn't go in. He couldn't imagine what it would be like after tomorrow, to have his twin away from him, buried under the surface of the earth.

Franco entered the kitchen and lit the candle, his thoughts agonized. He knew Roberto was dead, but he would never be gone. He was half of Franco, and Franco was half of him. Both men occupied the same space, defying all natural laws, which never applied to the human heart anyway.

"Franco?" Signora Esposito appeared in her robe and long white braid. "You couldn't sleep?"

"No."

"I heard you." Signora Esposito crossed to him and placed her hand on his forearm. "I'm sorry, I know how much you loved Roberto."

"Thank you. It's hard to believe he's gone." Franco looked around at the leftovers, covered by cloths and lids. "What do we have that's sweet?"

"Your *erbanetti*?"

Franco felt his chest tighten. The pastries made by Violetta. He couldn't bear to taste one now. "Anything else?"

"A nice *cassata*? Everyone remarked it was very good."

"I'd love some, with anisette. Something to help me sleep."

"I'll get it for you." Signora Esposito went to the counter, and Franco sat down at the table.

"I feel badly for Patrizio, all alone now."

"Yes, I hope you and Elvira adopt him." Signora Esposito came over with a glass of anisette.

"We will." Franco sipped the anisette, enjoying its licorice taste. "That will make Elvira happy, too."

"That's how it should be. All of us together in the house." Signora Esposito brought *cassata* on a plate, with a napkin and a fork.

Franco sighed. "I'm glad the guests are gone."

"There were so many."

"Yes, and did you see the other families? They're jealous. They want to be as big as we are. They're growing, but they're not as organized."

"They don't have you."

Franco smiled. "I don't disagree, but they want what we have. I should pick a successor to Roberto."

"You have time. The funeral's only tomorrow." Signora Esposito brought her own anisette to the table, then sat down, taking a sip. "This is delicious."

"Isn't it?" Franco forked into the *cassata*, which was good and lemony.

"Tomorrow we'll bury him, and that will be difficult." Signora Esposito sighed. "His men are taking it very hard."

"They're already jockeying for position."

"You're the King of Palermo. The *capo di tutti capi*, without question."

"Yes." Franco finished his anisette.

"By the way, I know you killed Roberto."

"What?" Franco wasn't sure he heard her correctly.

"I don't believe your story, about Don Bruno's men. You killed Roberto."

Franco made himself look offended. "What a thing to say! Of course I didn't."

"Yes, you did." Signora Esposito sipped her anisette. "I know you did because I know you so well. You don't know me as well. If you did, you would know I just poisoned you."

"What are you talking about?"

"It's in your anisette. You'll feel it soon, its effects."

Franco snorted, certain she was kidding. She had to be. "That's not possible."

"Yes, it is. It's time."

"For what?"

"Time for you to go. You killed Roberto, and you have to die for that. It's bad enough to kill your brother's wife, but it's far worse to kill your *brother*. What would your mother say?"

Franco thought she might be losing her mind. "My mother?"

"She wouldn't allow it. She would regret having favored you, as I do. She would punish you. So I'm punishing you."

Franco felt a sharp pain in his stomach. He broke into a sweat.

"I heard the oath you made that night to the men, when you were trying to get them on your side. You swore loyalty to them. They believed you, but it was a lie. You even betrayed your brother's loyalty. You were never loyal to anyone but yourself." Signora Esposito glared at him, her ferocity undimmed by age. "And I've been a fool to be loyal to you."

Franco rose, unsteady.

"You can't live on, after killing your twin. Your soul is dead. So I'm doing you a favor."

Franco's stomach cramped so hard he doubled over. His body began to shake.

"Now listen." Signora Esposito stood up, gathering her robe. "I'll offer you one last chance. Confess you killed Roberto, and I'll give you the antidote."

"The . . . antidote?" Franco asked, barely able to speak. Agony twisted his gut.

"I'll save your life if you tell me the truth. Did you do it or not?"

"I . . . did it," Franco managed to say. Pain wracked his entire body. "Give me . . . the antidote."

"I *knew* it."

"Give me—"

"There is no antidote." Signora Esposito folded her arms. "I lied."

Franco collapsed to the floor, writhing. "Why . . ."

"Because I'm so angry, I want to kill you twice. I gave you false hope. Now you don't have even that. You're going to die. It will be painful but not lengthy."

Franco began to convulse uncontrollably.

"Franco, you're not good for the family anymore. In time, your men would turn against you. You're not a king, you're a tyrant."

Franco flopped on the carpet like a fish on a dock.

"I'll tell Elvira you had a heart attack. She'll believe you died of a broken heart. Only I know the truth. You don't have a heart to break."

Franco gagged, spasming.

"Goodbye, Franco. Your punishment doesn't come from law. Nor does it come from men. It comes from a mother. It's a mother's justice."

Justice.

It was the last word Franco heard before he died.

CHAPTER NINETY-TWO

The next morning, Dante, Gaetano, and Lucia bade Alfredo goodbye in Mussomeli and set out for Palermo, making a happy caravan across the countryside. Dante rode next to Lucia in her dark spectacles, and Gaetano held Agostino on his saddle, ponying two chubby donkeys, each carrying three boys in fresh shirts and shorts, given them by the townspeople of Mussomeli.

The sun climbed a cloudless sky and the wind was temperate. They traveled slowly all day, the horses at a walk, the donkeys balking periodically, and the boys singing and laughing. They stopped for water at regular intervals and ate a big lunch prepared by the grateful townspeople. Nobody minded the slow pace except Dante, who gritted his teeth with impatience. As they got closer to Palermo, all he could think about was Baron Zito.

Dante looked over at Gaetano. "Where's Bagheria?"

Gaetano nodded that way. "I'll take you there after we drop the boys in Palermo."

"I don't mind going alone."

"No, I want to go with you." Gaetano shot him a knowing look. "I can help you."

"You're afraid of what I'll do, aren't you?"

"Yes. You want revenge, I want justice. Either way, I can't let you go alone."

"You can't stop me, Gaetano." Dante adored Gaetano, but could no longer avoid conflict on this matter. "I want to see my father face-to-face. He has to account to me for what he did."

Gaetano pursed his lips. "But I worry you'll act in the heat of the moment, out of emotion. You might do something rash."

"Whatever I do, I'll bear the consequences. If I go to prison, I go to prison. You did."

Lucia grimaced but didn't interrupt.

Gaetano shook his head. "It's not prison I worry about. I fear for your immortal soul. Injustice was done to you, but it's not rectified by another injustice."

"Would it be unjust if I killed Baron Zito?" Dante had to say it aloud because it was what they were talking about.

"He didn't kill you—"

"He may as well have."

"—and justice isn't yours to dispense."

"You tore up Tonelli's contracts. You dispensed justice."

"That was because we were in the country. In Palermo, we can appeal to the authorities."

"Gaetano, at last, be realistic. Did the authorities help you when I first went missing? How about when all those boys did? Will the *carabinieri* arrest Baron Zito, a wealthy nobleman, for a crime I can't prove?"

Gaetano sighed, anguished. "If they don't give us justice, then we look to God. He'll judge Baron Zito. You have to have faith, and hope. Hope isn't a feeling, it's an act."

"That's how you live your life. It's not how I live mine."

"I'm only trying to guide you, like a father."

"I'm not your son, I'm *his*."

Lucia frowned under her dark spectacles. "Dante, I agree with Gaetano, and I want to go, too."

"I wish you wouldn't."

"You're being too hotheaded. We have a future together, and I don't want to see you ruin it for the past." Lucia's beautiful mouth flattened, and Dante wondered if he would ever kiss her again.

"I can't go forward until I know who I am, who my family is. This is my battle, not yours or Gaetano's."

"But I love you."

"I love you, too. But I have to go alone. If you love me, stay here, both of you." Dante kicked his horse and rode off.

"Dante, no!" Lucia called back, but her cry was lost in the wind.

ONLY LATER DID LUCIA DISCOVER that her best knife was missing.

CHAPTER NINETY-THREE

Villa Zito was the largest property Dante had ever seen, but it had been left to ruin. He cantered up a long driveway flanked by overgrown prickly pear and flowering bushes. He approached the grand villa, its amber stones aglow in the late-day sun, but its façade crumbled in patches and shutters hung awry. Its balcony faced the sea, affording a breathtaking view, but exterior curtains meant to break the wind had tattered like flayed skin.

Dante reached the arched entrance, entered the courtyard, and dismounted, looking around. All of the shutters were closed, and bougainvillea and ivy overgrew many, sealing them permanently. The pebbles were unraked, and a fountain of four verdigris fish had gone dry. There were no people around, and the house seemed deserted.

"Baron Zito!" Dante shouted, his voice echoing. "Baron Zito!"

A moment later, a gray-haired servant came scurrying from a side door, blinking in the sun. "Signore, good afternoon. How may I be of service?"

"I'm here to see Baron Zito."

"And your name?"

"He knows me."

"May I tell him what this concerns?"

"No. He'll want to see me, I assure you."

"Oh dear." The servant bit his lip. "He doesn't take visitors. I'm not sure I can—"

"Tell him it's about a kidnapping."

"Oh my!" The servant jumped, scurried away, and vanished inside the door.

DANTE FOLLOWED THE SERVANT THROUGH the immense villa, past old room after old room filled with dirty rugs, dusty damask on the walls, empty glass cabinets, and bookshelves without books. The furniture was covered with muslin, and most of it was missing, leaving chairs facing nonexistent tables. Here and there hung family portraits in gilded frames, which left Dante wondering if they were *his* blood relations.

He followed the servant upstairs to the most private quarters. It was dim because the curtains were closed, and he spotted a mouse scooting from underneath its thick brocade.

Brocade.

Dante remembered his mother had taught him that word, and rage burned in his chest, at how cruel Baron Zito had been to her. He patted his pocket, reassuring himself Lucia's knife was there.

"This way." The servant held open a door, admitting Dante, and the sight took him aback.

Baron Zito was sitting in a bookless library behind a desk cluttered with papers, wine bottles, and rotted fruit. He must have been an elegant man in his day, but now his hair hung in greasy clumps, his cloudy gaze was unfocused, and his mouth had a grim downturn. His maroon dressing robe had stains on its black lapels, and he was still in his pajamas, showing underneath.

Baron Zito rose and walked around the desk, leaning on its top. "How much do you want? What's the demand?"

"What demand?"

"The ransom demand. Isn't that why you're here? You said it was about a kidnapping. Whoever took my Violetta sent you, didn't they? Aren't you the intermediary? The messenger?"

"What do you mean?" Dante felt mystified. He wondered if Baron Zito was crazy. He looked it.

"Why are you pretending? My Violetta was abducted from the convent. Her window had been broken open. Mother Superior came to tell me. They didn't see who took her. Nobody saw anything. Oh no, oh no." Baron Zito sagged, tears filming his eyes. "I have nothing left, no money, I owe taxes, she's lost, I'm lost, I can't pay a ducat, not a single one."

"Look, I have no ransom demand—"

"Please, have mercy, on her account. Can you imagine what she's going through? How terrified she is? Kidnapped, held against her will?"

"Yes, I can, I can imagine that exactly." Dante almost laughed at the irony, but he wasn't in a joking mood.

"What have they done to her? Where have they taken her? Whatever they want of me, she doesn't deserve what you've done. It's all my fault, I admit it, I have enemies, many of them, I've done wrong. Not Violetta, she doesn't deserve—"

"No child does. Not your son, either."

"I don't know what you mean." Baron Zito blinked with bewilderment. "My Davide died of drink in Belgium. My wife died years ago of a heart attack. I'm alone, all alone, and Violetta's been abducted—"

"Don't forget me, your illegitimate son. You had me kidnapped, taken from my mother at the Saint Rosalia festival. You paid your *gabellotto* Franco Fiorvanti to kidnap me, and he hired a man named Claudio to put me into the madhouse." Dante could see him listening in horror. "My name is Dante Michangeli."

"You're . . . *alive*?" Baron Zito's mouth dropped open. "No, you're supposed to be . . . to be . . ."

"*Dead?* You wanted me dead? Not just kidnapped, murdered?" Dante reached into his pocket, whipped out Lucia's knife, and backed Baron

Zito against the wall. Baron Zito withered on the spot, and Dante pressed the blade into the old noble's stringy throat.

"Kill me," Baron Zito croaked. "Kill me. Please."

"What?" Dante hadn't expected this reaction, and it threw him off balance.

"Kill me. I deserve it. I admit, I told Franco to kill you, he must have double-crossed me. I deserve to die. Kill me, kill me—"

"Why did you want your own son *killed*?"

"You're not my son."

"I don't believe you!"

"I'm telling the truth. You've got it wrong. Put me out of my misery." Baron Zito's hand went to his cheek, trembling. "Violetta's never coming back because I can't pay. They got it all wrong, too, everyone has it all wrong, all wrong—"

"Tell me why you did it! My own father!"

"I swear, I'm not your father."

"Then who is?"

Baron Zito swallowed, his Adam's apple going up and down. "Okay, I'll tell you."

CHAPTER NINETY-FOUR

Twilight fell, and Gaetano rode down the Via Maqueda with Agostino, leading the donkeys that carried the six other boys. Lucia had returned to the madhouse, fearful of the city, and Gaetano understood why, seeing the reactions to the boys. Families filled the streets during the *passeggiata*, talking and socializing, but they stopped abruptly when they spotted the caravan. They stared at the boys, pointed at their lopsided bodies, and recoiled at their bowed legs.

Gaetano turned onto Piazza della Vittoria and spotted the familiar crowd of *carabinieri* in front of the *Questura*. Their plumed caps turned to him, one after the other, when they saw the caravan approaching. Gaetano even recognized the officers who had thrown him out many years ago.

"What's this about?" one of the *carabinieri* called out, as the caravan reached the entrance. "You don't think you're bringing them here, do you?"

"Yes." Gaetano dismounted with Agostino, setting the boy down. "I'm Gaetano Catalano, in case you don't remember me. Please notify Marshal Rosselli that I'm here with these boys."

"What's going on? Who are they?"

"They were kidnapped from families in Palermo and put to work in a sulfur mine outside Mussomeli." Gaetano took the three boys from the first donkey and set them down, then the three from the second donkey and set them down.

"Are you serious? You found them?"

"Yes." Gaetano took Agostino's hand, and the boys lined up behind him. He headed for the entrance, and they followed like baby ducks.

"Good job, Gaetano!" one of the officers called out, then the other *carabinieri* joined in, bursting into applause. "*Bravo*, Gaetano!" "Welcome home, boys!"

Gaetano smiled, reminding himself to be humble.

But it wasn't easy.

After all, he wasn't a saint.

"MARSHAL ROSSELLI, DO YOU REMEMBER me?"

"Of course." Marshal Rosselli had grown older and crankier. "When did you get out of prison? And what's going on here? This isn't a nursery."

"These boys have been victims of a heinous crime. They were kidnapped from Palermo by one Enrico Tonelli, taken to Don Bruno Maresca's sulfur mine outside of Mussomeli, and forced to work as slaves. You should contact their parents and tell them the happy news of their sons coming home."

Marshal Rosselli blinked. "Is this a joke?"

"They need to be examined by a doctor, fed properly, and given the love and care every one of God's children deserves."

"Where did you get them? How did you find them?"

"I'll be happy to make a detailed statement later. First, I want you to notify the boys' parents. Each boy knows his full name, so finding his parents shouldn't be difficult." *Even for you*, Gaetano thought but didn't say.

"Hmph." Marshal Rosselli folded his arms. "What do you want out of this, Gaetano? The reward?"

"No."

"The credit, then."

"No."

"What's your relationship to the boys? I don't understand your involvement."

"I'm their lawyer. Now please, set about finding their parents. The reunions must take place tonight, or else."

"Or else what?"

"Or else I'll tell the parents *I* found their sons, and you didn't lift a finger." Gaetano met his eye evenly. "I bet their parents are well-heeled and influential. You could lose a job you neither deserve nor perform."

Marshal Rosselli had no reply.

LATER, GAETANO WATCHED FROM UNDER a palm tree across from the *Questura*. Well-dressed couples leapt from gleaming carriages and hustled inside the building, and their happy shouts were so loud that he could hear them outside. One reunion after the next took place, and each family left in joyful tears, hugging a son they loved and had missed.

The last boy leaving with his parents was little Agostino, who clung to his mother's neck. The happiness on the boy's face brought tears to Gaetano's eyes, and he watched the carriage drive away, sending a prayer of thanks to Saint Paul.

Gratitude filled Gaetano's heart, and peace calmed his soul. He had fought the good fight, he had kept the faith, and he had finished the race.

It was time to go home.

CHAPTER NINETY-FIVE

"Don Matteo!" Dante called, dismounting on the fly. He had raced from Villa Zito to Palermo, his heart pounding. Darkness was falling, and families were heading home after *passeggiata*.

"Dante!" Don Matteo broke into a smile. He stood in front of his office, talking with another man. "What a surprise! You've caught me just in time. Please meet my associate, Bartolomeo."

Dante nodded, curt.

"Where's Gaetano?"

"I don't know, I need to speak with you." Dante masked his intent.

"Certainly, let's go inside." Don Matteo bade Bartolomeo goodbye and admitted Dante into an entrance hall, then his fancy office. He turned on a lamp, which illuminated bookshelves full of legal books and an ornate desk behind two chairs. "Please, take a seat."

But Dante stood, barely controlling his fury. "*You're* my father."

"Pardon me?" Don Matteo asked, his smile fading.

"You heard what I said. You're my father, and you tried to have me killed."

"What?" Don Matteo recoiled, but guilt flickered across his lined face.

"I've just come from Baron Zito. He told me everything. You do legal work for him. You proposed a tax scheme to him, whereby you undervalued his properties. That was why he never cultivated his Bagheria estate. He couldn't afford the taxes on the income it would produce."

Don Matteo put up his hands, newly trembling. "Wait a minute—"

"You told Baron Zito you'd save him money on his taxes if he got someone to kill me. He knew a lowlife you didn't, his *gabellotto* Franco Fiorvanti, now Don Franco. But Franco double-crossed you both and instead of killing me, he had a man take me to the madhouse. A guard kept me there my *whole* life. Me! Your *son*!"

"No, listen." Don Matteo shuddered. "I can explain—"

"You wanted to *kill* me. *Me*, the son you fathered with your *niece*!"

Don Matteo gasped. "Hold on, your mother wasn't my blood relation. She's related only by marriage—"

"What difference does that make? She was your *niece*!" Dante advanced on Don Matteo, pushing the lawyer against his desk. He could see the resemblance between them now, but Dante had his mother's eyes, burned into his memory with love.

"Dante, you have to understand, she needed so much, she was lonely—"

"You took advantage of her! You preyed on her, your *niece*!"

"But, but, but," Don Matteo said, jittery, "these things happen, we fell in love—"

"How in love could you have been? You ruined her life! You tried to have her son killed!"

"I had to, I had no choice"—Don Matteo spoke faster, his words running together—"your mother wanted me to leave my wife, she was threatening to tell her everything, I couldn't let that happen, and your mother was demanding more and—"

"Your solution was *murder*? Your own son, a little boy! Does Donna Angelina know you're my natural father?"

"No, she could never bear it, think of *her*—"

"*You* didn't think of her!"

"I'm sorry, I know it was wrong, and when you came to the house with Gaetano that day, and he told me who you were, I was so glad, so grateful. I'm going to make it up to you, you'll see, give me the chance—"

"You pretended to care, to welcome me back home—"

"I *did* welcome you! I knew I could make it up to you, that's why. I know I can make it right—"

"Too late!" Dante withdrew his knife and put it to Don Matteo's throat. "You wanted me dead. There's only one way to make that right!"

"I'm sorry, I swear it! God help me!" Tears sprang to Don Matteo's eyes, and Dante pressed the knife against the pulsing vein in his neck.

"You disgust me! You deserve to die! What kind of a man *are* you?"

What kind of a man are you?

The question rang in Dante's ears.

What kind of a man are you?

Dante released Don Matteo, edging away in a sort of shock.

"Thank God!" Don Matteo made praying hands. "Thank you for showing mercy, Dante, I'll make it up to you—"

"I don't know what kind of man I am, but I know what kind of man I'm *not*. I'm *not you*. I'll be the *opposite* of you, in every way. I'll be a good man, a good husband, a good father. I'll be everything you're not. You're not worthy of me. You don't deserve another moment of my time, much less my loyalty. Do you know who *does*? *Gaetano!*"

"I'm so sorry—"

"You *fired* him because he searched for me, because he was going to uncover your filthy secret! He went to prison for *fifteen* years, for me! He lost *everything*, his career, his reputation, his family! He helped me find *you*! *That's* the kind of man I want to be! I want to be like *Gaetano!*"

Dante whirled around, left the office, and slammed the door behind him, his chest heaving. He stumbled outside in a teary daze, seeing people on the street as if they were far away. His head thundered, his heart ached.

Suddenly, he heard someone calling him and looked over to see

Gaetano riding toward him, his expression strained with fear. "Gaetano?"

"Dante, wait, don't!" Gaetano leapt from his horse. "Don't do it!"

"How did you know I was here?"

"I was going home from the *Questura* and I ran into Bartolomeo." Gaetano gripped Dante's shoulders. "Is *Don Matteo* your father?"

"Yes, I just saw him."

Gaetano gasped. "You didn't . . ."

"No, I didn't. That's not the man I want to be."

"Good boy!" Gaetano erupted with joy, embracing Dante. "I'm so proud of you, Dante. So proud. I love you, son."

"I love you, too," Dante told him, complete in the love only a father could give.

His chosen father.

CHAPTER NINETY-SIX

After bidding goodbye to Dante, Gaetano dropped his horse off at the stables and walked home through the streets of the Palermo he loved so well. The night was dark, but there were lights inside the houses, and he could hear the families chattering, laughing, and arguing, his fellow *Palermitani* either making love or at each other's throats.

A sensation of peace spread throughout his soul, and he breathed in the smells he knew since childhood, the rank odor of city cats and the fragrant perfume of lilies on a balcony. His hometown contained both, and he knew he couldn't accept one without the other. Life didn't work that way, and only God was perfect.

Gaetano turned the corner in his new neighborhood, since Maria had moved them to a different district while he was in prison. He'd never told her that he no longer needed to live near the church in which the Beati Paoli held their secret meetings. He no longer wanted to keep secrets from his wife.

Gaetano smiled as he approached his house, one of the most charming on the block, its two-story stone façade covered with verdant ivy. They rented the apartment on the first floor, and he twisted the knob on the lacquered door and stepped into an entrance hall, then crossed to their apartment door, opening it onto a warm golden interior filled with candlelight.

Gaetano stood at the threshold for a moment, taking in the sight. It made a beautiful picture, one any man would be lucky to come home to. His beloved Maria was sitting on a couch, her glossy head bent over her floral embroidery, and his two sons, Mario and Paolo, were reading in their chairs, buried in thick books. They had grown to be young men, and he had to get to know them all over again.

Gaetano vowed that he would spend every minute with his family from now on. They were his reward, and the only reward that mattered to him. He felt as if he were finally returning to his life, and he sensed it was a new life, a better life. Maybe even heaven on earth.

"Gaetano?" Maria looked up with a delighted smile.

"Papa!" the boys cried, setting aside their books.

"I'm home." Gaetano opened his arms. "It's over, and now, I'm all yours."

AND TO HIS DYING DAY, Gaetano would remember the child he had lost, saving the others.

CHAPTER NINETY-SEVEN

Sun blasted the cemetery with heat and light, and Sebastiano sat with his wife across from Don Franco's casket. Sebastiano hadn't loved the man, but he had respected him, so he mourned Don Franco and his own lost position as *consigliere*.

Sebastiano didn't know what would happen now, and neither did anybody else. The death of Don Franco, so soon after Don Roberto, rocked the family. The Fiorvantis started to fall apart, having no succession plan, and the business began to founder. Noblemen, businessmen, and shopkeepers didn't pay. Deals were broken and trips to markets canceled. Politicians and functionaries went empty-handed. Gossip and speculation spread. Disquiet reigned.

Sebastiano lifted his troubled gaze to the casket, surprised to meet the cool blue eye of Patrizio, Don Roberto's son, on the other side. The boy was only fourteen, but his gaze was mature and his eyes dry. The boy's equanimity took Sebastiano aback, given that it was the funeral of a favored uncle, on the heels of his father's death.

Sebastiano's mind raced. He realized that Patrizio had a claim as the next *capo di tutti capi*, since Don Franco had no male heir. Patrizio was Don Roberto's only son, so the men would acknowledge his legitimacy. They liked Don Roberto better than Don Franco anyway. Patrizio hadn't been involved in the business yet, but he could learn.

Sebastiano realized that opportunity had just stared him in the face. He resolved to go to Patrizio after the funeral to pay his respects. Later, he would suggest the boy aim for the head of the family and offer to be *consigliere*, since every boy king needed an advisor. Then, after Patrizio had risen to power, Sebastiano would do him in and take his place, as Don Franco had done to Don Roberto.

Sebastiano felt his spirits rise, his ambition resurrected. His career would soar from *bracciante* to *consigliere* to *capo di tutti capi*. The Fiorvantis might have been the first Mafia family in Sicily, but his would be even greater. He had younger brothers he could call on, and he had to seize power as soon as possible.

The notion inspired him, filling him with hope. Sicily was opening up to all men, the good and the bad, the peaceful and the violent, and every man would take his share. If the poor weren't permitted to go up, they would go around. It had ever been thus. As long as men contained both light and dark, there would be the righteous and the felonious.

Here, and in the world entire.

CHAPTER NINETY-EIGHT

Lucia labored in pain, pushing to deliver her baby. Sweat drenched her, and her nightgown stuck to her swollen belly. Gaetano's wife, Maria, held one hand, and Alfredo's wife, Simona, held the other. Her midwife was her best friend, Franca, who worked as a nurse at the new madhouse with Lucia. Dante, Gaetano, and Alfredo waited outside because there was only one room in the farmhouse.

"I can't do this!" Lucia cried, like her mother, Mafalda, had so many years ago.

"You can do it! Push, push!" Maria squeezed her hand. "Keep going!"

Simona squeezed her other hand. "Yes, yes, push! Push!"

Franca chimed in, "*Brava*, Lucia!"

Lucia remembered what her mother had told her. "Maybe I should count my blessings?"

"Good idea! What are they?"

"Dante!" Lucia loved her husband deeply, for they had saved each other. They'd both flourished under Baron Pisani's moral therapy.

"Good! What's another blessing?"

Lucia gritted her teeth. "You, my friends! I love you all!"

"Oh my, I see the head!" Franca cried excitedly. "Push one more time!"

Lucia pushed, feeling excruciating pain that vanished when she heard a baby's mild cry. "Thank God!"

"It's a girl!" Franca brought her the baby, who quieted quickly. "Look, how good!"

"She's so beautiful!" Lucia cradled the baby, gazing down at her. The infant was olive-skinned like Dante, which was fine with Lucia, as they had decided they would be grateful for any child God gave them. Her tiny nose was a bump, her mouth an adorable pucker, and her dark eyebrows matched a thatch of black hair.

"I love her already," Lucia said, her heart brimming. "Is it possible to love a baby as soon as you hold her?"

"Yes," the other mothers answered in happy unison.

Lucia's gaze fell on the coiled cord of purplish blood that connected her to her baby, as she had been connected to her mother, and so had every woman in the world, connecting them all, one to the other.

"Your name is Mafalda," Lucia told the baby, stroking her soft little cheek. She felt suffused with joy as well as grief, and somehow she sensed the presence of her beloved mother in this very room.

Tears filled her eyes, and she was overwhelmed by the memory of all she'd lost, all she'd found, and the long journey that led her to Dante and little Mafalda, so that they could become the most precious of all things.

A loving family.

AUTHOR'S NOTE

I love historical fiction, and every time I finish reading a novel with historical underpinnings, I always wonder how much was true. So I'd like to answer that question for you here, and to differentiate fact from fiction in *Loyalty*. This Note does not contain spoilers, but it will make more sense if you read it after you've read the novel.

I traveled all over Sicily to research *Loyalty* and also took videos and photos to illustrate the subject matter below, so you can see the sights in modern day. These materials make an instructive companion to the novel, whether you're in a book club or *a cappella*, and you can find them on my website.

The history of Sicily as depicted in the novel is true. Going to Sicily itself was an education, because there I realized that Sicily isn't completely Italian. In fact, some historians call Sicily "the world's island" because it has been conquered by so many peoples, owing to its location in the middle of the Mediterranean, valuable for trade and military reasons. Sicilians have been influenced by each culture, and the island's amazingly diverse history is reflected in its dramatic architecture, ruggedly beautiful terrain, delicious food, sibilant language, even the faces of its people. For those who want to learn more I recommend: Christopher Duggan, *A Concise History of Italy*; Mary Taylor Simeti, *On Persephone's Island*; Denis Mack Smith, *A History of Sicily: Modern Sicily After 1713*; John Julius Norwich, *Sicily: An Island at the Crossroads of History*; Louis Mendola and Jacqueline Alio, *The Peoples of Sicily: A*

Multicultural Legacy; and Louis Mendola, *Kingdom of the Two Sicilies, 1734–1861*.

The Fiorvanti family is fictional, but the origin of the Mafia depicted herein is true. As a lawyer, I thought I knew a lot about the Mafia, but I was surprised to trace its earliest roots to the luxuriant lemon groves around Palermo, arising from a unique set of circumstances in the 1800s, which combined legal, social, political, and even agricultural factors. For those who wish to learn more about the origin of the Mafia, I recommend: Helena Attlee, *The Land Where Lemons Grow: The Story of Italy and Its Citrus Fruit*; John Dickie, *Cosa Nostra: A History of the Sicilian Mafia*; Salvatore Lupo, *History of the Mafia*; and Anton Blok, *The Mafia of a Sicilian Village 1860–1960: A Study of Violent Peasant Entrepreneurs*. Every one of my novels, whether historical or contemporary, fleshes out the relationship between law and justice, and *Loyalty* is the best case in point to date.

There was a real-life secret society known as the Beati Paoli, but documentation is scant though its existence has been rendered in fiction, legend, and scholarship. The only thing everybody agrees on for certain is that they were based in the Capo district in Palermo and met under the church, which I visited and filmed for my website. Most commentators believe that the society was formed by right-thinking nobles in order to seek justice for the common man, like Sicilian Robin Hoods, because the law was so biased in favor of wealthy nobility. That is the Beati Paoli I chose to depict herein. It is not even known for certain whether the name *Beati Paoli* means the Blessed Society of St. Paul or reflects a devotion to the *Beato Paola* of Saint Francis of Paola. I went with the former, and it's beside the point with respect to the novel, because Gaetano's devotion to Saint Paul comes so clearly from the heart, not from any extrinsic society.

I should point out that some of the commentators and modern-day mobsters claim that the Mafia grew out of the Beati Paoli, claiming for themselves the standard of those fighting for the common man. The weight of serious scholarly authority is to the contrary and documents that the Mafia originated as depicted in the novel, growing out of the beautiful *giardini* of the Conca D'Oro.

The treatment for mental illness was horrific in this period. There really was an Ospizio di Santa Teresa in Palermo, a former convent converted to house the mentally ill, lepers, and the poor. The history of the institution is accurate, though Dottor Vergenti, its administrator when the book opens, is fictional. Baron Pietro Pisani, the administrator after Vergenti, was a real person, and I learned about his remarkable life when I was reading about Sicily. He really was the founder of "moral therapy," a term he coined, and sought to cure the mentally ill through humane treatment and exposure to the arts, music, and literature. A precursor to modern treatment in many ways, he described his method in his Instructions and his *Guida per la Real Casa de' Matti di Palermo* (1835), which I had translated from the Italian for my research. His encounters herein with fictional characters are imagined but are consistent with his biography, personality, and philosophy.

Baron Pisani actually did design and build his Real Casa dei Matti di Palermo, the Royal Madhouse of Palermo, and it still stands, though it has fallen into ruin. I visited the place, and you can see the video on my website. I also visited a reproduction of one of its cells, given by historian Dr. Sebastiano Catalano, and you can see that video on my website, too. Dr. Catalano's book *Le Stanze Ferite dalla Real Casa dei Matti al Manicomio di Palermo,* published in Italian, is an important work on the subject.

Baron Pisani's moral therapy brought him acclaim in Europe, and many luminaries visited the Real Casa dei Matti di Palermo, including Edgar Allan Poe, Alexandre Dumas (the elder), and Booker T. Washington. Tragically, a cholera outbreak swept through Sicily in 1837, and Baron Pisani was so dedicated to his patients that he refused to leave them. He died of cholera with those to whom he dedicated his life.

It is true that Sicily's enforcement of the Alhambra Decree expelled Jews from the island. The Sicilian Inquisition shows how law can perpetrate horrific injustice, in that it sanctioned the torture, murder, and expulsion of Sicily's Jews. It is also true that there were Jews who practiced their religion in secret, and those were called *marranos*, a Spanish derogatory term. Even today, there are few Jews in Sicily, and Palermo has made attempts to entice Jews to return, restoring a synagogue converted to a church during that terrible time. I visited the synagogue, and on my website you can see the video I took there.

The sulfur mines of those days really existed as described in the novel, and I went to an old sulfur mine and museum in the mining region of Caltanissetta, held sulfur ore in my hand, and got authentically nauseated. I was astounded to learn in my research that Booker T. Washington had visited the sulfur mines in Sicily around the time period of the novel and concluded there was no place on earth more hellish.

The cloistered Santa Caterina d'Alessandria convent really exists, on Piazza Bellini in Palermo. Its history in the novel is true, and at the time, there were about twenty such cloistered convents that baked and sold sweets in Palermo. It's also true that bakeries were permitted to sell bread, but not sweets, so as not to compete with the convents. Nowadays you can tour the Santa Caterina d'Alessandria convent, as I did, see how the nuns lived, visit their beautiful courtyard and garden, and buy their delicious pastries. (I'm still craving a *margherita*, a lemon tart.) Remarkably enough, they now offer a cookbook published in Italian, *I Segreti del Chiostro*, *The Secrets of the Cloister*. I took videos and photos at the convent, and you can see them on my website.

Porticello is a real fishing village, picturesque and charming. The Madonna del Lume church is also real and beautiful, but the event described herein is fictional. Likewise, Mussomeli is a real mountaintop town and completely charming, with homes of the period, Madonna dei Miracoli church, and Castello Manfredonico. You can see videos of Porticello and Mussomeli on my website.

Mount Pellegrino is real, as is the beautiful grotto of Saint Rosalia, Palermo's patron saint. I mentioned *ex voti* in the novel, and they exist, too. They're body parts in hammered silver, which are offered by the faithful in churches when they pray for intercession. *Ex voti* are at first glance primitive, but I found them beautiful and have quite a collection, which you can see on my website.

The food in the novel is delicious and true to the time in Sicily, as are the methods of its distribution, from clippers to donkey caravans to water sellers. During my trip, I basically took a food tour, enjoying every lemon dish of the Palermo area, fresh-caught sole from Porticello, and fresh-picked pistachios in Bronte, a revelation. I ate enough pistachio paste to turn green; I didn't mind, and neither would you. My favorite books about modern Sicilian cuisine are Ursula Ferrigno's *Cucina Siciliana*, Salvatore Farina's *Sweet Sensations of Sicily*, and Giorgio Locatelli's *Made in Sicily*.

It is true that delicious Marsala wine, from the city of Marsala on Sicily's west coast, gained popularity when bottled by the real-life Florio family and others. For those who want to learn more about the Florios, I recommend the splendid novel *The Florios of Sicily* by Stefania Auci, and its audiobook read by maestro Edoardo Ballerini.

Finally, there is wonderful classic fiction about Sicily: Giuseppe di Lampedusa, *The Leopard*; Giovanni Verga, *Little Novels of Sicily*; and Elio Vittorini, *Conversations in Sicily*. Those wishing to learn more about Sicily's folktales may want to read *The Collected Sicilian Folk and Fairy Tales of Giuseppe Pitrè*, translated and edited by Jack Zipes and Joseph Russo. Many end with a coda, like this one:

> And so they lived on, in contentment and peace,
> While we remain here, picking our teeth.

ACKNOWLEDGMENTS

Loyalty is a fascinating quality, and shaping its contours is a leitmotif through this novel. I regard myself as a loyal person and value loyalty in others, which is why my first thanks are to my readers, who have been loyal to me for years. Thank you so much to each and every one of you, and I know how grateful, lucky, and blessed I am in you. I love writing these books, but they are possible only because of you. You have my gratitude, forever.

Second thanks are to booksellers and librarians everywhere, who keep all of us reading and loving books. I didn't grow up in a houseful of books but found my lifelong love of them in the library, and now I'm lucky enough to have to-be-read piles falling over in every room of my house. Books center us, heal us, and connect us, and I believe that reading is fundamental to democracy. Case in point, as *Loyalty* suggests, the widespread illiteracy of Sicily in the 1800s was one reason the class system was fixed in place, denying opportunity and equality to so many. So thank you to booksellers and librarians, for all you do for all of us.

I love Sicily, and my research took me all over that amazing island. I was helped by a number of experts, who deserve thanks here. Thank you to historians Louis Mendola and Jacqueline Alio, who have written volumes about Palermo and Sicily's history, and were so patient in sharing their expertise. Thank you to historian Tania LoCicero and to Dr. Sebastiano Catalano, whose book I acknowledged in my author's note. Both Tania and Sebastiano showed me Baron Pisano's abandoned hospital and educated me on his psychiatric theories.

Thank you to Salvatore Equizzi for the culinary tour of Palermo, and to Irene at the historic Villa Igiea, and to Allison Scola. Thank you to Bartolomeo Alamio, who drove the getaway car when Italian authorities chased me off the grounds of Pagliarelli Prison, the maximum-security facility outside Palermo where many modern-day Mafiosi are serving their sentences. You can see the video on my website, and it was the most excellent adventure an author could have.

In Mussomeli, I was honored to meet Mayor Giuseppe Catania and councilwoman Rita Lamonica, who showed me around their beautiful town and told me about its history. In Porticello, I met the completely charming Francu at Trattoria Francu ù Piscaturi, which serves the best fish in Sicily. Thank you to Francu, a man of deep faith, who took me into his beloved Church of S.S. Madonna del Lume. Thanks to Francesco, with whom I toured Agrigento and Bronte, where I ate everything pistachio. Thanks to Fabrizio Testai, a genius guide who took me up Mount Etna only a week before it erupted. Yikes!

Of course, any mistakes herein are my own.

Thank you to my awesome team at G. P. Putnam's Sons, led by the amazing Ivan Held, who supports me at every step. Thank you to the great Sally Kim and to my genius editor, Mark Tavani, who improved this manuscript so much and is great fun besides. Thanks to Aranya Jain for her support, editorial comments, and good humor.

Thanks to Alexis Welby and Katie Grinch for their hard work in publicity. Thanks to Ashley McClay, Emily Mlynek, and Molly Pieper, who innovate in marketing every day. Thanks to the wonderfully talented Anthony Ramondo for a sensational cover yet again, and thanks to audiobook mavens Karen Dziekonski and Scott Sherratt. Lots of love and gratitude to the amazing sales reps at Putnam, who work so hard in such a tough job!

Thanks and love to my terrific agent Robert Gottlieb and his equally terrific colleague Erica Silverman of Trident Media Group. Finally, thanks to Nicole Robson, Sarah McEachern, and Aurora Fernandez, for all of their hard work.

Lots of love and thanks to my bestie/assistant Laura Leonard, who traveled with me to Sicily and supports me every day. Thanks and love to Nan Daley and Katie Rinda, who help with research, marketing, and everything else.

Thanks and love to my bestie Franca Palumbo. And finally, thanks and even bigger love to my amazing daughter, Francesca Serritella, a novelist in her own right with her wonderful debut *Ghosts of Harvard*. I couldn't be prouder of her and feel the same way about her as my father did of me, when he said:

"I was proud of her the day she came out of the egg."